W9-DEK-635

THE DRAGON KING

ALSO BY R. A. SALVATORE

The Crystal Shard
Streams of Silver
The Halfling's Gem
Homeland
Echoes of the Fourth Magic
Exile
Sojourn
Canticle
The Witch's Daughter
In Sylvan Shadows
Night Masks
The Legacy
The Fallen Fortress
Starless Night
The Woods Out Back
The Dragon's Dagger
The Chaos Curse
Siege of Darkness
*Sword of Bedwyr**
Dragonslayer's Return
*Luthien's Gamble**
Passage to Dawn

*The Crimson Shadow series

R.A. SALVATORE

THE DRAGON KING

WARNER BOOKS

A Time Warner Company

Warner Books, Inc., 1271 Avenue of the Americas, New York, NY 10020

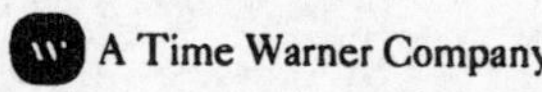
A Time Warner Company

Printed in the United States of America

ISBN 0-446-51728-3

Book design by Giorgetta Bell McRee

To Diane, and to Bryan, Geno, and Caitlin

Avon Sea
Dorsal Sea
N
Isle Marvis
Hale
Clywyd
Isle Caryth
Dun Varna
Gybi
Isle Bedwydrin
Bae Colthwyn
Krohlwyn
The Diamond Gate
Mennichen Dee
Land's End
Eriador
Fields of Eradoch
Colonsey
Bronegan
MacDonald's Swath
Chalmbers
Selling Run
Port Charley
Felling Downs
Monfort
Glen Albyn
Dun Caryth
Malpuissant's Wall
Baraduine
The Iron Cross
Princetown
Bennibeck
The Five Sentinels
Eornfast
Earn River
Dunkery River
Cumberland River
Glen Durritch
Dulsen
Berra
Bonny Fawddwy
Bangor
Mannington
Warchester
Deverwood
Lemmingbury
Speythenfergus Lake
Avon (Elkinador)
Ogniach Dee
The Straits of Mann
Corbin
Evenshorn
Lake Tummel
The Saltwash
Beachyhead
Darthemoor
Carlisle on Stratton
Darthemoor Wood
Stratton River
Newcastle
Gascony

THE DRAGON KING

PROLOGUE

The Avonsea Islands knew peace, but it was a tentative thing, founded on a truce that neither kingdom, Avon or Eriador, truly desired, a truce signed only because continuing the war would have been too costly for the outlaw king of Avon and too desperate for the ill-equipped and outmanned fledgling kingdom of Eriador.

In that northern land, the wizard Brind'Amour was crowned, and the excitement of the common people, an independent and rugged breed, was rightly high. But King Brind'Amour, grown wise by the passage of centuries, tempered his own hopes in the sobering understanding that, in mighty Avon, evil Greensparrow remained as king. For twenty years Greensparrow had held Eriador in his hand, giving him dominance of all the islands, and Brind'Amour understood that he would not so easily let go, whatever the truce might say. And Greensparrow, too, was a wizard, with powerful demonic allies, and a court that included four wizard-dukes and a duchess of considerable sorcerous power.

But though he was the only wizard in all of Eriador, alone in magical power against Greensparrow's court, Brind'Amour took comfort that he, too, had powerful allies. Most prominent among them was Luthien Bedwyr, the Crimson Shadow, who had become the hero of the nation and the symbol of Eriador free. It was

Luthien who slew Duke Morkney, Luthien who led the revolt in Montfort, taking back the city and restoring its true Eriadoran name of Caer MacDonald.

For now at least, Eriador was free, and all the people of the land—the sailors of Port Charley and the three northern islands, the fierce Riders of Eradoch, the sturdy dwarfs of the Iron Cross, the Fairborn elves, and all the farmers and fishermen—were solidly aligned behind their king and their land.

If Greensparrow wanted Eriador back in his unlawful grasp, he would have to fight them, all of them, for every inch of ground.

ENEMY OLD, ENEMY NEW

A simple spell brought him unnoticed past the guards, out from the main gates of the greatest city in all of Avonsea, mighty Carlisle on Stratton. Under cover of a moonless night, the man rushed along, fighting the rebellion, the inner turmoil, of his other self, the impatience of a being too long imprisoned.

"Now!" implored a silent call within him, the willpower of Dansallignatious. "Now."

Greensparrow growled. "Not yet, you fool," he warned, for he knew the risks of this journey, knew that to reveal himself to the Avonese populace, to show his subjects who and what he truly was, would surely overwhelm them. Dansallignatious, the other half of this man who was king, didn't agree, had never agreed, through all the years of Greensparrow's reign, through all the centuries before that since the time when the two, wizard and familiar being, had become one. To Dansallignatious, the revelation would only make them grovel all the more, would make Greensparrow greater in their eyes, would even cow the kings of neighboring countries into paying homage to the ultimate power that was Avon.

But then, Greensparrow reasoned, Dansallignatious would think that way; it was the way of his kind!

Through the fields the king ran, his feet hastened by a simple enchantment. Past the outlying farms, past the small huts where single candles behind windows showed that the folk were still awake. He felt a tug on his spine, an itch across his powdered skin.

"Not yet," Greensparrow implored Dansallignatious, but it was too late. The beast could no longer be contained. Greensparrow tried to run on, but a painful crack in his leg sent him sprawling in the thick grass. Then he was crawling, inching his way over a ridge, to roll down into the shelter of a grassy hollow.

His screams brought the farmers of three nearby cottages to their windows, peering out cautiously into the dark night. One man took up his ancient family sword, a rusted old thing, and dared to go out, moving slowly toward the continuing sound.

He had never heard such torment, such agony! It came from ahead, on the other side of a grassy bluff.

But then it quieted, suddenly, and the farmer thought that the man must have been killed.

Only then did he realize his own foolishness. Something behind that hill had apparently just murdered a man. What made him, a simple farmer with no experience or training with the sword, think that he would fare any better? Slowly, he began to back away.

Then he stopped, stricken.

A huge horned head lifted out of the shallow, rising, rising, ten feet, twenty feet above him. Lamplight orbs, yellow-green in color, reptilian in appearance, locked on to the man, showed him his doom.

The farmer's breath came in labored gasps. He wanted desperately to turn and run, but the sheer magnificence of the beast held him fast. Up came the dragon to the top of the bluff, great claws rending the earth as it moved, its wide-spread wings and tremendous bulk, eighty feet from horned head to swishing tail, blotting out the night sky.

"It feels good, Greensparrow," the beast said suddenly.

"Do not speak that name!" the beast then said, in the same thunderous voice, but with a different tone altogether.

"Greensparrow?" the farmer managed to whisper, confused, overwhelmed.

"Greensparrow!" insisted the dragon. "Do you not know your king? On your knees!"

The sheer power of the voice knocked the trembling farmer

over. He scrambled to his knees, bowing his head before this most awful of creatures.

"You see?" asked the part that was Dansallignatious. "They fear me, worship me!"

The words were barely out before the dragon's face twisted weirdly. The voice that signified Dansallignatious started to protest, but the words were blasted away as a huge gout of fire burst forth from the dragon's mouth.

The blackened corpse beside the melted sword was not recognizable.

Dansallignatious shrieked, outraged that his fun with the peasant had been cut short, but Greensparrow willed himself into flight then and the sheer freedom of the cool night air flowing over leathery wings brought such joy and exhilaration to the dragon king that all arguments seemed petty.

A crowd of farmers gathered about the side of the bluff the next day, staring at the scorched grass and the blackened corpse. The Praetorian Guards were called in, but, as was usually the case where the brutish, unsympathetic cyclopians were involved, they were of little help. Reports of the incident would go back to Carlisle, they promised, snickering as they watched the dead man's grieving family.

More than one of the folk gathered claimed to have seen a great winged beast flying about on the previous night; that, too, would be told in Carlisle.

Greensparrow, comfortably back in the slender, almost effeminate form that his subjects had come to know so well, the dark side of him that was Dansallignatious appeased by the night of freedom, dismissed the reports as the overactive imaginations of simple peasants.

"To be sure, even the fishing is better these days!" howled an exuberant Shamus McConroy, first hand on *The Skipper*, a fishing boat out of the village of Gybi, the north port of Bae Colthwyn on Eriador's windswept northeastern shore. So named for its tendency to leap headlong through the high breakers, half-clear of the water, *The Skipper* was among the most highly regarded vessels of Bae Colthwyn's considerable fishing fleet. She was a thirty-footer, wide and with one square sail, and a crew of eight, salty old seadogs all, with not a hair among them that wasn't turning to gray.

Old Captain Aran Toomes liked it that way, and steadfastly refused to train a younger replacement crew. "Got no time for puppies," the crusty captain grumbled whenever someone remarked that his boat was a doomed thing—"mortal as a man" was the saying. Toomes always accepted the ribbing with a knowing snarl. In Bae Colthwyn, on the Dorsal Sea, where the great killer whales roamed in huge packs and the weather turned ugly without warning, fishermen left widows behind, and more "puppies" drowned than reached manhood. Thus, the crew of *The Skipper* was a reckless bunch of bachelors, hard drinkers and hard riders, challenging the mighty Dorsal Sea as though God above had put the waves in their path as a personal challenge. Day after day, she went out further and faster than any other boat in the fishing fleet.

So it was this midsummer day, *The Skipper* running the breakers, sails full and straining. The weather seemed to shift every hour, from sunny bright to overcast, that curious mixture on the open water where a body was never quite comfortable, was always too hot or too cold. Younger, less experienced sailors would have spent a fair amount of time at the rail, bidding farewell to their morning meal, but *The Skipper*'s crew, more at home on the water than on land, took the dramatic changes in bowlegged stride.

And their spirits were higher than normal this fine day, for their land, beloved Eriador, was free once more. Prodded by a rebel army that had pushed all the way to the Avon city of Princetown, King Greensparrow of Avon had let Eriador out of his grasp, relinquishing the land to the people of Eriador. The old wizard Brind'Amour, a man of Eriadoran stock, had been crowned king in Caer MacDonald as the season had turned to summer. Not that life would be much different for the fisherfolk of Bae Colthwyn—except of course that they would no longer have to deal with cyclopian tax bands. King Greensparrow's influence had never really carried that much weight in the rugged land of northeastern Eriador, and not one in fifty of the people along the bay had ever gone further south than Mennichen Dee on the northern edges of the Fields of Eradoch.

Only the folk of southern Eriador, along the foothills of the Iron Cross mountain range, where Greensparrow's tyranny was felt in force, would likely see any dramatic difference in their day-to-day existence, but that wasn't the point of it all. Eriador was free, and that cry of independence echoed throughout the land, from the

Iron Cross to Glen Albyn, to the pinelands of the northeast and the splashing, rocky shoreline of Bae Colthwyn, to the three northern isles, Marvis, Caryth, and giant Bedwydrin. Simple hope, that most necessary ingredient of happiness, had come to the wild land, personified by a king that few north of MacDonald's Swath would ever glimpse, and by a legend come to life called the Crimson Shadow.

When the news of their freedom had come to the bay, the fleet had put out, the fishermen singing and dancing on the decks as though they honestly expected the waters to be fuller with fish, as though they expected the dorsal whales to turn and flee at the mere sight of a boat flying under the flag of Eriador old, as though they expected the storms to blow less fierce, as though Nature herself should bow down to the new king of Eriador.

What a wonderful thing is hope, and to all who saw her this season, and especially to the men who crewed her, it seemed as if *The Skipper* leaped a little higher and ran the dark waters a little faster.

Early that morning, Shamus McConroy spotted the first whale, its black dorsal fin standing higher than a tall man, cutting the water barely fifty feet off their starboard bow. With typical abandon, the eight seadogs hurled taunts and whisky bottles the great whale's way, challenging and cursing, and when that fin slipped under the dark water, moving away from the boat, they gave a hearty cheer and paid it no more heed. The least experienced of them had spent thirty years on the water, and their fear of the whales was long since gone. They could read the dangerous animals, knew when to taunt and when to turn, when to dump a haul of fish into the water as a diversion, and when, as a final stance, to take up their long, pointed gaff hooks.

Soon after, all signs of land long gone, Aran Toomes put the morning sun over his right shoulder, running *The Skipper* southeast toward the mouth of the straits between Eriador and the Five Sentinels, a line of brooding islands, more stone than turf. Toomes meant to keep his boat out for the better part of a week, putting a hundred miles a day behind him. His course would take him out to the north of Colonsey, the largest and northernmost of the Five Sentinels, and then back again to the bay. The water was colder out there, the old captain knew, just the way the cod and mackerel liked it. The other boats of Bae Colthwyn's fleet knew it, too, but few had the daring of *The Skipper*, or the confidence and sea know-how of Aran Toomes.

Toomes kept his course true for three days, until the tips of Colonsey's steep mountains were in sight. Then he began his long, slow turn, a hundred-and-eighty-degree arc, bringing her around to the northwest. Behind him, working furiously, drinking furiously, and howling with glee, his seven crewmen hauled in side-nets and long lines loaded with fish: beautiful, shiny, smelly, flopping cod and mack, and even blues, nasty little predators who did nothing more than swim and bite, swim and bite, never stopping long enough to finish devouring whatever unfortunate fish had given them the mouthful. Shamus McConroy worked a belaying pin wildly, thunking blues on the head until those tooth-filled mouths stopped their incessant snapping. He got a nasty bite on the ankle, cutting him right through his hard boots, and responded by hoisting the ten-pound blue by the tail and whacking it repeatedly against the rail, to the hoots and cheers of the others.

For the seadogs, this was heaven.

The Skipper was lower in the water halfway through the turn, her hold nearly full. The crew went down to one line, two men working it, while the other five sorted through the load, pulling out smaller fish that were still alive and tossing them over, wanting to replace them with bigger specimens. It was all a game at this point, a challenge for fun, for a dozen smaller fish were just as valuable as the eight bigger ones that would fill their space in the hold, but the old sailors knew that the long days went faster when the hands were moving. Here they were, full of fish three hundred miles from port, with little to do but keep the sail in shape and steer the damned boat.

"Ah, so we're not the only boat with the gumption and heads to come out for a full hold," Shamus remarked to Aran. Grinning at old Aran's skeptical look, Shamus pointed to the northern horizon, where a darker speck had become evident within the line of bluish-gray.

"A pity we've not a bigger hold," Aran replied lightheartedly. "We could have fished the waters clean before ever they arrived!" The crusty captain finished the statement by clapping the crewman hard on the back.

That brought a chuckle from Shamus.

The Skipper continued along its merry way, the weather crisp and clear, the sea high, but not choppy, and the fishing more for sport now than for business. It wasn't until later that afternoon that Aran Toomes began to grow concerned. That speck on the horizon was much larger now, and, to the captain's surprise, it showed no sail on its single, square-rigged mast; thus it was no fishing boat from Bae Colthwyn. It was moving, though, and swiftly, and it seemed to be angling to intercept *The Skipper.*

Toomes brought the fishing boat harder to port, turning more westerly.

A few moments later, the other boat corrected its course accordingly.

"What do you know?" Shamus asked as he came forward to join Toomes at the wheel.

"I don't know," Aran Toomes replied grimly. "That's what's got me to thinking."

By now, the crew of *The Skipper* could see the froth at the side of the approaching vessel, a turbulence that could only mean a bank of great oars, pulling hard. In all the Dorsal Sea, only one race normally used boats that could be so oared, as well as sailed.

"Huegoths?" Shamus asked.

Aran Toomes couldn't find the will to answer.

"What are they doing so far to the south and east?" Shamus asked rhetorically.

"We don't know that they're Huegoths!" Aran Toomes yelled at him.

Shamus went numb and silent, staring at Toomes. The captain, who could laugh at a dorsal whale, seemed truly unnerved by the thought that this approaching vessel might be a Huegoth longship.

"Huegoths be the only ones who run so swift with oars," remarked another of the crew. The long line was forgotten now.

Aran Toomes chewed at his bottom lip, trying to find some answer.

"She runs with beauty," Shamus remarked, his gaze fixed on the longship. It was true enough; the design of the ships of Huegoth barbarians was nothing short of beautiful, finer than anything else on the northern seas. The graceful longships, seventy feet in length, were both solid and swift and cut the swells with hardly a ripple.

"Empty the hold," Aran Toomes decided.

The expressions of the other seven ranged from eager to incredulous. For several of the crewmen, this command seemed impossible, ridiculous. They had risked much in coming out this far to the southwest, so long from port, and those risks had been accepted precisely for the prize of fish in the hold. Now the captain wanted to throw away their catch?

But the other four men, including Shamus McConroy, who had dealt with savage Huegoths before, agreed wholeheartedly with the call. Laden with several tons of fish, *The Skipper* could not outrun the longship; even empty, they could only hope to keep ahead of the Huegoths long enough for the oarsmen to tire. Even then, the Huegoths could put up a sail.

"Empty it clear!" roared Aran, and the crew went to work.

Toomes studied the wind more carefully. It was generally from the south, not a good thing considering that the Huegoths, who did not depend on the wind, were coming down from the north. If he tried to turn *The Skipper* about, he'd be running into headwinds, practically standing still on the water.

"Let's see how good you can turn," the captain muttered, and he angled back to the north. He'd go in close, cut right by the Huegoths. If *The Skipper* could survive that single pass, and avoid the underwater ram that no doubt stuck out from the front of the barbarian ship, Toomes would have the wind at his back while the longship turned about.

A few hundred yards separated the vessels. Toomes could see the activity on the barbarians' top deck, huge men running to and fro. He could see the tall, curving forecastle, carved into the likeness of a wolf.

Then he saw the smoke, rising up suddenly from the longship's center. For an instant, the captain thought the longship had somehow caught fire, thought that perhaps one of the galley slaves had sabotaged the Huegoth raiders. But Toomes quickly realized the truth, and knew that his dear ship was in worse trouble still.

"Get you behind a wall!" the captain yelled to his crew when the ships were less than a hundred yards apart, when he could make out individual Huegoths leaning over the rail, their expressions bloodthirsty.

Shamus ran forward with a huge shield that he kept in the hold. He placed it to cover as much of the captain at the wheel as possible, then crouched low beside Toomes.

Toomes had meant to go much closer, to practically dance with the Huegoth boat before executing his sharp turn, to port or to starboard, whichever way seemed to give the most light between the jockeying vessels. He had to commit sooner, though. He knew that now, with the black smoke billowing high.

He turned right, starboard, and when the longship's left bank began to drag in the water, pulling her to port, Toomes cut back to port harder than he had ever tried to turn *The Skipper*. The good ship seemed to hesitate, seemed to stand right up in the water, beams creaking, mast groaning. But turn she did, and her sails dipped for just an instant, then swelled with wind, racing her off in the new direction, which by comforting coincidence put *The Skipper* straight in line with Bae Colthwyn.

A barrage of flaming arrows soared out from the longship, a score of fiery bolts trailing black lines of smoke. Many fell short, most missed widely, but one did catch on the prow of *The Skipper*, and another found the starboard edge of the mast and sail.

Shamus McConroy was there in an instant, batting at the flames. Two other crewmen came right in with buckets, dousing the fires before they could do any real damage.

At the wheel, eyes locked on his adversary, Aran Toomes wasn't comforted. Now the longship's left bank pulled hard, while the right bank hit the water in reverse, pivoting the seventy-foot vessel like a giant capstan.

"Too fast," old Aran muttered when he saw the incredible turn, when he realized that *The Skipper* would have a difficult time getting past that devastating ram. Still, Aran was committed to his course now; he could not cut any harder, or try to pull back to starboard.

It was a straight run, wind in the sails of *The Skipper*, oars pounding the waters to either side of the longship. The little fishing boat got past the longship's prow and started to distance herself from the still-turning Huegoths. For an instant, it seemed as though the daring move might actually succeed.

But then came the second volley of flaming arrows, crossing barely thirty feet of water, more than half of them diving into the vulnerable sails. Shamus, still working to repair the minor damage from the first volley, took one right in the back, just under his shoulder blade. He stumbled forward while another man swatted his back furiously, trying to douse the stubborn flames.

That fire was the least of Shamus McConroy's problems. He

reached the wheel, verily fell over it, leaning heavily and looking close into Aran Toomes's grim face.

"I think it got me in the heart," Shamus said with obvious surprise, and then he died.

Aran cradled the man down to the deck. He looked back just once, to see *The Skipper*'s sails consumed by the flames, to see the longship, straightened now and in full row, banks churning the water on both sides, closing in fast.

He looked back to Shamus, poor Shamus, and then he was lurching wildly, flying out of control, as the devastating ram splintered *The Skipper*'s rudder and smashed hard against her hull.

Sometime later—it seemed like only seconds—a barely conscious Aran Toomes felt himself dragged across the deck and hauled over to the Huegoth ship. He managed to open his eyes, looking out just as *The Skipper*, prow high in the air, stern already beneath the dark canopy, slipped silently under the waves, taking with it the bodies of Shamus and Greasy Solarny, an old seadog who had sailed with Aran for twenty years.

As he let go of that terrible sight, focused again on the situation at hand, Aran heard the cries for his death, and for the death of the five other remaining crewmen.

But then another voice, not as gruff and deep, overrode the excited Huegoths, calming them little by little.

"These men are not of Avon," said the man, "but of Eriador. Good and strong stock, and too valuable to kill."

"To the galley!" roared one Huegoth, a cry quickly taken up by all the others.

As he was lifted from the deck, Aran got a look at the man who had saved him. He wasn't a small man, but certainly not of giant Huegoth stock, well-toned and strong, with striking cinnamon-colored eyes.

The man was Eriadoran!

Aran wanted to say something, but hadn't the breath or the chance.

Or the clarity. His life and the lives of his remaining crewmen had been spared, but Aran Toomes had lived a long, long time and had heard tales of the horrors of life as a Huegoth galley slave. He didn't know whether to thank this fellow Eriadoran, or to spit in the man's face.

DIPLOMACY

"Get out of that bed, Oliver!" came the yell, followed by a resounding pound. "Awaken, you half-sized mischief-maker!"

Siobhan slammed her open palm against the closed door again, then clenched her fists in frustration and half-growled, half-screamed as loudly as she could. "Why didn't you just go with Luthien?" she demanded, and pounded the door again. Then the energy seemed to drain from the slender and beautiful half-elf. She turned about and fell back against the door, brushed her long wheat-colored hair from her face, and took a deep breath to calm herself. It was mid-morning already; Siobhan had been up for several hours, had bathed and eaten breakfast, had seen to the arrangements in the audience hall, had discussed their strategy with King Brind'Amour, had even met secretly with Shuglin the dwarf to see what unexpected obstacles might be thrown in their path.

And Oliver, who had remained in Caer MacDonald to help Siobhan with all of these preparations, hadn't even crawled out of his fluffy bed yet!

"I really hate to do this," Siobhan remarked, and then she shook her head as she realized that a few short days with Oliver already had her talking to herself on a fairly regular basis. She rolled about to face the door and slipped down to one knee, drawing out a slender pick and a flat piece of metal. Siobhan was a member of the Cutters, a band of thieving elves and half-elves who had terrorized the merchants of Caer MacDonald when the city had been under the control of Greensparrow's lackey, Duke Morkney. Siobhan often boasted that no lock could defeat her, and so she proved it again now, deftly working the pick until her keen elven ears heard the tumblers of Oliver's door click open.

Now came the dangerous part, the half-elf realized. Oliver, too, had no small reputation as a thief, and the foppish halfling often warned people about uninvited entry to his private room. Slowly and gently, Siobhan cracked the door, barely an inch, then began sliding the metal tab about its edge. She closed her green eyes and let her sensitive fingers relay all the information she needed, and sure enough, halfway across the top of the door, she found something unusual.

The half-elf rose to her tiptoes, smiling as she came to understand the nature of the trap. It was a simple tab, wedged between door and jamb and no doubt supporting a pole or other item that was propping the edge of a hung bucket—probably filled with water.

Cold water—that was Oliver's style.

Carefully the graceful half-elf pushed the door a bit further, and then some more, until she exposed one edge of the supporting tab. Then she used her piece of flattened metal to extend the tab, and gently, so gently, she pushed the door a bit more. Now came the tricky part, as Siobhan had to slip into the room, contorting and sucking in her breath to avoid the doorknob. She barely fit, and had to push the door still more, nearly dislodging both tabs and sending the bucket—for she could now see that it was indeed a large bucket, suspended from the ceiling—into a spin that would soak her fine dress.

She paused for a moment and considered her predicament, resolving that if Oliver's little game ruined her outfit, the finest clothes she possessed, she would steal his treasured rapier blade, take it to a smithy friend, and have it tied into a knot!

The door creaked; Siobhan held her breath and slowly swiveled her hips into the room.

Her dress caught on the doorknob.

With a profound sigh, and a lament at how impractical this fashion statement truly was, Siobhan simply unstrapped the bulky garment and slid right out of it, leaving it on the knob as she wriggled around the door. She pulled the dress in behind her and gently closed the door, then turned about to a sight that opened wide her shining green eyes.

The door made a tinkling sound as it closed, drawing her attention. There, on the inside knob, hung Oliver's golden-brocade shoulder belt and baldric, lined with tiny bells. On the floor directly before the entrance was a green stocking, topped in silk. Further in lay a pair of green gauntlets, one on top of the halfling's signature purple velvet cape. Beyond the cape were a pair of shiny black shoes, impeccably polished. The line of strewn clothing continued with a sleeveless blue doublet, the second stocking, and a white silken undertunic, crumpled against the foot of a huge, four-posted bed. Oliver's wide-brimmed hat, one side pinned up tight and plumed with a huge orange feather, hung atop one of the corner posts—how the diminutive halfling ever got the thing up the seven feet to the top of it, Siobhan could only guess.

Siobhan let her eyes linger on the hat a moment, considering the feather, drooping as though it, too, had spent too many hours of the previous night in high partying.

With a sigh of resignation, Siobhan folded her dress carefully over her arm and crept closer. She covered her eyes and snickered when she spotted the halfling, facedown atop the oversized down comforter, arms and legs out wide to the sides and straddling a pillow that was larger than he. He was wearing his breeches (purple velvet, to match the cape), at least, but they were wrapped about his head and not where they belonged. The half-elf moved around the mounting stairs, a set of five for the little halfling, and right up to the side of the bed.

How might she wake the little one? she mused, and snickered again when Oliver let out a great snore.

Siobhan reached over and flicked a finger against Oliver's shining, naked buttock.

Oliver snored again.

Siobhan tickled him under the arm. The halfling started to roll over, but Siobhan, with a frightened squeal, put a hand on his shoulder and held him in place.

"Ah, my little buttercup," Oliver said, startling the half-elf. "Your bosom does so warm my body."

Siobhan couldn't tell for certain, but it sounded as if Oliver was kissing the pillow under the breeches-wrap.

Enough of that, Siobhan decided, and this time she reached over and gave the halfling a stinging slap.

Up popped his head, one pant-leg flopping over his face. Oliver blew a couple of times, but the material was too heavy to be moved that way. Finally the halfling reached up and slowly pushed the obstacle out of his eyes.

How those brown and severely bloodshot eyes widened when he saw Siobhan standing beside his bed in her petticoats, her dress over her arm! Oliver slowly shifted his gaze, to consider his own naked form, then snapped his gaze back to Siobhan.

"Buttercup?" the dazed halfling asked, and a smile widened over his face, his dimples shining through.

"Do not even think it," Siobhan replied evenly.

Oliver ran a hand over his neatly trimmed goatee, then through his long and curly brown locks, taking the pants off as he went, as he tried to piece together the events of the previous night. Most of it was a blur, but he remembered a certain maid-servant . . .

The halfling's eyes nearly fell from their sockets when he realized then that Siobhan wasn't in his room for any amorous reason, that she had come in to wake him and nothing more, and that he was . . .

"Oh!" Oliver wailed, spinning about to a sitting position. "Oh, you unabashed . . ." He stammered, choking with embarrassment. "Oh, where is my sword?" he howled.

Siobhan's eyes roamed down the halfling's chest and lower, and she gave a mischievous smile and a slight shrug of her shoulders.

"My rapier blade!" the flustered halfling corrected. "Oh, you . . ." Oliver fumed and leaped from the bed, fumbling with his breeches and nearly tripping over them as he struggled to put them over his moving feet. "In Gascony, we have a name for a woman such as you!" he said, spinning to face the half-elf.

Siobhan's fair features tightened into a threatening scowl.

"Dangerous," she said, a pointed reminder to the halfling.

Oliver froze, considering the word and considering this most beautiful of females. Finally, he gave up and shrugged. Dangerous was a good word for her, Oliver decided, in more ways than one.

"You could have knocked before entering my private room," said the halfling, in controlled tones once more.

"I nearly beat your door down," Siobhan retorted. "You have, perhaps, forgotten our meeting with King Bellick dan Burso of DunDarrow?"

"Forgotten it?" Oliver balked. He scooped up his silken undertunic and pulled it over his shoulders. "Why, I have spent all the night in preparation. Why do you think you have found me so weary?"

"The pillow was demanding?" Siobhan replied, looking to the disheveled bed.

Oliver growled and let it pass. He dropped suddenly to one knee, slapped aside the edge of the comforter to reveal the hilt of his rapier, then drew the blade out from between the mattresses. "I do not take lightly my so-important position," he said. "Halflings are more attu-ned . . ."

"A-too-ned?" Siobhan interrupted, mocking Oliver's Gascon accent, which seemed to extend every syllable of every word.

"Attu-ned!" Oliver gruffly answered. "Halflings are more attu-ned to the ways and likes of dwarfs than are peoples, and elfy-types!"

"Elfy-types?" Siobhan whispered under her breath, but she didn't bother to interrupt openly, for Oliver had hit his verbal stride. On he rambled about the value of halfling diplomats, of how they had stopped this war or that, of how they had talked "stupid human king-types" right out of their "jew-wels," family and otherwise. As he spoke, the halfling looked all around, then finally up, to see his hat atop the post. Not missing a syllable, Oliver flipped the rapier to catch it by the blade and threw it straight up, hilt first. It clipped the hat, lifting it from the post, and down both came.

Oliver caught the blade by the hilt above his head and moved it incredibly smoothly to poke the floor beside his bare, hair-topped foot, striking a gallant pose.

"So there," finished the halfling, who had regained his dignity, and on cue his hat fell perfectly atop his head.

"You have style," Siobhan had to admit. Then she added with a snicker, "And you are cute without your clothes."

Oliver's heroic pose disintegrated. "Oh!" he wailed, lifting the rapier and poking it down harder—and this time nicking the side of his foot.

Trying to hold to his fast-falling dignity, the halfling spun and ambled away, scooping his doublet, stockings, shoes, and gauntlets as he went. "I will find my revenge for this!" Oliver promised.

"I, too, sleep without any clothes," Siobhan said teasingly.

Oliver stopped dead in his tracks and nearly fell over. He knew that Siobhan was toying with him, hitting his amorous spirit where it could not defend itself, but the conjured image evoked by those six little words overwhelmed him, sent him into a trembling fit from head to hairy toe. He turned about, stammering for some retort, then just squealed in defeat and stormed to the door, grabbing his baldric as he passed.

Forgetting his own trap.

Down fell the supporting tab and over went the suspended bucket, dropping cold water all over the halfling, sending the brim of his great hat drooping low.

Oliver, cooled, turned back to Siobhan. "I meant to do that," he insisted, and then he was gone.

Siobhan stood in the room for a long while, shaking her head and laughing. Despite all the trouble this one caused, there was indeed something charming about Oliver deBurrows.

Oliver was back in form in time for the all-important meeting at the assigned house, a commandeered piece of real estate that had formerly belonged to a nobleman loyal to Greensparrow. The man had fled Eriador, and Brind'Amour had taken his house to use as the palace of Caer MacDonald, though most business was conducted at the Ministry, the huge cathedral that dominated the city. Oliver had dried off and somehow managed to get his wide-brimmed hat to stand out stiffly again—even the feather was properly rigid. Siobhan stared at that transformation incredulously, wondering if the halfling possessed more than one of the outrageous, plumed "chapeaus," as he called them.

Oliver sat on a higher stool on one side of a huge oaken table, flanking King Brind'Amour on the left, while Siobhan sat on the old wizard's right.

Across from them sat a quartet of grim-faced dwarfs. King Bellick dan Burso was directly across from Brind'Amour, his blue eyes locking intently with the wizard's—though Brind'Amour could hardly see them under the dwarf's tremendous eyebrows, fiery orange in hue, like his remarkable beard. So bright and bushy was that beard, and long enough for Bellick to tuck it into his belt, that it was often whispered that the dwarf king wore a suit of living flames. Shuglin, friend to the rebels who had conquered Caer MacDonald, sat beside Bellick, calm and confident. It had been Shuglin, a dwarf of Caer MacDonald and not of the Iron Cross, who had initiated this meeting and all the discussions between his mountain brethren and the new leaders of Eriador. Any alliance between the groups would benefit both, Shuglin realized, for these two kings, Bellick and Brind'Amour, were of like mind and goodly ilk.

Two other dwarfs, broad-shouldered generals, flanked King Bellick and Shuglin.

The formal greetings went off well, with Oliver doing most of the talking, as Brind'Amour had planned. This was their party, after all; through the emissary Shuglin, it had been Brind'Amour, and not Bellick, who had requested the summit.

"You know our gratitude for your help in overcoming Princetown," Brind'Amour began quietly. Indeed the dwarfs did know, for Brind'Amour had sent many, many messengers, all of them bearing gifts, to the stronghold of DunDarrow, the dwarfish underground complex nestled deep in the Iron Cross mountain range. Bellick's folk had arrived on the field outside of Princetown, Avon's northernmost city, just in time to cut off the retreat of the Avon garrison, which had been routed in Glen Durritch by the Eriadorans. With Bellick's sturdy force blocking the way, the victory had been complete. "Eriador owes much to King Bellick dan Burso and his warriors," Brind'Amour reaffirmed.

Bellick gave an accepting nod. "Princetown would have fallen in any event, even without our help," the dwarf replied graciously.

"Ah, but if the soldiers of Princetown had gotten back behind their so-high walls . . ." Oliver put in, though it was certainly not his place to interrupt.

Brind'Amour only chuckled, more than used to the halfling's often irreverent ways.

Bellick did not seem so pleased, a fact that made Brind'Amour eye him curiously. At first, the wizard thought that the dwarf had taken insult at Oliver's interruption, but then he realized that something else was bothering Bellick.

The dwarf king looked to Shuglin and nodded, and Shuglin stood solemnly and cleared his throat.

"Twenty Fairborn were slain yestereve in the foothills of the Iron Cross," he reported. "Not twenty miles from here."

Brind'Amour sank back in his high-backed chair and looked to Siobhan, who bit her lip and nodded her head in frustration. The half-elf had heard rumors of the battle, for her people, the Fairborn, were not numerous throughout Avonsea, and kept general tabs on each other. Now it seemed the number of Fairborn had diminished once again.

"Cyclopian raiders," Shuglin continued. "A group of at least a hundred."

"Never before have the one-eyes been so organized," Bellick added. "It would seem that your little war has riled the beasts from the deep mountain holes."

Brind'Amour understood the dwarf's frustration and the accusation, if that was what Bellick had just offered. The cyclopian activity along the northern foothills of the Iron Cross had indeed heightened tremendously since the signing of the truce with Greensparrow of Avon. Brind'Amour kept his gaze on Siobhan for a long moment, wondering how she would react. Then he looked to Oliver, and realized that his companions also understood that the cyclopian activity so soon after the truce was not a coincidence.

Shuglin waited for Brind'Amour to turn back to him before he resumed his seat. The wizard noted a slight nod from the black-bearded dwarf, an encouragement the beleaguered king of Eriador sorely needed at that time.

"The one-eyes have struck at several villages," Brind'Amour explained to Bellick.

"Perhaps they believe that with King Greensparrow no longer concerned with Eriador, the land is free for their pillaging," Bellick replied, and from his tone it seemed that he didn't believe that statement any more than did Brind'Amour. Both kings knew who was behind the cyclopian raids, but neither would speak it openly, especially since they hadn't yet reached any formal agreement with each other.

"Perhaps," Brind'Amour said. "But whatever the cause of the cyclopian raids, it only stands to reason that both your dwarfs and the folk of Eriador would profit from an alliance."

Bellick nodded. "I know what you're wanting from me and my kin, King Brind'Amour," he said. "You need a mountain army, protection from the one-eyes, and security against Greensparrow, should the Avon king decide to come calling once more. What I want to know is what you've to offer to my folk."

Brind'Amour was a bit surprised by the dwarf's straightforwardness. A diplomatic summit such as this could roll on for days before the obvious questions were so plainly asked. Shuglin had warned the wizard about the dwarf king's blunt style, and now, with so much trouble brewing and reports arriving daily about cyclopian raids, Brind'Amour found that he liked straightforward Bellick all the more.

"Markets," Brind'Amour replied. "I offer you markets. Both Caer MacDonald and Dun Caryth will be open for you, and with Eriador trying to establish her true independence, we shall be drilling a formal militia, and shall require many weapons."

"And none forge better weapons than your dwarfs," Siobhan quickly added.

Bellick put his elbows up on the oaken table and crossed his fingers in front of his hairy face. "You wish DunDarrow to become a city of Eriador," he said bluntly, and somewhat sourly.

"We considered an alliance of separate kingdoms," Brind'Amour replied without hesitation, "but I truly believe that—"

"That with DunDarrow under your control, you will get the supplies you so desperately need much more cheaply," interrupted Bellick.

Brind'Amour sat back once more, staring intently at the dwarf king. After a short pause, he started to respond, but Bellick cut him short with an upraised hand.

"It's true enough," the dwarf said, "and I admit that I would be doing much the same if I found myself in your tentative position. The king of Avon wants Eriador, not DunDarrow—by the stones, he'd not find us anyway, and not take us if he did!" The orange-bearded dwarf's voice rose excitedly, and his three brethren were quick to take up the cheer.

Oliver, wanting the floor, tapped Brind'Amour on the arm, but Bellick began again before the wizard could acknowledge the halfling.

"So I am not blaming you," Bellick said. "We came out of the mountains to Princetown because of what you and yours have done for our kin, those enslaved in the city and the mines, and in all of Eriador. We know you as dwarf-friend, no small title. And, to be truthful, DunDarrow, too, would profit by securing as tight an alliance with Eriador as you desire."

"None but the king of DunDarrow may rule in DunDarrow," said the dwarf warrior seated beside Shuglin.

"And he who rules in DunDarrow must be of Clan Burso," the other general added. "Of dwarven blood, and only dwarven blood."

Brind'Amour, Siobhan, and Oliver all understood that the interruptions had been planned, the words carefully rehearsed. Bellick wanted Brind'Amour to see his predicament clearly, even if the dwarf decided to join in with Eriador.

Brind'Amour began to respond, to offer the dwarfs all respect, but this time Oliver leaped from his chair and scrambled atop the table.

"My good fellow furry folk," the halfling began.

Shuglin groaned; so did Siobhan.

"I, too, am a citizen of Eriador," Oliver continued, ignoring the audible doubts. "In service to King Brind'Amour!" He said it dramatically, as if expecting some applause, and when none came, he seemed caught off guard, stumbling verbally for just a moment.

"But not a one rules Oliver deBurrows except for Oliver deBurrows!" With that, the halfling drew his rapier and struck a dramatic pose.

"Your point?" Bellick asked dryly.

"A duocracy," the halfling explained.

There came a round of murmurs and questions, no one having any idea of what a "duocracy" might be.

"Eriador is Brind'Amour's," Oliver went on. "In Eriador, he rules. And yet, he would not tell the Riders of Eradoch what to do in Mennichen Dee. Nor would he tell Gahris, who rules on Isle Bedwydrin, how to handle his affairs of state."

"Not unless he had to," Siobhan put in, drawing a sour look from the halfling.

"Please, I am speaking," Oliver huffed at her.

Siobhan winked at him, further throwing him off, but other than that, the half-elf let him go on.

"So it shall be with the dwarfs, but even more so," Oliver explained. He had to pause then, for a moment, as he considered the signals Siobhan was throwing his way. Was she merely teasing? As he considered the possibilities, the sheer beauty and intelligence of this most wonderful half-elf, Oliver hoped that she was not!

"You were saying," Brind'Amour prompted.

"I was?"

"So it shall be with the dwarfs, but even more so," Siobhan put in.

"Ah, yes!" beamed the halfling, and he brightened all the more when Siobhan offered yet another wink. "A duocracy. DunDarrow will become a city of Eriador, but the king of Eriador will have no say over matters of state within DunDarrow."

Both Bellick and Brind'Amour seemed somewhat intrigued, and also a bit confused.

"I have never heard of such a government," Brind'Amour put in.

"Nor have I," agreed Bellick.

"Nor have I!" Oliver admitted. "And since it hasn't been done before, it should work all the better!"

"Oliver is no supporter of government," Brind'Amour explained, noticing Bellick's confused expression.

"Ah," replied the dwarf, then to Oliver, "In this duocracy, what am I? Servant of Brind'Amour or king of DunDarrow?"

"Both," said the halfling. "Though never would I call one in the line of Burso Ironhammer a 'servant.' No, not that. Ally to Eriador, allowing Brind'Amour to determine all our course through the greater . . . er, larger, though certainly more boring, issues outside of Eriador."

"Sounds like a servant," one of the dwarven generals said distastefully.

"Ah, but it all depends upon how you look at it," Oliver replied. "King Bellick does not want to deal with such diplomatic matters as fishing rights or emissaries from Gascony. No, no, King Bellick would rather spend his days at the forge, I am sure, where any good dwarf belongs."

"True enough," admitted the orange-bearded king.

"In that light, it seems to me as if Brind'Amour was King Bellick's servant, handling all the troublesome pettiness of government while King Bellick beats his hammer, or whatever it is you dwarfs beat."

"And of course, in any matters that concern DunDarrow directly or indirectly, I would first inform you and seek your counsel and your decision," Brind'Amour cut in, wanting to keep Oliver's surprising momentum flowing.

The four dwarfs called for a break, then huddled in the corner, talking excitedly. They came back to the table almost immediately.

"There are details to be defined," Bellick said. "I would protect the integrity of DunDarrow's sovereignty."

Brind'Amour sagged in his chair.

"But," Bellick added, "I would be loving the expression on ugly Greensparrow's face when he hears that DunDarrow and Eriador are one!"

"Duocracy!" shouted Oliver.

They adjourned then, with more progress made than Brind'Amour had dared hope for. He left with Oliver and Siobhan, all three in fine spirits, and of course, with Oliver retelling, and embellishing, his inspirational interruption.

"I did notice, though," Brind'Amour remarked when the breathless halfling paused long enough for him to get a word in, "that in your little speech, you referred to my counterpart as *King Bellick*, while I was referred to as merely *Brind'Amour*."

Oliver started to laugh, but stopped short, seeing the wizard's serious expression. There were many people in the world whom Oliver did not want for enemies, and mighty Brind'Amour was at the very top of that list.

"It was not a speech," Oliver stammered, "but a performance. Yes, a performance for our hairy dwarf-type friends. You noticed my subtle error, and so did Bellick . . ."

"King Bellick," Brind'Amour corrected. "And I noticed that it was but one of your errors."

Oliver fumbled about for a moment. "Ah, but I knew you before you ever were king," he reminded the wizard.

Brind'Amour could have kept up the feigned anger all the day, taking pleasure in Oliver's sweat, but Siobhan's chuckling soon became infectious, and Oliver howled loudest of all when he realized that the wizard was playing games with him. He had done well, after all, with his improvisation of "duocracy," and it seemed as if the vital agreement between Bellick and Brind'Amour was all but signed.

Oliver noticed, too, the strange way Siobhan was looking at him. Respect?

* * *

Menster, in the southwestern corner of Glen Albyn, was much like any other tiny Eriadoran community. It had no militia, was in fact little more than a collection of a few houses connected by a defensive wall of piled logs. The people, single men mostly, farmed a little, hunted a lot, and fished the waters of a clear, babbling stream that danced down from the higher reaches of the Iron Cross. Menster's folk had little contact with the outside world, though two of the hamlet's younger men had joined the Eriadoran army when that force had marched through Glen Albyn on their way to Princetown. Both those young men had returned with tales of victory when the army came through again, heading west this time, back to Caer MacDonald.

And so there had been much rejoicing in Menster since the war. In years past, the village had been visited often by Greensparrow's tax collectors, and like most independent-minded Eriadorans, the folk of Menster were never fond of being under the shadow of a foreign king.

With the change in government, with Eriador in the hands of an Eriadoran, their lives could only get better, or so they believed. Perhaps they might even remain invisible to the new king of Eriador, an unnoticed little hamlet, untaxed and unbothered. Just the way they wanted it.

But Menster was not invisible to the growing cyclopian horde, and though the people of Menster were a sturdy folk, surviving in near-isolation on the rugged slopes of the Iron Cross, they were not prepared, could not have been prepared, for the events of one fateful midsummer's night.

Tonky Macomere and Meegin Comber, the two veterans of the Princetown campaign, walked the wall that night, as they did most nights, keeping watch over their beloved village. Meegin was the first to spot a cyclopian, ambling through the underbrush some forty yards from the wall.

"Graceful as a one-legged drunken bear," he whispered to Tonky, when the lanky man noted Comber's hand motion and moved over to his fellow guard.

Neither was overly concerned; cyclopians often came near to Menster, usually scavenging discarded animal carcasses, though sometimes, rarely, testing the readiness of the townsfolk. The village sat on a flat expanse of ground, cleared all about the irregular-shaped wall for more than a hundred feet. Given that cyclopians were terrible with missile weapons (having only one eye and little depth perception) and that the thirty or so hunter-folk of Menster were all expert archers, the defenders of the city could decimate a hundred one-eyes before the brutes could cross the fields. And cyclopians, so surly and chaotic, hating everything, even each other, rarely ever banded in groups approaching a hundred.

"Oops, there's another one," said Tonky, motioning to the right.

"And another behind it," added Comber. "Best that we rouse the folk."

"Most're up already," Tonky put in. Both men turned about to regard the central building of the hamlet, the town meetinghouse and tavern, a long and low structure well-lit and more than a little noisy.

"Let's hope they're not too drunk to shoot straight," Comber remarked, but again the conversation was lighthearted, and without much concern.

Comber set off then, meaning to run a quick circuit of the wall, checking the perimeter, then dart down and inform the village of potential danger. Menster had drilled for scenarios exactly such as this a thousand times and all thirty archers (excepting a few who indeed were too drunk), would be in place in mere seconds, raining death on any cyclopians that ventured too near. Halfway around his intended circuit, though, Comber skidded to a stop in his tracks and stood staring out over the wall.

"What do you see?" Tonky called as quietly as possible from across the way.

Comber let out a shriek.

Instantly the bustle halted in the central structure, and men and women began pouring forth from its doors, bearing longbows, heading for the wall.

Comber was shooting his bow by then, repeatedly, and so was Tonky, letting arrows fly and hardly aiming, for so great was the throng charging from the brush and across the clearing that it was almost impossible to miss.

More villagers scrambled up the wall and took up their bows, and cyclopians fell dead by the dozens.

But the one-eyes, nearly a thousand strong, could afford the losses.

All the wall seemed to groan and creak when the brutish masses slammed against it, setting ladders and chopping at the logs with great axes.

The folk of Menster remained controlled, emptied their quivers and called for more arrows, shooting point-blank at the brutes. But the wall was soon breached, cyclopians scrambling over the top and boring right through, and most of the folk had to drop their bows and take up sword or spear, or whatever was handy that might serve as a club.

In close, though, the defenders' advantage was lost, and so, both sides knew, was Menster.

It was over in a few minutes.

Suddenly Menster, or the utter carnage that had been Menster, was no longer an unnoticed and unremarkable little village to King Brind'Amour, or to anyone living along Eriador's southern border.

Chapter 3

BITTERSWEET

The first slanted rays of the morning sun roused Katerin O'Hale. She looked about her camp, to the gray ashes of the previous night's fire, to the two horses tethered under a wide elm, and to the other bedroll, already tied up and ready to pack away. That didn't surprise Katerin; she suspected that her traveling companion had found little sleep.

The weary woman dragged herself out from under the blankets, stood tall, and stretched away the pains of sleeping on hard ground. Her legs were sore, and so were her buttocks. For five days, she and Luthien had ridden hard to the north, across the breadth of Eriador, to the mainland's northwestern tip. Now, turning her back to the morning sun, Katerin could see the haze from the straits where the Avon Sea met the Dorsal, and through that haze, not so far away, loomed the ghostly gray forms of Isle Bedwydrin's rolling, melancholy hills.

Home. Both Katerin and Luthien had been raised on the island, the largest in Avonsea, save the mainland and giant Baranduine to the south and west. The two companions had spent nearly all of their lives on Bedwydrin, Luthien in Dun Varna, the largest city and seat of power, and Katerin across the way, on the western shores, in the hardy village of Hale. When she had hit her mid-teens, Katerin had gone to Dun Varna to train as a warrior in the arena, and there she had met Luthien.

She had fallen in love with the son of Eorl Gahris Bedwyr, and had followed him across the country, all the way into Avon at the head of an army.

The war was over now, at least for a while, and the two were going home. Not for a vacation, but to see Gahris, who, by all reports, lay near death.

Looking at the island, so near, and thinking of their purpose, Katerin understood that Luthien hadn't slept well the previous night. Likely he hadn't slept at all for several days. The woman looked all around, then crossed the small camp and climbed a rise, crouching low as she neared the top.

In a clearing beyond stood Luthien, stripped to the waist and holding *Blind-Striker*, the Bedwyr family sword.

What a marvelous weapon was that sword, its perfect blade of tightly wrapped metal gleaming in the morning sun, outshone only by its golden, bejeweled hilt, sculpted into the shape of a dragon rampant, the outstretched wings serving as a formidable crosspiece.

Katerin's shining green eyes did not linger long on the weapon, for more marvelous still was the specter of Luthien. He stood two inches above six feet, with wide shoulders and a broad chest, golden-tanned, and arms lined by strong and sinewy muscles that flexed and corded as he moved through his morning practice regimen. He was thicker, stronger, than he had been when they had fought in the arena in Dun Varna, Katerin decided. No more a boy, but a man. His eyes, striking cinnamon-colored orbs, the trademark of family Bedwyr, showed that change as well. They still held their youthful luster, but now that gleam was tempered by the intensity of wisdom.

Blind-Striker seemed to weave invisible strands into the air as it moved about Luthien, sometimes guided by one hand, sometimes by two. Luthien turned and dipped, came up high and arched gracefully downward, but though he was often facing her, Katerin did not fear that he would take any notice. He was a complete fighter, full of concentration despite his weariness, and his trance during his practice routine was complete. Up went *Blind-Striker*, straight over Luthien's head, held in both hands, the young man's arms and body perfectly squared. Slowly Luthien shifted to the side, letting go of the heavy sword with his right hand and bringing the weapon down inch by inch with his left. His right hand dragged along his left forearm during the descent, across the elbow, and over his biceps. Everything stopped together, left arm straight out, on the exact plane with his shoulders, while his right arm remained bent over his head, the tips of his fingers barely touching the left shoulder.

Katerin studied him for the long seconds as he held the pose. The sword was heavy, especially held horizontally, so far from his body, but Luthien's strong arm did not quiver. Katerin's eyes roved to the smaller details, to the intense eyes and Luthien's hair, long and wavy and a dark, rich shade of blond, showing highlights of red in the sun.

Katerin instinctively brought her hand to her own hair, a thick red mane, and she pulled it back from her face. How she loved Luthien Bedwyr! He was in her thoughts all the time, in her dreams—which were always pleasant when he was in her arms. He had left her, had left Bedwydrin, shortly after a tragic incident in which his best friend had been killed. Luthien had exacted revenge on the murderer and then had taken to the road, a road that had joined him up with Oliver deBurrows, highwayhalfling; a road that had led him to Brind'Amour, who was at that time a recluse living in a cave. It was Brind'Amour who had given to Luthien the crimson cape, thus resurrecting the legendary Crimson Shadow.

And that road, too, had led Luthien to Siobhan, beautiful Siobhan, who had become his lover.

That fact still pained Katerin greatly, though she and Siobhan had become friends, and the half-elf had confided that Luthien loved only Katerin. In reality, Siobhan was no longer a threat to Katerin's relationship with Luthien, but the proud woman could not easily shake the lingering image of the two together.

She would get over it, though. Katerin resolved to do that, and Katerin was not one to fail at anything she determined to do. Siobhan was a friend, and Luthien was Katerin's lover once more.

Once more and forever, he had promised, and Katerin trusted in that oath. She knew that Luthien loved her as much as she loved him. That love brought concern now, for, despite the strong pose, Luthien was plainly exhausted. They would cross Diamondgate this day, onto the shores of Isle Bedwydrin, and would make Dun Varna three or four days after.

Luthien would face Gahris once more. The father he had dearly loved, but the man, too, who had so disappointed the young Bedwyr. When his friend had been murdered, Luthien had learned the truth of the world under King Greensparrow. The young man had learned as well that his father lacked the courage and conviction he expected, for Gahris had sent Luthien's older brother away to die for fear of the evil, unlawful king. It had been a blow from which Luthien had never recovered, not even when Katerin had arrived in Caer MacDonald bearing the family sword and news that Gahris had taken up the revolt.

"We must be on the road at once if we are to catch the first ferry," Katerin called, breaking Luthien's trance. He turned to regard her, relaxing his taut muscles and letting *Blind-Striker*'s tip slip low. Not surprised by the interruption or the command, Luthien answered with a simple nod.

Ever since word had come to Caer MacDonald that Gahris, eorl of Bedwydrin, had taken ill, Katerin had hurried Luthien along. She understood that Luthien had to get to his father before the man died, to make peace with him else he might never find peace with himself.

Determined to make the ferry—for if they missed it, they would have to wait hours for the next—Katerin rushed off to pack her bedroll, while Luthien went to see to the horses. They were away in mere minutes, riding hard to the west.

Diamondgate was quite different from how Luthien remembered it. The place was so named because of the flat, diamond-shaped island, a black lump of stone, a hundred yards out from shore, halfway across the channel to Isle Bedwydrin. Here ran the ferries between Bedwydrin and the mainland, two dwarven-crafted barges, inching their way through the white-capped, dark water along thick guide ropes. These were marvelous constructions, flat and open and huge, but so perfectly geared that a single man could turn the crank to pull them, no matter how laden. One was always in operation, unless the weather was too foul, or great dorsal whales had been spotted in the channel, while the other was always down for maintenance. The folk could not be too careful when traversing the dark waters around Isle Bedwydrin!

All the main features of the place were the same: the ferries, the abundant stones, the giant wharves, and the old wharves, ghosts of another day, testament to the power of the sea. Even the weather was the same, dull and gray, the water dark and ominous, whipping into little whitecaps as it danced about the channel. Now, though, there were many great warships moored in the area, nearly half of the fleet Eriador had captured from Avon when the southern kingdom's invading army had landed in Port Charley. Also, several huge structures had been built on Diamondgate Island, barracks to house the three thousand cyclopians taken prisoner in that war. Most of those brutes were gone now—there had been an open revolt on Diamondgate in which many cyclopians had been killed, and Gahris Bedwyr had ordered the remaining groups to be split up, with most taken from the island to smaller, more manageable prison camps.

The structures on Diamondgate remained intact and in repair though, by order of King Brind'Amour, just in case a new group of prisoners was taken.

The companions rode down to the wharves and right onto the barge with their mounts, Katerin on a sturdy Speythenfergus gray and Luthien on Riverdancer, his prized Highland Morgan. The powerful Riverdancer was a remarkable stallion, shining white and well-muscled, with the longer hair that distinguished the short but powerful Highland Morgan breed. Few in all of Eriador, and none on Bedwydrin possessed a finer or more distinctive steed, and Riverdancer, more than anything else, drew attention to Luthien.

He heard the whispers before the barge even left the shore, heard men talking about the "son of Gahris" and "the Crimson Shadow."

"You should not have worn the cape," Katerin remarked, seeing his uneasiness.

Luthien only shrugged. Too late now. His notoriety had preceded him. He was the Crimson Shadow, the legend walking, and, though Luthien was sure he hadn't truly earned it, the common folk showed him great respect, even awe.

The whispers continued throughout the long and slow journey across the channel; as the ferry passed near to Diamondgate, scores of cyclopians lined the rocks, staring at Luthien, some hurling insults and threats. He simply ignored them; in truth, taking their outrage as confirmation of his heroics. He couldn't be comfortable with the pats on the back from his comrades, but he could accept cyclopian insults with a wide smirk.

The ferry was met on Bedwydrin's shore by all the dock hands, actually applauding as Luthien rode forth onto the wharf. Luthien's previous crossing, a daring escape from ambushing cyclopians, and, as it turned out, from a giant dorsal whale, had become legend here, and the companions heard many conversations—exaggerations, Luthien knew—referring to that event. Soon enough, Luthien and Katerin managed to slip away and were clear of the landing, riding free and easy along the soft turf of Isle Bedwydrin, their home. Luthien remained obviously uncomfortable, however.

"Is everything I do to be chronicled for all to read?" he remarked a short time later.

"I hope not everything," Katerin replied slyly, batting her eyes at Luthien when he turned to regard her. The woman of Hale had a good laugh then, thrilled that she could so easily draw a blush from Luthien.

The three subsequent days of riding passed swiftly and uneventfully. Both Luthien and Katerin knew the trails of Bedwydrin well enough to avoid any settlements, preferring the time alone with each other and with their thoughts. For the young Bedwyr, those thoughts were a tumult of stormy emotions.

"I have been to Caer MacDonald," he told Katerin solemnly when at last Dun Varna, and the large white estate that was his family home, came into view. "To Eradoch, as well, and I have ridden beside our king all the way to Princetown in Avon. But suddenly that world seems so far away, so removed from the reality of Dun Varna."

"It feels as though we never left the place," Katerin agreed. She turned to Luthien and they locked stares, sharing emotions. For both of them, the trip across the isle had been like a trot through memory, bringing them back to simpler and, in many ways, happier days.

Eriador was better off now, was free of Greensparrow, and no longer did the people of Bedwydrin, or of all the land, have to tolerate the brutal cyclopians. But for many years Greensparrow had been a name empty of meaning, a distant king who had no effect on the day-to-day lives of Luthien Bedwyr and Katerin O'Hale. Not until two dignitaries, Viscount Aubrey and Baron Wilmon, had arrived in Dun Varna, bringing with them the truth of the oppressive king, had Luthien understood the plight of his land.

There was peace in ignorance, Luthien realized, looking at that shining white estate nestled on the side of the hill facing the sea.

It had been only a year and a half since he had learned the truth of his world, and had gone out on the road. Only a year and a half, and yet all of reality had turned upside down for young Luthien. He remembered his last full summer in Dun Varna, two years previous, when he spent his days training for the arena, or fishing in one of the many sheltered bays near to the town, or off alone with Riverdancer. Or fumbling with Katerin O'Hale, the two of them trying to make some sense of love, learning together and laughing together.

Even that had changed, Luthien realized in looking at the beautiful woman. His love for Katerin had deepened because he had learned to honestly admit to himself that he did indeed love her, that she was to be his companion for all his life.

Still, there was something more exciting about those days past, about the unsure fumbling, the first kiss, the first touch, the first morning when they awoke in each other's arms, giggling and trying to concoct some story so that Gahris, Luthien's father and Katerin's formal guardian, wouldn't punish them or send Katerin back across the isle to the village of Hale.

Those had been good times in Dun Varna.

But then Aubrey had come, along with Avonese, the perfumed whore who had ordered the death of Garth Rogar, Luthien's dear friend. The two had opened Luthien's eyes to Eriador's subjugation, to the truth of the supposed Avonese nobility. Those pretentious fops had forced Luthien to spill his first blood—that of a cyclopian guard—and to take to the road as a fugitive.

"I wonder if Avonese remains in chains," Luthien remarked, though he had meant to keep the thought private.

"Eorl Gahris sent her south," Katerin replied. "At least, that is what one of the deckhands on the ferry told me."

Luthien's eyes widened with shock. Had his father freed the woman, the wretch who had caused the death of his dear friend? For an instant, the young Bedwyr despised Gahris again, as vividly as he had when he learned that Gahris, in an act of pure cowardice, had sent his older brother, Ethan, off to war to die because he feared that Ethan would cause trouble with Greensparrow's henchmen.

"In chains?" Luthien dared to ask, and he prayed that this was the case.

Katerin sensed his sudden anxiety. "In a box," she replied. "It seems that Lady Avonese did not fare well in the dungeon of Dun Varna."

"There are no dungeons in Dun Varna," Luthien protested.

"Your father made one especially for her," Katerin said.

Luthien was satisfied with that answer, and yet it was with mixed emotions that he entered Dun Varna and rode the red limestone and cobblestone streets to the grand entrance of House Bedwyr.

He and Katerin were met at the door by other reminders of their past, men and women they had not seen in more than a year, men and women both smiling and grim, glad for the young Bedwyr's return, and yet saddened that it should be on such an occasion as this.

Gahris's condition had worsened, Luthien was informed, and when the young Bedwyr went up to the room, he found his father sunk deep into the cushions of a large and soft bed.

The man's cinnamon eyes had lost their luster, Luthien realized as soon as he moved near to Gahris. His thick shock of silvery-white hair had yellowed, as had his wind-creased face, a face that had weathered countless hours under the Bedwydrin sun. The once-corded muscles on Gahris Bedwyr's arms had slackened, and his chest had sunken, making his shoulders seem even broader, though not so strong. Gahris was a tall man, three inches above Luthien and as tall as Luthien's older brother, Ethan.

"My son," Gahris whispered, and his face brightened for just a moment.

"What are you doing in bed?" Luthien asked. "There is so much to be done. A new kingdom to raise."

"One that will be better than the time of Greensparrow," Gahris replied, his voice barely a whisper. "And better than what was before Greensparrow. I know it will be so, because my son will play a hand in its formation." As he spoke, he lifted his arm and took Luthien by the hand. The old man's grip remained surprisingly strong, lending Luthien some hope.

"Katerin is with me," Luthien said, and turned to motion Katerin to the bedside. She drifted over, and the eorl's face brightened again, verily beamed.

"I had hoped to live to see my grandchildren," Gahris said, bringing more of a blush from Luthien than from Katerin. "But you will tell them about me."

Luthien started to protest that admission that Gahris was dying, but Katerin spoke first. "I will tell them," she promised firmly. "I will tell them of the eorl of Bedwydrin, whose people loved him, and who rid the isle of wretched cyclopians!"

Luthien looked back and forth between the two as Katerin spoke, and realized that any protests he might make would be obviously false and uncomforting. At that moment, the young man had to admit the truth to himself: his father was dying.

"Will you tell them of Gahris the Coward?" the old man asked. He managed a small chortle. "How I bent to the will of Greensparrow," he scolded. "And Ethan . . . ah, my dear Ethan. Have you heard anything . . . ?"

The question fell away as Gahris looked upon Luthien's grim expression, learning from that face that Ethan was truly gone to him, that Luthien had not found his brother.

"If ever you see him," Gahris went on, his voice even softer, "will you tell him of the end of my life? Will you tell him that, in the end, I stood tall for what was right, for Eriador free?"

Katerin eyed Luthien intently as the moments slipped past, realizing that her love was in a terrible dilemma at that moment, a crossroad that might well determine the path of his life. Here he was, facing Gahris once more, with one, and only one, chance to forgive his father. Gahris needed that forgiveness, Katerin knew, but Luthien needed it more.

Without saying a word, Luthien drew out *Blind-Striker* and lay it on the bed, across Gahris's legs.

"My son," Gahris said again, staring at the family sword, his eyes filling with tears.

"It is the sword of family Bedwyr," Luthien said. "The sword of the rightful eorl, Gahris Bedwyr. The sword of my father."

Katerin turned away and wiped her eyes; Luthien had passed perhaps his greatest test.

"You will take my place when I am gone?" Gahris asked hopefully.

As much as he wanted to comfort his father, Luthien couldn't commit to that. "I must return to Caer MacDonald," he said. "My place now is beside King Brind'Amour."

Gahris seemed disappointed for just a moment, but then he nodded his acceptance. "Then you take the sword," he said, his voice stronger than it had been since Luthien had entered the room, stronger than it had been in many days.

"It is your—" Luthien began to protest.

"It is mine to give," Gahris interrupted. "To you, my chosen heir. Your gift of forgiveness has been given and accepted, and now you accept from me the family sword, now and forever. This business with Greensparrow is not finished, and you will find more use for *Blind-Striker* than I, and better use. Strike hard for family Bedwyr, my son. Strike hard for Eriador!"

Luthien reverently lifted the sword from the bed and replaced it in its scabbard. The verbal outburst had cost Gahris much energy, and so Luthien bade his father rest and took his leave, promising to return after he had cleaned up from the road and taken a meal.

He kept his promise and spent the bulk of the night with his father, talking of the good times, not the bad, and of the past, not the future.

Gahris Bedwyr, eorl of Bedwydrin, died peacefully, just before the dawn. Arrangements had already been made, and the very next night the proud man was set adrift in a small boat, into the Dorsal Sea that was so important to the lives of all in Dun Varna. No successor was immediately named; rather, Luthien appointed a steward, a trusted family friend, for as he had explained to his father, Luthien could not remain in Dun Varna. Bigger issues called out to him from Caer MacDonald; his place was with Brind'Amour, his friend, his king.

Luthien and Katerin left Dun Varna the very next day, both of them wondering if they would ever again look upon the place.

Katerin noticed the change in Luthien immediately. He slept well and rode alert and straight as they made their way back to the south, to Diamondgate and then to the mainland.

Katerin worried about him for a long while, seeing that he was not grieving for his loss. She couldn't understand this at first—when she had lost her own father, to a storm on the Avon, she had cried for a fortnight. Luthien, though, had shed few tears, had stoically placed his hand on his father's chest as Gahris lay in the small boat and had pushed it away, as if he had pushed Gahris from his mind.

Gradually, Katerin came to realize the truth, and she was glad. Luthien wasn't grieving now because he had already grieved for Gahris, on that occasion when the young man had been forced to flee the law of Bedwydrin. To Luthien, Gahris, or the man he had thought Gahris to be, had died on the day the young Bedwyr learned the truth about his brother Ethan and about his father's cowardice. Then, when Katerin had arrived in Caer MacDonald, bearing *Blind-Striker* and news that Bedwydrin was in open revolt against Greensparrow, Luthien's father had come alive once more.

Luthien, Katerin now realized, had viewed it all as a second chance, borrowed time, a proper way to bid farewell to the redeemed Gahris. Luthien's grieving had been long finished by the time he knelt by his dying father's bed. Now his cinnamon eyes no longer seemed full of pain. Gahris had made his peace, and so had his son.

Chapter 4

GYBI

Proctor Byllewyn stood solemnly on the sloping parapet of the Gybi monastery, staring out from his rocky perch to the foggy waters of Bae Colthwyn. More than a hundred gray ghosts slipped through that mist, Colthwyn fishing boats mostly, tacking and turning frantically, all semblance of formation long gone. The sight played heavy on the shoulders of the old proctor. These were his people out there, men and women who looked to him for guidance, who would give their lives at his mere word. And indeed, it had been Proctor Byllewyn's decision that the fishing boats should go to meet the invaders, to keep the fierce Huegoths busy out on the dark and cold waters and, thus, away from the village.

Now Byllewyn could only stand and watch.

The captains tried to stay close enough for their crews to shoot their bows at the larger vessels of the Huegoths, but they had to be perfect and swift to keep away from the underwater rams spearheading those terrible Huegoth longships. Every so often, one of the fishing boats didn't turn swiftly enough, or got held up by a sudden swirl of the wind, and the horrible cracking sound of splintering wood echoed above the waters, above the shouted commands and the terrified screams of the combatants.

"Twenty-five Huegoth longships have entered the bay, by last accounting," said Brother Jamesis, standing at Byllewyn's side.

"It is only an estimate," Jamesis added when the proctor made no move to reply.

Still the old man stood perfectly still and unblinking, only his thick shock of gray hair moving in the wind. Byllewyn had seen the Huegoths before, when he was but a boy, and he remembered well the merciless and savage raiders. In addition to the rowing slaves, twenty on a side, the seventy-foot longships likely carried as many as fifty Huegoth warriors, their shining shields overlapped and lining the upper decks. That put the number in the bay at more than twelve hundred fierce Huegoths. Colthwyn's simple fishing boats were no match for the deadly longships, and the men on the shore could only hope that the brave fishermen would inflict enough damage with their bows to dissuade the Huegoths from landing.

"One of the raiders flies the pennant of *The Skipper*, upside down, on its forward guide rope," the somber Jamesis further reported, and now Byllewyn did flinch. Aran Toomes and all the crewmen of *The Skipper* had been dear, long-standing friends.

Byllewyn looked down the sloping trail to the south, to the village of Gybi. Already many of the townsfolk, the oldest and the youngest, were making their way along the red-limestone mile-long walk that climbed the side of the knoll to the fortress monastery. The more able-bodied were down by the wharves, waiting to support the crews when the fishing boats came rushing in. Of course, the small fleet had not put out with any intentions of defeating the Huegoths at sea, only to buy the town time for the people to get behind the monastery's solid walls.

"How many boats have we lost?" Byllewyn asked. With the refugees now in sight, the proctor was considering ringing the great bell of Gybi, calling in the boats.

Jamesis shrugged, having no definite answer. "There are Colthwyn men in the water," he said grimly.

Byllewyn turned his gaze back to the mist-shrouded bay. He wished that the skies would clear, just for a moment, so that he could get a better feel for the battle, but he realized that the shroud was in truth a blessing for the fishermen. The Colthwyn fisherfolk knew every inch of these waters, could sail blindly through them without ever getting near the shallows or the one reef in the area, a long line of jagged rocks running straight out into the bay just north of the monastery. The Huegoth mariners also understood the ways of the sea, but these were foreign waters to them.

Byllewyn did not ring the bell; he had to trust in the fisherfolk, the true masters of the bay, and so it went on, and on.

The cries only intensified.

Stubbornly, the proud fisherfolk kept up the seaborne resistance, darting all around the larger Huegoth vessels, boats working in pairs so that if the Huegoth made a sudden turn to intercept one of them, the archers on the second would find their line of sight opened for a stern rake on the longship. Still, the fisherfolk had to admit that they were doing little real damage to the Huegoths. A dozen Colthwyn boats had been sent under the dark waters, but not a single Huegoth had gone down.

Captain Leary of the good boat *Finwalker* noted this fact with great concern. They were making the Huegoths work hard, peppering them with arrows and probably wounding or killing a few, but the outcome seemed assured. The more boats the Colthwyn defenders lost, the more quickly they would lose more. When a dozen additional Colthwyn ships were caught and sunk, the support for the remaining boats would be lessened, and all too soon it would reach the point where the defenders had to flee back to port, scramble out of their boats helter-skelter, and run the path to the monastery.

The defenders needed a dramatic victory, needed to send one of those seemingly impregnable longships to its watery death. But how? Arrows certainly wouldn't bring one down and any attempt at ramming would only send the Colthwyn boat to the bottom.

As he stood in thought, *Finwalker* rushed past the wolf's-head forecastle of a longship, close enough so that the captain could see the Huegoth's ram under the water. The Huegoth was in the midst of a turn, though, with little forward momentum, and *Finwalker*'s crew got off a volley of arrows, taking only a few in return as the boat glided past.

Leary looked to the woman at the wheel. "North," he instructed.

The woman, Jeannie Beens, glanced over her shoulder, to the longship and the two Colthwyn boats that had been working in conjunction with *Finwalker*. If she turned north, she would leave the Colthwyn boats behind, for one of them was sailing southeast, the other due west. The Huegoth, though, was facing north, and with those forty oars would soon leap in pursuit.

"North," Leary said again, determinedly, and the steerswoman obeyed.

Predictably, the Huegoth came on, and though the wind was from the southeast, filling *Finwalker*'s sails, the longship was swift in the pursuit. Even worse, as soon as the general battle, and the other two Colthwyn boats, were left behind, the Huegoths put up their own single square sail, determined to catch this one boat out from the pack and put it under.

Leary didn't blink. He told his archers to keep up the line of arrows, and instructed the steerswoman on the course he wanted.

Jeannie Beens stared at him blankly when she deciphered the directions. Leary wanted her to swing about, nearly out of the bay, and come back heading south much closer to the shore.

Leary wanted her to skim the reef!

The tide was high, and the rocks would be all but invisible. There was a break along the reef—Nicker's Slip, the narrow pass was called—that a boat could get through when the water was this high, but finding that small break when the rocks were mostly submerged was no easy task.

"You've sailed these waters for ten years," Captain Leary said to the woman, seeing her uncertainty. "You'll find the Slip, but the longship, turning inside our angle and flanking us as they pursue, will only get their starboard side through." Leary gave a mischievous wink. "Let's see how well half a longship sails," he said.

Jeannie Beens set her feet wide apart and took up the wheel more tightly, her sun-and-wind-weathered features grim and determined. She had been through Nicker's Slip on two occasions: once when Leary wanted to show her the place for no better reason than to prove to her that she was a fine pilot, and a second time on a dare, during a particularly rowdy party when a dorsal whale had been taken in the bay. On both of those occasions, though, the tide had been lower, with the rocks more visible, and the boats had been lighter, flat-bottomed shore-huggers that drew only a couple of feet. *Finwalker*, one of the largest fishing boats this far north in the bay, drew nine feet and would scrape and splinter if Leary tried to put her through when the tide was low, might even rub a bit now, with the water at its highest. Even worse for Jeannie was the damned fog, which periodically thickened to obscure her reference points.

When the high dark outline of the monastery dipped behind her left shoulder, Jeannie Beens began her wide one-hundred-eighty-degree turn back to the south. As Leary had predicted, the Huegoth turned inside *Finwalker*, closing some ground and giving chase off the fishing boat's port stern. Now the Huegoth archers had a better angle and their bows twanged mercilessly, a rain of arrows, broadheads, and flaming bolts falling over *Finwalker*.

Two crewmen fell dead; a third, trying to put out a fire far out on the mast's crossbeam, slipped overboard and was gone without a cry. Leary himself took an arrow in the arm.

"Keep to it!" the captain yelled to Jeannie.

The woman refused to look back at their pursuers, and blocked out the growing shouts of the Huegoths as the longship rapidly gained. The wind did not favor *Finwalker* any longer; her turn had put the stiff breeze straight in off her starboard bow. Her sails had been appropriately angled as far as possible, and she made some headway, but the Huegoths dropped their sail altogether, and the pounding oars drove the longship on.

More arrows sliced in; more of *Finwalker*'s crew fell. Jeannie heard the roars, heard even the rhythmic beating of the drum belowdecks on the longship, prodding the rowing slaves on.

Huegoths called out taunts and threats, thinking they had the boat in their grasp.

Jeannie blocked it all out, focused on the shoreline, its features barely distinguishable through the heavy mist. There was a particular jag signaling the reef line, she knew, and she pictured it in her mind, trying hard to remember it exactly as it had appeared on those two occasions when she had gone through Nicker's Slip. She focused, too, on the bell tower of Gybi monastery and on the steeple of the meetinghall in the town, further ahead to the south, recalling the angle. She had to calculate their angle so that the two towers would line up, three fingers between them, at the moment *Finwalker* passed the jag and entered the reef line.

Leary gave a shout and fell to his knees beside her, holding his now bleeding forehead. Beyond him, Jeannie noted the bloody arrow that had just grazed him, embedded deep into *Finwalker*'s rail, its shaft shivering.

"Hold steady," Leary implored her. "Hold . . ." The captain slumped to the deck.

Jeannie could hear the oars pounding the water; smoke began to drift about her as more of the flaming arrows found their deadly hold. She heard a Huegoth call out—to her!—the barbarian apparently excited to find that a woman was on board.

Jeannie couldn't help but glance back, and saw that a pair of massive Huegoths were standing along the forward edge of the longship, preparing to leap aboard *Finwalker*. The longship could not come up beside *Finwalker*, Jeannie realized, because its oars would keep it too far away for the Huegoths to board. But positioned just to the side and behind, the prow of the longship could get within a few feet of the fishing boat.

They weren't much further away than that right now, and Jeannie wondered why her fellows weren't shooting the brazen Huegoths dead. Then she realized, to her horror, that none of *Finwalker*'s crew could take to their bows. Most of the crew lay dead or wounded on the deck, and those who could still function were too busy battling fires to battle the fierce men of Isenland!

Jeannie turned her eyes back to the reef and the shore, quickly determined her angle and made a slight adjustment, putting a few extra feet between *Finwalker* and the longship.

She saw the jag, instinctively lifted her hand up between the images of the bell tower and the steeple, thumb and little finger tucked back tight.

Three fingers—almost.

Finwalker groaned and shook, her starboard side scraping hard. She leaned hard, but came through, and though her seaworthiness had surely been compromised, the reef was behind her.

The longship did not fare so well. Her prow hit the rocks, bouncing her to the right, and she plowed on, her left bank of oars splintering and catching, swinging her about. Nicker's Slip was a narrow pass, and as the seventy-foot craft hooked and turned, her stern crunched sidelong across the gap, into the reef. Huegoths tumbled out by the dozen, and those poor slaves at the oars fared little better as the great ship split in half, to be battered and swallowed by the dark waters.

Jeannie Beens saw none of it, but heard the cheers from those crewmen still standing. She pulled *Finwalker* hard to starboard, angling for shore, for she knew that the boat was taking water and was out of the fight.

The little boat had scored even, one-to-one, but more importantly, the daring heroics of *Finwalker* did not go unnoticed, not by the Bae Colthwyn fisherfolk nor by the Huegoth raiders. Leary's decision had been based on the captain's belief and hope that this was not a full-scale invasion force, but a powerful probe into Gybi's defenses. No doubt the Huegoths meant to go into the town, but Leary didn't think they had the manpower to lay siege to the monastery, and didn't think they meant to stay for long.

As it turned out, he was right. The Huegoths had not expected to suffer any considerable losses on the water, certainly hadn't believed they would lose a longship, and soon after the incident, the raiders turned their prows back out to the open sea and sped off into the veil of fog.

The fisherfolk of Gybi could not claim victory, though. They had lost almost twenty boats, with twenty others damaged, and more than a hundred folk lost to the cold waters of the bay. In a town of three thousand, that meant that almost every family would grieve that night.

But Leary's daring and Jeannie Beens's grit and skill had bought them time, to plan or to flee.

"The Huegoths will be back in force," Brother Jamesis said at the all-important meeting that night in the monastery.

"They have a base somewhere near here," Leary reasoned, his voice shaky, for the wounded man had lost a lot of blood. "They could not have sailed all the way from Isenland, only to turn about to sail all the way back, and that before they even resupplied in the town!"

"Agreed," said Proctor Byllewyn. "And if their base is near Colthwyn, then it is likely they will return, in greater numbers."

"We must assume the worst," added another of the brothers.

Proctor Byllewyn leaned back in his seat, letting the conversation continue without him while he tried to sort things through. Huegoths hadn't been seen so close to Eriador's shores in such numbers in many, many years. Yet now, just a few months after the signing of the truce with King Greensparrow, the barbarian threat had returned. Was it coincidence, or were those events linked? Unpleasant thoughts flitted through Byllewyn's mind. He wondered if the Huegoths were working secretly with Greensparrow. Perhaps it was less contrived than that, though certainly as ominous: that the Isenlanders had merely come to the conclusion that with the two nations of Avonsea separated, with Eriador no longer afforded the protection of the mighty Avon navy or the promise of severe retribution from the powerful King Greensparrow and his wizard-duke allies, the plunder would be easily gotten. Proctor Byllewyn recalled an incident a few years before, when he was returning from a pilgrimage to Chalmbers. He had witnessed a Huegoth raiding ship overtaken by an Avon warship. The longship had been utterly destroyed and most of the floundering Huegoths left in the water to drown or to feed the dorsal whales. And those few Huegoths who had been plucked from the sea found their fate more grim: keel-hauling. Only one Isenlander had been left alive, and he had been set adrift in a small boat, that he might find his way back to his king and tell of the foolishness of raiding the civilized coast. That vivid memory made Byllewyn think even less of the possibility that the Huegoth king would have allied with Greensparrow.

"As far as the Huegoths know, Eriador has little in the way of warships," Brother Jamesis was saying, a related line of thought that brought the proctor back into the conversation.

Byllewyn looked around at the faces of those gathered, and he began to see a dangerous seed germinating there. The people were wondering if the break from Avon and the protective power of Greensparrow was a good thing. Most of the men and women in the room, besides Byllewyn and Captain Leary, were young, and did not remember, or at least did not appreciate, Eriador before Greensparrow. In the face of such a disaster as the Huegoths, it was easy to judge the years under Greensparrow in a softer light. Perhaps the unfair taxes and the presence of brutish cyclopians was not such a bad thing when viewed as protection from greater evils . . .

Byllewyn, fiercely independent, knew that this was simply not true, knew that Eriador had always been self-sufficient and in no need of protection from Avon. But those determined notions did little to dispel the very real threat that had come so suddenly to Gybi's dark shores.

"We must dispatch an emissary to Mennichen Dee in Eradoch," he said, "to enlist the riders in our defense."

"If they are not dancing about the Iron Cross with the good King Brind'Amour," another man remarked sarcastically.

"If that is the case," Byllewyn interrupted, defeating the rising murmurs of discontent before they could find any footing, "then our emissary must be prepared to ride all the way to Caer MacDonald."

"Yes," said the same sarcastic fisherman, "to the throne seat, to beg that our needs not be ignored."

The proctor of Gybi did not miss the vicious tone of the voice. Many of the locals had voiced their opposition to the anointment of the mysterious Brind'Amour as king of Eriador, declaring that Byllewyn, the long-standing proctor of Gybi, would be the better choice. That sentiment had been echoed across much of northeastern Eriador, but the movement had never gained much momentum since Byllewyn himself had put an end to the talk. He wondered now, given the grim mood, how long it would be before he would be dissuading similar opinions once more.

"Caer MacDonald, then!" another man growled. "Let us see if our newly proclaimed king has any bite in him."

"Here, here!" came the agreeing chorus, and Byllewyn sat back thoughtfully in his chair, his fingertips tapping together before his eyes. He didn't doubt that Brind'Amour—that anyone who could wrest control from Greensparrow—had bite, but he was also pragmatic enough to realize that, with the kingdoms separate once more, many ancient enemies, Huegoth and cyclopian, might indeed see Eriador as vulnerable. The arrival of Huegoths would be a major test for Brind'Amour, one that the new king could not afford to fail.

The proctor of Gybi, a man of small ambition and generous heart, would pray for him.

Chapter 5

SOUGLES'S GLEN

"Ah, we'll be eating well when the money starts a'flowing outa Caer MacDonald!" exclaimed Sougles Bellbanger, a rugged dwarf with hair and beard the color of rich tea. He hoisted his flagon high into the crisp night air.

Ten of his fellows, sitting about a huge bonfire, did likewise, all looking to the stars shining brightly and clearly visible through the break in the forest above this small glen.

"Keep it quiet!" yelled yet another of the bearded folk, who was curled up on a bedroll not so far away. Beside him, a dwarf snored loudly, and so when his call to the partying group at the fire went unnoticed, he slapped the snoring dwarf instead, just for the satisfaction.

"Sleeping on this night!" Sougles howled derisively. "Plenty of time for that after we've sold our goods."

"After we've spent the gold we've got for selling our goods!" corrected one of the others, and again, the mugs came up high into the air.

"And after we get the gold, you'll all be too weary to spend it properly," grumbled the dwarf from the bedroll. "And I'll be helping meself, thank you."

That brought still more wild cheering from the gathering at the fire, along with many snorts. They were tough and ready dwarfs of DunDarrow; they could party all this night, go into the little settlement—Menster, it was called—in the morning, then spend the rest of the day selling their goods and quickly giving back most of the gold to the folk of Menster in exchange for ale and good food, and then comfortable lodgings before they made their trek back into the mountains to the nearest entrances of DunDarrow. That was the way it would work, now that Brind'Amour was king, now that Bellick dan Burso was in Caer MacDonald signing a pact to make Eriador and DunDarrow as one.

And so they partied, howled and drank, tore off huge chunks of venison and threw the bones at the complainer in the bedroll. It went on most of the night, ending only in surprise as a ragged human, bleeding from the forehead, stumbled into camp.

Up came the dwarfs and out came their weapons, huge axes, short, thick swords, and heavy hammers that could spin through the air and take down a target at thirty paces.

The man, seemingly oblivious to his surroundings, stumbled further, nearly tripping headlong into the fire. Two dwarfs had him in an instant, propping him by the arms.

"What're you about?" demanded Sougles.

The man whispered something too low for the dwarf to hear, considering the grumbling conversations erupting all about. Sougles called for quiet and moved closer, cocking his head to put his ear in line with the man's lips.

"Menster," the man repeated.

"Menster?" Sougles asked loudly, and the word hushed his fellows. "What about Menster?"

"Them," whispered the man, and he slumped.

"Them?" Sougles asked loudly, turning to his companions.

"Them!" one of the dwarfs yelled in response, pointing to the dark line of trees, to the bulky shapes moving within those shadows.

In all of Avonsea, in all the world, no two races hated each other more profoundly than did cyclopians and dwarfs, and when the one-eyes came howling out of the brush, thinking to overwhelm the dwarvish encampment, they found themselves running headlong into a wall of determination. Outnumbered nearly ten to one as the horde poured in, the dwarfs locked in a ring about their fire, fighting side to side, hacking and slashing with abandon, and singing as though they were glad for the fight. Every so often, one of the dwarfs would manage to reach back to retrieve a flaming brand, for dwarfs enjoyed nothing more than putting the hot end of a burning stick into the bulbous eye of a cyclopian.

A sword in each hand, Sougles Bellbanger slashed out the knees of any cyclopian that ventured near, and more often than not, the cunning dwarf managed to thrust his second sword into the wounded brute's torso before it ever hit the ground.

"Oh, good sport!" Sougles yelled often, and though they were taking some hits, and a couple had gone down, the dwarfs heartily agreed. In only a few moments, a score of cyclopians lay dead or dying, though still more poured from the trees to take up the fight.

It went on and on; those dwarfs who had been caught without their boots on felt the puddles of blood rising up to mid-ankle. Half an hour later, they were still fighting, and still singing, all traces of drink pushed from their blood by fiery adrenaline. Every time a dwarf fell, he was pushed back, and the ring tightened defensively. They were running out of room, Sougles knew, for he could feel the heat of the fire licking at his backside, but by this time the cyclopians had to clamber over their own dead to get near the fighting. And the ranks of one-eyes were indeed thinning, with many others running off into the woods, wanting no part of this deadly dwarven brigade.

Sougles believed that they would win—all the dwarfs held faith in their battle prowess. The fire, untended for so long, was burning low by this time and had become a heap of charred logs and glowing ashes, bluish flames rising to lick the cold air every so often. Sougles worked hard to devise a plan where he and his fellows might make use of that; perhaps they could retreat part of the line over the dying fire, using it as a weapon, kicking embers up at the one-eyes. Yes, he decided, they could launch a fiery barrage at the cyclopian line and then come roaring back across the embers, charging hard into the confused brutes.

Before Sougles could begin to pass word of the move, though, the fire seemed to execute a plan of its own. Blue flames exploded high into the air, changing hue to bright white, and all the embers flew out onto the backs of the dwarfs, nipping at them, stinging them and singeing their hair. Even worse, the mere surprise of the explosion destroyed the integrity of the dwarvish defensive ring. Dwarfs jumped, not in unison, and the cyclopians, who did not seem so startled, were quick to wedge in between their bearded adversaries, to separate the dwarfs. Soon Sougles, like many of his fellows, found himself battling cyclopians frantically on all sides, slashing and dodging, ducking low and running about. He did well, killed another one-eye and cut yet another's legs out from under it. But the experienced dwarf knew that he could not keep up the pace, and understood that one hit—

Sougles felt the crude spear burrow deep into the back of his shoulder. Strangely, he had no sensation of burning pain, just a dull thud, as though he had been punched. He moved to respond, but alas, his arm would not lift to his mind's call. Seeing the opening, a second one-eye howled and charged straight in.

Across came Sougles's other blade, somehow parrying the thrust of the charging brute and turning the one-eye aside.

But then Sougles was hit in the other side, and behind him the spearwielder prodded wildly, bending the dwarf forward, and then to the ground, where the one-eyes fell over him with abandon.

Some distance from the action and the fire, the cyclopian leader looked down at the person standing next to him, his one eye scrunched up with anger. "Yer should'a done that afore," the brute scolded.

The young woman gave a shake of her head, though her neatly coiffed blond hair hardly moved. "Magic cannot be rushed," she declared, and turned away.

The cyclopian watched her go, not so certain of her motives. It never seemed to bother the duchess much when one-eyes died.

Upon his return to Caer MacDonald, Luthien reported immediately to Brind'Amour the news that Eorl Gahris of Bedwydrin was dead. The old wizard was truly saddened and offered his condolences to Luthien, but the young man merely nodded his acceptance and begged his leave, which the king readily granted.

Coming out of the Ministry, the sun gone in the west and the stars beginning to twinkle above, Luthien knew where to go to find Oliver. The Dwelf, a tavern in the rougher section of the city with a reputation for catering to nonhumans even in Duke Morkney's time, had become the most popular sitting room in the city. "Here the Crimson Shadow laid plans for the conquest of Caer MacDonald," claimed the fairly accurate rumors, and so the small tavern had gained a huge celebrity. Now sturdy dwarvish guards lined the entryway, while a discriminating elf walked the line, determining which would-be patrons might enter.

Luthien, of course, was allowed entry without question, both dwarfs and the elf going to proper military posture as he passed. So used was he to the behavior, the young Bedwyr hardly gave it a thought as he swept into the crowded room.

He found Oliver and Shuglin sitting together on high stools at the bar, the dwarf huddled over a mug of thick, foaming ale and Oliver leaning back, holding a glass of wine up before the nearest light source that he might properly inspect its coloring. Tasman, the bartender, noted Luthien's approach and nodded grimly at the young man, then motioned toward Luthien's two friends.

Luthien came up between them, putting his hands on their backs. "My greetings," he said quietly.

Oliver looked into the young man's cinnamon eyes and knew immediately what had happened. "How fares your father?" he asked anyway, thinking that Luthien would need to talk about it.

"Gahris has passed," Luthien replied evenly, stoically.

Oliver started to offer his condolences, but saw by the look on Luthien's face that the young man was dreading that. Instead the halfling lifted his glass once more and called out loudly, "To Gahris Bedwyr, eorl of Bedwydrin, friend of Caer MacDonald, thorn in the buttocks to Greensparrow. May he find just rewards in the world that is after our own!"

Many others in the Dwelf hoisted their mugs and called out, "Hear, hear!" or "Gahris!"

Luthien stared long and hard at his diminutive friend, the halfling who always seemed to know how to make things better. "Has the alliance been signed?" the young Bedwyr asked, wanting—needing—to change the subject.

Oliver's bright face went grim. "We were that close," he said, holding thumb and index finger a fraction of an inch apart. "But then the stupid one-eyes . . . "

"Fifteen dwarfs," Shuglin added. "Slaughtered near the village that used to be called Menster."

"Used to be called?" Luthien's voice was weak.

" 'Kindling' would be a better name now," explained Oliver.

"The agreement was in hand," Shuglin went on. "A duocracy, Oliver called it, and both kings, Brind'Amour and Bellick dan Burso, thought it a most splendid arrangement."

"Greensparrow, he would not have liked it," Oliver remarked. "For he would have found the mountains blocked by an army of dwarfs loyal to Eriador."

"But after the slaughter in Sougles's Glen—that's what we've named the place—King Bellick has decided to take matters under advisement," Shuglin said and drowned the bitterness with a great draining gulp of his ale.

"But that makes no sense," Oliver protested. "Such a fight should show clearly the need for alliance!"

"Such a fight shows clearly that we might not want to be involved," Shuglin grumbled. "King Bellick is considering a retreat to our own mines and our own business."

"That would be so very stupid . . ." Oliver started to say, but a threatening look from Shuglin told him that the matter was not up for debate.

"Where is Bellick?" Luthien asked. Unlike Oliver, whose view was apparently clouded by hope, and by his own prideful desire that his suggestion of duocracy be the determination of history's course, the young Bedwyr understood Bellick's hesitance. It was likely that the dwarf king was not even secure in his trust of the Eriadorans, perhaps even wondering whether Brind'Amour, and not Greensparrow, was behind the raids, using them for political gain.

"In Brind'Amour's house still," replied Oliver. "He will go to the mines on the morrow, and then return in a ten-day."

Luthien was not really surprised at the news. The cyclopian raids had become so frequent that many sourly called this the Summer of the Bleeding Hamlet. But that fact only made it even more clear to Luthien that the dwarfs should join with the folk of Eriador. What they needed now was to erase all suspicions between the sides, to put the blame for the raids squarely where it belonged: with the cyclopians, and with the one who was spurring them on.

"Would King Bellick desire revenge for Sougles's Glen?" Luthien asked Shuglin, and the dwarf's face brightened immediately, shining wherever it showed around his tremendous bluish-black beard.

"Then arrange for a dwarvish force to accompany me into the mountains," Luthien went on.

"You have spoken to Brind'Amour about this?" Oliver put in.

"He will not oppose it," Luthien assured the halfling.

Oliver shrugged and went back to his wine, obviously not convinced.

Neither was Luthien, actually, but the young Bedwyr would take his problems one at a time.

And he found another one waiting for him when he caught up to Brind'Amour later that same evening, the wizard standing atop the highest tower of the Ministry, alone with the stars. Brind'Amour politely listened to all of Luthien's plans and arguments, nodding his head to keep the young man talking, and it took some time before Luthien even began to understand that something was deeply troubling his friend.

"All in good order," Brind'Amour said when Luthien decided that he had babbled enough. "Fine idea including the dwarfs; they're the best in the mountains, after all, and eager to spill cyclopian blood. And if Greensparrow is behind the raids—and we both know that he is—let Bellick's folk see the proof, if there is any proof, firsthand."

Luthien's smile was blown away a moment later.

"You cannot go."

Luthien's jaw dropped open. "But . . ."

"I need you," Brind'Amour said plainly. "We have more trouble, worse trouble, brewing in the east."

"What could be worse than cyclopians?"

"Huegoths."

Luthien started to protest, until the response truly sank in. Huegoths! Among Eriador's, among all of Avonsea's, oldest enemies and worst nightmares.

"When?" Luthien stammered. "A rogue vessel or coordinated raid? Where? How many ships . . . ?"

Brind'Amour's steady hand, patting the air gently before the young Bedwyr, finally calmed him to silence. "I have spoken with an emissary from the village of Gybi on Bae Colthwyn," the king explained. "It was a substantial attack, more than a score of longships. They did not come ashore, but they would have, except for the courage of Gybi's folk."

Luthien did not immediately reply, trying to collect his wits in the face of such disturbing news.

"We know in our hearts that Greensparrow uses the cyclopians to daunt the solidarity of our kingdom," Brind'Amour went on, "and to destroy any potential alliance between Eriador and Dun-

Darrow. I suspect that the king of Avon has not in any way surrendered Eriador to the Eriadorans, as the truce would indicate."

"And thus you believe that Greensparrow might also be in league with the Huegoths," Luthien reasoned.

Brind'Amour shook his head halfheartedly. He did indeed fear that to be the case, but he honestly couldn't see how the wizard-king of Avon could have forged such an alliance. Huegoths respected physical might. They had little use for the "civilized" folk of Avon, and open hatred for wizardry. Brind'Amour, a sturdy northman himself, might be able to deal with them, but by all appearances Greensparrow was a fop, a physical weakling, who made no secret of his magical powers. Furthermore, even though an alliance with the Huegoths would strengthen Avon's position, Brind'Amour didn't believe that Greensparrow would want to deal with the barbarian Isenlanders.

"The man will gladly deal with cyclopians," Luthien reminded him when he spoke that thought aloud.

"He will gladly dominate stupid one-eyes," Brind'Amour corrected. "But no king who is not Huegoth will bend the will of the fierce Isenlanders."

"Even with wizardry?"

Brind'Amour sighed, having no answer. "Go to Gybi," he bade Luthien. "Take Oliver and Katerin with you."

The request disappointed the young Bedwyr, who sorely wanted to go into the mountains in search of the raiding cyclopian forces, but he did not complain. Luthien understood the importance of handling the Huegoths, though he wanted badly to believe that the raid on Gybi might be a coincidence, and not a long-term threat.

"I have already sent word to the Riders of Eradoch," Brind'Amour explained. "A fair-sized force is nearing Gybi now, to bolster their defenses, and watches have been ordered along all the eastern coast as far south as Chalmbers."

Luthien saw then how important Brind'Amour considered the appearance of the Huegoths, and so the young Bedwyr did not argue the command. "I will make my preparations," he said and bowed, then turned to leave.

"Siobhan and the Cutters will accompany Shuglin into the mountains," Brind'Amour said to him, "to gather as much information as possible on the cyclopians. They will be waiting for you when you return." Brind'Amour gave a wink. "I will use some magic to facilitate your journey, that you might get your chance to put *Blind-Striker* to good use on the bloodshot eyes of cyclopians."

Luthien looked back to the old king and smiled, genuinely grateful.

Brind'Amour's return smile disappeared the moment Luthien was out of sight. Even if Greensparrow wasn't behind the Huegoth raid, the fledgling kingdom of Eriador was in serious trouble. Brind'Amour had brought about his victory over Avon in large part through hints to Greensparrow from the Gascons that they favored a free Eriador, that they might even enter the war on Eriador's side. But Brind'Amour had received such subtle aid from the vast southern kingdom of Gascony only by promising some very favorable port deals. Now, with the presence of the Huegoths, the new king had been forced to send word south to Gascony that the eastern stretches of Eriador, including the important port of Chalmbers, were not to be approached without heavy warship escort.

The Gascons would not be pleased, Brind'Amour knew; they might even come to the conclusion that Eriador was a safer place for their merchant ships under the protective rule of Greensparrow. One word to that effect from Gascony to the Avon king might launch Eriador back into an open war with Avon, a war that Brind'Amour feared they could not win. Avon had many more people, with a better trained and better equipped army and vicious cyclopian allies. And though Brind'Amour believed himself a wizardous match for Greensparrow, he couldn't ignore the fact that, as far as he could tell, he was Eriador's sole magical strength, while Greensparrow had at least four wizard-dukes and the duchess of Mannington in his court.

And if the mighty Huegoths, too, were in Greensparrow's hand . . .

The situation in Gybi had to be dealt with at once and with all attention, Brind'Amour knew. Luthien, Katerin, and Oliver were his best emissaries for such a mission, and the king had already dispatched nearly two-score of his own warships, almost half of his fleet, from Diamondgate, to sail around the northern reaches of Eriador and meet up with Luthien in Gybi.

The king of fledgling Eriador spent all that night atop the Ministry, thinking and worrying, looking for his answers in the stars, but finding nothing save potential disaster.

THE DUCHESS OF MANNINGTON

She was a small woman, slender and with her golden hair neatly cropped. She wore many valuable jewels, including a diamond hairpin and a brooch that glittered in the softest of lights. By all measures, Deanna Wellworth, the duchess of Mannington, was most elegant and sophisticated, undeniably beautiful, and so she seemed out of place indeed in the cold and rugged Iron Cross, surrounded by smelly, burly cyclopians.

The one-eyed leader, a three-hundred-pounder that stood halfway between six and seven feet, towered over Deanna. The brute could reach out with one hand and squash her flat, so it seemed, and, considering the tongue-lashing Deanna was now giving, the cyclopian appeared as though it wanted to do just that.

But Deanna Wellworth was hardly concerned. She was a duchess of Avon, one of Greensparrow's court, and with Duke Paragor of Princetown killed by Brind'Amour of Eriador, she was perhaps the strongest magician in all of Avon except for the king himself. She had a protection spell ready now, and if Muckles, the cyclopian leader, swung a hand out at her, it would burst into flames that the one-eye could not extinguish in any way short of leaping into the Avon Sea.

"Your murderers are out of control," Deanna ranted, her blue eyes, soft in hue to appear almost gray, locked on the face of ugly Muckles.

"We kill," the cyclopian responded simply, which was about the only way Muckles could respond. What flustered Deanna most about this assignment in the God-forsaken mountains was the fact that stupid Muckles was probably the smartest of the cyclopian group!

"Indiscriminately," Deanna promptly added, but she shook her head, seeing that the one-eye had no idea of what that word might mean. "You must choose your kills more carefully," she explained.

"We kill!" Muckles insisted.

Deanna entertained the thought of calling in Taknapotin, her familiar demon, and watching the otherworldly beast eat Muckles a little bit at a time. Alas, that she could not do. "You killed the dwarfs," she said.

That brought howls of glee from all the cyclopians nearby, brutes who hated dwarfs above anything. This tribe had lived in the Iron Cross for many generations and had occasionally run into trouble with the bearded folk of secret DunDarrow. The cyclopians thought that the woman's statement was the highest compliment anyone could pay them.

Deanna hardly meant it that way. The last thing Greensparrow wanted was an alliance between Eriador and DunDarrow. By her reasoning, any threat to DunDarrow would only strengthen the dwarfs' resolve to ally with Brind'Amour.

"If the result of your killing the dwarfs . . ."

"Yerself helped!" Muckles argued, beginning to catch on that Deanna was truly angered about the massacre.

"I had to finish what you stupidly started," Deanna retorted. Muckles began to counter, but Deanna snapped her fingers and the brute staggered backward as though it had been punched in the mouth. Indeed, a small line of blood now trickled from the side of Muckles's lip.

"If your stupidity has brought the dwarfs together with our enemies in Eriador," Deanna said evenly, "then know that you will face the wrath of King Greensparrow. I have heard that he is particularly fond of cyclopian skin rugs."

Muckles blanched and looked around at his grumbling soldiers. Such rumors about fierce Greensparrow were common among the cyclopians.

Deanna looked across the encampment, to where the dozen dwarf heads were drying out over a smoky firepit. Disgusted, she stormed away, leaving Muckles with her threats and a score of nervous subordinates. She didn't bother to look back as she passed from the small clearing into a wider meadow, where she was expected.

"Do you truly believe that the killings will ally DunDarrow with Brind'Amour?" asked Selna, Deanna's handmaid, and the only human out here in the wretched mountains with her.

Deanna, thoroughly flustered, only shrugged as she walked by.

"Do you really care?" Selna asked.

Deanna stopped dead in her tracks and spun about, curiously regarding this woman, who had been her nanny since childhood. Did Selna know her so very well?

"What do you imply by such a question?" Deanna asked, her tone openly accusing.

"I do not imply anything, my Lady," Selna replied, lowering her eyes. "Your bath is drawn, in the cover of the pine grove, as you commanded."

Selna's submissive tone made Deanna regret speaking so harshly to this woman who had been with her through so very much. "You have my gratitude," the duchess said, and she paused long enough for Selna to look up, to offer a smile of conciliation.

Deanna was very conscious of the shadows about her as she undressed beside the steaming porcelain tub. The thought of cyclopians lewdly watching made her stomach turn. Deanna hated cyclopians with all her heart. She thought them brutish, uncivilized pigs, as accurate a description as could be found, and these weeks in the mountains among them had been nothing short of torture for the cultured woman.

What had happened to her proud Avon? she wondered as she slipped into the water, shuddering at the intensity of the heat. She had given Selna a potion to heat the bath, and feared that the handmaid had used too much, that the water would burn the skin from her bones. She quickly grew accustomed to it, though, and then poured in a second potion. Immediately the water began to churn and bubble, and Deanna put her weary head back on the rim and looked up through the pine boughs to the shining half-moon.

The image brought her back through a score and two years, to when she was only a child of seven, a princess living in Carlisle in the court of her father the king. She was the youngest of seven, with five boys and a girl ahead of her, and thus far removed from the throne, but she was of that family nonetheless, and now remained as the only surviving member. She had never been close to her siblings, or to her parents. "Deanna Hide-away," they called her, for she was ever running off on her own, finding dark places where she could be alone with her thoughts and with the mysteries that filtered through her active imagination.

Even way back then, Deanna loved the thought of magic. She had learned to read at the age of four, and had spent the next three years of her life immersed in all the tomes detailing the ancient brotherhood of wizards. As a child, she had learned of Brind'Amour, who was now her enemy, though he was thought long-buried, and of Greensparrow, and how thrilled the young girl had been when that same Greensparrow, her father's court mystic, had come to her on a night such as this and offered to tutor her privately in the art of magic. What a wonderful moment that had been for young Deanna! What a thrill, that the lone surviving member of the ancient brotherhood would choose her as his protégée!

How then had Deanna Wellworth, once in line for the throne of Avon, wound up in the Iron Cross, serving as counsel to a rogue band of bloodthirsty cyclopians? And what of the folk of the Eriadoran villages they had routed, and of the dwarfs, massacred for reasons purely political?

Deanna closed her eyes, but couldn't block out the terrible images of slaughter; she covered her ears, but couldn't stop the echoing screams. And she couldn't stop the tears from flowing.

"Are you all right, my Lady?" came the stark question, shattering Deanna's visions. Her eyes popped open wide to see Selna standing over her churning tub, the woman's expression concerned, but in a way that seemed strange and unsettling to Deanna.

"Are you spying on me?" the duchess demanded, more sharply than she had intended. She realized her error as soon as she snapped out the words, for she knew that her tone made her appear guilty.

"Never that, my Lady," Selna replied unconvincingly. "I only returned with your blanket, and saw the glisten of tears in the moonlight."

Deanna rubbed her hand across her face. "A splash from the tub, and nothing more," she insisted.

"Do you long for Mannington?" Selna asked.

Deanna stared incredulously at the woman, then looked all around, as though the answer should be obvious.

"As do I," Selna admitted. "I am glad that is all that is troubling you. I had feared—"

"What?" Deanna insisted, her tone razor sharp, her soft eyes flashing dangerously.

Selna gave a great sigh. Deanna had never seen her act this cryptic before, and didn't like it at all. "I only feared," the handmaid began again, but stopped short, as if searching for the words.

Deanna sat forward in the tub. "What?" she demanded again.

Selna shrugged.

"Say it!"

"Sympathy for Eriador," the handmaid admitted.

Deanna slumped back in the hot water, staring blankly at Selna.

"Have you sympathy for Eriador?" Selna dared to ask. "Or, the God above forbid, for the dwarfs?"

Deanna paused for a long while, trying to gauge this surprising woman she had thought she knew so well. "Would that be so bad?" she asked plainly.

"They are our enemies," Selna insisted. "Sympathy for Eriador..."

"Decency for fellow humans," Deanna corrected.

"Some might see it as weakness, however you describe it," the handmaid answered without hesitation.

Again Deanna was at a loss for a reply. What was Selna implying here? The older woman had often served as Deanna's confidante, but this time Selna seemed removed from the conversation, as though she knew something Deanna did not. Suddenly, Deanna found that she didn't trust the woman, and feared that she had already revealed too much.

The water was cooling by this time, so Deanna rose up and allowed Selna to wrap her in the thick blanket. She dressed under cover of the pine grove and went to her tent, Selna following close behind.

The duchess's sleep was fitful, full of images that she could not block out or explain away. She felt a coldness creeping over her, a darkness deeper than the night.

She awoke in a cold sweat, to see a pair of red-glowing eyes staring down at her.

"Mistress," came a rasping, familiar voice, the voice of Taknapotin, Deanna's familiar demon.

The groggy duchess relaxed at once, but her relief lasted only as long as the second it took her to realize that she had not summoned the demon. Apparently, the beast had come from the fires of Hell of its own accord!

She saw Taknapotin's considerable array of gleaming teeth as the demon, apparently recognizing her concern, smiled widely.

No, not of its own accord, Deanna realized, for that simply could not be. Demons were creatures brought to the world by human desires, but who, other than Deanna Wellworth, could so summon Taknapotin? For a moment, Deanna wondered if she had somehow called to the fiend in her sleep, but she quickly dismissed that possibility. Bringing a demon to the material world was never that easy.

There could be only one answer then, and it was confirmed when next Taknapotin spoke.

"You are relieved of your duties here," the beast explained. "Go back to your place in Mannington."

Greensparrow. Only Greensparrow was powerful enough to summon Deanna's familiar demon without the duchess knowing about it.

"Duke Resmore of Newcastle will guide the cyclopian raiders," Taknapotin went on.

"By whose command?" Deanna asked, just because she needed to hear the name out loud.

Taknapotin laughed at her. "Greensparrow knows that you have little heart for this," the fiend said.

Selna, Deanna realized. Her handmaid, among her most trusted confidantes for the last twenty years, had wasted no time in reporting her sympathies to Greensparrow. The notion unsettled Deanna, but she was pragmatic enough to set her emotions aside and realize that her knowledge of the informant might be put to profitable use.

"When may I leave this wretched place?" Deanna asked firmly. She worked hard to compose herself, not wanting to appear as though she had been caught at anything treasonous. Of course it was perfectly logical that she would not want to be here with the one-eyes—she had protested the assignment vehemently when Greensparrow had given it to her.

"Resmore is outside, talking with Muckles," the fiend answered with a snicker.

"If you are finished with the task for which you were summoned, then be gone," Deanna growled.

"I would help you dress," Taknapotin replied, grinning evilly.

"Be gone!"

Instantly the beast vanished, in a crackling flash that stole Deanna's eyesight and filled her nostrils with the thick scent of sulfur.

When the smoke, and Deanna's vision, cleared, she found Selna at the tent flap, holding Deanna's clothing over her arm. How much this one already knew, the duchess mused.

Within the hour, Deanna had wished Resmore well and had departed the mountains, via a magical tunnel the duke of Newcastle had conveniently created for her. Trying to act as if nothing out of place had happened, indeed, trying to seem as though the world was better now that she was in her proper quarters in Mannington's palace, she dismissed Selna and sat alone on the great canopy bed in her private room.

Her gaze drifted to the bureau, where sat her bejeweled crown, her trace to the old royal family. She thought back again to that day so long ago, when drunk with the promise of magical power she had made her fateful choice.

Her thoughts wound their way quickly through the years, to this point. A logical procession, Deanna realized, leading even to the potential trouble that lay ahead for her. The cyclopians were not happy with her performance in the mountains, and rightly so. Likely, Muckles had complained behind her back to every emissary that came out of Avon. When Cresis, the cyclopian duke of Carlisle, heard the grumbles, he had probably appealed to Greensparrow, who had little trouble getting to Selna and confirming the problem.

"As it is," Deanna said aloud, her voice full of grim resignation, "let Resmore have the one-eyes and all their wretchedness." She knew that she would be disciplined by Greensparrow, perhaps even forced to surrender her body to Taknapotin for a time, always a painful and exhausting possession.

Deanna only shrugged. For the time being, there was little she could do except shrug and accept the judgments of Greensparrow, her king and master. But this was not the life Deanna Wellworth had envisioned. For those first years after her family's demise, she had been left alone by Greensparrow, visited rarely, and asked to perform no duties beyond the mostly boring day-to-day routines of serving the primarily figurehead position as duchess of Mannington. She had been thrilled indeed when Greensparrow had called her to a greater service, to serve in his stead and sign the peace accord with Brind'Amour in Princetown. Now her life would change, she had told herself after delivering the agreement to her king. And so it had, for soon after Greensparrow had sent her to the mountains, to the cyclopians, staining her hands with blood and shadowing her heart in treachery.

She focused again on the crown, its glistening gemstones, its unkept promises.

The dwarf howled in pain and tried to scamper, but the hole he was in was not wide and the dozen cyclopians prodding down at him with long spears scored hit after stinging hit.

Soon the dwarf was on the ground. He tried to struggle to his knees, but a spear jabbed him in the face and laid him out straight. The cyclopians took their time in finishing the task.

"Ah, my devious Muckles!" roared Duke Resmore, a broad-shouldered, rotund man, with thick gray hair and a deceivingly cheery face. "You do so know how to have fun!"

Muckles returned the laugh and clapped the huge man on the back. For the brutal cyclopian, life had just gotten a little better.

MASTERS OF THE DORSAL SEA

Huegoth!" cried one of the crewmen, a call seconded by another man who was standing on the crosspiece of the warship's mainmast.

"She's got up half a sail, and both banks pulling hard!" the man on the crosspiece added.

Luthien leaned over the forward rail, peering out to sea, amazed at how good these full-time seagoers were at discerning the smallest details in what remained no more than a gray haze to his own eyes.

"I do not see," remarked Oliver, standing beside Luthien.

"It can take years to train your eyes for the sea," Luthien tried to explain. (And your stomach, he wanted to add, for Oliver had spent the better part of the week and a half out of Gybi at the rail.) They were aboard *The Stratton Weaver*, one of the great war galleons captured from the Avon fleet in Port Charley now flying under Eriador's flag. In favorable winds, the three-masted *Weaver* could outrun any Huegoth longship, and in any condition could outfight three of the Huegoth vessels combined. With a keel length of nearly a hundred feet and a seasoned crew of more than two hundred, the galleon carried large weaponry that could take out a longship at three hundred yards. Already the crew at the heavy catapult located on the *Weaver*'s higher stern deck were loading balls of pitch into the basket, while those men working the large swiveling ballistae on the rail behind the foremast checked their sights and the straightness of the huge spears they would soon launch the barbarians' way.

"I do not see," Oliver said again.

"Fear not, Oliver, for Luthien is right," agreed Katerin, whose eyes were more accustomed to the open waters. "It can take years to season one's eyes to the sea. It is a Huegoth, though—that is evident even to me, though I have not been on the open sea in many months."

"Trust in the eyes of our guides," Luthien said to the halfling, who appeared thoroughly flustered by this point, tap-tapping his polished black shoe on the deck. "If they call the approaching vessel as a Huegoth, then a Huegoth it is!"

"I do not see," Oliver said for the third time, "because I have two so very big monkey-types blocking the rail in front of me!"

Luthien and Katerin looked to each other and snorted, glad for the relief that was Oliver deBurrows when battle appeared so imminent. Then, with great ceremony, they parted for the halfling.

Oliver immediately scrambled up to the rail, standing atop it with one hand grasping a guide rope, the other cupped over his eyes—which seemed pointless, since the brim of his huge hat shaded his face well enough.

"Ah yes," the halfling began. "So that is a Huegoth. Curious ship. One, two, three . . . eighteen, nineteen, twenty oars on each side, moving in harmony. Dip and up, dip and up."

Luthien and Katerin stared open-mouthed at each other, then at the tiny spot on the horizon.

"Oh, and who is that big fellow standing tall on the prow?" Oliver asked, and shuddered visibly. The exaggerated movement tipped Luthien off, and he sighed and turned a doubting expression upon Katerin.

"I would not want to fight with that one," the halfling went on. "His yellow beard alone seems as if it might scrape the tender skin from my halfling bones!"

"Indeed," Luthien agreed. "But it is the ring upon his finger that I most fear. See how it resembles the lion's paw?" Now it was Luthien's turn to feign a shudder. "Knowing Huegoth savagery and cunning, it is likely that the claws can be extended to tear the face from an adversary." He shuddered again, and with a grinning Katerin beside him, began to walk away.

Katerin gave him a congratulatory wink, thinking that he had properly called Oliver's bluff.

"Silly boy," the irrepressible halfling shouted after them. "Can you not see that the ring has no more than jew-wels where the retracted claws should be? Ah, but the earring . . ." he said, holding a finger up in the air.

Luthien turned, meaning to respond, but saw Katerin shaking her head and realized that he could not win.

"Fine eyes," remarked Wallach, the captain of *The Stratton Weaver*. He aimed his sarcasm squarely at Oliver as he and Brother Jamesis of Gybi walked over to join Luthien and Katerin.

"Fine wit," Katerin corrected.

"How long until we close?" Luthien asked.

Wallach looked out to the horizon, then shrugged noncommittally. "Could be half an hour, could be the rest of the day," he said. "Our friends in the longship are not running straight for us. They travel to the southeast."

"Do they fear us?" Luthien asked.

"We would overmatch them," replied Wallach confidently. "But I've never known Huegoths to run from any fight. More likely, they're wanting to take us near to Colonsey, into shallower waters where they might beach us, or at least outmaneuver us."

Luthien smiled knowingly at Wallach. This captain had been chosen to lead *The Stratton Weaver* out of Gybi because he, more than any other commanding one of the warships, was familiar with these waters. Wallach had lived in the settlement of Land's End on Colonsey for more than a dozen of his fifty years, and had spent nearly every day of that decade-and-two upon the waters of the Dorsal.

"They will think they have the advantage as we near the island," Katerin remarked slyly.

Wallach chuckled.

"We do not wish to fight them," Luthien reminded them both. "We have come out alone to parley, if that is possible." That was indeed the plan, for *The Stratton Weaver* had left her support fleet of thirty galleons in Bae Colthwyn.

"Huegoths aren't much for talking," Katerin remarked.

"And they respect only force," added Wallach.

"If we have to cripple the longship, then so be it," said Luthien. "We'll take them as bloodlessly as possible, but on no account will we let them slip from our grasp."

"Never that," said Jamesis, whose face had become perpetually grim since the arrival of the fierce Huegoths in the bay, since his peaceful existence in the quiet monastery had been turned upside down.

Luthien carefully studied the monk. He thought the folk of Gybi quite impressive for allowing him to execute his plan of parley. With thirty galleons at their disposal, the folk wanted nothing more than to exact revenge on the Huegoths for the loss of so many good men in Bae Colthwyn. But whatever their desires, the bell tower in Gybi had tolled wildly when Luthien and his companions had arrived, answering the call from Gybi to the new king. And the celebration had exploded yet again when the Eriadoran fleet had come into view north of the bay, rushing hard under full sail. Thus, Proctor Byllewyn had gone along with Luthien's desires and *The Stratton Weaver* had put out to sea, an armed and capable emissary, a diplomat first, a warship second.

"Run up the flag of parley," Luthien instructed Wallach. The young Bedwyr's gaze never left Jamesis as he spoke, searching for the monk's approval. Jamesis had argued against Luthien coming out here, and had found much support in the debate, even from Katerin and Oliver.

"The white flag edged in blue is known even to the Huegoths," Jamesis said grimly. "An international signal of parley, though Huegoths have been known to use it to get advantageously near to their opponent."

"The man's eyes, they are so blue!" exclaimed Oliver from the rail, the perfect timing to break the tension. Jamesis and Wallach cast the halfling a sidelong glance, but Luthien and Katerin only chuckled knowingly. Oliver couldn't see the Huegoth's eyes, they knew, couldn't see the oars of the longship, could hardly make out the vessel at all within the gray haze. But how wonderfully the halfling could play the game! Luthien had come to calling Oliver "the perfection of bluff" for good reason indeed.

A few minutes later, the flag of parley went up high on the mainmast of *The Stratton Weaver*. Wallach and the others watched carefully as more minutes slipped by, but, though the lookouts assured the captain that the Huegoths were close enough to discern the flag, the longship didn't alter her course or slow in the least.

"Running for Colonsey," Wallach repeated.

"Follow her in, then," Luthien instructed.

The captain cocked an eyebrow the young Bedwyr's way.

"You fear to give chase?" Luthien asked him.

"I would feel better about it if my king's second wasn't aboard," Wallach replied.

Luthien glanced nervously about.

Wallach knew that his simple logic had stung the young man, but that didn't stop him from ramming home his point. "If the Huegoths are in league with Greensparrow, as we fear, then wouldn't Luthien Bedwyr be a prize to give to the man? I'll not want to see Greensparrow's expression when the Crimson Shadow is handed over to him."

The argument was growing tedious to Luthien, one he had been waging since the meeting at Gybi when it was decided that the first course would be an attempt of parley with the Huegoths. Luthien had insisted that he be on the lone ship running out of the harbor. Even Katerin, so loyal to the young Bedwyr, had argued against that course, insisting that Luthien was too valuable to the kingdom to take such risks.

"The Crimson Shadow was a prize that Morkney of Montfort wanted to give to Greensparrow," Luthien replied. "The Crimson Shadow was a prize that General Belsen'Krieg promised to the evil king of Avon. The Crimson Shadow was a prize that Duke Paragor of Princetown coveted above all else."

"And they are all dead for their efforts," Brother Jamesis finished for him. "And thus you feel that you are immortal."

Luthien started to protest, but Oliver beat him to it.

"Can you not see?" the halfling asked, scrambling down to Luthien's side. "You say that my sometimes so unwise friend here is too valuable, but his value is exactly that which you wish to protect him from!"

"Oliver is right," added Katerin, another unexpected ally. "If Luthien hides behind the robes of Brind'Amour, if the cape is not seen where it is needed most, then the value of the Crimson Shadow is no more."

Wallach looked to Jamesis and threw up his hands in defeat. "Your fate is not ours to decide," the monk admitted.

"To Colonsey, then," said Wallach and he turned for the helm.

"Only if you think that the wisest course for your ship," Luthien said abruptly, turning the captain about. "I would not have you sailing into danger by my words. *The Stratton Weaver* is yours, and yours alone, to command."

Wallach nodded his appreciation of the sentiment. "We knew the danger when we came out," he reminded Luthien. "And every person aboard volunteered, myself chief among them. To a man and woman, we understand the perils facing our Eriador, and are willing to die in defense of our freedom. If you were not aboard, my friend, I would not hesitate to give chase to the longship, to force the parley, even if all the Huegoth fleet lay in wait!"

"Then sail on," Luthien bade him. With nods, both Wallach and Jamesis took their leave.

The Stratton Weaver angled inside the longship, turning to the east, but the Huegoths rowed fiercely and the galleon could not cut her off. Still, they got close enough for the barbarians to get a clear glimpse of the flag of parley, and the Huegoth reaction proved telling.

The longship never slowed, continuing on her way to the southeast. The great galleon took up the chase, and soon the gray tips of Colonsey's mountainous skyline were in plain sight.

"You still believe they are trying to beach us?" Luthien asked Wallach sometime later.

"I believe they were running for aid," Wallach explained, pointing out to starboard, where yet another longship was coming into sight, sailing around the island.

"Convenient that another was out and about and apparently expecting us," Luthien remarked. "Convenient."

"Ambushes usually are," Wallach replied.

A third Huegoth ship was soon spotted rowing in hard from port, and a fourth behind it, and the first vessel put up one bank of oars and turned about hard.

"We do not know how they will play it," Luthien was quick to say. "Perhaps now that the longship has its allies nearby, the Huegoths will agree to the parley."

"I'll allow no more than one of them to get close," Wallach insisted. "And that only under a similar flag of truce." He called up to his catapult crew then, ordering them to measure their aim on the lone ship to starboard. If a fight came, Wallach meant to sink that one first, giving *The Stratton Weaver* an open route out to deeper waters.

Luthien couldn't disagree, despite his desire to end these raids peacefully. He remembered Garth Rogar, his dearest of friends, a Huegoth who had been shipwrecked at a young age and washed up on the shores of Isle Bedwydrin. Luthien had unintentionally played a hand in Garth's death by defeating the huge man in the arena. If it had been Luthien who had gone down, Gahris would never have allowed the down-pointing-thumb signal that the defeated be vanquished.

Logically, Luthien Bedwyr held no fault in Garth Rogar's death, but guilt was never a slave to logic.

And so Luthien had determined to honor Garth Rogar's memory in this trip to Gybi and out onto the waters of the Dorsal Sea by resolving the conflict with the Huegoths as peacefully as possible. Despite those desires, Luthien could not expect the men and women who crewed *The Stratton Weaver* to leave themselves defenseless in the face of four longships. Wallach and his crew had been brave beyond the call of duty in merely agreeing to come out here alone.

"We could be in for a fight," Luthien said to Katerin and Oliver when he returned to their side at the forward rail.

Oliver looked out at the longships, white froth at their sides from the hard pull of oars. Then he looked about the galleon, particularly at the catapult crew astern. "I do so hope they are good shots," the halfling remarked.

With the odds suddenly turning against them, both Luthien and Katerin hoped so as well.

A call from above told them that a fifth longship had been spotted, and then a sixth, both following in the wake of the ship to starboard.

"Perhaps it was not so good an idea for the king's closest advisor to personally come out this far," Oliver remarked.

"I had to come out," replied Luthien.

"I was talking about myself," Oliver explained dryly.

"We've never run from a fight," Katerin said with as much resolve as she could muster.

Luthien looked into her green eyes and saw trepidation there. The young man understood completely. Katerin was not afraid of battle, never that, but this time, unlike all of the battles of Eriador's revolution, unlike all of the real battles that either she, or he, had ever fought, the enemy would not be cyclopian, but human. Katerin was as worried about killing as she was about being killed.

Captain Wallach verily raced the length of the deck, readying his crew. "Point her to the forward ship," he instructed the catapult gunners, for the longship coming straight at the galleon was the closest, and the fastest closing.

"Damn you, put up your flag of parley," the captain muttered, finally coming to the forward rail alongside the three companions.

As if on cue, the approaching longship's banks of oars lifted out of the water, the long and slender craft quickly losing momentum in the rough seas. Then a horn blew, a note clear and loud, careening across the water to the ears of *The Stratton Weaver*'s anxious crew.

"War horn," Katerin said to Wallach. "They're not up for parley."

Horns rang out from the other five longships, followed soon after by howls and yells. On came the vessels, save the first, which sat in the water, as if waiting for the galleon to make the first move.

"We cannot wait," Wallach said to an obviously disappointed Luthien.

"Three more to port!" came a cry from above.

"We'll not run out of here," remarked Katerin, studying the situation, seeing the noose of the trap drawing tight about the galleon.

Wallach turned back to the main deck, ordering the sails dropped to battle-sail, tying them down so that the ship could still maneuver without presenting too large a target for the Huegoth archers and their flaming arrows.

Luthien turned with him, and noticed Brother Jamesis approaching, his expression as grim as ever. Luthien matched the man's stare for a short while, but in truth it had been Luthien's decision to parley, it had been Luthien's doing that had put the crew in jeopardy. The young Bedwyr turned back to the water, then felt Jamesis's hand on his shoulder.

"We tried as we had to try," the monk said unexpectedly, "else we would have been no better than those we now, it would seem, must fight. But fear not, my Lord Bedwyr, and know that every longship we sink this day . . ."

"And there will be many," Wallach put in determinedly.

". . . will be one less to terrorize the coast of Bae Colthwyn,"

". . . will be one less to terrorize the coast of Bae Colthwyn," Jamesis finished.

Wallach looked to Luthien then, and motioned to the nearest longship, as if seeking the young man's approval.

It was not an easy choice for a man of conscience such as Luthien Bedwyr, but the Huegoths had made it clear that they were up for a battle. On the waters all about *The Stratton Weaver* horns were blowing wildly and calls to the Huegoth god of war drifted across the waves.

"They view battle as an honorable thing," Katerin remarked.

"And that is what damns them," said Luthien.

The ball of flaming pitch soared majestically through the afternoon sky, arcing delicately and then diving like a hunting bird that has spotted its quarry. The longship tried to respond—one bank of oars fell into the water and began to churn the ship about.

Too late. The gunners aboard the galleon had taken a full ten minutes to align the not-so-difficult shot. The longship did a quarter-turn before the missile slammed in, catching it square amidships, nearly knocking it right over.

Luthien saw several Huegoths, their furred clothing ablaze, leap overboard. He heard the screams of those others who could not get away. But the longship, though damaged, was not finished, and the oars fell back into the water and on it came.

Shortly thereafter, the Huegoth leader showed himself, rushing up to the prow of his smoking vessel, raising his sword in defiance and shouting curses the galleon's way.

To Luthien, the man's pride was as evident as his stupidity, for the ten other longships (for two more had joined in) were still too far away to offer support. Perhaps the Huegoth didn't understand the power of a war galleon; more likely, the battle-lusting man didn't care.

Wallach turned the galleon broadside to the longship. Another ball of pitch went out, hissing in protest as it crunched through several oars to fall into the water. On the longship came; the barbarian leader climbed right atop the sculpted forecastle, lifting his arms high to the sky.

He was in that very position, crying out to his battle-god, when the ballista-fired spear drove through his chest, hurling his broken body half the length of the longship's deck.

Still the vessel came on, too close now for the catapult, which Wallach ordered to move on to another target. Both ballistae opened up, though, as did a hundred archers, bending back great longbows, sweeping clear the deck of the Huegoth ship.

But still it came on.

The ballistae concentrated on the waterline near to the oars, their spearlike missiles cracking hard into the Huegoth hull.

"Move us!" Captain Wallach cried to his helmsman, and the man, and all those helping with the rigging, were trying to do just that. The Eriadoran crew couldn't believe the determination of the Huegoths. Most of the barbarian crew was certainly dead; the Eriadorans could see the bodies lying thick about the longship's deck. But they could hear the drumming of the slave drivers, the rhythmic beat, and though the slaves now surely outnumbered the captors many times over, the slaves didn't know it!

The Stratton Weaver slipped ahead a few dozen yards, and the longship, with no one abovedecks to steer her, did not compensate. The vessel crossed close in the galleon's wake, though, close enough so that her right bank of oars splintered on the great warship's stern, close enough so that three crewmen aboard the galleon were able to drop a barrel of flaming oil onto her deck.

That threat was ended, but the other Huegoths came on side by side, ten longships working in perfect concert. The catapult crew worked furiously, the ballistae fired one great spear after another, and another Huegoth vessel was sent to the bottom, a third damaged so badly that it could not keep up with its brethren.

Archers lined the rails, and their volleys were returned by Huegoth arrows and spears, many tipped with flame. Luthien had his bow out, too, and he took down one Huegoth right before the man could heave a huge spear the galleon's way. Oliver and Katerin and many others, meanwhile, worked at tending to the increasing number of wounded, and at putting out the stubborn fires before they could cause real damage.

Captain Wallach seemed to be everywhere, encouraging his warriors, calling out orders to his helmsman. But all too soon, the great galleon shuddered under the force of a ram, and the awful sound of cracking wood came up through the open hatches of *The Stratton Weaver*'s deck.

Grappling hooks soared over the rail by the dozen. Luthien drew out *Blind-Striker* and ran along, cutting ropes as fast as he could, while archers bent back their bows and let fly repeatedly, hardly taking the moment to aim.

The young Bedwyr could not believe the courage and sheer ferocity of the Huegoths. They came on without regard for their safety, came on with the conviction that to die in battle was a holy thing, a death to be envied.

There came a second shudder as a longship rammed them to port, then a third as another charged head-on into the *Weaver*'s prow, nearly destroying itself in the process. Soon there seemed to be as many Huegoths aboard the galleon as Eriadorans, and even more continued to pour over the rail.

Luthien tried to get to Wallach, who was fighting fiercely near to the prow. "No!" the young Bedwyr cried, and pulled up, staring in horror, as one Huegoth impaled the captain with the sharp prong of a grapnel. The rope went taut immediately, hurling the screaming Wallach over the rail.

Luthien jumped, startled, as a Huegoth bore down on him from the side. He knew the barbarian had him, that his hesitation in the face of such brutality had cost him his life.

But then the barbarian stopped short and turned to look curiously at a foppishly dressed halfling balancing along the rail, or more particularly, at the halfling's rapier, its slender blade piercing the man's ribs.

The Huegoth howled and leaped up, meaning to catch hold of Oliver and take the halfling over with him, but even as he found his footing, it was knocked away by the sure swipe of a belaying pin, cracking hard against the side of the man's knee. Over the rail he tumbled, and Katerin managed to pop him again, right in the head, before he disappeared from sight.

"I do so like fighting better atop my dear Threadbare," Oliver remarked.

"Think of the battle in the Ministry," Luthien said to them both. "Our only chance is to get as many together in a defensive group as possible."

Katerin nodded, but Oliver shook his head. "My friend," he said evenly, "in the Ministry, we survived because we ran away." Oliver looked around, and the others didn't have to follow his gaze to understand that this time, out on the open sea, there could be no retreat.

The valiant crew of *The Stratton Weaver* fought on for more than an hour, finding their first break when they came to a stand-off. Luthien, Katerin, Oliver, and fifty men and women held the high stern deck, while a hundred Huegoths on the main deck below pulled prisoners and cargo off the badly listing galleon. The prospects for the Huegoths fighting their way up the two small ladders to the higher deck were not good, but then, with their ships fast filling with captured booty and prisoners and *The Stratton Weaver* fast filling with water, they really didn't have to.

Luthien saw this, as did the others, and so they had to come up with the strength for a last desperate charge. There was no hope of winning, they all knew, and no chance of escape.

Then a brown-robed figure was brought forward and thrown to the deck by a huge Huegoth.

"Brother Jamesis!" Luthien cried.

The monk pulled himself up to his knees. "Surrender your sword, my friend," he said to Luthien. "Rennir of Isenland has assured me that he will accept it."

Luthien looked around doubtfully to his fellows.

"Better the life of a galley slave than the watery death!" peaceable Jamesis pleaded.

"Not so!" cried one Eriadoran, and the woman untied a guide rope, took it under her arm and leaped out, soaring heroically into the Huegoth throng. Before her companions could move to follow or to stop her, though, a long spear came up and stabbed her hard, dropping her to the deck. Huegoths fell over her like wolves. Finally she came out of the tangle, in the grasp of one huge barbarian who ran her to the rail and slammed her face hard upon it.

He let go then, and somehow the woman managed to hold her footing, but just long enough for another barbarian to skewer her through the belly with a long trident. The muscled man lifted her trembling form high off the deck and held the macabre pose for a long moment before tossing her overboard.

"Damn you!" Luthien cried, starting down the ladder, his knuckles white with rage as he clutched his mighty sword.

"No more!" wailed Jamesis, the monk's desperation bringing Luthien from his outrage. "I beseech you, son of Bedwyr, for the lives of those who follow you!"

"Bedwyr?" mumbled a curious Rennin, too low for anyone to hear.

Looking back at the fifty men and women in his wake, Luthien ran out of arguments. He was partly responsible for this disaster, he believed, since he had been one of the chief proponents of sending a lone ship out to parley. The entirety of Luthien's previous experience with Huegoths had been beside his friend Garth Rogar in Dun Varna, and that man was among the most honorable and reasonable warriors the young Bedwyr had ever known.

Perhaps due to that friendship, Luthien hadn't been prepared for the savage men of Isenland. Now a hundred Eriadorans, or even more, were dead, and half that number had already been hauled aboard the longships as prisoners. His cinnamon eyes moist with frustration, Luthien tossed *Blind-Striker* down to the main deck.

Sometime later, he and his companions watched from the deck of a Huegoth longship as *The Stratton Weaver* slipped quietly under the waves.

Chapter 8

PROSPECTS

Luthien heard the whips cracking on the decks of other Huegoth vessels, heard the cries of the unfortunate Eriadoran sailors as they were shuffled belowdecks and chained to benches. Some of the prisoners on his own longship were treated similarly, and it seemed as if Luthien and his friends would find no escape. The grim prospects of a life as a galley slave loomed large before the young Bedwyr, but he was more afraid for his closest companions than for himself. What would the Huegoths make of Oliver, who was obviously too small to row? Would the foppish halfling become a source of entertainment, a longship jester subject to the whims of the brutal barbarians? Or would the fierce men of Isenland simply jettison him overboard like so much useless cargo?

And what of Katerin? For Katerin, and the half dozen other women captured in the battle, Luthien feared even more. Huegoth raiders were away from home for long, long stretches, time counted in months more than in weeks. What pleasures might the merciless barbarians make of such a delicacy as Katerin O'Hale?

A violent shudder brought the young Bedwyr from the dark thoughts, forced him to focus on the reality instead of the prospects. Fortunately, Katerin and Oliver were on the same longship as he, and they, along with Luthien and Brother Jamesis, had thus far not been so much as scratched. It would stay that way, Luthien told himself determinedly. He resolved that if the barbarians meant to kill Oliver, or if they tried to harm Katerin in any way, he would fight them again, this time to the most bitter end. He had no weapons save his bare hands, but in defense of Oliver and especially Katerin, he held faith that those hands would be deadly.

The Huegoths were quite proficient in the role of captors, Luthien soon realized, for he and all the others were properly secured with thick ropes and guarded closely by a score of huge warriors. When that was finished, a selection process began on the longship, a magnificent vessel that Luthien figured to be the flagship of the fleet. Old and used-up galley slaves, men too weak and malnourished to continue to pull to the demands of the barbarians, were dragged onto the deck, while newer prisoners were ushered below and chained in their place. Luthien knew logically what the Huegoths meant to do, and his conscience screamed out at him to take action, any action. Still, the barbarians kept their intentions just mysterious enough for the young Bedwyr and the others, particularly those slaves who looked upon the sun for the first time in weeks, to hold out some hope. That hope, that thought that they all might indeed have something to gain through obedience and something to lose by causing trouble, proved paralyzing.

Thus, Luthien could only close his eyes as the replaced galley slaves, withered and beyond usefulness in the cold eyes of the Huegoths, were pushed overboard.

"I, too, will find such a fate," Oliver said matter-of-factly. "And I do so hate the water!"

"We do not know that," whispered Brother Jamesis, his voice trembling. Jamesis had facilitated the surrender, after all, and now he was watching the fruits of his action. Perhaps it would have been better for them all if they had battled to the last on the sinking *Weaver.*

"I am too small to row," Oliver replied. He was surprised to find that his greatest lament at that moment was that he had not found time to explore the intriguing possibilities with Siobhan.

"Quiet," Luthien sharply bade them both. "There is no gain in giving the Huegoths ideas."

"As if they do not already know!" said Oliver.

"They may think you a child," Katerin put in. "Huegoths have been known to take in orphaned children and raise them as Isenlanders."

"Such a comforting thought," Oliver said sarcastically. "And tell me, what will become of me when I do not grow?"

"Enough!" Luthien commanded, sheer anger causing his voice to rise enough to get the attention of the nearest Huegoth guard. The huge man looked Luthien's way and issued a low growl, and the young Bedwyr smiled meekly in reply.

"We should not have let them bind us," Luthien lamented out of the side of his mouth.

"We could have stopped them?" Oliver asked.

The group quieted as a band of barbarians came toward them, led by Rennir, the Huegoth leader.

"I must protest!" Brother Jamesis called immediately to the large man.

Rennir's white teeth showed clearly within the bushy blond hair that covered his face. His teasing expression revealed that he had heard similar words before, that he had watched "civilized" folk witness Huegoth justice on previous occasions. He stalked toward Jamesis so boldly that the monk shrank back against the rail and Luthien and the others thought for a moment that Rennir would simply heave Jamesis into the sea with the floundering slaves.

"We had an arrangement," Jamesis said, much more humbly, when the Huegoth leader stopped right before him. "You guaranteed the safety . . ."

"Of your men," Rennir was glad to finish. "I said nothing about the slaves already within my longships. Where would I put you all?" The Huegoth turned a wry smile over his shoulder, back to the chuckling group of his kinsmen standing near.

Brother Jamesis searched hard for some rational argument. Indeed, the Huegoth was holding true to the wording of their agreement, if not the spirit. "You do not have to execute those who have served you," Jamesis stuttered. "The island of Colonsey is not so far away. You could drop them there . . ."

"Leave enemies in our wake?" Rennir thundered. "That they might wage war with us once more?"

"You would find fewer enemies if you possessed the soul of a human," Luthien offered, drawing Rennir's scowl his way. Rennir began a slow and ominous walk toward the young Bedwyr, but

Luthien, unlike Jamesis, did not shrink back. Indeed Luthien stood tall, jaw firm and shoulders squared, and his cinnamon-colored eyes locked on the gray orbs of the giant Huegoth. Rennir came right up to him, but though he was taller by several inches, he did not seem to tower over Luthien.

The dangerous stares lasted for a long while, neither man speaking or even blinking. Then Rennir seemed to notice something—something about Luthien's appearance—and the Huegoth leader visibly relaxed.

"You are not of Gybi," Rennir stated.

"I ask you to retrieve those men in the sea," Luthien replied.

Several barbarians began to chuckle, but Rennir held up his hand, no mirth crossing his deadly serious features. "You would show mercy if those in the sea were of Isenland blood?"

"I would."

"Have you?"

The surprising question nearly knocked Luthien over. What in the world was Rennir talking about? Luthien searched frantically for some response, realizing that his answer now might save the lives of the poor slaves. In the end, he could only shake his head, though, not understanding the Huegoth's intent.

"What is your name?" Rennir asked.

"Luthien Bedwyr."

"Of Isle Bedwydrin?"

Luthien nodded and glanced over at Oliver and Katerin, who could only shrug in reply, as confused as he.

"Have you?" Rennir asked again.

It clicked in Luthien's head. Garth Rogar! The man was referring to Garth Rogar, Luthien's dearest friend, who had been pulled from the sea by Luthien and raised in the House of Bedwyr as a brother! But how could Rennir possibly know? Luthien wondered.

At that critical moment, it didn't matter, and Luthien didn't have the time to debate it. He squared his shoulders once more, looked sternly into Rennir's gray eyes, and said with all conviction, "I have."

Rennir turned to his fellows. "Drag the slaves from the water," he commanded, "and pass word to the other boats that none are to be drowned."

Rennir turned back to Luthien, the Huegoth's face wild, frightening. "That is all I owe to you," he stated and walked away. As he did, he put a lewd stare over Katerin, then chuckled.

"You owe me a place beside my men," Luthien stated, stopping Rennir short. "If they are to row, then so am I!"

The Huegoth thought on that for a moment, then threw his head back and roared heartily. He didn't bother to look back again as he joined his fellows.

The longships moved in a wide formation around the western shore of Colonsey. This somewhat surprised Luthien and his companions, who thought the barbarians would put out to the open sea. They learned the truth when they came into a sheltered bay, passing through a narrow opening, practically invisible from the sea, into a wide and calm lagoon.

A hundred longships were tied up along the rocky beach. Further inland, up the rocky incline, dozens of stone and wood huts dotted the stark landscape, and smoke wafted out of many cave openings.

"When did this happen?" a stunned Brother Jamesis muttered.

"And what of Land's End?" Luthien asked, referring to the small Eriadoran settlement around to the eastern side of the island. If this many Huegoths had formed a base on Colonsey, it did not bode well for the hundred or so people in the rugged, windswept settlement. Luthien understood the trouble the barbarians had gone to, and realized then beyond any doubt that their attacks on Bae Colthwyn were not intended as minor raids. They had wood here, in large supply, though there was little on rocky Colonsey, and Luthien took note that there were many Huegoth women among those gathering at the shore to greet the returning longships. This was a full-scale invasion, and Luthien grimaced as he thought of the misery that would soon befall his dear Eriador.

Slaves were not normally taken off the longships when they were in harbor, and as the other boats put in, most of the Huegoths clambered over the side, splashing into shore, leaving just a few guards behind. Luthien's thoughts immediately turned to the potential for escape, but he was surprised when Rennir's boat put in and a group of Huegoths came and gathered him up with his three companions, ushering them roughly ashore.

Luthien never got the obvious questions out of his mouth when he stumbled onto the rocky beach, Rennir taking him by the collar and dragging him along to the largest hut of the settlement.

"Beg before Asmund, who is king!" was all the Huegoth said as he pulled Luthien past the guards and into the open single-roomed structure.

His hands still bound behind his back, Luthien stumbled down to one knee. He recovered quickly, forced himself not to look back as he heard Katerin, or Jamesis, perhaps, go down behind him. As calmly as he could manage, Luthien straightened himself on his knees, regaining a measure of dignity before he looked upon the Huegoth king.

Asmund was an impressive figure indeed, barrel-chested, with a huge gray beard, brown, weathered skin, and light blue eyes so intense that they seemed as if they could bore holes through hard wood.

But Luthien hardly noticed the king. He was more stricken by the sight of the man standing casually beside the great Asmund.

A man with cinnamon-colored eyes.

THE ERIADORAN TIE

Ethan," Katerin muttered in disbelief.

Gasping for breath, Luthien started to rise and was promptly grabbed by Rennir. Luthien growled and pulled away from the huge man, determined to stand before Asmund, and especially before Asmund's escort. It was Ethan, obviously, but how his brother had changed! A stubbly beard graced his fine Bedwydrin features and his hair had grown much longer. The most profound change, though, was the man's eyes, intense and wild, perfectly dangerous.

"You know him?" Oliver whispered to Katerin.

"Ethan Bedwyr," Katerin said loudly. "Luthien's brother."

"Ah, so I see," said Oliver, taking note of the distinct resemblance between the men, particularly in the rare cinnamon coloring of their eyes. Then, as he realized the truth of this impossible situation, the halfling's jaw dropped in speechless astonishment.

Asmund, seeming quite amused, turned Ethan's way, giving the floor to the Eriadoran.

Luthien's heart and hopes soared. "My brother," he said breathlessly as Ethan walked over to him.

The older Bedwyr pushed Luthien down to the floor. "No more," he said.

"What are you doing?" Katerin cried out, rushing to intervene.

"A woman of spirit!" howled huge Asmund as Rennir grabbed the thrashing Katerin in his massive arms.

"What is wrong with you?" Luthien demanded of Ethan, rolling up to one knee and staring hard at his brother. He looked to Rennir, then back to Ethan, pleading, "Stop him!"

Ethan shook his head slowly. "No more," he said again to Luthien, but he did indeed turn to Rennir and bade the man to let go of Katerin O'Hale.

"If you're thinking that I'm to be grateful, then you're thinking wrong!" Katerin roared at him, moving up to face him squarely. "You are on the wrong side of the ropes, son of Gahris!"

Ethan tilted his head back, his features taking on a look that seemed both distant and superior. He never blinked, but neither did he lash out at Katerin.

"You are with them," Luthien stated.

Ethan looked at him incredulously, as though that much should have been obvious.

"Traitor!" Katerin growled.

Ethan's hand came up and Katerin turned away, fully expecting that she would be slapped.

The blow never came, though, as Ethan quickly regained his composure. "Traitor to whom?" he asked. "To Gahris, who banished me, who sent me away to die?"

"I searched for you," Luthien put in.

"You found me," Ethan said grimly.

"With Huegoths," Luthien added, his tone derisive. More than a few barbarians around him growled.

"With brave men," Ethan retorted. "With men who would not be ruled by an unlawful king from another land!"

That gave Luthien some hope concerning the greater situation at least. Perhaps this Huegoth invasion wasn't in any way connected to Greensparrow.

"You are Eriadoran!" Katerin yelled.

"I am not!" Ethan screamed back at her. "Count me not among the cowards who cringe in fear of Greensparrow. Count me not among those who have accepted the death of Garth Rogar!" He looked Luthien right in the eye as he finished the thought. "Count me not among those who would wear the colors of Lady Avonese, the painted whore!"

Luthien breathed hard, trying to sort out his thoughts. Ethan here! It was too crazy, too unexpected. But Ethan did not know of all that had transpired, Luthien reminded himself. Ethan likely thought that things were as he had left them in Eriador, with Greensparrow as king and Gahris as one of his many pawns. But where did that leave Luthien? Even if he convinced Ethan of the truth, could he forgive his brother for allying with savage Huegoths against Eriador?

"How dare you?" Luthien roared, struggling to his feet.

"Greensparrow—" Ethan began to counter.

"Damn Greensparrow!" Luthien interrupted. "Those ships that your newfound friends attacked were Eriadoran, not Avonese. The blood of fellow Eriadorans is on your hands!"

"Damn you!" Ethan yelled back, slamming into Luthien so forcefully that he nearly knocked his younger brother over once more. "I am Huegoth now, and not Eriadoran. And all ships of Avonsea serve Greensparrow."

"You murdered—"

"We wage war!" Ethan snapped ferociously. "Let Greensparrow come north with his fleet, that we might sink them, and if Eriadorans also die in the battle, then so be it!"

Luthien looked from Ethan to Asmund, the Huegoth king smiling widely, and smugly, as though he was thoroughly enjoying this little play. It struck Luthien that his brother might be more of a pawn than an advisor, and he found at that moment that he wanted nothing more than to rush over and throttle Asmund.

But in looking back to Ethan, Luthien had to admit that his brother didn't seem to need any champion. Ethan's demeanor had changed dramatically, had become wild to match the raging fires in his eyes. Gahris's actions in banishing Ethan had come near to breaking the man, Luthien realized, and in that despair, Ethan had found a new strength: the strength of purest anger. Ethan seemed at home with the Huegoths, so much so that the realization sent a shudder coursing through Luthien's spine. He had to wonder if this really was his brother, or if the brother he had known in Dun Varna was truly dead.

"Greensparrow will not come north," Luthien said quietly, trying to restore some sense of calm to the increasingly explosive discussion.

"But he will," Ethan insisted. "He will send his warships north, one by one or in a pack. Either way, we will destroy them, send them to the bottom, and then let the weakling wizard who claims an unlawful throne be damned!"

He would have gone on, but Luthien's sudden burst of hysterical laughter gave him pause. Ethan tilted his head, tried to get some sense of why his brother was laughing so, but Luthien threw his head back, roaring wildly, and would not look him in the eye. Ethan turned to Katerin instead, and to Luthien's other companions, but they offered no explanation.

"Are you mad, then?" Ethan said calmly, but Luthien seemed not to hear.

"Enough!" roared Asmund, and Luthien stopped abruptly and stared hard at his brother and the Huegoth king.

"You do not know," the younger Bedwyr brother stated more than asked.

Ethan's wild eyes calmed with curiosity and he cocked his head, his unkempt hair, even lighter now than Luthien remembered it, hanging to his shoulder.

"Greensparrow no longer rules in Eriador," Luthien said bluntly. "And his lackeys have been dispatched. Montfort is no more, for the name of Caer MacDonald has been restored."

Ethan tried to seem unimpressed, but how his cinnamon-colored eyes widened!

"'Twas Luthien who killed Duke Morkney," Katerin put in.

"With help from my friends," Luthien was quick to add.

"You?" Ethan stammered.

"So-silly barbarian pretender-type," Oliver piped in with a snap of his green-gauntleted fingers, "have you never heard of the Crimson Shadow?"

That name brought a flicker of recognition to Ethan; it seemed as if the legend had spread wider than the general political news. "You?" Ethan said again, pointing and advancing a step toward Luthien.

"It was a title earned by accident," Luthien insisted.

"But of course you have heard of Oliver's Bluff," the halfling interrupted, skipping forward and stepping in front of Luthien, so that his head was practically in Ethan's belly, and puffing his little chest with pride.

Ethan looked down at Oliver and shook his head.

"It was designed for Malpuissant's Wall," the halfling began, "but since the wall was taken before we ever arrived, we executed this most magnificent of strategies on Princetown itself. That is right!" Oliver brought his hand up right in Ethan's face and snapped his fingers again. "The very jew-wel of Avon taken by the forces of cunning Oliver deBurrows!"

"And you are Oliver deBurrows?" Ethan surmised dryly.

"If I had my so-fine rapier blade, I would show you!"

A dangerous scowl crossed Ethan's features, one that Asmund did not miss. "That can be arranged, and quickly!" the Huegoth king said with a snort, and all the barbarians in the tent began to laugh and murmur, apparently pleased at the prospect of a duel.

Luthien's arm swept around the dramatically posing Oliver and pushed the halfling back. Luthien knew well his brother's battle prowess and he wasn't keen on the idea of losing his little halfling friend, however annoying Oliver might sometimes be.

"It is all true," Luthien insisted to Ethan. "Eriador is free, under King Brind'Amour."

Ethan turned back to find Asmund staring hard at him, searching for some confirmation or explanation of the unknown name. Ethan could only shrug, for he had never heard of this man Luthien claimed was now ruling the northern kingdom of Avonsea.

"He was of the ancient brotherhood," Luthien explained, seeing their skepticism. "A very mighty . . ." Luthien paused, realizing that it might not be a good thing to reveal Brind'Amour's true profession to the Huegoths, who distrusted magic. "A very mighty and wise man," Luthien finished, but he had already said too much.

"The ancient brotherhood," Ethan said to Asmund, "thus, the king of Eriador, too, is a wizard."

Asmund snorted derisively.

The fact that Ethan betrayed that secret so matter-of-factly gave Luthien some idea of how far lost his brother truly was. Luthien needed something to divert the conversation, he realized, and he only had one card to play. "Gahris is dead," he said calmly.

Ethan winced, but then nodded his acceptance of the news.

"He died peacefully," Luthien said, but again, Ethan didn't seem very concerned.

"Gahris died many years ago," Ethan remarked. "He died when our mother died, when the plague that was Greensparrow swept across Eriador."

"You are wrong!" Katerin O'Hale said boldly. "Gahris made certain that no cyclopians remain alive on Bedwydrin, and Lady Avonese—"

"The whore," Ethan sneered.

Katerin snorted, not disagreeing in the least. "She died in the dungeon of House Bedwyr."

"There are no dungeons in House Bedwyr," Ethan said doubtfully.

"Eorl Gahris built one just for her," Katerin replied.

"What is this all about, Vinndalf?" Asmund asked.

Ethan turned to his king and shrugged once again, in truth, too surprised to sort through it all.

"Vinndalf?" Luthien echoed.

Ethan squared his shoulders. "My proper name," he insisted.

Now Luthien could no longer contain his mounting anger. "You are Ethan Bedwyr, son of Gahris, who was eorl of Bedwydrin," the younger brother insisted.

"I am Vinndalf, brother of Torin Rogar," Ethan retorted.

Luthien moved to respond, but that last name caught him off his guard. "Rogar?" he asked.

"Torin Rogar," Ethan explained, "brother of Garth."

That took the wind from Luthien. He wanted to meet the brother of Garth Rogar—that thought reverberated in his mind. He sublimated it, though, realizing that such a meeting was for another time. For now, Luthien's duty was clear and straightforward. Fifty lives depended on him, and the ante would be even greater if the Huegoths continued their raids along Eriador's coast. All that Luthien had discovered in this meeting, particularly the fact that the Huegoths did not know of recent events in Eriador, and thus could not be in any alliance with Avon, had given him hope. That hope, though, was tempered by the specter of this man standing before him, by Ethan, who was not Ethan.

"Then my greetings to Vinndalf," Luthien said, surprising Katerin, who stood scowling at his side. "I come as emissary of King Brind'Amour of Eriador."

"We asked for no parley," Asmund said.

"But you know now that your attacks on Eriadoran ships and coast do no harm to Greensparrow," Luthien said. "We are not your enemies."

That brought more than a few laughs from the many Huegoths in the hut, and laughter from outside as well, confirming to

Luthien that this meeting of the lost brothers had become a public spectacle.

"Ethan," Luthien said solemnly. "Vinndalf, I am, or was, your brother."

"In a world from which I was banished," Ethan interrupted.

"I looked for you," Luthien said. "I killed the cyclopian who murdered Garth Rogar, and then I looked for you, to the south, where you were supposedly heading."

"I took him there," Oliver had to say, if for no other reason than the fact that the halfling couldn't stand being on the sidelines of any conversation for so long.

"I, too, considered our father dead," Luthien went on, "though I assure you that in the end the man redeemed himself."

"He thought of you on the night he died," Katerin put in. "His guilt weighed heavily on him."

"As it should have," said Ethan.

"Agreed," Luthien replied. "And I make no excuses for the world from which you fled. But that world is no more, I promise. Eriador is free now."

"What concern have we of your petty squabbles?" Asmund asked incredulously. As soon as he regarded the man, Luthien realized that the Huegoth feared that Luthien might be stealing some fun here. "You speak of Greensparrow and Eriador as though they are not the same. To us, you are *degjern-alfar*, and nothing more!"

Degjern-alfar. Luthien knew the word, an Isenland term for any who was not Huegoth.

"And I am Huegoth," Ethan insisted before Luthien could make any points about his Eriadoran blood. Ethan looked to a nodding Asmund. "Huegoth by deed."

"You are a Huegoth who understands the importance of what I say," Luthien added quickly. "Eriador is free, but if you continue your raids, you are aiding Greensparrow in his desires to take us back under his evil wing." For the first time, it seemed to Luthien as if he had gotten through to his stubborn brother. He knew that Ethan, whatever his claim of loyalty, was thrilled at the idea that Eriador had broken free of Avon, and Luthien knew, too, that the thought that the Huegoth actions, that Ethan's own actions, might be aiding the man who had, by sending the plague, murdered their mother and broken their father, was truly agonizing to Ethan.

"And what would you ask of me?" the older Bedwyr brother asked after a short pause.

"Desist," said Oliver, stepping in front. Luthien wanted to slap the halfling for taking center stage at that critical point. "Take your silly boat and go back to where you belong. We have four-score warships—"

Luthien pushed Oliver aside, and when the halfling tried to resist, Katerin grabbed him by the collar, spun him about and scowled in his face, a look that conjured images in Oliver of being thrown to the floor and sat upon by the woman.

"Join with us," Luthien said on a sudden impulse. He realized how stupid that sounded even as the words left his mouth, but he knew that the last thing one should do to a Huegoth (as Oliver had just done) was issue a challenge of honor. Threatening King Asmund with eighty galleons would force the fierce man to accept the war. "With nearly four-score warships and your fleet, we might—"

"You ask this of me?" Ethan said, slapping himself on the chest.

Luthien straightened. "You are my brother," he said firmly. "And were of Eriador, whatever your claim may now be. I demand that you ask of your king to halt the raids on Eriador's coast. For all that has happened, we are not your enemies."

Ethan snorted and didn't even bother to look over his shoulder at Asmund. "Do not put too much weight on my ability to influence my Huegoth brothers," Ethan said. "King Asmund, and not I, decides the Huegoth course."

"But you were willing to go along," Luthien accused, his face twisting in sudden rage. "While Eriadorans died, Ethan Bedwyr did nothing!"

"Ethan Bedwyr is dead," the man called Vinndalf replied.

"And does Vinndalf not remember all the good that Luthien Bedwyr brought to his younger life?" Katerin asked.

Ethan's broad shoulders slumped for just an instant, a subtle indication that Katerin had hit a chord. Ethan straightened quickly, though, and stared hard at Luthien.

"I will beg of my king to give you this much," Ethan said evenly. "On mighty Asmund's word, we will let you leave, will deliver you and Katerin and your puffy and puny friend back to the coast of Bae Colthwyn, south of Gybi."

"And the others?" Luthien asked grimly.

"Fairly taken," Ethan replied.

Luthien squared up and shook his head. "All of them," he insisted. "Every man and woman returned to Eriador, their home."

For a long moment, it seemed a stand-off. Then Rennir, who was enjoying it all, crossed the room to Ethan and handed the man *Blind-Striker*. Ethan looked long and hard at the sword, the most important relic of his former family. After a moment, he chuckled, and then, eyeing Luthien in an act of open defiance, he strapped the magnificent weapon about his waist.

"You said you were no longer of family Bedwyr," remarked Luthien, looking for some advantage, and trying to take the edge from his own rising anger. Seeing Ethan—no, Vinndalf—wearing that sword was nearly more than Luthien could take.

"True enough," Ethan replied casually, as though that fact was of no importance.

"Yet you wear the Bedwyr sword."

Now it was Ethan's turn to laugh, and Rennir and Asmund, and all the other Huegoths joined in. "I wear a weapon plundered from a vanquished enemy," Ethan corrected. "Fairly won, like the men who will serve as slaves. Take my offer, former brother. Go, and with Katerin. I cannot guarantee her safety here, and as for your little friend, I can assure you that he will find a most horrible fate at the hands of the men of Isenland, who do not accept such weakness."

"Weakness?" Oliver stammered, but Katerin slapped her hand over his mouth to shut him up before he got them all killed.

"All of them," Luthien said firmly. "And I'll have the sword as well."

"Why should I give to you anything?" Ethan asked.

"Do not!" roared Luthien as the laughter began to mount around him once more. "I ask for nothing from one so cowardly as to disclaim his heritage. But I'll have what I desire, by spilled blood if not by family blood!"

Ethan's head tilted back at that open challenge. "We have fought before," he said.

Luthien didn't answer.

"I was victorious," Ethan reminded.

"I was younger."

Ethan looked to Asmund, who made no move.

"The slaves are not yours to give," said Rennir. "The capture was mine."

Ethan nodded his agreement.

"Fight for the sword, then," offered Asmund.

"All of them," Luthien said firmly.

"For the sword," Ethan corrected. "And for your freedom, and the freedom of Katerin and the little one. Nothing more."

"That much, save the sword, was already offered," Luthien argued.

"An offer rescinded," said Ethan. "You challenged me openly. Now you will see it through, though the gain is little more than what you would have found without challenge, and the loss—and you will lose—is surely greater!"

Luthien looked to Asmund and saw that he would find no sympathy there, and no better offers. He had stepped into dynamics that he did not fully understand, he realized. It seemed to Luthien as though Asmund had desired this combat from the moment the king learned that Luthien and Ethan were brothers. Perhaps it was a test of Ethan's loyalty, or more likely, brutal Asmund just thought it would be fine sport.

Behind Luthien, Katerin O'Hale's voice was as grim as anything the young Bedwyr had ever heard. "Kill him."

The words, and the image they conjured, nearly knocked Luthien over. He was hardly conscious, his breath labored, as his companions were pushed away, as Rennir handed him a sword, as Ethan drew out *Blind-Striker* and began a determined and deadly approach.

SIBLING RIVALRY

Ethan's initial swing brought Luthien's swirling thoughts back to crystal clarity, his survival instincts overruling all the craziness and potential for disaster. The weapon Rennir had given him was not very balanced, and was even heavier than the six-pound, one-and-a-half-handed *Blind-Striker*. He took it up in both hands and twisted hard, dipping his right shoulder and laying the blade angled down.

Blind-Striker hit the blocking blade hard enough for Luthien to realize that if he hadn't thrown up the last-second parry, he would have been cut in half.

"Ethan!" he yelled instinctively as a rush of memories—of fighting in the arena, of training as a young boy under his older brother's tutelage, of sharing quiet moments beside Ethan in the hills outside of Dun Varna—assaulted him.

The man who was known as Vinndalf didn't respond to the call in the least. He backed up one step and sent *Blind-Striker* around the other way, coming straight in at Luthien's side.

Luthien reversed his pivot, and his grip, dropping his left shoulder this time, launching the heavy weapon the other way and cleanly picking off the attack. Ahead came Luthien's left foot; the logical counter was a straightforward thrust.

Ethan was already moving, directly back, out of harm's way and not even needing to parry the short attack. That done, he took up his sword, the magnificent Bedwyr sword, in both hands and began to circle to his right.

Luthien turned with him. He could hardly believe that he had so thrust at his own brother, that if Ethan had not been so quick, he would be lying on the floor, his guts spilling. Luthien dismissed such images. This was for real, he told himself; this was for his very life and the lives of his dearest friends, as well. He could not be distracted by contrary feelings, could not think of his opponent as his brother. Now he tried to remember again the arena in Dun Varna, tried to remember the style of Ethan's moves.

Ethan dropped his shoulder and came ahead in a quick-step, lunging for Luthien's lead knee. The attack stopped short, though, before *Blind-Striker* even tapped Luthien's parrying blade, and Ethan threw himself to the side, his other foot rushing right beside his leading leg, turning him in a complete circuit. Down to one knee he went, both hands on his sword as it came across in a devious cut.

Luthien had seen the trick before and was long out of danger before Ethan even finished.

Ethan had been a mature fighter when last they had battled, and so Luthien thought it unlikely that his tactics would have changed much. But Luthien had been young on that occasion, a novice fighter just learning the measure of single combat.

That was his advantage.

Ethan was up to his feet, dropping one hand for balance and charging hard in the blink of an eye, *Blind-Striker* going left, right, straight ahead, then right again. Steel rang against steel, Luthien working furiously to keep the deadly blade at bay. Those attacks defeated, Ethan took up the weapon in both hands and chopped hard at Luthien's head, once, twice, and then again.

Luthien beat them all, but stumbled backward under the sheer weight of the furious blows. He wanted to offer a fast counter, but this sword, half-again as heavy as the weapon he was used to carrying, would not allow for any quick response. And so he backed away as wild-eyed Ethan forged onward, slamming with abandon.

Now Luthien concentrated on conserving his strength, on picking off the attacks with as little motion as possible. He willingly gave ground, came near to the hut wall and shifted his angle so that, propelled by yet another brutal blow, he went right out the door into the dazzling daylight.

A throng of Huegoths swarmed about the battling brothers; Luthien saw Katerin and Oliver come to the door, Rennir roughly pushing them aside to make way for grinning Asmund.

Oh, this was great play for the fierce Isenlanders, Luthien realized.

The uneven and stony ground somewhat took away Ethan's advantage of wielding the lighter and quicker weapon. Suddenly footwork was of the utmost importance, and no warrior Luthien had ever met, with the possible exception of fleet-footed Oliver deBurrows, was better at footwork than he. Luthien skittered right along the uneven ground, deftly trailing his heavy sword to pick off any of pursuing Ethan's attacks. He came to a spot where the ground sloped steeply and saw his chance. Up Luthien went, beyond *Blind-Striker*'s reach as Ethan came by below him, and then down Luthien charged in a fury, suddenly pressing his brother with a series of momentum-backed chops.

Perfectly balanced, Ethan was up to the defense, picking off or dodging each blow. It occurred to Luthien then, when he thought he had gained an advantage, that the endgame of this combat would not go well. Win or lose, the young Bedwyr would find himself in a bind. Would it be to the death? And if so, how could Luthien possibly kill his own brother? And even if it wasn't to the death, Luthien understood that he had much to lose, and so did Ethan, for Ethan had likely only gained acceptance among the fierce barbarians through skill in battle. Now, in this encounter, if Ethan lost their respect . . .

Luthien didn't like the prospects, but he had no time to pause and try and discern another way out. Ethan went up high on the sloping stone, trying to get the angle above him, and he had to work furiously to keep up.

Out came *Blind-Striker* in a wicked thrust, suddenly, as the brothers picked their way up the stone. Luthien couldn't possibly get his heavier blade in line in time, nor could he dodge in the difficult position, so he rolled instead, out from Ethan and then down the slope, coming lightly to his feet some twenty feet below his brother.

He heard Katerin cry out for him, and Oliver's groan in the midst of the cheers of a hundred bloodthirsty Huegoths.

Down came Ethan, spurred on by his comrades, but Luthien was not going to grant him the higher ground. Off sped the younger Bedwyr, running away from the slope. Ethan yelled out as he pursued, even going so far as to call his brother a coward.

Luthien was no coward, but he had learned the advantage of choosing his ground. So it was now, with Ethan fast closing. Luthien turned along the beach to a small jetty, skipping gingerly atop its stones. Now he had the high ground, but Ethan, so enraged, so full of adrenaline, did not slow, came in hacking wildly, thrusting *Blind-Striker* this way and that, searching for a hole in Luthien's defenses.

There was no such hole to be found; Luthien's blocks were perfect, but Ethan did manage to sidle up the rocks as he attacked, gradually coming near to Luthien's level. Luthien saw the tactic, of course, and could have stopped it by shifting to directly block his brother, but he had something else in mind.

Up came Ethan. Luthien's sword started for the man's knees and Ethan jumped back, launching a vicious downward cut.

Luthien's thrust had been a feint; before he ever got close, and as Ethan started the obvious counter, the young Bedwyr moved back a step, reversed his grip on his heavy sword, and shifted it, not to block *Blind-Striker*, but to deflect the sword. As Ethan's weapon scraped by, Luthien turned his blade over it and shoved it down for the rocks, and off-balance Ethan could not resist. Sparks flew from *Blind-Striker*'s fine tip as the gleaming blade dove into a crevice between the stones.

From his lower angle, Ethan could not immediately pull it out. One step up would allow him to extract the blade, yet he could not make that step. He had lost a split second, and against cunning Luthien, a split second was too long.

Endgame.

Luthien knew it, but had no idea of what to make of it. Images of Katerin and Oliver as Huegoth prisoners flashed in his mind, yet his fledgling Eriador would not likely survive his victory. His foot slipped out from under him suddenly, and down he went to the stone, his sword bouncing away. He rolled up to a sitting position, holding his bruised and bleeding hand.

Ethan stood over him, *Blind-Striker* in hand. In looking into his eyes, those trademark Bedwyr eyes, Luthien thought for a moment that his brother would surely kill him.

Then Ethan paused, seeming unsure of himself, a mixture of frustration and rage. He couldn't do it, could not kill his brother, and that fact seemed to bother the man who called himself Vinndalf more than a little.

Blind-Striker came in to rest at the side of Luthien's neck.

"I claim victory!" Ethan bellowed.

"Enough!" roared Asmund before Ethan had even finished. The Huegoth king said something to the man standing beside him, and a host of Huegoths moved to join the brothers.

"Into the King's Hall!" one of them commanded Ethan, while two others roughly hoisted Luthien to his feet and half-carried him across the beach, past the hundred sets of curious eyes, Oliver's and Katerin's among them, and into King Asmund's quarters. There, Luthien was thrown to the floor, right beside his standing brother, and then all the Huegoths, save Asmund himself, quickly departed.

Luthien spent a moment looking from the seated king to his brother, then slowly rose. Ethan would not look at him.

"Clever boy," Asmund congratulated.

Luthien eyed him skeptically, not knowing what he was driving at.

"You had him beaten," Asmund said bluntly.

"I thought so, but—" Luthien tried to reply.

Asmund's laughter stopped him short.

"I claim victory!" Ethan growled.

Asmund abruptly stopped his laughing and stared hard at Ethan. "There is no dishonor in defeat at the hands of a skilled warrior," the Huegoth insisted. "And by my eyes, your brother is as skilled as you!"

Ethan lowered his gaze, then sighed deeply and turned to Luthien. "You tricked me twice," he said. "First in putting my blade between the rocks, and then by pretending to stumble."

"The stones were wet," Luthien protested. "Slick with weeds."

"You did not trip," Ethan said.

"No," Asmund agreed. "He fell because he thought it better to fall." The king laughed again at the incredulous expression that came over Luthien. "You would not kill Ethan," the keen leader explained. "And you held faith that he would not kill you. Yet if you defeated him, you feared that, though our agreement would be honored concerning the sword and the release of you and your friends, any chance of the greater good, of ending our raids along your coast, would be destroyed."

Luthien was truly at a loss. Asmund had seen through his ploy so easily and so completely! He had no answer and so he stood as calmly as he could manage and waited for the fierce king's judgment.

Ethan seemed more upset by it all than did Asmund. He, too, could not deny the truth of Asmund's perception. When *Blind-Striker* had gone into that crevice, Luthien had gained a seemingly insurmountable advantage, and then Luthien had fallen. In retrospect, Ethan had to admit that his brother, so balanced and so in command of his movements, could not have slipped at that critical moment.

Asmund spent a long while studying the pair. "You are the only Eriadorans I have come to know in heart," he said finally. "Brothers of a fine stock, I admit."

"Despite my intended slip?" Luthien dared to ask, and he relaxed more than a little when Asmund laughed again.

"Well done!" the king roared. "Had you beaten Ethan, your gain would have been your life and the lives of your two closest companions. And the sword, no small thing."

"But the price would have been too high," Luthien insisted. "For then our parley would have been ended, and Ethan's standing in your eyes might have been lessened."

"Would you die for Eriador?" Asmund asked.

"Of course."

"For Ethan, who we now name Vinndalf?"

"Of course."

The simple way Luthien answered struck Ethan profoundly, forced him to think back on his days in Dun Varna with his younger brother, a boy, then a man, he had always loved. Now Ethan was truly wounded, by his own actions, by the notion that he might have killed Luthien in their duel. How could he have ever let his rage get so much control over him?

"Would Ethan die for you?" Asmund asked.

"Yes, he would," Luthien replied, not even bothering to look to his brother for confirmation.

Asmund roared with laughter again. "I like you, Luthien Bedwyr, and I respect you, as I respect your brother."

"No more his brother," Ethan remarked before he could consider the words.

"Always," Asmund corrected. "If you were not his brother still, you would have claimed victory with your sword and not your mouth."

Ethan lowered his gaze.

"And I would have struck you dead!" Asmund yelled, coming forward, startling both Ethan and Luthien. The king calmed quickly and moved back into his chair. "When we earlier spoke, you claimed that we were not enemies," he prompted to Luthien.

"We are not," Luthien insisted. "Eriadorans fight Huegoths only when Huegoths attack Eriador. But there is a greater evil than any enmity between our peoples, I say, a stain upon the land—"

Asmund patted his hand in the empty air to stop the speech before Luthien could get into the flow. "You need not convince me of the foulness of Avon's king," the Huegoth explained. "Your brother has told me of Greensparrow and I have witnessed his wickedness. The plague that swept Eriador was not confined to your borders."

"Isenland?" Luthien asked breathlessly.

Asmund shook his head. "It never reached our shores because those afflicted at sea daren't ever return," he explained. "Our priests discovered the source of the plague, and ever since, the name of Greensparrow has been a cursed thing.

"You were the best friend of Garth Rogar," the king said suddenly, changing the subject and catching Luthien off guard. "And Torin Rogar is among my closest of friends."

This was going quite well, Luthien dared to hope. He was certain that he, Oliver, and Katerin would be granted their freedom; now he wanted to take things to the next level.

"Garth Rogar was the only Huegoth I came to know in heart," he said. "Representative of a fine stock, I say!"

Again Asmund bellowed with laughter.

"We are not your enemy," Luthien said determinedly, drawing the king into a more serious mode.

"So you say," he remarked, leaning forward in his chair. "And is Greensparrow your enemy?"

Luthien realized that he was moving into uncharted ground here. His gut instinct told him to yell out "Yes," but formally, such a proclamation to a foreign king could turn into serious trouble.

"You hinted at an alliance between our peoples to wage war on Greensparrow," Asmund went on. "Such a treaty might be welcomed."

Luthien was at once hopeful and tentative. He wanted to respond, to promise, but he could not. Not yet.

Asmund watched his every movement: the way his hands clenched at his side, the way he started to say something, then bit back the words. "Go to your King Brind'Amour, Luthien Bedwyr," the Huegoth leader said. "Deliver to me within the month a formal treaty naming Greensparrow as our common enemy." Asmund sat back, smiling wryly. "We have come for war, in the name of our God and by his will," he proclaimed, a not-so-subtle reminder to Luthien that he was dealing with a fierce people here. "And so we shall fight. Deliver your treaty or our longships will lay waste to your eastern coast, as we had planned."

Luthien wanted to respond to that challenge as well, to counter the threat with the promise of many Eriadoran warships to defend against the Huegoths. Wisely, he let it pass. "A month?" he asked skeptically. "I can hardly get to Caer MacDonald and back within the month. A week to Gybi—"

"Three days in a longship," Asmund corrected.

"And ten days of hard riding," Luthien added, trying not to think of the suffering the galley slaves would surely know in delivering him so far, so fast.

"I will send your brother to Gybi to serve as emissary," Asmund conceded.

"Send him to Chalmbers, directly west of here," Luthien asked. "A shorter ride on my return from Caer MacDonald."

Asmund nodded. "A month, Luthien Bedwyr, and not a day more!"

Luthien was out of arguments.

With that, Asmund dismissed him and Ethan, who was charged with making the arrangements to deliver Luthien, Katerin, Oliver, and Brother Jamesis back to the Eriadoran mainland. The other fifty Eriadorans were to remain as prisoners, but Luthien did manage to get a promise that they would not be mistreated and would be released if and when the treaty was delivered.

Within the hour, the ship was ready to depart. Luthien's three companions were on board, but the young Bedwyr lingered behind, needing a private moment with his brother.

Ethan seemed truly uncomfortable, embarrassed by the entire situation, of his choices and of his role in the Huegoth raids.

"I did not know," he admitted. "I thought that all was as it had been, that Greensparrow still ruled in Eriador."

"An apology?" Luthien asked.

"An explanation," Ethan replied. "And nothing more. I do not control the actions of my Huegoth brothers. Far from it. They only tolerate me because I have shown skill and courage, and because of the tale of Garth Rogar."

"I did go south to find you," Luthien said.

Ethan nodded, and seemed appreciative of that fact. "But I never went to the south," he replied. "Gahris commanded me to go to Port Charley, then to sail to Carlisle, where I would be given a rank of minor importance in the Avon army and sent to the Kingdom of Duree."

"To battle beside the Gascon army in their war," Luthien put in, for he knew well the tale.

Ethan nodded. "To battle, and likely to die, in that distant kingdom. But I would not accept that banishment and so chose one of my own instead."

"With the Huegoths?" Luthien was incredulous.

Ethan shook his head and smiled. "Land's End," he corrected. "I went south from Bedwydrin for a while, then turned east, through MacDonald's Swath. My destination became Gybi, where I paid handsomely for transport, in secret, to the Isle of Colonsey. I believed that I could live out my life quietly in Land's End. They ask few questions there."

"But the Huegoths came and crushed the settlement," Luthien accused, and his voice turned grim as he spoke of the probable deaths of many Eriadorans.

Ethan shook his head and stopped his brother's errant reasoning. "Land's End remains intact to this day," Ethan replied. "Not a single man or woman of that settlement has been injured or captured."

"Then how?"

"My boat never got there, for it was swamped in a storm," Ethan explained. "The Huegoths pulled me from the sea; chance alone put them in my path, and it was simple chance, simple good fortune, that the captain of the longship was Torin Rogar."

Luthien rested back on his heels and spent a long moment

digesting the story. "Good fortune for you," he said. "And for Eriador, it would seem."

"I am pleased by what you have told me of our Eriador," Ethan said, unstrapping *Blind-Striker* and handing it back to Luthien. "And I am proud of you, Luthien Bedwyr. It is right that you should wear the sword of family Bedwyr." Ethan's face grew grim and uncompromising. "But understand that I am Huegoth now," he said, "and not of your family. Deliver your treaty to my king or we—and I—will fight you."

Luthien knew that the words were a promise, not a threat, and he believed that promise.

POLITICS

Incredibly, less than two weeks after leaving the Huegoth encampment in Colonsey, Luthien and Oliver had the great Ministry of Caer MacDonald in sight. They had covered hundreds of miles, by sea and by land, and Riverdancer and Threadbare were haggard. Katerin had not returned with them; rather, she had gone south from Gybi by longship, with Ethan and Brother Jamesis, headed for the Eriadoran port city of Chalmbers.

"The journey back should be easier," Luthien remarked to his exhausted companion. "We shall use Brind'Amour's magics to cross the land. Perhaps our king will accompany us, wishing to sign the treaty personally with Asmund of Isenland."

Oliver grimaced at the young Bedwyr's continued optimism. All along the journey, the halfling had tried to calm Luthien down, had tried to temper that bubbly optimism with some very real obstacles that Luthien apparently was not counting on. So far, Oliver had tried to be subtle, and apparently it wasn't working.

He pulled Threadbare up short, and Luthien did likewise with Riverdancer, sidling up to the halfling, following Oliver's gaze to the great cathedral. He figured that Oliver just wanted a moment with the spectacular view of this city that had become their home.

"Brind'Amour will not agree," Oliver said bluntly.

Luthien nearly toppled from his mount, sat staring open-mouthed at his diminutive companion.

"My bumpkin-type friend," the halfling explained, "there is a little matter of a treaty."

Luthien thought Oliver was referring to the pending treaty with Asmund. Was the halfling saying that Brind'Amour would never agree to terms with the Huegoths? The young Bedwyr moved to argue the logic, but Oliver merely rolled his eyes and gave Threadbare a kick, and the skinny yellow pony trotted on.

The two friends stood before Brind'Amour in the audience room at the Ministry within the hour, with Luthien happily spilling the details of the Huegoth advance, and the potential for a truce. The old wizard who was Eriador's king beamed at the news that the Huegoths were not in league with Greensparrow, but that wide smile gradually diminished, and Brind'Amour spent more time looking at worldly Oliver than at Luthien, as the young Bedwyr's full tale began to unfold.

"And all we need do is deliver the treaty within the month to King Asmund," Luthien finished, oblivious to the grim mood about him. "And Greensparrow be damned!"

If the young Bedwyr expected Brind'Amour to turn cartwheels in joy, he was sorely disappointed. The king of Eriador eased back in his great chair, rubbing his white beard, his eyes staring into empty air.

"Should I pen a draft for you?" Luthien asked hopefully, though he was beginning to catch on that something was surely amiss here.

Brind'Amour looked at him directly. "If you do, you must also pen a fitting explanation to our Gascon allies," he replied.

Luthien didn't seem to understand. He looked to Oliver, who only shrugged and reminded him again that there was a treaty that might get in the way.

Suddenly Luthien understood that Oliver hadn't been doubting the potential treaty between Brind'Amour and Asmund, but about a treaty that had already been signed.

"Nothing is ever as easy as a bumpkin-type would think," the halfling said dryly.

Luthien decided that he would have to speak to Oliver about that bumpkin reference, but this was neither the time nor the place.

"There is a matter of a treaty signed by myself and the duchess of Mannington, acting on King Greensparrow's behalf," Brind'Amour clarified, taking up the halfling's argument. "We are not at war with Avon, and our truce does not include a provision for acceptable invasions."

The sarcasm stung Luthien profoundly. He understood the pragmatism of it all, of course, but in his mind Greensparrow had already broken the treaty many times over. "Sougles's Glen," he said grimly. "And Menster. Have you forgotten?"

Brind'Amour came forward at once, eyes gleaming. "I have not!" he yelled, the sheer strength of his voice forcing Luthien back a step. The old wizard calmed at once and eased himself to a straight posture. "Cyclopian raids, both," Brind'Amour said.

"But we know that Greensparrow was behind them," Luthien replied, full of determination, full of frustrated rage.

"What is known and what can be proven are oft two very different things," Oliver remarked.

"True enough," agreed the king. "And on strictly moral grounds, I agree with you," he said to Luthien. "I have no discomfort with the morality of launching a war, with Huegoth allies, against the king of Avon. Politically, though, we would be inviting complete disaster. Any attack on Avon would not rest well with the lords of Gascony, for it would disrupt their trade with both our kingdoms and make a mockery of their aid to us, playing the role of victims, in the previous war. They would not help us this time, I fear. They might even offer some warships to Greensparrow, that the war, and particularly the Huegoth threat, be quickly ended."

Luthien clenched his fists at his sides. He looked to Oliver, who only shrugged, and then back to Brind'Amour, though he was so angry that he was viewing a wall of red more than any distinct forms. "If we do not ally with Asmund," he said slowly, emphasizing each word, "then we will be forced into a war with the Huegoths."

Brind'Amour agreed with the assessment, nodding and then giving a small chuckle. "The ultimate irony," he replied. "Might it be that Eriador will join in common cause with Avon against the Huegoths?"

Luthien rocked back on his heels.

"Oh, yes," Brind'Amour assured him. "While you were on the road, King Greensparrow's emissary reached out to me, begging alliance against the troublesome barbarians of Isenland."

"But what of Menster?" Luthien protested. "And what of Sougles's Glen, and all the other massacres perpetrated by—"

"By the one-eyes," Oliver interrupted. "My pardon," he quickly added, seeing Luthien's dangerous glower, "I am but playing the role of the Gascon ambassador."

"Cyclopians prompted by Greensparrow!" Luthien growled back at him.

"You know that and I know that," Oliver replied, "but the Gascons, they are another matter."

"Oliver plays the role well," Brind'Amour remarked.

Luthien sighed deeply, trying to calm his rising ire.

"Greensparrow has prompted the raids," the Eriadoran king said to soothe him.

"Greensparrow will never accept Eriador free," Luthien replied.

"So be it," said Brind'Amour. "We will deal with him as we can. While you were gone, our forces were not idle. Siobhan and the Cutters have been working with King Bellick dan Burso's dwarfs, and have discovered the whereabouts of a large cyclopian encampment."

"So we ally with Greensparrow against the Huegoths at sea, while we fight against his allies in the mountains," Luthien said distastefully.

"I told you that you would not so much enjoy politics," Oliver remarked.

"As of now, I don't know what we shall do," Brind'Amour answered. "But there are many considerations to every action when one speaks for an entire kingdom."

"Surely we will attack the cyclopians," Luthien said.

"That we shall," Brind'Amour was glad to assure him. "I do not believe that our Gascon allies would protest any war between Eriador and the cyclopians."

"One-eyes, ptooey!" spat Oliver. "In Gascony, we consider a cyclopian eye an archery target."

Luthien was far from satisfied, but he realized that he was involved in something much bigger than his personal desires. He would have to be satisfied; at least he might soon get the chance to exact revenge for the folk of Menster.

But there was something deeper tugging at his sensibilities as he and Oliver exited the audience room in search of Siobhan. He had just over two weeks remaining to deliver the treaty or Eriador would be at war once more with the Huegoths—and Luthien would be at war with his own brother.

Oliver kept beside his sullen friend for the rest of the day, from a long quiet stay at the Dwelf to a walk along the city's outer wall. Luthien wasn't speaking much and Oliver didn't press him, figuring that the young man had to get through all the shocks—Ethan siding with the Huegoths and the reality of political intrigue—on his own.

Shortly before sunset, with news that Siobhan would be back in the city that night, Luthien's face brightened suddenly. In looking at him, Oliver understood that the young man had come up with yet another plan. Hopefully a better-informed course of action than his previous ideas, Oliver prayed.

"Do you think that Brind'Amour would ally with the Huegoths if Greensparrow was first to break the treaty?" Luthien asked.

Oliver shrugged noncommittaly. "I can think of better allies than slavers," he said. "But if the gain was the potential downfall of King Greensparrow, then I think he might be convinced." Oliver eyed Luthien, and particularly, Luthien's wry smile, suspiciously for a short while. "You have an idea to entice Greensparrow into action against Eriador?" the halfling asked. "You think you can get him to break the treaty?"

Luthien shook his head. "Greensparrow already has broken the treaty," he insisted, "merely by inciting the cyclopians against us. All we need to do is get proof of that conspiracy—and quickly."

"And how do you mean to accomplish such a task?" Oliver wanted to know.

"We will go to the source," Luthien explained. "Siobhan will return this night with information about the cyclopian encampment. No doubt Brind'Amour will order action against that band immediately. All we have to do is get there first and get our proof."

Oliver was too surprised to find any immediate response. Vividly, though, the halfling didn't miss Luthien's reference to "we."

LIVING PROOF

Luthien and Oliver eased up side by side toward the top of the boulder. They could hear the bustle of the cyclopian encampment below, in a stony clearing surrounded by pines, boulders, and cliff walls. Luthien glanced to the side as he neared the rim, then moved quickly to pull the wide-brimmed hat from Oliver's head.

Oliver started to cry out in protest, but Luthien anticipated such a reaction and put his hand over the halfling's mouth, motioning with the other hand for Oliver to remain quiet.

"I tell you once to give me back my hat," the halfling whispered.

Luthien handed it over.

"And for you," the halfling went on, "and your woman friend," he added quickly, recalling all the times Katerin had also so bullied him, "if you ever put your dirty hand over my mouth again, I will bite you hard."

Luthien put his finger to pursed lips, then pointed in the direction of the cyclopian encampment.

Up rose the pair, Luthien merely extending to his full height, Oliver having to find one more foothold. They eased over the boulder's rim together, looking down on their adversaries. From this angle, the camp seemed almost surreal, too vivid with its brightness against the backdrop of the dark night. The companions spotted several small campfires, but these could not account for the almost daylight brilliance within the encampment, or for the fact that the light had not been so visible from any other vantage point, as though it was somehow contained within the perimeter of the camp.

Luthien immediately understood that magic had to be its source, but he knew that cyclopians did not use magic. The one-eyed brutes certainly were not smart enough to unravel the mysteries of the magical arts.

But Luthien could not deny what he saw. Everything in the clearing, the scores of cyclopians milling about, the uneven shapes of the many stones, the rack of weapons against the cliff wall opposite his perch, was vividly clear, stark in outline.

Luthien looked to Oliver, who only shrugged, similarly mystified. "Cyclopian wizard?" the halfling mouthed.

Both turned back to the encampment and found their answer as a broad-shouldered, large-bellied man walked into view, laughing cheerily as he talked with a large cyclopian. He wore a dark-colored tabard, richly embroidered, that hung to his knees. Even from this distance, Luthien could see the sheen on his hose, indicating that they were silk, or some other exotic and expensive material, and the buckles of his shoes gleamed as only the purest silver could.

"I count two eyes on that one," Oliver whispered.

Luthien was nodding. He didn't recognize the man, but the presence of magic and the rich, regal dressings led him to believe that he could guess the man's title. This was one of Greensparrow's dukes; this was all the proof that Brind'Amour would need.

The man, laughing still, clapped his cyclopian companion hard on the back, then reached up and put a fur-trimmed cap with a golden insignia sewn into its front atop his thick gray hair. Another cyclopian came by and handed him a huge mug, which he lifted to his beardless face and nearly drained in one gulp.

Some of the contents spilled out, running down the man's considerable jowls, and the cyclopian burst out in laughter. The man followed suit, roaring wildly.

"Brind'Amour will laugh louder than he when we deliver this one to Caer MacDonald," Luthien whispered.

"How are we to get to him?" Oliver asked the obvious question.

If this was indeed a wizard, then capturing him in the impending battle would be near to impossible.

Luthien smiled wryly and held out the edge of his marvelous crimson cape. The Crimson Shadow could get into that encampment undetected, no matter how bright the light!

"You mean to sneak in and steal him away?" Oliver asked incredulously.

"We can do it," Luthien replied.

Oliver groaned softly, rolled over to put his back against the boulder, and slumped down from the rim. "Why is it always 'we'?" he asked. "Perhaps you should find another to go with you."

"But Oliver," Luthien protested, coming down beside his friend, his smile still wide, "you are the only one who will fit under the cape."

"Oh, lucky Oliver," grumbled the halfling.

They moved away from the camp, to inform the nearest elves of their plan. More than two hundred dwarfs were in the area, along with the forty elves and half-elves, including Siobhan, that now comprised the spying band known as the Cutters. The original plan was to go in hard and fast under the cries of "Sougles's Glen!" and slaughter every cyclopian. Luthien, with help from Siobhan, had convinced the fierce dwarfs otherwise, had shown them the potential for greater good by exercising restraint until the proof they needed could be found.

Luthien and Oliver were back at their high perch soon after, waiting for the majority of one-eyes to drift off to sleep, or at least for the light to go down somewhat. An hour passed, then another. The sliver of the waning moon moved low in the western sky, and was soon swallowed up by turbulent black clouds. The rumble of distant thunder tingled under their feet.

The man Luthien had targeted as a duke continued to laugh and to drink, sitting about a fire, throwing bones with a handful of brutish cyclopians. Even with the magical cape, there was no way that Luthien could get near to him without a fight.

But then came a break. The man belched loudly and stood up, brushing the dust and twigs from his tabard. He drained the rest of his mug, belched again, and walked away, toward the perimeter of the encampment, just to the right and below the watching companions.

"Whatever goes in . . ." Oliver whispered.

He and Luthien slipped down the back side of the boulder and crept along in the darkness, inching their way in the general direction to intercept the man. Soon they were following a steady stream of sound, and spotted the man standing beside a tree, supporting himself with one hand, while the other held up the front of his tabard. He was fully twenty yards from the encampment, with most of that distance blocked by tangled trees and shrubs.

"Do not get too close," Oliver warned. "It seems that he has a missile weapon."

Luthien stifled a nervous chuckle and inched his way in. He froze as he stepped on one stick, which cracked apart loudly. Oliver froze in place, too, a horrified expression on his face.

The companions soon realized that they had nothing to worry about. The drunken man was oblivious to them, though he was barely ten feet away. Luthien considered his options. If he rushed up and punched hard but did not lay the man low, his cry would surely alert the cyclopians. Certainly Luthien couldn't strike with his sword, for he wanted the man alive.

The threat should suffice, Luthien decided, and with a look about for Oliver, who was suddenly not to be seen, the young Bedwyr drew out *Blind-Striker*. Luthien couldn't dare call out for his missing halfling friend, so he took a deep and steadying breath, rushed the last few feet, and lifted his blade up before the man's face.

"Silence!" Luthien instructed in a harsh whisper, bringing the finger of his free hand to pursed lips.

The man looked at him curiously and continued his business, as though the possibility of capture hadn't yet occurred to him.

Luthien wagged the blade in the air. The man, startled from his stupor, widened his eyes suddenly and straightened. Thinking that he was about to cry out, Luthien lunged forward, meaning to put his swordtip right to the man's throat.

But the man was faster, his motion simpler. His hand moved from the tree and in a single arc, yanked a talisman from his tabard and swished in a downward swipe. A field of shimmering blue came up before him.

Luthien's momentum was too great for him to react. *Blind-Striker*'s tip hit the field and threw sparks, and the sword was violently repelled, flying back over Luthien's head, yanking his arm painfully. Luthien, though, was still moving forward, and he, too, couldn't avoid the shield. He yelped and rolled his shoulder defensively, barely brushing the bluish light. But that was all the repelling magic needed, and the young Bedwyr found himself flying backward, off his feet, to crash into the trees.

The jolly wizard's laugh was stifled before it ever began, as he felt a sting in his belly. He looked down to see Oliver, standing on his side of the repelling field, rapier drawn and poking.

"Aha!" said the halfling. "I have gone around your silly magics and am inside your so-clever barrier." Oliver's beaming expression suddenly turned sour and he looked down. "And my so-fine shoes are wet!" he wailed.

The man moved fast; so did Oliver, meaning to stick him more forcefully. But to the halfling's horror, a single word from the wizard transformed his rapier blade into a living serpent, and it immediately turned back on him!

And the wizard's huge and strong hands were coming for him as well! Right for his throat.

Oliver cried out and threw his rapier over his head, then moved to dodge. The attack never came, though, for the blade-turned-serpent struck the repelling shield and rebounded straight out, hitting the wizard square in the face. Now it was Duke Resmore's turn to cry out, reaching frantically for the writhing snake.

Oliver darted between the man's legs, turned about and grabbed the edges of his tabard. Up the halfling scrambled, taking the serpent's place as the man threw it to the ground. Oliver grabbed on to one ear for support, and the man's head jerked backward, his mouth opening to cry out. Oliver promptly stuffed his free hand into that mouth.

Luthien came around the edge of the shield, *Blind-Striker* in hand. Some of the cyclopians the duke had left behind were heading in their direction and calling out the name of "Resmore." They had to go, and quickly, Luthien knew, and if this wizard, Resmore, would not cooperate, Luthien meant to strike him dead.

"My gauntlets, they are leather, yes?" Oliver asked.

"Yes."

"But he is biting right through them!" Oliver squealed. Out came the hand, and the wizard-duke wasted no time.

"A'ta'arrefi!" he cried.

Barely twenty yards away, a host of cyclopians cried out.

Two running strides brought Luthien up to the man, and a solid right cross to the jaw dropped him where he stood, forcing Oliver to leap away, rolling in the twigs.

"One-eyes!" the halfling groaned as he came up, but he found some hope when he spotted his rapier, the blade whole again. "Take his silly cap, and let us go!"

Luthien shook the pains out of his bruised hand and moved to comply, realizing that the insignia on that cap might suffice. He stopped, though, as Oliver spoke again.

"Do you smell what I smell?" the halfling asked.

Luthien paused, and indeed he did, an all-too-familiar odor. Sulfurous, noxious. The young Bedwyr looked to Oliver, then turned to follow Oliver's gaze, back over his shoulder, to a spinning ball of orange flames, quickly taking the shape of a bipedal canine with goatlike horns atop its head and eyes that blazed with the red hue of demonic fires.

"Oh, not again," the beleaguered halfling moaned.

The monster's howl split the night.

"Let me guess," Oliver said dryly. "You are A'ta'arrefi?"

The creature was not large, no more than four feet from head to tail, but its aura, that sensation of might that surrounded every demon, was nearly overwhelming. Luthien and Oliver had battled enough of the fiends to know that they were in serious trouble, a fact made all the more obvious when A'ta'arrefi opened wide its fanged maw, wide enough, it seemed, to swallow Oliver whole!

Above them all, a bolt of lightning crackled through the rushing black clouds, a fitting touch, it seemed, to this hellish scenario. The sudden light showed the companions that cyclopians were all about them now, fanning out in the woods and keeping a respectable distance, whispering that this was the Crimson Shadow.

Luthien hardly gave the brutes a thought, focusing, as he had to, on the caninelike demon.

Out of that huge maw came a forked tongue, a hissing bark, and A'ta'arrefi, with speed that stunned the companions, leaped forward, dancing in the unholy symphony of the angry storm.

Oliver screamed. Luthien did, too, and raised *Blind-Striker*, though he knew that he could not be quick enough to intercept the charge.

And then he was blinded, and so was Oliver, and so were the cyclopians, as a lightning stroke came down right in front of him. Luthien felt his muscles jerking wildly, felt his hair dancing, and realized that he had been lifted right off the ground by the terrific impact. Somehow he came back down on his feet and held his tentative balance, though he soon enough realized that, with the demon charging, he might have been wiser to fall to the side.

But the expected attack never came, and Luthien heard before he saw, that battle had been joined in the woods about him. He heard the twang of elvish bows, the thunder of a dwarven charge, the cries of surprised and quickly dying cyclopians.

Finally, Luthien's vision cleared, and he saw that A'ta'arrefi was no more—no more than a blackened forked tongue lying on the ground at Luthien's feet.

As abrupt as the lightning bolt came the downpour, a torrent of rain hissing through the trees. Luthien pulled the hood of his crimson cape over his head, purely an instinctual movement, made with hardly a thought, for the young man was surely dazed.

Resmore's groan brought Luthien back to the situation at hand. He shook the dizziness from his head and turned to the prone duke. He couldn't stifle a burst of laughter as he spotted Oliver, sitting beside the man, the halfling's usually curly hair straightened and standing on end.

"Boom," the foppish halfling muttered and toppled to lie across the duke. The jarring woke the man.

Luthien skidded down atop him to hold him in place.

"I will deliver you personally to King Greensparrow," the dazed and drunken Resmore slurred.

Luthien slugged him again to silence him, and when the man went still, Luthien lay atop the pile, spreading his shielding crimson cape to hide them all. He wanted to get up and join in the fight, but he understood the importance of his inaction, both to safeguard his all-valuable prisoner and to ensure that the magic-wielder could not wake up again and get into the fray.

Besides, Luthien soon realized, it was all going the way of the dwarfs and elves. Vengeance fueled the chopping axes and pounding hammers, and none could fight better in the darkness than elves, and none were better with deadly bows. The cyclopians had been caught by surprise, and even worse for them, they had been sitting within a brightly lit encampment and were now perfectly blind to the night.

Luthien thought he would have to fight, though, when he heard one terrified one-eye come rushing out of the brush, sloshing through the growing mud puddles, running straight for the unseen pile of bodies. The young Bedwyr turned slowly, so as not to give up the camouflage, and he spotted the cyclopian, looking back desperately over its shoulder, at about the same instant it ran smack into Resmore's repelling shield.

Back the one-eye flew, meeting up with a pair of dwarfs as they burst out of the brush.

"I didn't think he'd have the guts to charge!" one of the dwarfs roared, coming to his feet and promptly bringing his axe into the stunned cyclopian's backbone.

"Nor did myself!" howled the other, caving in the one-eye's skull with his heavy hammer.

"His children should be proud!" the first dwarf proclaimed.

"His children should be orphans!" cried the second, and off they ran, happily, looking for more one-eyes to smack.

Luthien eased his head back down, shifted himself more completely under the cape. It was better to stay out of this one, he decided.

Chapter 13

EVIDENCE AND ERRORS PAST

The return to Caer MacDonald was heralded by cries of vengeance sated and by trumpets blowing triumphantly along the city's walls. Word of their victory had preceded Luthien and his forces, as well as the whispers that a wizard, one of Avon's dukes, had been captured in the battle.

Luthien and Oliver flanked Resmore every step of the way, with weapons drawn and ready. The duke hadn't said much; not a word, in fact, other than a stream of threats, invoking the name of Greensparrow often, as though that alone should send his captors into a fit of trembling. He was tightly bound, and often gagged, but even with that, Luthien held *Blind-Striker* dangerously near to the man's throat, for the young Bedwyr, more experienced than he wanted to be with the likes of wizard-dukes, would take no chances with this man. Luthien had no desire to face A'ta'arrefi, or any other demon again, nor would he let Resmore, his proof that Greensparrow was not honoring the truce, get away.

Men, women, and many, many children lined the avenues as the victorious procession entered Caer MacDonald. Siobhan and Shuglin led the way, with the elvish Cutters in a line behind their leader, and twenty dwarfs following Shuglin. In the middle of this powerful force walked Luthien, Oliver, and their most valuable prisoner. Another score of dwarfs took up the rear, closely guarding the dozen ragged cyclopian prisoners. If the bearded folk had been given their way, all the cyclopians would have been slaughtered in the mountains, but Luthien and Siobhan had convinced them that prisoners might prove crucial now, for all the politics of the land. Aside from these forty soldiers returning to Caer MacDonald, the rest of the bearded folk, along with another dozen cyclopian prisoners, had remained in the Iron Cross, making their way to Dun-Darrow to bring word of the victory to King Bellick dan Burso.

Cheers accompanied the procession every step along the main way of Caer MacDonald; many tossed silver coins or offered fine wine or ale, or plates heaped with food.

Oliver basked in the moment, even standing atop his pony's back at one point, dipping a low bow, his great hat sweeping. Luthien tried to remain vigilant and stoic, but couldn't contain his smile. At the front of the column, though, Siobhan and Shuglin paid the crowd little heed. These two exemplified the suffering of their respective races at the hands of Greensparrow. Shuglin's folk, those who had been caught, had long been enslaved, working as craftsmen for the elite ruling and merchant classes until they outlived their usefulness, or gave their masters some excuse to send them to torturous labor in the mines. Siobhan's folk had fared no better in the last two decades. Elves were not numerous in Avonsea—most had fled the isles for parts unknown many years before Greensparrow's rise—but those who were caught during the rein of the evil king were given to wealthy homes as servants and concubines. Siobhan, with blood that was neither purely elven nor purely human, was on the lowest rung of all in Greensparrow's racial hierarchy, and had spent many years in the service of a merchant tyrant who had beaten and raped her at will.

So these two were not smiling, and would not rejoice. For Luthien, victory had come when Eriador was declared free; for Shuglin and Siobhan, victory meant the head of Greensparrow, staked up high on a pole.

Nothing less.

King Brind'Amour met them in the plaza surrounding the Ministry. Purposefully, the king made his way past Siobhan and Shuglin, holding up his hand to indicate that they should wait to tell their tale. Down the line he went, his eyes locked on one man in particular, and he stopped when he came face-to-face with the prisoner.

Brind'Amour reached up and pulled the gag from the man's mouth.

"He is a wizard," Luthien warned.

"His name is Resmore," Oliver added.

"One of Greensparrow's dukes?" Brind'Amour asked the man, but Resmore merely "harrumphed" indignantly and lifted his fat face in defiance.

"He wore this," Oliver explained, handing the expensive cap over to his king. "It was not so much a trick for me to take it from him."

Luthien's sour expression was not unexpected, and Oliver purposefully kept his gaze fixed on his king.

Brind'Amour took the hat and turned it in his hands, studying the emblem: a ship's prow carved into the likeness of a rearing stallion, nostrils flared, eyes wild. "Newcastle," the Eriadoran king said calmly. "You are Duke Resmore of Newcastle."

"Friend of Greensparrow, who is king of all Avonsea!" a flustered Resmore replied.

"And king of Gascony, I am so sure," Oliver added sarcastically.

"Not by treaty," Brind'Amour reminded Resmore calmly, the old wizard smiling at the duke's slip. "Our agreement proclaims Greensparrow as king of Avon and Brind'Amour as king of Eriador. Or is it that you deem the treaty immaterial?"

Resmore was sweating visibly now, realizing his error. "I only meant . . ." he stammered, and then he stopped. He took a deep breath to steady himself and lifted his chin proudly once more. "You have no right to hold me," he declared.

"You were captured fairly," Oliver remarked. "By me."

"Unlawfully!" Resmore protested. "I was in the mountains, by all rights, in land neutral to our respective kingdoms!"

"You were on the Eriadoran side of the Iron Cross," Brind'Amour reminded him. "Not twenty miles from Caer MacDonald."

"I know of no provisions in our treaty that would prevent—" Resmore began.

"You were with the cyclopians," Luthien promptly interrupted.

"Again, by word of the treaty—"

"Damn your treaty!" Luthien shouted, though Brind'Amour tried to calm him. "The one-eyes have been raiding our villages, murdering innocents, even children. At the prompting of your wretched king, I say!"

A hundred voices lifted in accord with the young Bedwyr's proclamation, but Brind'Amour's was not among them. Again the king of Eriador, skilled in matters politic, worked hard to quiet them all, fearing that a mob would form and his prisoners would be hanged before he could gather his evidence.

"Since when do one-eyes need the prompting of a human king to raid and pillage?" Resmore sarcastically asked.

"We can prove that this very band you were captured beside was among those participating in raids," Brind'Amour said.

"Of which I know nothing," Resmore replied coolly. "I have only been with them a few days, and they have not left the mountains in that time—until you illegally descended upon them. Who is the raider now?"

Brind'Amour's blue eyes flared dangerously at that last remark. "Pretty words, Duke Resmore," he said grimly. "But worthless, I assure you. Magic was used in the massacre known as Sougles's Glen; its tracings can still be felt by those attuned to such powers."

Brind'Amour's not-so-subtle proclamation that he, too, was a wizard seemed to unnerve the man more than a little.

"Your role in the attacks can be proven," Brind'Amour went on, "and a wizard's neck is no more resistant to the rope than is a peasant's."

The mob exploded with screams for the man's death, by hanging or burning, or whatever method could be quickly expedited. Many seemed ready to break ranks and beat the man. Brind'Amour would hear none of it, though. He motioned for Luthien and the others to take Resmore and the cyclopians into the Ministry, where they were put into separate dungeons. Resmore was assigned two personal guards, elves, who were quite sensitive to magic, who stood over the man continually, swords drawn and ready.

"We should thank you for your role in the capture," Luthien remarked to Brind'Amour, walking the passageways along the smaller side rooms in the great structure beside Oliver and their king.

"Oh yes," Oliver piped in. "A so-very-fine shot!"

Brind'Amour slowed enough to stare at his companions, his expression showing that he did not understand.

"In the mountains," Luthien clarified. "When Resmore called in his demon."

"You faced yet another hellish fiend?" Brind'Amour asked.

"Until your so-booming bolt of lightning," Oliver replied. "On came the beast for Luthien—he would not approach my rapier blade, you see."

"A'ta'arrefi, the demon was called," Luthien interrupted, not willing to hear Oliver's always-skewed perspective.

Still Brind'Amour seemed not to understand.

"He resembled a dog," Luthien added, "though he walked upright, as a man."

"And his tongue was forked," Oliver added, and it took the halfling's two companions a moment to decipher that last word, which Oliver's thick Gascon accent made sound as though it was two separate words, "for-ked." The halfling's gesture helped in the translation, for he put two wiggling fingers up in front of his mouth.

Brind'Amour shrugged.

"Your lightning bolt," Luthien insisted. "It could not have been mere chance!"

"Say it plainly, my boy," the wizard begged.

"Resmore's demon ran for us," Luthien replied. "He was but five paces from me when the storm broke, a sting of lightning rushing down."

"Boom!" Oliver yelled. "Right on the head."

"And all that was left of A'ta'arrefi was his blackened tongue," said Luthien.

"For-ked," Oliver finished.

Brind'Amour rubbed his white beard briskly. He had no idea of what the two were talking about, for he hadn't even been looking that way; Brind'Amour had been so engrossed with events in the east and south that he had no idea Luthien and Oliver had even gone into the mountains with Siobhan, let alone that they were facing a demon! Still, it seemed perfectly impossible to him that the lightning bolt was a natural accident. Luthien and Oliver were lucky indeed, but that was too far-fetched. Obviously a wizard had been involved. Perhaps it was even Greensparrow himself, aiming for Luthien and hitting Resmore's fiend by mistake. "Yes, of course," was all that he said to the two. "A fine shot, that. Demons are easy targets, though; stand out among mortals like a giant among halflings."

Luthien managed a weak smile, not convinced that Brind'Amour was speaking truthfully. The young Bedwyr had no other explanation, though, and so he let it go at that. If there was something amiss, magically speaking, then it would be Brind'Amour's concern, and not his own.

"Come," the wizard bade, moving down a side passage. "We have perhaps found the link between Greensparrow and the cyclopians, thus our treaty with Avon may be deemed void. Let us draw up the truce with King Asmund of Isenland and begin to lay our plans."

"We will fight Greensparrow?" Luthien asked bluntly.

"I do not yet know," Brind'Amour replied. "I must speak with our prisoners, and with the ambassador from Gascony. There is much to do before any final decisions can be made."

Of course there was, Luthien realized, but the young Bedwyr held faith then that he would not be battling against his brother. Greensparrow's treacherous hand had been revealed in full; Resmore was all the proof they needed. Visions of sailing the fleet up the Stratton into Carlisle beside the Huegoth longships danced in Luthien's mind.

It was not an unpleasant fantasy.

Brind'Amour entered the dimly lit room solemnly, wearing his rich blue wizard robes. Candles burned softly from pedestals in each of the room's corners. In the center was a small round table and a single stool.

Brind'Amour took his place on the stool. With trembling hands, he reached up and removed the cloth draped over the single object on the table, his crystal ball. It was with trepidation and nervous excitement that the wizard began his incantation. Brind'Amour didn't believe that Greensparrow had launched a bolt for Luthien that had accidentally destroyed Resmore's familiar demon. In lieu of that, the old wizard could think of only one explanation for Luthien's incredible tale: one of his fellows from the ancient brotherhood of wizards had awakened and joined in the effort. What else might explain the lightning bolt?

The wizard fell into his trance, sent his sight through the ball, into the mountains, across the width and breadth of Eriador, then across the borders of time itself.

"Brind'Amour?"

The question came from far away, but was insistent.

"Brind'Amour?"

"Serendie?" the old wizard asked, thinking he had at last found one of his fellows, a jolly chap who had been among his closest of friends.

"Luthien," came the distant reply.

Brind'Amour searched his memory, trying to remember which wizard went by that vaguely familiar name. He felt a touch on his shoulder, and then was shaken.

Brind'Amour came out of his trance to find that he was in his divining room at the Ministry, with Luthien and Oliver standing beside him. He yawned and stretched, thoroughly drained from his night's work.

"What time?" he asked.

"The cock has crowed," Oliver remarked, "has eaten his morning meal, put a smile on the beaks of a few hen-types, and is probably settled for his afternoon nap!"

"We wondered where you were," Luthien explained.

"So where were you?" Oliver asked.

Brind'Amour snorted at the halfling's perceptive question. He had been physically in this room—all the night and half the day it would seem—but in truth, he had visited many places. A frown creased his face as he considered those journeys now. The last of them, to the isle of Dulsen-Berra, central of the Five Sentinels, haunted him. The vision the crystal ball had given him was somewhere back in time, though how long ago he could not tell. He saw cyclopians scaling the rocky hills of the island. Then he saw their guide: a man he recognized, though he was not as fat and thick-jowled as he was now, a man Brind'Amour now held captive in the dungeons of this very building!

In the vision, Resmore carried an unusual object, a forked rod, a divining stick. So-called "witches" of the more remote villages of Avonsea, and all across wild Baranduine, used such an object to find water. Normally a divining rod was a form of the very least magic, but this time, Resmore's rod had been truly enchanted. Guided by it, Resmore and his one-eyed cronies had found a secret glen and the blocked entrance to a cave. Several wards exploded, killing more than a few cyclopians, but there were more than enough of the brutes to complete the task. Soon enough, the cave mouth was opened and the brutes rushed in. They returned to Resmore in the grassy glen, dragging a stiff body behind them. It was Duparte, dear Duparte, another of Brind'Amour's closest friends, who had helped Brind'Amour in the construction of the Ministry and had taught so many Eriadoran fisherfolk the ways of the dangerous dorsal whales.

All the long night Brind'Amour had suffered such scenes of murder as his fellows were routed from their places of magical sleep. All the long night he had seen Resmore and Greensparrow, Morkney and Paragor, and one other wizard he did not know, flush out his helpless, sleeping fellows and destroy them.

Brind'Amour shuddered visibly, and Luthien put a comforting hand on his shoulder.

"They are all dead, I fear," Brind'Amour said quietly.

"Who?" Oliver asked, looking around nervously.

"The ancient brotherhood," the old wizard replied—and he truly seemed old at that moment! "Only I, who spent so long enacting magical wards against intrusion, seem to have escaped the treachery of Greensparrow."

"You witnessed all of their deaths?" Luthien asked incredulously, looking at the crystal ball. By Brind'Amour's tales, many, many wizards had gone into the magical slumber those centuries before.

"Not all."

"Why did you look?" Oliver asked.

"Your tale of the encounter with Resmore," Brind'Amour replied.

"You did not send the lightning," Luthien reasoned. "Thus you believed that one of your brothers had awakened, and had come to our aid."

"But that is not the case," Brind'Amour said.

"You said you did not find them all," Oliver reminded.

"But none are awake; of that I am almost certain," Brind'Amour replied. "If any of them were, my divining would have revealed them, or at least a hint of them."

"But if you did not send the lightning . . ." Luthien began.

Brind'Amour only shrugged, having no explanation.

The old wizard sighed and leaned back in his chair. "We erred, my friends," he said. "And badly."

"Not I," Oliver argued.

"The ancient brotherhood?" Luthien asked, pausing only to shake his head at Oliver's unending self-importance.

"We thought the land safe and in good hands," Brind'Amour explained. "The time of magic was fast fading, and thus we faded away, went into our slumber to conserve what remained of our powers until the world needed us once more.

"We all went into that sleep," the wizard went on, his voice barely above a whisper, "except for Greensparrow, it seems, who was but a minor wizard, a man of no consequence. Even the great dragons had been destroyed, or bottled up, as I and my fellows had done to Balthazar."

Luthien and Oliver shuddered at the mention of that name, a dragon they knew all too well!

"I lost my staff in Balthazar's cave," the wizard continued, turning to regard Luthien. "But I didn't think I would ever need it again—until after I awoke to find the land in the darkness of Greensparrow."

"This much we knew," Luthien said. "But if Greensparrow had been such a minor wizard, then how did he rise?"

"What a great error," Brind'Amour said to himself. "We thought magic on the wane, and so it was, by our standards of the art. But Greensparrow found another way. He allied with demons, tapped powers that should have been left alone, to rebuild a source of magical power. We should have foreseen this, and warded against it before our time of slumber."

"I do so agree!" Oliver chimed in, but then he lowered his gaze as Luthien's scowl found him.

"You should have seen me!" Brind'Amour said suddenly, his face flashing with the vigor of a long past youth. "Oh, my powers were so much greater then! I could use the art all the day, sleep well that night, then use it again all the next day." A cloud seemed to pass over his aged features. "But now, I am not so strong. Greensparrow and his cohorts find most of their strength through demonic aid, a source I cannot, and will not, tap."

"You destroyed Duke Paragor," Luthien reminded.

Brind'Amour snorted, but managed a weak smile. "True," he admitted. "And Morkney is dead, and Duke Resmore, his demon somehow taken from him, is but a minor wizard, and no more a threat." Again he looked to Luthien, his face truly grim. "But these are but cohorts of Greensparrow, who is of the ancient brotherhood. These dukes, and the duchess of Mannington, are mortals, and not of my brotherhood. Minor tricksters empowered by Greensparrow."

Luthien saw that his old friend needed his strength at that moment. "When Greensparrow is dead," he declared, "you, Brind'Amour, king of Eriador, will be the most powerful wizard in all the world."

Oliver clapped his hands, but Brind'Amour only replied quietly, "Something I never desired."

"Leave us," Brind'Amour instructed as he entered the dungeon cell below the Ministry. The small room was smoky, lighted by a single torch that burned in an unremarkable wall sconce beside the door.

The two elvish guards looked nervously to each other, and to the prisoner, but they would not disobey their king. With curt bows, they exited, though they stubbornly took up positions just outside the cell's small door.

Brind'Amour closed that door, eyeing Resmore all the while. The miserable duke sat in the middle of the floor, hands bound behind his back and shackled by a tight chain to his ankles. He was also gagged and blindfolded.

Brind'Amour clapped his hands and the shackles fell from Resmore's wrists. Slowly, the man reached up and removed first the blindfold and then the gag, stretching his numb legs as he did so.

"I demand better treatment!" he growled.

Brind'Amour circled the room, muttering under his breath and dropping a line of yellow powder at the base of the wall.

Resmore called to him several times, but when the old wizard would not answer, the duke sat quiet, curious.

Brind'Amour completed the powder line, encompassing the entire room, and looked at the man directly.

"Who destroyed your demon?" Brind'Amour asked directly.

Resmore stuttered for lack of an answer; he had thought, as had Luthien and Oliver, that Brind'Amour had done it.

"If A'ta'arrefi—" Brind'Amour began.

"A wizard should be more careful when uttering that name!" Resmore interrupted.

Brind'Amour shook his head slowly, calmly. "Not in here," he explained, looking to the line of yellow powder. "Your fiend, if it survives, cannot hear your call, or mine, from in here, nor can you, or your magic, leave this room."

Resmore threw his head back with a wild burst of laughter, as if mocking the other. He struggled to his feet, and nearly fell over, for his legs were still tingling from sitting for so long. "You should treat your peers with more respect, you who claim the throne of this forsaken land."

"And you should wag your tongue more carefully," Brind'Amour warned, "or I shall tear it from your mouth and wag it for you."

"How dare you!"

"Silence!" the old wizard roared, his power bared in the sheer strength of his voice. Resmore's eyes widened and he fell back a step. "You are no peer of mine!" Brind'Amour went on. "You and your fellows, lackeys all to Greensparrow, are a mere shadow of the power that was the brotherhood."

"I—"

"Fight me!" Brind'Amour commanded.

Resmore snorted, but the scoff was lost in his throat as Brind'Amour launched into the movements of spellcasting, chanting heartily. Resmore began a spell of his own, reaching out to the torch and pulling a piece of fire from it, a flicker of flame to sting the older wizard.

It rolled out from the wall at Resmore's bidding, flaring stronger right in front of Brind'Amour's pointy nose, and Resmore snapped his fingers, the completion of his spell, the last thrust of energy that should have caused the lick of flame to burst into a miniature fireball. Again, Resmore's hopes were abruptly quashed as his flame fell to the floor and elongated, something he never intended for it to do.

Brind'Amour continued his casting, aiming his magic at the conjured flame, wresting control of it and strengthening it, transforming it. It widened and gradually took the shape of a lion, a great and fiery cat with blazing eyes and a mane that danced with the excitement of fire.

Resmore paled and fell back another step, then turned and bolted for the door. He hit a magical wall, as solid as one of stone, and staggered back into the middle of the room, gradually regaining his senses and turning to face the wizard and his flaming pet.

Brind'Amour reached down and patted the beast's flaming mane.

Resmore cocked his head. "An illusion," he proclaimed.

"An illusion?" Brind'Amour echoed. He looked to the cat. "He called you an illusion," he said. "Quite an insult. You may kill him."

Resmore's eyes popped wide as the lion's roar resounded about the room. The cat dropped low—the duke had nowhere to run!—and then sprang out, flying for Resmore. The man screamed and fell to the floor, covering his head with his arms, thrashing for all his life.

But he was alone in the dirt, and when at last he dared to peek out, he saw Brind'Amour standing casually near the side of the room, with no sign of the flaming lion to be found, no sign that the cat had ever been there.

"An illusion," Resmore insisted. In a futile effort to regain a measure of his dignity, he stood up and brushed himself off.

"And am I an illusion?" Brind'Amour asked.

Resmore eyed him curiously.

Suddenly Brind'Amour waved his arms and a great gust of wind hit Resmore and hurled him backward, to slam hard into the magical barrier. He staggered forward a couple of steps and looked up just as Brind'Amour clapped his hands together, then threw his palms out toward Resmore. A crackling black bolt hit the man in the gut, doubling him over in pain.

Brind'Amour snarled and brought one hand sweeping down in the air. His magic, the extension of his fury, sent a burst of energy down on the back of stooping Resmore's neck, hurling him face-first into the hard dirt.

He lay there, dazed and bleeding, with no intention of getting back up. But then he felt something—a hand?—close about his throat and hoist him. He was back to his feet, and then off his feet, hanging in midair, the hand choking the life from him.

His bulging eyes looked across to his adversary. Brind'Amour stood with one arm extended, hand grasping the empty air.

"I saw you," Brind'Amour said grimly. "I saw what you did to Duparte on the Isle of Dulsen-Berra!"

Resmore tried to utter a denial, but he could not find the breath for words.

"I saw you!" Brind'Amour yelled, clenching tighter.

Resmore jerked and thought his neck would surely snap.

But Brind'Amour threw his hand out wide, opening it as he went, and Resmore went flying across the room, to slam the magical barrier once more and fall to his knees, gasping, his nose surely broken. It took him a long while to manage to turn about and face terrible Brind'Amour again, and when he did, he found the old wizard standing calmly, holding a quill pen and a board that had a parchment tacked to it.

Brind'Amour tossed both items into the air, and they floated, as if hung on invisible ropes, Resmore's way.

"Your confession," Brind'Amour explained. "Your admission that you, at King Greensparrow's bidding, worked to incite the cyclopians in their raids on Eriadoran and dwarvish settlements."

The items stopped right before the kneeling duke, hanging in the empty air. He looked to them, then studied Brind'Amour.

"And if I refuse to sign?" he dared to ask.

"Then I will rend you limb from limb," Brind'Amour casually promised. "I will flail the skin from your bones, and hold up your heart, that you may witness its last beat." The calm way he said it unnerved Resmore.

"I saw what you did," Brind'Amour said again, and that was all the proof the poor duke needed to hear to know that this terrible old wizard was not bluffing. He took up the quill and the board and quickly scratched his name.

Brind'Amour walked over and took the confession personally, without magical aid. He wanted Resmore to see his scowl up close, wanted the man to know that Brind'Amour had seen his crimes, and would neither forget, nor forgive.

Then Brind'Amour left the room, crossing through the magical wall with a single word.

"You will no longer be needed here," Resmore heard him say to the elves. "Duke Resmore is a harmless fool."

The dungeon door banged shut. The single torch that had been burning in the place was suddenly snuffed out, leaving Resmore alone and miserable in the utter darkness.

THE PRINCESS AND HER CROWN

She sat before the mirror brushing her silken hair, her soft eyes staring vacantly through space and time. The bejeweled crown was set on the dresser before her, the link to her past, as a child princess. Beside the crown sat a bag of powder Deanna used to brighten the flames of a brazier enough to open a gate from Hell for the demon Taknapotin.

She had been just a child when that bag had become more important to her than the crown, when Greensparrow had become closer to her than her own father, the king of Avon. Greensparrow, who gave her magic. Greensparrow, who gave her Taknapotin. Greensparrow, who took her father's throne and saved the kingdom after a treacherous coup by a handful of upstart lords.

That was the tale Deanna Wellworth had been told by those loyal to the new king, and repeated to her by Greensparrow himself on the occasion of their next meeting. Greensparrow had lamented that, with his ascent to the throne, she was now out of the royal line. In truth, it mattered little because Greensparrow was a wizard of the ancient brotherhood, after all, blessed with long years, and would surely outlive Deanna, and all of her children, if she had any, and all of their children as well. But Greensparrow was not unsympathetic to the orphaned girl. Mannington, a not-unimportant port city on the western shore of Avon, would be her domain, her private kingdom.

That was the story Deanna Wellworth had heard since her childhood and for all of her adult life; that was the tale the sympathetic Greensparrow had offered to her.

Only now, nearing the age of thirty, had Deanna come to question, indeed to dismiss, that story. She tried to remember that fateful night of the coup, but all was confusion. Taknapotin had come to her and whisked her away in the dark of night; she vividly heard the screams of her siblings receding behind her.

O noble rescuer . . . a demon.

Why hadn't Taknapotin, a fiend of no small power, rescued her brothers and sister as well? And why hadn't the fiend and, more importantly, Greensparrow, who was easily the most powerful individual in the world, simply halted the coup? His answers, his excuses, were obvious and straightforward: there was no time; we were caught by surprise.

Those questions had often led Deanna to an impenetrable veil of mystery, and it wasn't until many years later that the duchess of Mannington came to ask the more important questions. Why had she been spared? And since she was alive after the supposed murderers had been executed, then why hadn't she been placed in Carlisle as the rightful queen of Avon?

Her stiff brush scraped hard against her head as the now-familiar rage began to mount inside of her. For several years, Deanna had suspected the betrayal and had felt the anger, but until recently she had suppressed those feelings. If what she feared had truly happened those two decades ago, then she could not readily excuse her own role in the murder of her mother and father, her five brothers and her sister.

"You look so much like her," came a call from the doorway.

Deanna looked into the mirror and saw Selna's reflection, the older woman coming into the room with Deanna's nightclothes over her arm. The duchess turned about in her seat to face the woman.

"Your mother," Selna explained with a disarming smile. She walked right over and put her hand gently against Deanna's cheek. "You have her eyes, so soft, so blue."

It was like a religious ceremony for the handmaid. Weekly at least, over the last twenty years, Selna, who had been her nanny in the days when her father ruled Avon, would brush her hand against Deanna's cheek and tell her how much she looked like her murdered mother. For so many of those years, Deanna had beamed under the compliment and begged Selna to tell her of Bettien, her mother.

What a horrible irony that now seemed to the enlightened woman!

Deanna rose and walked away, taking the nightclothes.

"Fear not, my Lady," Selna called after her. "I do not think our king will punish you for your weakness in the Iron Cross."

Deanna turned sharply on the woman, making her jump in surprise. "Has he told you that personally?" she asked.

"The king?"

"Of course, the king," Deanna replied. "Have you spoken with him since our return to Mannington?"

Selna appeared shocked. "My Lady," she protested, "why would his most royal King Greensparrow deem to talk with—"

"Have you spoken with him since we left the Iron Cross?" Deanna interrupted, speaking each word distinctly so that Selna could not miss the implications of the question.

Selna took a deep breath and lifted her jaw resolutely.

She feels safe within the protection of Greensparrow, Deanna mused. The duchess realized that her anger may have caused her to overstep her good judgment. If Selna's calls to Greensparrow were easily answered—perhaps the king had given her a minor demon to serve as courier—then Deanna's anger might soon bring Greensparrow's probing eye her way once more, something she most certainly did not want at this crucial hour.

"My apologies, dear Selna," Deanna said, moving over to put her hand on the woman's arm. Deanna dropped her gaze and gave the most profound of sighs. "I only fear that your perception of my weakness beside the cyclopians has lessened me in your view."

"Never that, my Lady," the handmaid said unconvincingly.

Deanna looked up, her soft blue eyes wet with tears. Ever since her childhood, Deanna had been good at summoning those; she called them "sympathy drops."

"It is late, my Lady," Selna said tersely. "You should retire."

"It was weakness," Deanna admitted with a slight sniffle. She noted that Selna's expression shifted to one of curiosity.

"I could not bear it," Deanna went on. "I hold no love for Eriadorans, and certainly none for dwarfs, but even the bearded folk seem a high cut above those ghastly one-eyes!"

Selna seemed to relax somewhat, even managed a smile that appeared sincere to Deanna.

"I only fear that my king and savior has come to doubt me," Deanna lamented.

"Never that, my Lady," Selna insisted.

"He is all the family that I have," Deanna said, "except for you, of course. I could not bear to disappoint him, and yet, that, I fear, is exactly what I have done."

"It was a task for which you of princessly temperament were not well-equipped," Selna said.

Princessly temperament. Selna often used that curious phrase when speaking to Deanna. Often the young woman wanted to yell in the face of it. If she was so attuned to royalty, then why was Greensparrow, and not she, who was of rightful blood, sitting on Carlisle's throne?

Deanna forced the angry thoughts deep within her. She let the tears come then, and wrapped Selna in a tight hug, holding fast until the woman remarked that it was time for her to go.

The duchess dashed those tears away in the blink of an eye as soon as Selna was safely out of the room. The hour was late, and she had so much to do this night! She spent a long moment looking at the dresser, at the crown and the bag, gathering her strength.

The hours passed. Deanna moved out of her room to make sure that all those quartered near her were asleep. Then she went back to her private chamber, closed and magically sealed the door, and went to her wardrobe, producing a small brass brazier from a secret compartment she had fashioned in its floor.

Not long after that, Taknapotin sat comfortably on her bed.

"A'ta'arrefi was not so formidable," the cocksure demon remarked.

"Not with the power of the storm I sent to you," Deanna replied coolly.

"Not so difficult a thing to channel the energy," Taknapotin admitted. "And so A'ta'arrefi is gone, poof!"

"And Resmore is out of the way, dead or in the dungeons of Caer MacDonald or DunDarrow," Deanna said.

"And we are one step closer to the throne," Taknapotin said eagerly.

Deanna still could not believe how easy this part of her plan had been. She had merely dangled the carrot of supreme rulership in front of Taknapotin and the fiend had verily drooled at the thought of overthrowing Greensparrow. This was the weakness of evil, Deanna realized. In alliance with such diabolical creatures, one could never securely hold any trust.

Not if one was wise.

Deanna walked over to the dresser and took up the crown, the link to her heritage, the one item that Greensparrow had managed to retrieve after the defeat of the usurpers. The one item that Greensparrow had given to her personally, begging her to keep it safe as a remembrance of her poor family.

"I do not think that any others need die," Taknapotin remarked. "Surely you are closest now, with Paragor and Resmore gone."

"Ah, but what of Duke McLenny of Eornfast in Baranduine?" Deanna asked. "He is wise to the world, my pet. So wise." The duchess chuckled silently at the irony of that statement.

"He suspects?"

Deanna shrugged. "He watches everything from the privacy of that wild land," she said. "Removed from the scene, he might better judge the players."

"Then he is a danger to us," the demon reasoned.

Deanna shook her head. "Not so." She turned from the mirror, holding the delicate crown in both hands. "Not to us."

Taknapotin looked at her curiously, particularly at the way her hands were clenched about that all-important crown.

Deanna's voice changed suddenly, dropping a complete octave as she began her chant. *"Oga demions callyata sie,"* she recited.

Taknapotin's eyes blazed brighter as the beast felt the impact of the chant, a discordant recital that pained any creature of Hell to its black heart. "What are you doing?" the fiend demanded, but it knew all too well. Deanna was issuing the words of banishment, a powerful enchantment that would send Taknapotin from the world for a hundred years!

She continued her chant, bravely, for the fiend rose up powerfully from the bed, fangs gleaming. The enchantment was powerful, but not perfect. Deanna couldn't be sure that it would work, in part because in her heart, in the heart of any wizard who has tasted such power, she could not fully desire to be rid of the demonic ally. She continued, though, and when Taknapotin, struggling and trembling, managed to take a step closer to her, she lifted high the crown that was her heritage, the gift of Greensparrow, the item that she now believed held more value than its gems or its memories. With a knowing smirk, Deanna twisted the metal viciously.

A sizzling crackle of black energy exploded from the crown, stunning Deanna and temporarily interrupting her chant. But it affected Taknapotin all the more. That crown was the demon's real tie to the world. It had been empowered by Greensparrow, the true master, and given to Deanna for reasons greater than nostalgia.

"You cannot do this!" Taknapotin growled. "You throw away your own power, your chance of ascension."

"Ascension into Hell!" Deanna yelled back, and with her strength renewed by the pitiful sight of the writhing agonized fiend, she took up her chant once more, uttering every discordant syllable through gritted teeth.

All that remained of Taknapotin was a black stain on her thickly carpeted floor.

Deanna threw down the twisted crown and stamped her foot upon it. It was the symbol of her foolishness, the tie to a kingdom—*her* kingdom—and to a family she had unwittingly brought down.

Though she had just enacted perhaps the most telling and powerful magical feat of her young life, and though Taknapotin, the demon that gave to her a great part of her power, was gone from her forever, Deanna Wellworth felt strangely invigorated. She went to her mirror and took up a vial, supposedly of perfume, but in truth, filled with a previously enchanted liquid. She sprayed the liquid generously over her mirror, calling to her closest friend.

The mirror misted over, and the fog seemed within the glass as well. Gradually the center cleared, leaving a distinct image within the foggy border.

"It is done?" asked the handsome, middle-aged man.

"Taknapotin is gone," Deanna confirmed.

"Resmore is in the care of Brind'Amour, as we had hoped," said the man, Duke Ashannon McLenny of Baranduine.

"I wish that you were here," Deanna lamented.

"I am not so far away," Ashannon replied, and it was true enough. The duke of Baranduine resided in Eornfast, a city directly across the Straits of Mann from Mannington. Their connection in spirit was even closer than that, Deanna reminded herself, and, though she was more scared than she had ever been, except of course for that terrible night twenty years before, she managed a smile.

"Our course is set," Deanna said resolutely.

"What of Brind'Amour?" Ashannon asked.

"He searches for a friend of old," Deanna replied, for she had heard the wizard's call. "He will unwittingly answer my call."

"My congratulations to you, Princess Deanna Wellworth," Ashannon said with a formal bow and the purest of respect. "Sleep well."

They broke the connection then, both of them needing their rest, especially since their respective demons were no more. Deanna was truly charmed by the man's respect, but it was she who owed the greatest debt in their friendship. Ashannon had been the one to open her eyes. It was the duke of Baranduine, who had ruled the largest clan of the island when Deanna's father was king of Avon, who had figured out the truth of the coup.

Now Deanna believed him, every word. Ashannon had told her as well the truth about her crown: that it was the key to Taknapotin, a tie in an unholy triangle that included Greensparrow and allowed the king to keep her under close scrutiny. That crown was the link that had allowed Greensparrow to call in Deanna's demon so easily that night in the Iron Cross. That crown, both by enchantment and by the subtle feelings of guilt that it incessantly forced upon poor Deanna, was the key that allowed Greensparrow to keep her locked under his spell.

"No," Deanna reminded herself aloud. "It was only one of the keys."

She walked determinedly across the room and gathered up her robe. Selna's room was only three doors down the hall.

In the duke's private room in Eornfast, Ashannon McLenny watched his mirror cloud over and then gave a great sigh.

"No turning round'about now," said a voice behind him, that of Shamus Hee, his friend and confidant.

"If ever I had meant a round'about, I'd not have told Deanna Wellworth the truth of Greensparrow," the duke replied calmly.

"Still, 'tis a scary thing," Shamus remarked.

McLenny didn't disagree. He, above perhaps any man in the world, understood Greensparrow's power, the network of spies, human and diabolical. After the coup in Avon, Ashannon McLenny had thought to break Baranduine free of the eastern nation's clutches, but Greensparrow had put an end to that before it had ever begun, using Ashannon McLenny's own familiar demon against him. Only the duke's considerable charm and wits had allowed him to survive that event, and he had spent the subsequent decade proving his value and his loyalty to the Avon king.

"I'm still not knowing why Greensparrow ever kept the lass alive," Shamus mumbled. "Seems a cleaner thing to me if he had just wiped all the Wellworths from the world."

"He needed her," McLenny answered. "Greensparrow didn't know how things would sort out after the coup, and if he could not cleanly take the throne, then he would have put the lass there, though he would have been in the shadows behind her, the true ruler of Avon."

"Wise at the time, but not so much now, so it seems," remarked Shamus with a chuckle.

"Let us hope that is the case," said McLenny. "Greensparrow has slipped, my friend. He has lost a bit of his rulership edge, perhaps through sheer boredom. Events in Eriador are proof enough of that, and, perhaps, a precursor to our own freedom."

"A dangerous course," said Shamus.

"More dangerous to Deanna by far than to us," said McLenny. "And if she can succeed in her quest, if she can even wound Greensparrow and steal his attention long enough, then Baranduine will at long last know independence."

"And if not?"

"Then we are no worse off, though I will surely lament the loss of Deanna Wellworth."

"You can break the ties to her and her little plan that easily, then?"

Ashannon McLenny nodded, and there was no smile upon his face as he considered the possibility of failure.

Shamus Hee let it go at that. He trusted Ashannon's judgment implicitly; the man had survived Greensparrow's Avon coup, after all, whereas almost all of the other sitting nobles at the time had not. And Shamus understood that McLenny, whatever his personal feelings for Deanna (and they did indeed run deep), would put Baranduine first. He had seen the man's face brighten with hope when they had first learned from Deanna Wellworth that

Brind'Amour of the ancient brotherhood was alive and opposing Greensparrow.

Yes, Shamus understood, McLenny was a man for the ages, more concerned with what he left behind than with what he possessed. And what he meant to leave behind was a free Baranduine.

DRESSED FOR BATTLE

Yes, my dear deJulienne," Brind'Amour said absently, leaning back in his throne, chin resting heavily in his palm. "DeJulienne," he muttered derisively under his breath. The man's name was Jules!

The other man, dressed all in lace and finery, and spending more time looking at his manicured fingernails than at Brind'Amour, continued to spout his complaints. "They utter such garish remarks," he said, seeming horrified. "Really, if you cannot keep your swine civilized, then perhaps we should put in place a wide zone of silence about the wall."

Brind'Amour nodded and sat up straighter in his throne. The argument was an old one, measuring time from the formation of the new Eriadoran kingdom. Greensparrow had sent Praetorian Guards to Malpuissant's Wall to stand watch on the Avon side, and from the first day of their arrival, bitter verbal sparring had sprung up between the cyclopians and the Eriadorans holding the northern side of the wall.

"Uncivilized," Brind'Amour replied casually. "Yes, deJulienne, that is a good word for us Eriadorans."

The fop, Avon's ambassador to Caer MacDonald, tilted his head back and struck a superior pose.

"And if you ever speak of my people again as 'swine,'" Brind'Amour finished, "I will prove your point exactly by mailing your head back to Carlisle in a box."

The painted face drooped, but Brind'Amour, seeing his friends enter the throne room, hardly noticed. "Luthien Bedwyr and Oliver deBurrows," the king said, "have you had the pleasure of meeting our distinguished ambassador from Carlisle, Baron Guy deJulienne?"

The pair moved near to the man, Oliver bobbing to stand right before him. "DeJulienne?" the halfling echoed. "You are Gascon?"

"On my mother's side," the fop replied.

Oliver eyed him suspiciously, not buying a word of it. It had become common practice among the Avon nobles to alter their names so that they sounded more Gascon, a heritage that had become the height of fashion. To a true Gascon like Oliver, imitation did not ring as flattery. "I see," said Oliver, "then it was your father who was a raping cyclopian."

"Oliver!" Luthien cried.

"How dare you?" deJulienne roared.

"A true Gascon would duel me," Oliver remarked, hand on rapier, but Luthien grabbed him by the shoulders, easily lifted him off the ground, and carried him to the side.

"I demand that the runt be punished," deJulienne said to Brind'Amour, who was trying hard not to laugh.

"With my rapier blade I will write my so-very-long name across your puffy Avon breast!" Oliver shouted.

"He suffers from the war," Brind'Amour whispered to deJulienne.

"Phony Gascon-type!" Oliver yelled. "If you want to be truly important, why do you not stand on your knees and pretend you are a halfling?"

"I should strike him down," deJulienne said.

"Indeed," replied the king, "but do have mercy. Oliver killed a hundred cyclopians personally in a single battle and has never quite gotten over it, I fear."

DeJulienne nodded, and then, as the impact of the statement hit him fully, blanched even paler than his chalky makeup. "I will spare him then," the man said quickly.

"I trust our business is finished?" Brind'Amour asked.

The Avon ambassador bowed curtly, spun on his heel, and stalked from the room.

"Jules!" Oliver called after him. "Julie, Julie!"

"Did you really see that as necessary?" Brind'Amour asked when Oliver and Luthien came to stand before him once more.

Oliver tilted his head thoughtfully. "No," he answered at length, "but it was fun. Besides, I could tell that you wanted the fool out of here."

"A simple dismissal would have sufficed," Brind'Amour said dryly.

"Baron Guy deJulienne," Luthien snorted, shaking his head in disbelief. Luthien had tasted more than his fill of the foppish Avon aristocracy, and he had little use for such pretentious fools. The woman who had sent him on the road from Dun Varna in the first place, the consort of yet another self-proclaimed baron, was much like deJulienne, all painted and perfumed. She had used the name of Avonese, though in truth her mother had titled her "Avon." Seeing the ambassador of Avon only reaffirmed to Luthien that he had done well in giving the throne over to Brind'Amour. After the war, the Crimson Shadow could have likely claimed the throne, and many had called for him to do just that. But Luthien had deferred to Brind'Amour, for the good of Eriador—and, the sight and smell of deJulienne pointedly reminded him, for the good of Luthien!

"I should have sticked him in his puffy Avon breast," Oliver muttered.

"To what end?" Brind'Amour asked. "At least this one is harmless enough. He is too stupid to spy."

"Beware that facade," Luthien warned.

"I have fed him information since he arrived," Brind'Amour assured the young man. "Or should I say, I have fed him lies. DeJulienne has already reported to Greensparrow that nearly all of our fleet is engaged in a war with the Huegoths, and that more than twenty Eriadoran galleons have been sunk."

"Diplomacy," Luthien said with obvious disdain.

"Government, ptooey!" Oliver piped in.

"On to other matters," Brind'Amour said, clearing his throat. "You have done well, and I offer again my congratulations and the gratitude of all Eriador."

Luthien and Oliver looked to each other curiously, at first not understanding the change that had come over Brind'Amour. Then their faces brightened in recognition.

"Duke Resmore," Luthien reasoned.

"The wizard-type has admitted the truth," Oliver added.

"In full," Brind'Amour confirmed. The king clapped his hands twice then, and an old man, dressed in brown robes, moved out from behind a tapestry.

"My greetings, once more, Luthien Bedwyr and Oliver deBurrows," he said.

"And ours to you!" Luthien replied. Proctor Byllewyn of Gybi! The mere presence of the man told Luthien that the treaty with the Huegoths had been drawn.

Brind'Amour stood up from his throne. "Come," he bade the others. "I have already spoken with Ethan and Katerin and word has gone out to the Dorsal Sea. King Asmund should have arrived in Chalmbers by now, thus I will open a path that he and Ethan might join with us."

And Katerin, Luthien hoped, for how he missed his dear Katerin!

It was no small feat convincing suspicious Asmund to walk through the magical tunnel that Brind'Amour erected between Caer MacDonald's Ministry and the distant city of Chalmbers. Even after Katerin and Brother Jamesis had gone through, even after the Huegoth king had agreed, Ethan practically had to drag him into the swirling blue lights.

The walk was exhilarating, spectacular, each step causing a mile of ground to rush under their feet. Chalmbers was fully three hundred miles from Caer MacDonald, but with Brind'Amour's enchanted gate, the six men (including two strong Huegoth escorts, none other than Rennir and Torin Rogar) stepped into the Ministry in mere minutes.

"I do not approve of your magics!" Asmund said, defeating any greetings before they could even be offered.

"Time is pressing," Brind'Amour replied. "Our business is urgent."

Rennir and Torin Rogar grumbled.

"Then why did you not walk through the blue bridge to us?" Asmund asked suspiciously.

"Because Avon's ambassador is in Caer MacDonald," was all that

Brind'Amour would reply. "This is the center, whether the Huegoths choose to join with Eriador's cause or not."

Luthien looked at the old wizard with true surprise; Brind'Amour's stern demeanor hardly seemed a fitting way to greet the Huegoths, especially since they were proposing an alliance that went opposite the traditions of both peoples!

But Brind'Amour did not back down, not in the least.

"I am weary," Asmund declared. "I will rest."

Brind'Amour nodded. "Take our guests to their rooms in the northeastern wing," he said to Luthien, nodding in that direction to emphasize the area. Luthien understood; deJulienne was quartered in the southeastern wing, and Brind'Amour wanted to keep the Avonese ambassador and Asmund as far apart as possible.

"I will do it," Oliver offered, cutting in front of Luthien. He turned and winked at Luthien, then whispered, "You show Lady Katerin to her room."

Luthien didn't argue.

"You are sure that all is well with you?" Luthien asked softly.

Katerin rolled over, facing away from the man. "You need to ask?" she said with a giggle.

Luthien wasn't joking. He put a hand on Katerin's shoulder and gently, but firmly, turned her back to face him. He said not a word, but his expression stole the mirth from teasing Katerin.

"Ethan was with me the whole time," she replied in all seriousness. "He is still your brother, despite his claims, and still my friend. He would have aided me, but in truth, I needed no protection or assistance. As rough as they might be, the Huegoths are honorable enough, by my eyes."

"You would not have agreed with that when we were on Colonsey," Luthien reminded her, and she had to admit that to be true. When they had first been captured, when *The Stratton Weaver* had been sent under the waves, Katerin was quite sure that her life would become a miserable thing, enslaved in the worst possible way by the savage Isenlanders.

"I am not for understanding them," she admitted. "But their demeanor changed as soon as the treaty was proposed by Asmund. I spent much time with Ethan and the Huegoths in Chalmbers, many hours out on the longship, and I was not threatened, not even insulted, in the least. No, my love, the Huegoths are fierce enemies, but loyal friends. I hold all confidence in the alliance, should it come to pass."

Luthien rolled onto his back and lay quiet, staring at the ceiling. He trusted fully in Katerin's judgment, and was filled with excitement.

But also with trepidation—for the war, if it came, would be brutal, far worse than the battles Eriador had fought to win its tentative freedom from Avon. Even with Huegoth allies, the Eriadorans would be sorely outnumbered by the more prosperous kingdom to the south. Even with the Huegoth longships and the captured Avon galleons, the Eriadoran fleet would not dominate the seas.

Luthien chuckled softly as he considered the irony of his current fears. When Princetown had fallen, that same spring only a few short months before, Luthien had wanted to press the war all the way to Carlisle. Brind'Amour had warned against such a desperate course, reminding his young friend of Greensparrow's power.

"Find your heart, my love," Katerin said, shifting so that her face was above Luthien's, her silken red hair cascading over his bare neck and shoulders.

Luthien pulled her down to him and kissed her hard. "You are my heart," he said.

"As is Eriador," Katerin quickly added. "Free of Greensparrow and free of war."

Luthien put his chin on her shoulder. Gradually a smile widened on his face; gradually the fires came again into his cinnamon eyes.

"It is all but done," Luthien remarked as he and Brind'Amour left the table after a long and private session with Asmund and Ethan.

"Your brother shows wisdom far beyond his thirty years," Brind'Amour said. "He has led Asmund down this road of alliance."

"It was Asmund who first proposed the treaty," Luthien reminded.

"And since that time, Ethan has taken the lead in making Asmund's wish a reality," replied Brind'Amour. "He is loyal to his king."

That remark stung the young Bedwyr, who did not like to think of Ethan as a Huegoth, whatever Ethan might claim. He stopped in the corridor, letting Brind'Amour get a couple of steps ahead of him. "To both his kings," he replied when his friend turned back to regard him.

Brind'Amour thought on that a moment, considered Ethan's work in the discussions, and nodded his agreement. Ethan's actions on behalf of Eriador had been considerable in the sessions; on several occasions he had openly disagreed with Asmund, and had even managed to change the Huegoth's mind once or twice.

Brind'Amour's nod set Luthien moving again. He caught up to his king, and even swept Brind'Amour up in his wake, taking the lead the rest of the way to the war room, where Siobhan, Katerin, Oliver, and Shuglin waited anxiously.

"It will be finished and signed this night," Brind'Amour confided.

Smiles were exchanged all about the oval table, on which was set a map of Avonsea. The mirth fell away when it reached Oliver, though, the halfling standing solemnly atop a stool.

"What is your pain?" Luthien asked bluntly. "An alliance with the Huegoths gives us a chance."

"Do you know how many innocent Avon people-types the Huegoth barbarians will destroy?" the halfling asked, reminding them of the reality of their newfound friends. "How many now work the oars of their longships? How many would they have thrown into the sea when we were captured, had not the one called Rennir recognized Luthien as one owed a debt?"

True enough, they all had to admit. They were about to get into bed with the devil, it seemed.

"We cannot change the Huegoth ways," Brind'Amour said at length. "We must remember that Greensparrow is the most immediate threat to our independence."

"To Eriador whole," Oliver replied, not backing down. "But do not be so quick to tell that to the next man sent bob-bobbing in the deep waters because his life with Asmund's people has taken his strength."

Katerin slammed her fist on the table in frustration; Shuglin, who had no experience with Huegoths and considered their slaves as unfortunate people too far removed for consideration at that point, glared at Oliver.

Luthien, though, nodded at his little friend, somewhat surprised by Oliver's enlightened view of things. Oliver had never been one to hesitate from separating a wealthy merchant from his purse, but Oliver, Luthien silently reminded himself, was the one who used to buy many winter coats, then find some minuscule complaint with them that he might justify throwing them out in the street—where the homeless orphans promptly found them and gathered them up.

Siobhan, too, saw the truth in Oliver's words and she walked up beside him, and, in front of everyone, kissed him.

Oliver blushed and swayed, nearly toppling from the stool. As was his way, the halfling quickly regained his dignity.

"The Huegoths are not the best moral choice as allies," Katerin agreed, "but we can trust them to keep their part in the alliance."

"But should we accept them at all?" Siobhan asked.

"Yes," Brind'Amour replied immediately, in a tone that showed no room for debate. "I, too, despise many of the Huegoth customs, slavery highest among them. Perhaps we might do something about that at another time. But for now, the foremost problem is Greensparrow and his cyclopians, who, even Oliver must agree, are far worse than the Huegoths."

Everyone looked to Oliver, and, feeling important, he nodded for Brind'Amour to continue.

"We cannot defeat Greensparrow without Huegoth aid," the Eriadoran king went on. Even with that aid, Brind'Amour doubted the outcome, but he kept that unsettling thought private. "Once Eriador is truly free, once Greensparrow is thrown down, then our power and influence will increase many times over."

"We war for freedom, not power," Luthien had to say.

"True freedom will grant us power beyond our borders," Brind'Amour explained. "Then we might properly deal with the Huegoths."

"You cannot go to war with an ally," Oliver retorted.

"No," Brind'Amour agreed, "but as allies, our influence upon Asmund will be much greater. We'll not change the Huegoth ways, any way short of complete war, and I do not think that any of us has the heart to take battle all the way to Isenland." He paused to watch the shaking heads, confirming his proclamation.

"I, too, would choose differently than the Huegoths as allies if any choice was to be made," Brind'Amour went on. "Your own Gascony, Oliver, cannot be counted on for any overt aid, though

Lord de Gilbert has promised Eriador a lenient credit line should war come."

"A promise he probably has also extended to Avon," a snickering Oliver admitted, and the tension broke apart.

"Then we are agreed?" Brind'Amour asked when the nervous laughter subsided. "Asmund is our ally."

Luthien seconded the call, just beating Shuglin to the mark. Katerin came next, followed by Siobhan and finally, with a great and dramatic sigh, Oliver. There was one other voice to be heard in this debate, Brind'Amour knew, but he would have to deal with that problem later.

Brind'Amour moved up to the table's edge and took up a pointer. "Ethan has helped," remarked the wizard, who suddenly did not seem so old to Luthien. "He, too, understands the benefit of keeping the Huegoths as far from land as possible."

"Ethan knows the truth of Eriador now," Luthien put in.

"Thus, and Asmund has tentatively agreed, the Huegoth ships will sail in formation east of the Eriadoran Dorsal fleet, which itself will sail east of the Five Sentinels." Brind'Amour ran the pointer down the eastern shores of the island line.

"What of Bangor, Lemmingburg, and Corbin?" Katerin wanted to know, referring to three Avon coastal towns, clearly marked on the wizard's detailed map. "And what of Evenshorn, on the northern fringes of the Saltwash? If the ships are to sail *outside* the Five Sentinels, how are we to wage war with all the eastern towns of Avon?"

"We are not," Brind'Amour replied without hesitation. "Avon is Greensparrow. Avon is Carlisle. When Carlisle falls, so shall Avon!" He banged the pointer's tip on the point where the twin rivers both known as Stratton joined, in the southwestern section of the southern kingdom.

"The Five Sentinels are a long way from Carlisle," Siobhan remarked. "A roundabout route, and certainly longer and more dangerous than simply sailing along the Avon coast."

"But this course will keep the Huegoths offshore," Oliver piped in.

"And," said Brind'Amour slyly, "it will lessen the chance of an engagement with Avon's fleet."

"I thought that was the point," Shuglin said, looking confused.

Brind'Amour shook his head and waved his free hand, running

the pointer down the wide channel between the Five Sentinels and the eastern shore of Avonsea. "If we battle with Avon's fleet here," he explained, "and they are victorious, they will still have time to sail all the way around to the south, to do battle with our second fleet before it enters the River Stratton."

All the others moved closer to the table as the wizard spoke, his tone making it clear that he had thought this out completely and carefully.

"Also," the king explained, "let us keep our alliance with Asmund secret from Greensparrow. Surely the presence of Huegoth longships so close will make him nervous. And nervous leaders make mistakes!"

Brind'Amour again paused to consider the affirming nods, drawing strength from the others. It was clear that the wizard was doing a bit of gambling here, and a bit of praying.

"The attack will be four-pronged," he explained. "Half our fleet and the Huegoths will sail outside the Five Sentinels, securing the outer islands, and then swinging to the west for the mouth of the Stratton. A second fleet, already on its way to Port Charley from Diamondgate, will go south, through the Straits of Mann, and come into the Stratton from the east."

Luthien and Katerin exchanged nervous glances at that. Both understood the danger of this second move, for the fleet would be caught in narrow waters between the two strongholds of Mannington and Eornfast.

"The largest land force," Brind'Amour went on, moving the pointer appropriately, "will strike out from Malpuissant's Wall, securing Princetown, then sweeping down the open farmlands between Deverwood and the southern spurs of the Iron Cross, a straight run for Carlisle."

"Might they be held up at Princetown?" Oliver asked.

"By all reports, the city remains virtually defenseless," Brind'Amour said with confidence. "Neither the wizard-duke nor the garrison has been replaced."

"And the fourth prong?" Luthien asked impatiently, guessing that this last, and perhaps most important, move would likely be his to lead.

"Straight south from Caer MacDonald," Brind'Amour answered. "Collecting King Bellick's dwarfs and pressing straight through the mountains."

Luthien eyed that intended line. The Iron Cross was no easy traverse, even with a dwarvish army leading the way, and worse, it was widely accepted that the bulk of Greensparrow's cyclopian allies, including the highly trained and well-armed Praetorian Guards, were encamped along that same route. Even if those obstacles were overcome, it wouldn't get much easier for the Eriadoran army once the mountains were crossed, for that pocket of Avon, tucked into the nook between the Straits of Mann and the southern and western reaches of the Iron Cross, was the most populous and fortified region in all of Avonsea. Towns dotted the banks of all three rivers that ran from the mountains into Speythenfergus Lake, culminating with mighty Warchester, the second city of Avon, with walls as high as those of Carlisle itself!

Finally, a resigned Luthien looked to Katerin and shrugged, managing a smile.

The woman only shook her head; now that the true scope of their undertaking had been laid out before them, it seemed a desperate, almost impossible attempt.

Chapter 16

THE DECLARATION

The group was back in the war room later that afternoon, this time joined by Proctor Byllewyn and Brother Jamesis. The two men of Gybi talked excitedly about the prospects of war with Avon, but both of them, particularly Proctor Byllewyn, seemed to Luthien to be holding some serious reservations. The young Bedwyr didn't know how much Brind'Amour had told them of the previous meetings, but he could guess what was troubling them.

All eyes went to the door as Brind'Amour entered, his features locked. "This will be our last meeting," he said with all confidence, "until we rejoin at Carlisle's gates."

Murmurs of approval rolled about the table. Luthien kept his eyes on the men of Gybi—Proctor Byllewyn's wide smile showed that he was more than a little intrigued.

"I will entertain the ambassadors from Gascony and Avon presently," Brind'Amour explained. "The charges will be openly declared."

"War should not be declared until our armies are ready to march," Byllewyn interjected.

"But they are," Brind'Amour insisted. "Even the force from Gybi."

Byllewyn's expression turned dour. "You and I still have much to discuss," he protested quietly, calmly.

"Not so," replied Brind'Amour. "With all deference to your position, good proctor, and with all understanding that I am in desperate need of your influential cooperation, I cannot undo what has been done."

"You have signed a treaty with Asmund?" Byllewyn asked, his tone growing sharp.

There it was, Luthien realized. The men of Gybi, so recently under siege by the Huegoths, were not thrilled at the prosect of an alliance with King Asmund.

Brind'Amour shook his head fiercely, his huge white beard flopping from shoulder to shoulder. "Of course not," he replied. "My signature will not be penned until that of Proctor Byllewyn is in place on the document."

"You presume—" the proctor began.

"That you have the best intent of Eriador in mind," Brind'Amour interrupted.

Byllewyn rested back in his chair, not knowing how to respond.

Brind'Amour turned and whistled and the door opened immediately. In strode a tall, powerful-looking woman, handsome but fierce, with black hair and black eyes and the assured gait of a true warrior.

"Kayryn Kulthwain, the leader of the Riders of Eradoch," Brind'Amour explained, though she needed no introduction. She was well-known to the people in the room, particularly to the two men of Gybi.

"My greetings," Byllewyn extended, standing in salute to this warrior, a close ally of the folk of Bae Colthwyn. Byllewyn had met with Kayryn many times in Mennichen Dee for the great trading carnivals, and the two shared great respect and great friendship.

"Kayryn Kulthwain," Brind'Amour said again, "the duchess of Eradoch."

The title brought a moment of stunned silence.

"Duchess?" Katerin echoed incredulously.

"It is time for us to put our kingdom in line," Brind'Amour explained. "Wouldn't you agree, Duke Byllewyn, who is second in line to the throne of Eriador?"

Byllewyn slumped back down in his seat, overwhelmed. Brother Jamesis, beaming from ear to ear, put a comforting hand on his shoulder. All about the oval table, expressions shifted from ecstatic to confused, encompassing every emotion in between.

"A logical choice, would you not agree?" Brind'Amour asked them all. "Who in the land is more experienced in matters of state than our dear Proctor Byllewyn of Gybi?"

"False flattery to seal a necessary alliance?" Byllewyn asked slyly.

"Well-earned respect," Brind'Amour assured him, "though I admit that the alliance is necessary."

"None in this room, none in all of Eriador, would dispute the choice," Luthien piped in, and those words were indeed important from this man, the Crimson Shadow, perhaps the only man in all of Eriador whose claim as second in line for the throne of Eriador was greater than Byllewyn's. Luthien understood the importance of this as did Brind'Amour, for Gybi was viewed by most of northern Eriador as the spiritual center of the kingdom.

"I demand that the Huegoths be kept in close check," the proctor said at length. "I'll not have them slaughtering and enslaving innocents, Eriadoran or Avonese!"

"We have formulated our plans with exactly that in mind," assured Brind'Amour, who was happy to have Gybi serve as his moral conscience. "They will be kept offshore as much as is possible, and when they do come to land, they will be escorted by an Eriadoran force of at least equal strength."

Byllewyn chewed on that information for many seconds. "We will meet with Asmund when this is concluded," he finally agreed. "My folk will not sail beside the Huegoths, though!"

Brind'Amour was already nodding. "My hope is that the militia of Gybi will run with the Riders of Eradoch to lead the charge from Malpuissant's Wall," Brind'Amour explained. "With both Byllewyn and Kayryn Kulthwain to guide them, the march to Carlisle will go smoothly."

Byllewyn nodded his approval, and both Brind'Amour and Luthien sighed, realizing that the major obstacle in properly launching this war had just been overcome. Without the support of Gybi, the support from Eradoch would have been tentative indeed. Now, with Proctor Byllewyn and Kayryn Kulthwain in agreement and fully in the fold, northeastern Eriador's proud and independent folk would take part in the campaign with all their hearts.

"Ethan will be my link to the Huegoths," Brind'Amour explained, "and to the eastern Eriadoran fleet."

"I am thinking that you put much stock in a man who has proclaimed his allegiance to King Asmund," Oliver interjected.

Brind'Amour conceded the point. "He is Bedwyr," the Eriadoran king replied, as though that alone should suffice.

"I will go with the Huegoths," Brother Jamesis unexpectedly volunteered. "I understand their ways," he said in the face of the doubting expressions. "And their honor."

Brind'Amour looked to Byllewyn, who nodded his agreement.

"Very well, then," the king said. "My two eastern arms are thus secured." He paused, his gaze settling on Katerin. The woman understood what he was asking of her. In the previous war, Katerin had served well as emissary to Port Charley. She among them best understood the seafolk of western Eriador. Katerin was of that same stock.

"I will ride out for Port Charley this day," she agreed, ignoring the crestfallen expression that came over Luthien at the proclamation.

"I will get you there more quickly than any horse," Brind'Amour said with a smile.

"I will go with her," came Luthien's not-unexpected call.

Brind'Amour smiled and did well to hide his chuckle. "You will strike due south," the king replied. "At my side, with Shuglin and Bellick and the dwarfs, with Siobhan and the Fairborn, and with the militia of Caer MacDonald. Praetorian Guards await us, my young friend, and their hearts will surely sink at the knowledge that the Crimson Shadow, the man who outmaneuvered legendary Belsen'Krieg, has come against them."

Luthien couldn't deny the logic, or dismiss the call of his country. "Then Oliver will go with Katerin," he decided, and it made sense, for the halfling had been with Katerin during her first mission as ambassador to Port Charley.

Oliver started to protest, but Siobhan, sitting beside him, kicked him in the ankle. He looked to her and went silent, realizing that this one's heart was for Eriador first, for him second.

"I hate boats," was all the complaint the halfling offered, though his blue eyes, so obviously full of longing, locked on to the fair Siobhan as he spoke.

"Then it is settled," Brind'Amour said. "Now let us turn our discussion to the meeting I must soon hold with the ambassadors. We each will have a role to play."

* * *

Felese Raymaris de Gilbert was a tall and slender man with soft gray eyes and dark hair, neatly coiffed, and a clean-shaven, unblemished face. His posture was perfect, but he did not appear rigid; his dress was fashionable and rich, but he did not appear foppish. And unlike many Gascon (and Avonese) lords, he did not reek from an overabundance of perfume. His hands, though manicured, were not soft from luxury.

Felese had been chosen by the Gascon lords to represent them to the tough Eriadorans for just these reasons. The man had a lord's appearance, but a workingman's sensibilities, a rare combination that had set him in good standard in the court of Brind'Amour.

He stood now beside puffy Guy deJulienne in Brind'Amour's audience room, facing the grim-faced king of Eriador. DeJulienne's gaze was more centered on the king's companions standing behind the throne, particularly on the gaily dressed halfling who stood beside the fair half-elf named Siobhan.

Oliver eyed the foppish Avonese as well, winking and blowing kisses at the man.

It was a strange scene for the two ambassadors, and Felese was worldly enough to know that something important was brewing. Brind'Amour sat in his customary throne, but a second seat had been brought in and placed beside the first. It was empty, and Felese, suspicious and wary, hoped that Brind'Amour meant to announce that he would soon wed, or something as innocuous as that.

Judging from the king's companions, standing with perfect posture in a line behind the chairs, he didn't think so. Anchoring the line to Brind'Amour's left stood the tough dwarf with the bushy blue-black beard, Shuglin by name. Beside him stood Proctor Byllewyn of Gybi, a most important man in Eriador, and next to him, a fierce-looking black-haired woman, obviously a warrior. Then, at the king's left shoulder, stood Katerin O'Hale, a fiery woman Felese longed to know better. Looking to Brind'Amour's right, the ambassador was reminded of the impossibilities of such a tryst, though, for there stood Luthien Bedwyr, the famed Crimson Shadow, slayer of Duke Morkney and hero of the last war.

And also, Katerin's lover.

Beside Luthien came Oliver deBurrows, a fellow Gascon, that most curious of fellows. Felese liked Oliver quite a bit, mostly because of the way the halfling unnerved deJulienne, whom Felese did not like at all. Anchoring the line on Brind'Amour's right stood the half-elf Siobhan, a former slave, leader of the notorious Cutters, a band of Fairborn who had ever been a thorn in the side of those who would unlawfully rule Eriador.

Felese looked them over carefully, trying to guess the intent. It was the presence of Kayryn Kulthwain, the one he did not know, who finally tipped him off. This was no announcement of a future queen of Eriador, Felese realized, for these were Brind'Amour's generals!

"I do appreciate your coming here on such short notice," Brind'Amour said casually.

"We are entertaining a great guest?" deJulienne asked, nodding to the empty chair.

"A fellow king," Brind'Amour replied.

"Huegoth?" Felese asked hopefully, for news that the war on the eastern shores was at its end would have been most welcome to the Gascon.

Brind'Amour didn't miss that excited smile, and he also noticed that deJulienne didn't seem so pleased.

The Eriadoran king shook his head. "No," he replied. "Not Huegoth." Then, without dragging out the suspense, Brind'Amour motioned to one of the guards standing in front of a side door. The man opened the door and an orange-bearded dwarf, regally attired in a flowing purple tabard hanging loosely over gleaming silver mail, strode confidently into the room.

Both ambassadors went down to one knee as the orange-bearded dwarf walked past to take his seat beside Brind'Amour.

"I trust that you two are familiar with King Bellick dan Burso of DunDarrow?" Brind'Amour asked, and he did well to hide his smile at the hint of a frown tugging at the edges of Guy deJulienne's mouth.

"I am honored, good King Bellick," said Felese sincerely.

"My friend Brind'Amour has spoken well of you," Bellick answered, and neither ambassador missed the importance of the fact that Bellick had not referred to Eriador's leader as "King Brind'Amour."

"I, too, am honored," said deJulienne.

Bellick snorted derisively and looked to Brind'Amour.

"I have summoned you here to announce a truce," Brind'Amour explained, then looked to his dwarvish friend. "More than a truce," he corrected. "Know you that the kingdoms of Eriador and DunDarrow are now one."

Felese wore a grin, though he realized that the situation in Avonsea might soon deteriorate. DeJulienne, though, openly gawked, obviously displeased by the prospect of taking such unwelcome news to his merciless king!

"Under Eriador's flag?" Felese asked.

Brind'Amour looked to Bellick, and both shrugged. "Perhaps we will design a new flag," Brind'Amour said with a laugh, for they hadn't even thought of such minor details.

"But you, Brind'Amour, will speak for DunDarrow in Eriador's dealings with Gascony?" Felese pressed, thinking that this might work out well for his merchant kingdom.

"Well-reasoned," replied Brind'Amour.

Guy deJulienne could hardly contain himself; he knew by the fearful flutter of his heart that something bigger would be revealed here.

Brind'Amour saw his discomfort, and so he played along, enjoying the spectacle. "All goods traded between Gascony and DunDarrow will flow through Port Charley," he explained. "Port Charley to Caer MacDonald, and then distributed to the dwarvish encampments in the Iron Cross."

Guy deJulienne was trembling.

"And what of the east?" Felese pressed. "When will Chalmbers be opened to Gascon trade?"

"The fighting in the east is ended," Brind'Amour announced, and it seemed to him as if deJulienne was having trouble drawing breath. How the Eriadoran king was enjoying this! "The men of Isenland will not fight in the face of Eriador's fleet."

"A stolen fleet!" deJulienne blurted before he could help himself.

Brind'Amour shrugged and chuckled, willing to concede that irrelevant point. "However gotten, the fleet flies under Eriador's flag, and the fierce Huegoths will not battle with these ships, for they have no desire to give aid to Greensparrow, who is Eriador's enemy."

The words sent a shock ripple through the gathering, sent murmurs along the line behind the Eriadoran king and even from the guards standing at the room's three doors. All of those waves seemed to gather heavily on the shoulders of the foppish diplomat from Avon.

Baron Guy deJulienne worked very hard to control himself, to steady his breathing. Had Brind'Amour just declared war with Avon?

"Surely we have not come together on this glorious occasion to hurl insults," said Felese, trying to soothe things. The news of the Caer MacDonald–DunDarrow alliance was marvelous, the news of cessation of hostilities with the Huegoths even better, and Felese didn't want the continuing animosity between Eriador and Avon to put a damper on this bright situation. From Gascony's greedy perspective, it was better for all if the two kingdoms of Avonsea were at peace.

"Insults?" deJulienne managed to stammer. "Or threats?"

"Neither," Brind'Amour said sternly, coming out of his seat to stand tall over the foppish man. Felese tried to intervene, but the powerful wizard simply nudged him aside. "Know you that there will be no peace between Eriador and Avon as long as Greensparrow sits on Avon's throne," Brind'Amour proclaimed, as overt a gesture of war as could be made.

"How dare you?" deJulienne said breathlessly.

"My good King Brind'Amour," soothed the shocked Gascon ambassador.

Brind'Amour relaxed visibly, but did not sit down and did not let the scowl diminish from his face. "We asked for peace," he explained. "In good faith earlier this same year, we signed in Princetown with Duchess Deanna Wellworth, who spoke for King Greensparrow of Avon, a binding document for peace."

"Binding!" echoed deJulienne loudly, pointing an accusing finger and seeming to gain a fleeting moment of momentum.

Oliver blew him a kiss and the distraction gave Brind'Amour the upper hand.

"Broken!" the Eriadoran king roared, coming forward, and the stunned deJulienne skittered backward and nearly tumbled. Brind'Amour did not pursue him physically, but his verbal tirade continued the assault. "Broken by cyclopians, working for your treacherous king! Broken by the spilled blood of Eriadoran innocents in hamlets along the Iron Cross!

"Broken," shouted Brind'Amour, motioning to his stern-faced fellow sitting calmly in the second throne, "by the spilled blood of DunDarrow's dwarfs."

"Be not a fool!" deJulienne pleaded. "We have Huegoths to contend with, and so many other . . ."

Brind'Amour waved his hand and the terrified man fell silent. "We of Eriador have a more pressing enemy." Then, responding with his trump card, Brind'Amour motioned again to the two guards standing at the door over to the side of the room. Again the door was opened and a miserable Resmore was dragged in by two elven escorts.

Felese stood back in thoughtful posture, his hand stroking his fashionable goatee.

"Now you know your enemies, foolish pawn of Greensparrow," Brind'Amour said to deJulienne. "Go to your king. War is at your door!"

The man of Avon, horrified, ran from the room, but Felese remained, seeming truly intrigued. "A friend of Greensparrow's?" he asked, indicating Resmore, who was in a crouch on the floor, seeming barely conscious.

"The duke of Newcastle," Brind'Amour replied. "Sent into the mountains by Greensparrow to incite the cyclopians into war against Eriador and DunDarrow. I will furnish Duke Resmore's complete confession for you to take to your lords."

The man nodded. He had no intention of committing Gascony to the war, and Brind'Amour didn't ask for, or expect, such a pledge. All that the king of Eriador needed was for Gascony to stand with him in spirit or, at the least, to remain neutral.

"I will send my messengers at once," Felese replied, and bowed and turned to leave. He looked back at Brind'Amour and nodded, all the confirmation the king of Eriador needed. Then he left the room, his mind whirling with the possibilities. For the Gascons, this situation might well prove profitable. No matter the outcome, both sides would soon need tons of supplies.

Back in the audience room, Brind'Amour motioned to the guard at the door on the opposite side of the room, and when they unlocked it, it nearly burst apart as King Asmund and Ethan stormed in.

"You did not introduce your other ally," Ethan explained. "My king feels slighted."

"I did not reveal the most potent of my weapons," Brind'Amour replied, bidding Asmund to take the unoccupied throne at Bellick's side, Brind'Amour's own.

The proud Huegoth puffed out his chest and accepted the seat of honor, satisfied with the gesture and with the description of his warriors as Brind'Amour's "most potent" of weapons.

OPENING MOVES

I will keep Asmund and my people from bloodlust," Ethan assured Luthien quietly. The two of them stood along the side wall of a small, unfurnished chamber. A few feet away, Brind'Amour worked his magic, opening a tunnel through the stone and across the miles, a fast run to Chalmbers. King Asmund, Proctor Byllewyn, and Brother Jamesis stood beside the old wizard, the two men of Gybi waiting patiently, but the Huegoth king obviously anxious.

Ethan looked to Asmund and couldn't suppress a grin. It had taken him a long time to convince Asmund to come through the tunnel to Caer MacDonald. Now, though Asmund desperately wanted to get back to the Dorsal Sea and his fleet, it seemed as though another battle would have to be fought.

Luthien was too busy scrutinizing Ethan to take note of the sight that had brought a smile to his brother's face. The younger Bedwyr was encouraged by Ethan's continuing shift back toward their family. Ethan's unsolicited promise to keep the Huegoths in line during the war showed that the man cared deeply about Eriador. How deeply? Luthien had to ask himself, and as yet he had no answer. In that same promise, Ethan had referred to the Huegoths as "my people," a notion that Luthien was finding harder to dispute.

The two walked over to the others as Brind'Amour, clearly growing weary from his extensive use of magic over the last few days, completed the passage. This was the old wizard's second magical tunnel this day, having earlier delivered Kayryn Kulthwain back to Eradoch, where she would gather her forces.

"My folk will join with me in Chalmbers," Proctor Byllewyn explained.

"They have sailed from Gybi already," Jamesis added. "Escorted by the thirty galleons of Eriador's Dorsal fleet."

"Our fishing boats will remain in dock there," the proctor went on. "It is not so far a march from Chalmbers to Malpuissant's Wall, where my folk of Gybi will meet with the forces of Dun Caryth and Glen Albyn, as well as Kayryn Kulthwain and her fierce riders."

"Out with you then," insisted Brind'Amour. "Captain Leary leads the Eriadoran fleet and anticipates your return."

Proctor Byllewyn and Brother Jamesis bowed curtly and said their farewells, promising victory, then entered the tunnel without hesitation.

"One of your longships awaits you at Chalmbers's dock," Brind'Amour said to the nervous Huegoth king.

"Will it wait long enough for me to walk?" Asmund asked, managing a slight chuckle. Rennir followed suit, laughing exuberantly, but the king's other Huegoth escort was distracted at that moment.

"Luthien Bedwyr," Torin Rogar called, joining Luthien and Ethan at the side of the room. "We never found chance to speak of my kin who was your friend."

"We will meet again," Luthien promised.

"In celebration," said Torin determinedly. He clapped Luthien on the shoulder, then nodded to Ethan and moved back to join his king. He and Rennir stepped into the swirling blue mists together, paving the way for Asmund.

"I look forward to our meetings when this is at its end, King Brind'Amour," said Asmund. "We have much to learn from each other."

Brind'Amour took the huge man's wrist in a firm and sincere clasp. Luthien and Ethan exchanged hopeful looks at the encouraging words.

"Do not tarry," Asmund ordered Ethan, and with a deep breath to steady his nerves, the Huegoth king went into the magical tunnel.

"Eriador free," Luthien said as he and Ethan walked to the spot.

Ethan turned to him, curiously at first, but his expression gradually and surely changed to one of excitement. "Eriador free," Ethan offered, "my brother."

They hugged each other tightly, and for that short moment, Luthien felt as close to Ethan as he had through all their years together in Dun Varna. At that moment, Luthien understood that Ethan could proclaim whatever heritage he desired, but the truth of it was that he and Luthien were of the same blood, were indeed, as Ethan had just generously offered, brothers.

"Until we meet again," Ethan said.

"At the gates of Carlisle!" Luthien called as his brother disappeared from sight, lost in the fast pace of the swirling blue mists.

"A pity there weren't more of you," Brind'Amour snickered under his breath. Luthien looked at him curiously, not understanding the comment.

"Your father sired two fine sons," the old wizard explained. "A pity there weren't more of you." Brind'Amour walked past Luthien, patting him comfortingly on the shoulder, then exited the room, heading for his bed and some much-needed rest.

Luthien stood for a long while watching the wizard's tunnel diminish and then disappear altogether. He missed Ethan already! The last year or so, since he and Oliver had stumbled into Brind'Amour's secluded mountain cave, then into a revolt against Duke Morkney that quickly degenerated into open rebellion against Avon, had been such a wild ride for the young Bedwyr that he had hardly given his absent brother much thought. Ethan, to his knowledge, had been far away in the Kingdom of Duree, fighting with Greensparrow's loaned troops beside the Gascon army.

Only when Luthien had finally returned to Dun Varna and seen Gahris on his death bed, had he found time to focus attention on his past, on his lost brother and his redeemed father.

Then, suddenly, Ethan had been thrown back into Luthien's life. Luthien's emotions swirled as had Brind'Amour's tunnel, moving along at a pace no less swift, but with a destination far less clear. Ethan was returned, perhaps, but Gahris was dead. That much was certain.

Luthien's father was dead.

The young Bedwyr bit his lip hard, trying to hold the tears in check. Eriador needed him, he reminded himself. He was the Crimson Shadow, the hero of the last war and destined to lead this war. He could not stand facing a blank wall in an empty room and weep for what had gone before. He could not . . .

But he did.

"I will deliver Brind'Amour's head unto you," the woman promised.

King Greensparrow rested back comfortably in his plush throne, throwing both his legs over one arm of the great chair and studying closely the fingernails of one hand. The pose did little to diminish Deanna's suspicion that the king was greatly agitated. He had called to her through an enchanted mirror, a call she had at first decided not to answer. The urgency of his tone, though, could not be ignored, and Deanna had concluded quickly that if she did not go to her own enchanted mirror in her private quarters, Greensparrow would likely show up in Mannington, something the duchess most definitely did not want to see!

"Where is Taknapotin?" Greensparrow asked, the question Deanna had feared all along.

Deanna put on a perplexed look. "Where should the fiend be?" she replied.

"I want to know."

"In Hell, I would suppose," Deanna answered. "Where Taknapotin belongs." Greensparrow didn't believe any of her explanation, Deanna realized by his sour expression. He was indeed closely tied to the fiend he had given to her, as she had suspected. Now the king had her backed into a corner because he could not contact his demonic spy.

Deanna silently congratulated herself on the power of her dismissal of Taknapotin. Her enchantment and the breaking of the crown had apparently blasted the fiend from the world and put him beyond even Greensparrow's considerable reach.

—Unless the king was bluffing, Deanna suddenly feared. Unless Taknapotin was sitting in Greensparrow's throne room, out of view, sharing a diabolical joke with the merciless king of Avon.

Deanna understood that her fears showed clearly on her face.

She quickly composed herself and used that involuntary expression to her benefit.

"I have not been able to contact him since . . . since Selna . . ."

Greensparrow's eyes widened—too much, Deanna realized, for the name of Selna had struck him profoundly, confirming to the duchess that her handmaid was indeed yet another of Greensparrow's spies.

". . . since Selna broke my crown," Deanna lied. "I fear that Taknapotin took offense, for the demon has been beyond my call—"

"Broke your crown?" Greensparrow interrupted, speaking each word slowly and evenly.

For a moment, Deanna expected the man to fly into a fit of rage, but he composed himself and relaxed in his chair, settling comfortably.

He is angry about Selna and the crown, Deanna told herself, but he is relieved, for he believes the lie, and now thinks that I am still his willing puppet.

"The crown was indeed a link between you and your demon," Greensparrow confirmed.

And between you and my demon, Deanna silently responded.

"I enchanted it those years ago, when first you came into your power," Greensparrow said.

When you murdered my family, came Deanna's angry thoughts.

"I will find another way back to Taknapotin," the king offered. "Or to another fiend, equally malicious."

Deanna wanted to divert him from that course, but she realized that she would be walking dangerous ground. "I will not wait," she said. "I can destroy Brind'Amour without Taknapotin, for I have my brother wizards and their fiends at my call."

"You must not fail in this!" Greensparrow said suddenly, forcefully, coming forward in the throne, so close to his mirror that his appearance became distorted, his pointy nose and cheeks looming larger and more ominous. "It will all dissolve when Brind'Amour is dead. Eriador's armies will fall into disarray that we might destroy them one by one."

"Brind'Amour will die within the week," Deanna promised, and she feared that she might be correct.

A wave of Greensparrow's hand broke the contact then, to Deanna's ultimate relief.

Back in Carlisle's throne room, the king motioned for the two huge and ugly one-eyed cyclopians holding the enchanted mirror to be gone, then turned to Duke Cresis. DeJulienne, returned from Caer MacDonald, stood beside the brute, twitching nervously. He had been the bearer of ill tidings, after all, not an enviable position in Greensparrow's court!

Greensparrow's laugh put the ambassador at ease; even militant Cresis seemed to relax somewhat.

"You do not trust her?" Cresis reasoned.

"Deanna?" Greensparrow answered lightly. "Harmless Deanna?" Another burst of laughter followed, and deJulienne chimed in, but stopped and cleared his throat nervously when Greensparrow sat up abruptly, his face going stern. "Deanna Wellworth is too filled with guilt to be a threat," Greensparrow explained. "And rightly so. To turn against me, she must explore her own past, wherein she will discover the truth."

Cresis was nodding at every word, deJulienne noticed, and he realized that the brutish duke of Carlisle had obviously heard all of this before. DeJulienne had not, though, and he was perplexed as to what his king might be hinting.

"Deanna was my link to the throne," Greensparrow said bluntly, looking deJulienne right in the eye. "She unwittingly betrayed her own family, giving me personal items from each of them."

DeJulienne started to ask the obvious question, but stopped short, realizing that if what Greensparrow was hinting at was the truth of Avon's past, then his king was a usurper and murderer.

"All that I feared from Deanna was the loss of Taknapotin," Greensparrow explained, looking back to Cresis. "But if that fool handmaid broke the crown, then I understand why I have not been able to make contact, a situation that should be easily rectified."

"What of the coming war?" Cresis asked. "The Eriadorans will soon march, and sail."

"Fear Eriador?" Greensparrow scoffed. "The ragtag farmers and fisherfolk?"

"Who won the last war," deJulienne reminded, and he regretted the words as soon as he spoke them, as soon as he saw the dangerous scowl cross Greensparrow's hawkish features.

"Only because of my absence!" the king roared angrily.

Greensparrow sat trembling, his bony knuckles turning white as he clasped the edges of his throne.

"Indeed, my mighty King," deJulienne said with a submissive bow, but it was too late for the man.

Greensparrow snapped a fist into the air, then extended his long fingers. Beams of light, a rainbow of hues, shot out from each of them, joining and swirling into one white column, roughly the length and breadth of a sword blade.

The king sliced his arm down, the magical blade following.

DeJulienne's left arm fell to the floor, severed at the shoulder.

The man howled. "My King!" he gasped, clutching at the spurting blood.

With a growl, Greensparrow brought his hand in a straight-across cut down low.

Off came deJulienne's left leg and the man toppled to the floor, his lifeblood gushing out from the garish wounds. He tried to call out again, but only managed a gurgle. He did lift his remaining arm in a feeble attempt to block the next strike.

It was taken off at the elbow.

"My absence was the cause of our defeat," Greensparrow said to Cresis, ignoring the squirming, shivering man on the floor. "That, and the incompetence of those I left in charge!

"And because of Gascony," Greensparrow reasoned. "The Gascons thought a free Eriador would profit them greatly; little did they realize the importance of Carlisle's protection from Huegoths and other such troubles.

"This time," Greensparrow went on, coming right out of his seat and pointing a finger to the air, "this time, the Gascons understand the truth of pitiful Eriador and will not ask that we make peace." The king gingerly stepped over the now-dead deJulienne. He noticed Cresis then, noting particularly the worried look on the ugly face of his duke.

"This is exactly what we wanted!" Greensparrow yelled, and howled with laughter. "We prodded Eriador and foolish Brind'Amour declared war."

Cresis relaxed somewhat, remembering that this was indeed the outcome that he and Greensparrow had plotted when they had sent the cyclopian tribes into raiding actions against Eriador and DunDarrow.

"They have perhaps fifty of our ships remaining," Greensparrow went on, accounting for the twenty the Huegoths had reportedly sent to the bottom. "The mere fact that so many of our fine warships were lost to those savages only confirms that the Eriadoran fisherfolk can hardly sail the great galleons." Greensparrow flashed Cresis a wild, maniacal look. "Yet we have more than a hundred, crewed by experienced sailors and cyclopian warriors. Half the Eriadoran fleet will soon enter the Straits of Mann. I have a like number of warships waiting to scuttle them."

"It could be a costly battle," pragmatic Cresis dared to interrupt.

"Not so!" yelled Greensparrow. "When the ships of Baranduine join in, another hundred strong, then that threat is ended."

The eager king grew more excited with every word, savoring the anticipation of complete victory. "Brind'Amour will then think himself vulnerable on his western shore and he will have to turn his forces about for Montfort before he ever gets out of the mountains."

It seemed perfectly easy and logical, and so Cresis again allowed himself to relax. Greensparrow came right up to him, put a hand on his shoulder.

"That is assuming that the old wizard is even alive at that time," he whispered in the cyclopian's ear. Then he leaped away, taking care to avoid the gore that had been his ambassador to Caer MacDonald.

"Do not underestimate Deanna Wellworth, my one-eyed friend," Greensparrow explained. "With the powers of my dukes and their demons at her bidding, Deanna will catch the old wizard and show him that the time of his magics are long past."

Greensparrow stopped suddenly and went silent. He had to find a way to contact Taknapotin once more. Or to get Deanna another demon, if that was his only choice.

"Easy enough!" he shouted, though Cresis had no idea what he was talking about.

The cyclopian was comforted anyway. Cresis had been with Greensparrow all the score-and-two years of the king's reign. In fact, Cresis, once an ambassador from the cyclopian tribes to Avon's rightful king, had been an instrument of Greensparrow's rise. The brute had personally murdered four of the five sons of the king, Deanna Wellworth's brothers. His reward had been a position as Carlisle's duke, and in the years of his service, Cresis had learned to trust in Greensparrow's merciless power. Well-advised were those who feared the king of Avon.

DeJulienne was yet another testament to that truth.

The next time Luthien saw Brind'Amour, the wizard was again at work evoking a magical tunnel. This time the destination was due west, not east, to Port Charley.

This parting would be no less difficult for Luthien than the last. Oliver and Katerin stood patiently by as the gray wall transformed into a bluish fog and gradually began to swirl. To Luthien's surprise, Oliver held Threadbare's reins in hand, the ugly yellow pony standing quietly.

Oliver's gaze kept drifting to the back of the room, where stood Siobhan, the half-elf seeming cool and impassive. It took Oliver a long while to even get her attention. Then, he merely offered her a resigned look, and lifted his hand, in which he held both of his green gauntlets, to the tip of his wide brim in salute.

Siobhan nodded slightly, and Oliver's heart skipped a beat as he caught a glimpse of the true pain in Siobhan's green eyes. She was sad that he was leaving!

Bolstered by that thought, the romantic halfling stood tall—relatively speaking—and stared resolutely at the widening passageway.

Katerin caught it all, and managed a slight, confused smile. She moved away from Oliver and over to Luthien, sweeping him up in her wake and going to the furthest corner from the others.

"Oliver and Siobhan?" she whispered incredulously.

"I know nothing," Luthien answered truthfully.

"The way she looked at him," Katerin remarked.

"The way I look at you," Luthien added.

That gave Katerin pause. She had been so caught up in the tumultuous events preceding the war, she hadn't even realized the pain her lover was feeling. Studying Luthien's expression now, she finally understood. He had found Ethan, only to lose Ethan again, and now she, too, was going from his side—and all of them were walking into danger.

"You needn't go," Luthien pleaded. "Oliver could serve as Brind'Amour's eyes."

"Then all that our king will see is a ship's rail and the water below it," Katerin quipped, a not-so-subtle reminder that the halfling wasn't the most seasoned of sailors.

A long moment of silence passed between them as they stood, staring deeply at one another. They could find another emissary for Brind'Amour, they both knew that, and Katerin could remain at Luthien's side. But it was not to be. Among Brind'Amour's tight court, Katerin was best suited for this most-important mission. These few had been the leaders of the revolution, and now were taking their rightful places as the generals of the war. Their duty was to Eriador, and personal feelings would have to wait.

Both Luthien and Katerin came to this complete understanding together, silently and separately.

"Perhaps I could go with you, then," Luthien offered on a sudden impulse. "I, too, am of Isle Bedwydrin, and familiar with the ways of the sea."

"And then again I would have a Bedwyr son by my side, protecting me," Katerin remarked, a bit of sarcasm creeping into her soft tone. "Perhaps Brind'Amour could recall Ethan, for he, too, is of our island home."

A twang of jealousy came over Luthien, showing clearly on his face.

"And Ethan's surely the cuter," Katerin continued.

Luthien's eyes widened; he didn't even realize that he had been taken until Katerin burst out in laughter and kissed him hard on the cheek.

Her face grew serious once more as she moved back from the man, though. "Your place is with our king," she explained firmly. "You are the Crimson Shadow, the symbol of Eriador free. In truth, I believe that Oliver, your most-noted sidekick, should remain with you and Brind'Amour as well, but perhaps his absence will not detract from your presence, and his presence on the ships should help me keep the coastal folk from forgetting their king."

Her words ended the debate once and for all, clearly spelling out to Luthien the duty before him, and before Katerin. As she went on, though, Katerin's face grew grim, and she offered more than one glance at Siobhan, standing still by the door at the back of the room.

"You will march across the land in the company of Siobhan," Katerin said.

Luthien sighed and tried to empathize with the emotions he knew Katerin must be feeling. Siobhan was his old lover, after all, and Katerin knew that all too well. But Luthien had thought that painful situation a thing of the past, had thought that he and Katerin had resolved Siobhan's rightful place as their common friend.

He started to protest, gently, but again Katerin burst out in laughter and kissed him hard, this time staying close and moving her lips to his.

"Let us hope you are not so gullible when facing an emissary of Greensparrow's," the woman whispered.

Luthien held her all the tighter, squeezed her close until Brind'Amour announced that the tunnel was complete, that it was time for Oliver and Katerin to go.

"You mean to take the pony?" Brind'Amour asked Oliver, and from his weary tone it seemed to Luthien that he had asked that question many times already.

"My Threadbare likes boats," Oliver replied. He looked to Luthien and snapped his fingers in the air. "And you did not believe me when I said that I rode my horse all the way from Gascony!" he declared. Then he motioned and whispered to the yellow pony, and Threadbare knelt down so that little Oliver could climb up into the saddle. With one last look to Siobhan, Oliver entered the tunnel, and with one last look to Luthien, Katerin followed.

And so it began, that same day, the gathering clouds, moving into their respective positions east of the Five Sentinels, along Malpuissant's Wall, outside of Caer MacDonald's southern gate, and along the docks of Port Charley.

The proper declarations had been sent; the invasion of Avon began.

FRONT-RUNNERS

Of all the paths to be taken by Eriador's forces, the one looming before Luthien's group was by far the most uncertain. In the east and the west, the army moved by sea, along routes often traveled and well-defined. From Malpuissant's Wall, the Riders of Eradoch and Proctor Byllewyn's militia swept across open, easy terrain. But within the hour of departing Caer MacDonald's southern gate, the forerunners of Luthien's group, including Luthien, Siobhan, and the other Cutters, were picking their careful way among boulder tumbles and treacherous trails, often with a sheer cliff on one side, rising high and perfectly straight, and a drop, just as sheer, on the other.

The force, nearly six thousand strong, could not move as a whole in the narrow and difficult terrain, but rather, as a plodding mass flanked by a series of coordinated patrols. Organization was critical here; if the scouting patrols were not thorough, if they missed even one unremarkable trail in the crisscrossing mountains, disaster could come swiftly. The main group, nearly a third of the soldiers with their king among them, all of the supply carts and horses, including Luthien's shining stallion, Riverdancer, would be vulnerable indeed to ambush. Most of the soldiers were more concerned with getting their supplies and horses through the impossible trails and with building impromptu bridges and shoring up the crumbling trails than with watching for enemies. Most of them carried shovels and hammers, not swords, and if some of the cyclopian enemies, particularly the highly trained Praetorian Guards, managed to slip through the front groups unopposed, the march of the entire force might be suddenly stalled.

It was Luthien's job to make sure that didn't happen. He had dispersed the remaining four thousand into groups of varying sizes. Five hundred spearheaded the main group's march, marking the trails Brind'Amour would follow; five hundred others followed the plodding force, leaving open no back door. In the rougher terrain off the main trail, things were less structured. Patrol groups ranged from single scouts (mostly reclusive men who had lived for many years in these parts of the Iron Cross) to supporting groups of a hundred warriors, sweeping designated areas, improvising as they learned each section of these rarely traveled mountains. Luthien and Siobhan moved together, along with a dozen elven Cutters. Sometimes the pair were in sight of all their twelve companions, other times they felt so completely alone in the vast and majestic mountains.

"I will feel all the better when we have met with Bellick's folk," Luthien remarked as they traveled along one open area, picking their way across the curving sides of great slabs of stone. Looking above him, a hundred feet higher on the face of the mountain, Luthien saw two elves emerge from a small copse of trees, nimbly running along the steep stone. He marveled at their grace and wished, as he stumbled for the hundredth time, that he had a bit of the elvish blood in him!

Siobhan, following the young Bedwyr's steps, didn't disagree, but her response was halfhearted at best, and made Luthien turn about to regard her. She, too, stopped, matching his stare.

The nearly two hundred elves accompanying Caer MacDonald's army had made no secret of their trepidations concerning the route that might come before them when they linked with the dwarvish army. King Bellick had explained that his dwarfs were hard at work in trying to open tunnels to get the force more easily through the Iron Cross. While elves and dwarfs got along well, the Fairborn had little desire to stalk through deep and dark tunnels. That simply was not their nature.

Siobhan had argued that point during the final preparations—

successfully, Luthien had thought. Even if Bellick's folk could open a tunnel, it was decided that only the main group, laden as they were with carts and supplies, would go underground, while the rest continued their overland sweep to the south. So it confused Luthien now, for just a moment, that Siobhan appeared so glum.

"Oliver?" the young Bedwyr reasoned.

Siobhan didn't answer, just motioned with her delicate chin that Luthien should move along. He complied, satisfied that he had hit the mark. He knew the pain that he was feeling at his separation from Katerin, especially since he understood that his love was sailing into great danger. Might it be that Siobhan was feeling much the same about her separation from Oliver?

The notion brought a giggle to Luthien's lips. He cleared his throat, even faked a stumble to help cover the laughter, not wanting to deride the half-elf.

Siobhan understood the ruse, though, understood that Luthien's giggle was a fair indication of what she might expect from others. She took it stoically and continued on without a word.

Shadows came fast and deep with the setting sun, and though the month of August was not yet gone, the night air was much cooler, a chilling reminder to all the soldiers that they could not afford to get bogged down in the mountains, or get chased back into the Iron Cross once they broke free into the northern fields of Avon.

Luthien and Siobhan made contact with the other Cutters in their area, determining how they might set a perimeter to ensure that every passable trail in this region was well-watched. Just a few hundred yards behind their line, a group of nearly seventy warriors was setting camp.

Siobhan found a hollow for her and Luthien, surrounded by high stones on three sides and partially capped by an earthen overhang. Within it they were sheltered from the wind. Luthien even dared to set a small fire in one deep nook, knowing that any light which spilled out of the deep hollow would be meager indeed.

It was a bit awkward for the young Bedwyr—and for his companion, too, he realized—to be so alone together on this quiet summer's eve. They had been lovers, passionate lovers, and there remained an undeniable attraction between them.

Luthien sat against the wall near to the opening, pulling his crimson cape tight about him to shield him from the nipping wind. He tried to lock his gaze on the dark line of the trail below, but kept glancing back at beautiful Siobhan as she reclined near to the glowing logs. He remembered some of the times he and Siobhan had shared in Caer MacDonald, back when the city had been called Montfort, when Morkney had been duke and life had been simpler. A smile widened on Luthien's face as he thought of his initial meeting with Siobhan. He had gone to rescue her, thinking her a poor, battered slave girl, only to find out that she was one of the leaders of the most notorious thieving band in all of Montfort! The mere recollection of his image of Siobhan as a helpless creature made Luthien feel the fool; never in his life had he met a person less in need of rescuing!

She was his friend now, as dear to him as anyone could ever be.

Just his friend.

"They'll not come out this late," Siobhan remarked, drawing him from his thoughts.

Luthien agreed. "The mountain trails are too dangerous at night, unless the one-eyes carried such a blaze of torches that would alert all the soldiers of Eriador. We can consider our watch at its end."

Siobhan nodded and turned away.

Sitting against that cold stone, Luthien Bedwyr realized how fortunate he truly was. Katerin knew that he and Siobhan would travel together, and yet she had gone out to Port Charley willingly, saddened to be separated from Luthien, but with not a word to him concerning his relationship with his traveling companion. Katerin trusted him fully, and Luthien understood in his heart that her trust was not misplaced. Feelings for Siobhan remained strong within him; he could not deny her beauty, or that his love for her had, in many ways, been real. But Siobhan was a friend, a dear and trusted companion, and nothing more. For Katerin O'Hale was the only woman for Luthien Bedwyr.

He knew that, felt that, without any regrets, and Katerin knew him well enough to trust him completely.

Indeed, sitting there that night, with only the occasional crackle from the fire and the groaning of the wind through the stones, with the beauty of the stars and Siobhan to keep him company, Luthien Bedwyr fully appreciated the good fortune that had come into his life. With warm thoughts of his Katerin filling his mind, he drifted off to sleep.

Siobhan was not as comfortable. She kept a quiet watch over Luthien and when she was certain that he was asleep, she drew out a folded parchment from a pocket. Still watching Luthien, the half-elf eased it open and leaned near to the fire, that she might read it once more.

To my dearest half-elven-type Siobhan,
From this halfling so gallant and true,
The wind blows of war, thus I must be gone,
The fairest rose no more in my view.

But fear not, for not miles nor sea,
Not mountains nor rivers nor one-eyes,
Can block our thoughts, me for you, you for me,
Or blanket our hearts with disguise.

With summer-type breezes tickling my hairy chin,
Upon my palm rested to gaze at your beauty.
Would that I were not so needed now
Alas for hero-bound duty!

I go, but not for long!
Oliver

The half-elf closed the letter carefully and replaced it in her pocket. "Foolish Oliver," she whispered with a shake of her head, wondering what she was getting herself into. She took up a stick and prodded the embers, managing to stir forth a small flicker of fire from the nearly consumed logs.

What might Oliver be thinking, she wondered, and she sighed deeply, realizing that the halfling's amorous advances might make her seem quite ridiculous. Oliver carried a well-earned reputation as a charmer among the scullery maids and other less-worldly women, but those who better understood the ways of the wide world, who recognized the truth of the halfling's boasts and stolen finery, saw that side of Oliver as more than a bit of a joke. His fractured poems, like the one in the letter, could make quite an impression on a young girl, or a woman locked in drudgery, who did not read the works of the accomplished bards, but Siobhan was no tittering schoolgirl. She saw the halfling clearly.

Why, then, did she miss Oliver so damned much?

The half-elf looked across the way to Luthien and managed a chuckle at his mounting snores. The flame was gone now, the fire nothing more than a pile of orange-glowing embers, but its heat was considerable, and comfortable, and so Siobhan settled back and, with a final look to make sure the trail remained clear, let sleep overtake her.

A sleep filled with thoughts of a certain highwayhalfling.

The next day was dreary and cold, threatening rain. A heavy fog enshrouded the mountains, rising up from the river valleys to meet with the low-hanging clouds so that all the world seemed gray. Sound was muffled almost as much as sight, and it took Luthien and Siobhan some time to locate those Cutters camped nearby.

One of the elves suggested a delay, waiting until the fog had lifted, but Luthien couldn't agree to that.

"The ships are sailing," he reminded. "And the riders have gone out from Malpuissant's Wall. Even as we sit here talking they are likely closing in on Princetown."

There came no further arguments, and so the group carefully plotted their lines of probing forays, and split apart, with two elves waiting at the spot on the main trail for the lead runners of the rear supporting force.

Luthien and Siobhan moved steadily, their fellow scouts lost to them almost as soon as they had set out. They felt alone, so very alone, and yet, they knew they were not. They were deep into the Iron Cross now, many miles further than they had been on the occasion of Luthien's capture of Duke Resmore. The other scouting bands were near, they knew, and so, likely, were cyclopians.

It wasn't long before the pair's fears were confirmed. Luthien led the way up a rocky bluff, creeping to its ridge and peering over.

Below him, down a short and steep decline, in a clearing edged by rocks, lay a cyclopian camp. A handful of the brutes milled about the blackened remains of the previous night's fire, gathering together their supplies. One of them polished a huge sword, another sharpened the tip of its heavy spear, while a pair of the brutes off to the side pulled on their heavily padded silver and black uniforms—regalia that Luthien and Siobhan knew all too well.

"Praetorian Guards," the young Bedwyr whispered when Siobhan, bow in hand, was in place beside him. "A pity it wasn't this easy when we sought proof of Greensparrow's involvement. Better than facing a wizard!"

"Praetorian Guards in the neutral mountains proves nothing," Siobhan reasoned. She went silent, crouching a bit lower as one of the brutes moved toward her and Luthien, carrying a bucket of dirty water. Oblivious to the pair, the one-eye splashed the water against the rocks at the bottom of the decline and turned back to camp.

Luthien nodded, conceding the point to Siobhan, then eyed the half-elf slyly. "But now we are formally at war," he remarked, "and an enemy is before us."

Siobhan scrutinized the camp carefully. "Seven of them, at least," she replied. "And we are but two." She looked all about, and Luthien did as well, but none of their allies were apparent.

Their gazes eventually met, melting into a communal smile and shrug. "Kill them quick," was all the advice that Siobhan offered.

Luthien drew out *Blind-Striker* and studied the moves of the brutes. One was near the fire, collecting warm embers in a pouch, but the others were all about the perimeter of the stony clearing, appearing as no more than gray shadows in the fog.

"Soon to be six," the young Bedwyr promised, and over the ridge he went, slipping fast and silent down the decline.

A brute to the right yelled out, and Luthien broke into a full charge. He bore down on the cyclopian; it came up and drew out a sword to meet the charge.

An arrow whistled right over the young Bedwyr's shoulder, startling him, forcing him to lurch to the left. The stunned cyclopian threw up its arms wildly, dodged and yelled, and caught the arrow deep in its shoulder. Worse for the brute, Luthien deftly followed the momentum of his reaction. The young Bedwyr went down to one knee in a complete spin and came across, both hands clinging tightly to *Blind-Striker*. The fine sword gashed the brute in the side of the ribs and tore across its chest, opening a wide wound.

It fell away dying, but Luthien hardly noticed. He put his feet under him and rushed out to the side, a few running steps to the right, lifting his sword high to defeat the chopping axe of yet another cyclopian. Luthien quickly shifted his blade diagonally, pushing the brute's weapon out wide, then punched straight ahead, slamming *Blind-Striker*'s crafted hilt into the one-eye's face.

The fabulous crosspiece, sharp-edged sculptures of dragon wings, cut a deep gash along the side of the brute's single eye, and the cyclopian retreated a couple of staggering steps, red blood washing away its vision.

Luthien had no time to follow, for yet another one-eye came in hard, forcing him to pivot fast and half-turn to the left, swiping down desperately with his sword to pick off a thrusting spear.

Siobhan, another arrow set and ready, followed Luthien's rush to the right, thinking to lead him in with a killing shot. She caught movement out of the corner of her eye, though, and halted her swinging bow, leaving it locked steady in the wake of her companion. A cyclopian had circled out of the rocks and now bore down on Luthien from behind.

It crossed into view and the half-elf let fly, knowing she had to be perfect, knowing that she had but one shot to save her friend.

The arrow plunged deep into the brute's head, dropping it straight to the ground without so much as a grunt.

Her arms moving in perfect harmony, Siobhan put up another arrow and let fly, this time grazing the chest of the staggered brute Luthien had punched in the face. It fell back another few steps, buying Luthien precious time.

But Siobhan's aid was at an abrupt end. She wheeled back across the encampment to the left, taking a bead on a pair of cyclopians crossing the clearing for the rocky climb to her position. Off flew the arrow, slamming one in the belly and doubling it over.

Siobhan barely had time to grin, watching its companion dive desperately behind the cover of some rocks, when she realized that another brute had slipped out of the mist and was standing right over her, its axe up high.

"Eight," the half-elf lamented.

The speartip rushed ahead in three rapid thrusts, but Luthien managed to parry and dodge, shifting his hips out of harm's way each time. He had his back to Siobhan now, but guessed that she could not help him as yet another one-eye came rushing in at his back.

Luthien measured the footsteps and twirled aside at the very last moment, barely avoiding being skewered. The off-balance brute lurched past, nearly taking out its companion.

The young Bedwyr put his feet back under him quickly and charged in, hoping to score some hits amidst the confusion, but these were Praetorian Guards, well-trained veterans. While its stumbling companion regained its footing the other brute stepped in front, spear whipping across to pick off Luthien's series of attacks.

Luthien kept up the barrage, then cut hard down and to the side, defeating a spear thrust from the second one-eye. He rushed back to the left, forcing the first to retreat, then pivoted back, swinging his sword about.

The thrusting spear slipped past him, in front of him, and Luthien went right around the other way in a complete circle, going down low, trying to come in under the one-eye's defenses.

In response, the cyclopian thrust its speartip straight to the ground and ran out behind the blocking weapon.

Luthien rolled right under the defense, using his sword to keep the brute's weapon-arm extended. The other cyclopian was fast returning and so the young Bedwyr struck out hard and fast with his free hand, crunching the brute's nose.

Then Luthien had to leap back and break, squaring up once more against the pair. On they came, showing more respect this time, offering measured attack routines that Luthien could easily defeat, but keeping up their common defense, keeping the young Bedwyr at bay.

Gradually the cyclopians increased their tempo, working in unison, giving Luthien no opportunities and inevitably putting him back on his heels.

Purely on instinct, Siobhan tossed her bow into the air and caught it in both hands down low on one end. She snapped out like a snake, stepping into the swing and smacking the brute across the face, staggering it backward. Again without thinking, the lightning-fast half-elf tossed her bow once more, catching it in one hand while her other went to her quiver and pulled out an arrow.

Before the axe-wielding cyclopian could even take a step forward to get near to her, she pulled back and let fly, point-blank.

The brute fell away into the fog.

Siobhan wheeled back to see the other cyclopian out from behind the rocks and in full charge. Behind it came its companion, holding its belly still, and crawling in a futile attempt to keep up.

No time for another arrow, Siobhan realized, so she dropped the bow and rushed ahead, drawing her short and slender sword as she went. She came to the lip of the ridge and leaped high and far, over the slashing sword of her adversary. She stuck her own sword down as she flew past, scoring a hit on the one-eye's shoulder, but since she was sailing past, there was little force behind the strike and the cyclopian was not badly wounded.

Siobhan hit the ground running, skipping gingerly down the treacherous slope. So fast had she moved that the crawling one-eye never realized the danger, and Siobhan finished it with a single stroke to the back of its neck as she skittered past.

The other brute came on in a fast, but respectful, pursuit, following Siobhan as she ran out of the clearing to the left, away from Luthien's continuing battle.

Luthien realized that he had to do something dramatic, and quickly, for the third one-eye, dazed and bloody, but not down, would soon join in. He launched *Blind-Striker* into a series of cunning and vicious thrusts and slashes, all parried, but Luthien used the momentum to break contact and run ahead toward the back end of the small clearing. He scrambled up the side of a waist-high boulder, then leaped out far to the side, narrowly avoiding the lumbering thrust of one pursuing brute. Luthien came down at the one-eye's side, facing away and with open ground before him. He threw himself backward—exactly the opposite of what the turning cyclopian expected. The brute didn't question the luck, though, and swung its spear about, thinking to skewer the man.

Then it understood the ruse, for Luthien snapped in a counterclockwise spin as the spear thrust harmlessly past. Down the young Bedwyr went and across came *Blind-Striker*, scoring a wicked hit on the cyclopian's hip. The brute leaped out to the side, sprawling across the same boulder Luthien had climbed, and rolling off its side, thinking that the wicked sword would soon come in for the killing blow.

But Luthien couldn't follow the attack, for the second one-eye was back in, forcing the young Bedwyr into a defensive posture once more.

None in all of Avonsea could navigate without their sight as well as the Fairborn, who spent so many dark nights dancing among the trees. Thus, the thick mists aided Siobhan as she outdistanced the pursuing cyclopian. She took a roundabout route, smiling grimly as she came upon the body of the cyclopian she had shot point-blank, her bow on the ground just a few feet away.

The half-elf heard the grunts of the out-of-breath one-eye closing. She skittered to the bow and scooped it up and when the brute came out of the fog, it saw its doom.

The cyclopian lifted its thick arms defensively, calling out for mercy, and if the fight had been over, if Luthien had not been in desperate straits just a few yards away, Siobhan might have held her shot. Not now, though; not with the certainty that if she took her attention away from this "prisoner," the one-eye would waste no time in tackling her and choking the life out of her.

The arrow zipped between the upraised arms, bounced off the cyclopian's heavy breastplate, and ricocheted at an upward angle, driving through the brute's throat. The cyclopian stood for a moment longer, waving its arms stupidly, but gradually it sank to its knees, its dying words no more than indecipherable gurgles.

Siobhan immediately turned her attention to Luthien, engaged with two, soon to be three, cyclopians. She considered dropping her bow and drawing out her sword once more, charging to his side, but she feared she didn't have the time.

"Down!" she yelled, praying that her friend would understand.

Luthien, not sure, but without any real options, threw himself into a backward roll. He was barely halfway down when the arrow sliced the air over his head, right in front of his face, thudding solidly into the chest of one cyclopian. The brute ran backward a few steps, weirdly, flapping its arms like a dying chicken before falling into the dirt.

The other cyclopian, following Luthien's move, made the mistake of taking note of its faltering companion. That instant of hesitation gave the young Bedwyr all the room he needed. As he came around in his roll, he tucked his feet under him and reversed direction, staying low, his leading sword crossing under the defenses of the distracted brute. *Blind-Striker* dove into the one-eye's belly, running at an upward angle, through the brute's diaphragm and into its lungs.

The cyclopian tumbled backward and Luthien couldn't help but follow, coming to rest atop the dead brute.

An arrow just to the side alerted the young Bedwyr that the one remaining cyclopian had rejoined the fight. Siobhan had missed, he noted with some concern, but fortunately the arrow had come close enough to force the cyclopian into a desperate, off-balance dodge. Luthien tugged hard on *Blind-Striker*, but to no avail, for the blade was truly stuck. With a frustrated growl, Luthien scrambled out from the tangle barehanded.

Regaining its balance, the one-eye tried a halfhearted chop, but Luthien brought his arm against the side of the heavy axe and pushed it out wide. Then he waded in with a series of heavy blows, left and right, left and right, and the brute staggered away.

Stubbornly the cyclopian put up its axe defensively, fending off Luthien's pursuit, and shook its head, fast regaining its senses. A wicked grin crossed its face as soon as it realized that the man had no weapon.

Luthien didn't see the shot, didn't hear a whistle in the air or the crack of bone at the impact. As though it simply appeared from nowhere, the butt of an arrow was sticking out from the side of the cyclopian's knee. With a howl, the cyclopian dropped and Luthien waded in, again easily turning out the axe. Grunting with every heavy blow, Luthien pounded the brute into the dirt.

Siobhan was beside him then, grinning as she surveyed the battleground.

"Six dead and one captured," Luthien remarked, offering a wink and draping an arm across the shoulder of his slender companion.

Siobhan wriggled away. "Seven dead," she corrected, indicating the ridge line, "for one came out of the mist."

Luthien nodded his admiration.

"Four clean kills for me," Siobhan announced, "and you must share all three of yours, and the capture."

Luthien's smile disappeared.

"That makes six for me," the half-elf figured, "and but two for the legendary Crimson Shadow!" She skipped away then, quite pleased with herself.

A dumbfounded Luthien watched her as she searched through the camp. Gradually his smile returned. "Challenge accepted!" he called, confident that in the course of this campaign he would be given ample opportunity to catch up.

The captured cyclopian was ferried back along the lines to the main group, where Brind'Amour had no trouble in hypnotizing the brute and garnering valuable information. Other skirmishes along the line brought in more prisoners, who only confirmed what the first one-eye had revealed: a large force of cyclopians, mostly Praetorian Guards, was making its way into a wide valley some twenty miles or so to the south.

With that general description in hand, Brind'Amour then used his crystal ball to send his eyes far ahead. He located the force and was pleased. The Eriadorans would meet up with Bellick's dwarvish army halfway to the one-eyes, and then the brutes would be in for a warm welcome indeed!

Luthien and Siobhan were brought forward to speak for Brind'Amour when contact with Bellick's army was finally made. They came in sight of their allies—five thousand grim-faced dwarfs, armored in glittering mail and shining shields, and with an assortment of weapons, mostly axes and heavy hammers—on a wide and fairly open stretch of windblown stone. Bellick was there, along with their friend Shuglin.

Luthien and Siobhan could hardly catch their breath at the sight of the spectacle. Hope flooded through the young Bedwyr; with such allies as these, how could Eriador lose?

"Surely the one-eyes are in for a nasty surprise," Siobhan whispered at his side.

"Dwarvish fighters," Luthien replied, imitating Oliver's thick Gascon accent. "But, oh, how bad they smell!"

He turned to offer a wink to his half-elven companion, but lost it in the face of the forlorn look Siobhan threw his way.

Luthien cleared his throat and let it go, wondering again just how much was going on between Siobhan and Oliver.

THE VALLEY OF DEATH

Their leader is wise," Brind'Amour remarked, surveying the rough and broken terrain to the south.

The others gathered about the old wizard offered no arguments to the observation. The cyclopians had made haste long after sunset, not setting their camp until the steep walls of the valley were behind them.

Brind'Amour sat down on a stone, rubbing his thick white beard, trying to improvise a plan of attack.

"Not so many," the dwarf Shuglin offered. "We counted campfires, and unless they're fifty to one about the flames, they're not more than half our number."

"Too many, then," Luthien interjected.

"Bah!" snorted the battle-hungry dwarf. "We'll run them down!"

Brind'Amour listened to it all distantly. He had no doubt that his fine force, with two-to-one odds in their favor, would overwhelm the Praetorian Guards, but how expensive might an open battle be? Eriador could not afford to lose even a quarter of its force while still in the mountains, not with so much fortified ground to cover before they ever got near Carlisle.

"If we hit them hard straight on and on both flanks," Siobhan asked, "spreading our line thin so that they believe we are greater in number than we truly are, how might they react?"

"They will break ranks and run," Shuglin replied without hesitation. "Ever a coward was a one-eye!"

Luthien was shaking his head; so was Bellick. Brind'Amour spoke for them. "This group is well-trained and well-led," the old wizard answered. "They were wise enough, and disciplined enough, to get out of the valley before setting camp. They'll not run off so readily."

A sly sparkle came into the man's blue eyes. "But they will fall back," he reasoned.

"Into the valley," Siobhan added.

"Using the valley walls to tighten our lines," agreed Bellick, catching on to the idea.

"Into the valley," Luthien echoed, "where groups of archers will be waiting."

A long moment of silence passed, all the gathered leaders exchanging hopeful smiles. They knew that the cyclopians were well-disciplined, but if they could force a retreat into the vale, then make the one-eyes think they had walked into an ambush, the resulting chaos might just send them into full retreat—and fleeing enemies inflicted little damage.

"If they do not break ranks from our initial attack, then we will be dangerously thin," Brind'Amour had to put in, just a reminder that this might not be so easy as it sounded in theory.

"We will overrun them anyway," stern Shuglin promised, slapping a hammer across his open palm to accentuate his point. Looking at that grim expression, Brind'Amour believed the dwarf.

All that was left was to divide the forces accordingly. Luthien and Siobhan would collect most of the scouting groups, including all of the elvish Cutters, and filter south in two quiet lines, slipping past the cyclopian encampment and moving over the valley rims to take up defensible positions on the slopes. Bellick and Shuglin were charged with ordering the frontal line, nine thousand strong, more than half of them dwarfs.

Brind'Amour begged out of the detail planning, for the wizard understood that he would have to find a place to fit in. Magic would be a necessary ingredient, particularly in the initial assault, if they wanted to get the one-eyes moving. But the wizard knew that he had to be careful, for if he revealed himself too fully, any cyclopians who got out of the mountains would begin a whirlwind of talk that would stretch all the way to Carlisle.

The old wizard had just the enchantment in mind, subtle, yet devilishly effective. He just had to figure out how best to pull it off.

The two flanking lines, five hundred in each, set out that night, quiet archers moving swiftly. Luthien and Siobhan stayed together, spearheading the line that passed the cyclopian encampment on the east. They came over the rim of the valley shortly before dawn, picked their careful way down the slopes, searching out positions even as they heard the first rumbles of battle to the north.

Nearly two thousand Eriadoran soldiers flanked the charge on the right, another two thousand on the left, but it was the center of that line, the rolling thunder of five thousand grim-faced, battle-hungry dwarfs, that sent the Praetorian Guards into a frenzy. The leading groups of cyclopians were simply overwhelmed, buried under the weight of stomping boots, but as Brind'Amour had reasoned, the force was well-trained and they regrouped accordingly, ready to make a determined stand.

Then Brind'Amour went to work. The cyclopians recognized that they were outnumbered, but apparently had the notion to stand and fight. Holding two mugs filled with clear water, the wizard swept one arm out to the left, and one to the right, chanting all the while and dancing slightly, moving his feet in prescribed fashion.

The water flew out of the mugs and seemed to dissipate in midair, but in truth, it merely spread so thin as to be nearly invisible.

The curtain widened as Brind'Amour injected more of his magical energy, encompassing all of the dwarvish and Eriadoran line. In the dust and tumult, the enchanted liquid took shape as an indistinguishable mirror, effectively doubling the image of the charging force.

The cyclopian leaders were not fools. They had no specific head count, of course, but it quickly became clear to them that this raging army outnumbered them three or four to one, and they would simply be overrun. As expected, as hoped for, the call went through the cyclopian ranks to break and retreat to the narrower ground of the valley to the south.

Those cyclopians who did not turn and run fast enough found themselves quickly engaged with fierce dwarfs, usually two or three at a time.

But the bulk of the Praetorian Guard force did get out, heads bent and running swiftly. Orders continued to filter from group commander to group commander, efficiently, just the way Brind'Amour and his cohorts had expected. As the one-eyes came to the steep-walled entrance of the valley, the plan shaped out in full. Two-thirds of the cyclopian force would form a delaying line across the valley mouth, slowing their furious enemies, while the rest of the one-eyes scrambled up the slopes, east and west, finding high, defensible ground that would put the Eriadorans and their dwarvish allies at a sore disadvantage.

From their concealed perches, Luthien, Siobhan, and a thousand other archers waited patiently, letting the one-eyes charge in, letting the delaying line stretch out, and letting those others begin their ascent.

A fierce battle began almost immediately at the valley mouth, as the three groups of the Eriadoran charge converged. Still the furious dwarfs led the way, pounding the much larger cyclopians fearlessly. A dwarf fell dead for every one-eye, but the sheer weight of the line forced the Praetorian Guards slowly backward.

A one-eyed general stood on the slopes not so far below Luthien, barking out orders, calling for his soldiers to bolster a rocky outcropping that would serve as their first blocking point on this, the eastern wall.

Luthien unfolded his bow and pinned it; the general would be his first kill of the day.

"Eriador free!" he shouted, the signal, and off flew his arrow, unerringly, taking the cyclopian in the back and launching the brute into a headlong dive down the side of the valley. All around Luthien, and all along the higher ground across the way, the Eriadoran archers popped up from their concealment, letting fly a rain of deadly arrows on the surprised cyclopians.

"Eriador free!" Luthien cried again, scrambling up from behind a stone ridge, drawing out his sword and leaping down to the next lower footing. Siobhan, letting fly her second arrow, and killing her second cyclopian, started to yell out to him, to ask him where he was going, but she let it go, actually finding it within her to laugh aloud at her excited companion.

The arrow volley continued; in several spots, cyclopians and Eriadorans came into close melee. The Eriadorans held the higher ground, though, and with the archery support, most of those skirmishes ended with several cyclopians dead and the rest leaping fast to get away.

But the valley floor was no better a place for the surprised one-eyes. The delaying line held for a short while, but as it was pushed inevitably back by the dwarfs and Eriadorans pouring into the valley, all semblance of order broke down, into a melting pot of sheer chaos. Clouds of dust rose from the floor, rocks tumbled away from the valley walls thunderously, and cries of victory and of agony echoed from stone to stone.

Siobhan soon found herself out of targets, her vision limited by the thick dust, and the cyclopians falling back down the valley wall. She took up her bow and scrambled over the ridge, picking her way carefully down and calling for Luthien.

She spotted a group of cyclopians stubbornly coming up, just a few yards to the side and a dozen or so yards below her. Immediately, her bow came up and she drew out an arrow, but she hesitated for just a moment, looking ahead of the one-eyes in a desperate attempt to find Luthien. Surely they were moving along the same path he had descended; surely they had come upon him, or soon would!

The leading one-eye, a huge, three-hundred pound, muscular brute, put a hand on an outcropping and threw up a leg, then heaved itself to stand atop the high stone. The cyclopian overbalanced forward, and screamed out, and Siobhan understood its frenzy as, out of the hollow below that ridge, came the blade of a familiar sword. *Blind-Striker* went right through the brute, tearing out its back, and Luthien came up fast, retracting the sword and shoulder-blocking the cyclopian right back over the outcropping.

It fell atop the next in line, and that one, in turn, tumbled atop the third.

Up came the young Bedwyr, dropping his bloody sword to the stone and taking up his bow. One, two, three, went his arrows, each scoring a hit, each nudging on the falling tumble.

"Damn you," Siobhan muttered, and she managed to get one arrow away, nailing one of the cyclopians who had moved out of the line. Then the half-elf watched, amazed and inspired, as Luthien took up his sword once more, called out for "Eriador free!" and leaped down from the outcropping, quickly catching the bouncing jumble of one-eyes and hacking away with abandon.

Siobhan quickly surmised that her reckless young friend had that situation well under control, so she moved off, looking for more targets. Not an easy proposition, the half-elf discovered when she was only fifty feet above the valley floor, for the rout was on in full. Both lines had broken apart, but Bellick's skilled dwarvish warriors formed into tight battle groups, most resembling wedges, that sliced any attempted cyclopian formations apart. Cyclopian stragglers, separated from their ranks, were immediately overwhelmed by the supporting Eriadorans, buried under a barrage of hacking swords and axes, stuck by spears from several directions at once, or simply tackled and crushed under the weight of the rolling army.

At the valley mouth, Brind'Amour watched it all with satisfaction. He had done well—they all had—for now those cyclopians who managed to escape the ambush would flee all the way back to Avon with word of an invading army twice its actual size.

Several times as large, the wizard mused, for he knew that panicking, retreating soldiers had a way of making the enemy even greater than it truly was, even greater than a simple wizard's trick had made it appear!

The wizard spotted one skirmish, on the lower slopes of the western valley wall, where a handful of cyclopians had taken cover within a protective ring of huge stones. A group of elves were trying to get at them, but the ground favored the one-eyes.

Brind'Amour began to chant once more, lifted his arms out to the side and, as his words brought forth the magical energy, swept his arms together, clapping his hands.

The stones of the cyclopians' defensive ring rolled together suddenly, squeezing the brutes, crushing a couple, and leaving the rest out in the open.

The elves were on them immediately, slender swords darting through the desperate defenses of the scrambling brutes, laying them low in a matter of seconds. One of the elves stood tall on the closed stones, shaking his head. He looked to the east, saw Brind'Amour standing quietly, and saluted the old wizard.

Then he and his fellows ran off, for there remained more cyclopians yet to kill.

Brind'Amour sighed and walked into the valley, reciting an old religious verse that he knew from his younger days those centuries before, when he had used his magics to help construct the fabulous Ministry cathedral.

"The Valley of Death," the verse was called, and barely a few feet in, the wizard began to step across the corpses of cyclopians, dwarfs, and humans.

A fitting title.

Luthien ran along a narrow ledge higher up the valley wall, looking for some alternate route, or some wider spot, for a group of fleeing cyclopians were close behind. The one-eyes didn't know that he was there, but they would figure it out soon enough. Luthien glanced left, up the steep wall, a climb he could not even attempt. Then he looked right, down toward the valley floor, hoping to see Siobhan or some other friendly archer taking a bead on those trotting behind him. All that he saw was a thick dust cloud; he would find no allies that way.

The path wound on, narrow and dangerous.

Luthien didn't know how many cyclopians were back there, but there were several, at least, and he had no desire to fight against unfavorable odds up here, with so little ground for maneuvering. He resigned himself to do just that, though, and he considered his resources and how he might strike hard and fast to better even the odds. A bow shot might kill the first in line—if he was lucky enough, that falling one might take the second with it, or at least slow the others so that Luthien could let fly a couple of more arrows. But what if he missed, or if his first shot didn't drop the leading cyclopian, but only slowed the brute?

Luthien went around another bend, resolved to use his sword alone, and not his bow. He would turn and make his stand, he decided. As he came around, he saw that the ledge widened in this one area, a depression in the cliff wall several feet deep.

With a sigh of relief, Luthien skipped to the back wall, pulled the hood of his magical cape over his head and stood very still. Only seconds later, he could hear the closing cyclopians, lumbering on and talking of climbing to the valley rim and escaping.

The one-eyes came around the bend; peeking out from under the hood, Luthien counted as they passed. The seventh, and last, came into view as the first moved on past the wider area.

The notion flitted through Luthien's mind that he had been wise to run ahead, and not to stop and fight this desperate crew. That wise thought was abruptly washed away, though, as the daring young Bedwyr realized that the back end of this cyclopian line might make for easy targets. Hardly conscious of the move, Luthien rushed out from the wall, shouldering the trailing cyclopian right over the ledge. Luthien stopped, facing the drop, then pivoted a complete turn, coming around hard with *Blind-Striker* to smash the next cyclopian across the hip as the startled brute spun about to register the attack.

Luthien dug in hard, clenched tightly on his blade with both hands, and forced that second brute over the ledge as well. The third, already on the narrower path, howled and turned about, sword at the ready. Luthien rushed right up to it, keeping it out of the wider area so that its friends could not flank him. Two of those one-eyes, thinking they had been caught from behind by the nasty Eriadorans, only increased their pace, running off as fast as they could manage along the narrow ledge. The other two stopped and turned, calling to their battling companion.

Luthien worked his blade furiously, not letting the cyclopian off its heels for a moment. "I have them!" the man yelled, looking over his shoulder as though expecting reinforcements.

His cavalier attitude and his dress told the brute fighting him much. "The Crimson Shadow!" the foolish cyclopian yelled out. That was all its companions needed to hear. With typical cyclopian loyalty, they bid their engaged friend farewell and ran off.

Terror drove the cyclopian fighting Luthien to daring, reckless attack routines. It dropped one foot back, retreating half a step, then came forward in a rush, lowering its shoulder, hoping that the bold tactic would catch its opponent off his guard.

It didn't. Luthien merely dropped back a step and slipped to the side, around the wall into the wider area. *Blind-Striker* slid easily through the cyclopian's ribs as it stumbled past.

Luthien was fast to withdraw the blade, jumping back to defensive posture. The cyclopian stood perfectly still, groaning, trying to turn about to face the swordsman squarely. It finally managed to do so, just in time to see the bottoms of Luthien's feet as the young man leaped out and double-kicked, blasting the wounded brute from the ledge.

Luthien was up in an instant. "The Crimson Shadow, true

enough," he called to the tumbling cyclopian. He took a breath and ran off along the narrow path in pursuit of the four who had fled. Confident that they would not stop to wait for the pursuit, Luthien slid *Blind-Striker* back into its scabbard and pulled his folding bow from his back, extending and pinning it as he ran.

The frightened cyclopians were reckless on the treacherous path and Luthien gained little ground. He did get one shot, though, and made the most of it, nailing the trailing one-eye in the back of the calf as it rounded one bend. It stumbled out of sight, but Luthien knew it could not escape. Out came his sword and on he charged, slowing to a determined stalk as he neared that bend.

He found the brute leaning heavily against the wall, crouching low, holding a sword in one hand and its bleeding calf with the other. Its companion, a dozen feet further along the ledge, waited anxiously.

Luthien casually strode forward and whacked at the injured one-eye. It picked off the straightforward attack, but nearly toppled for the weight of the blow. Its companion howled and started forward, but Luthien put an end to that, sent the one-eye running off, merely by shifting *Blind-Striker* to his left hand, then reaching back with his right to pull the bow off his shoulder.

"Your friend has fled," he said to the injured cyclopian. "I'll accept your surrender."

The brute lowered its sword and started to straighten, then came ahead suddenly in a rush, thrusting boldly.

In a single movement, Luthien brought the tip of his bow straight across, right to left, then turned the bow tip up and swept it back across, taking the thrusting sword out wide. Out came *Blind-Striker* to stick the off-balance brute through the heart. It fell heavily against the wall and slowly sank to the ground, its lifeless eye staring coldly at Luthien.

The young Bedwyr looked ahead and could tell that the narrow ledge didn't go on much further, spilling out into wider terrain. There was no way that he could get to the fleeing cyclopians before they reached that area. With a sigh, Luthien looked back to the valley floor, then scanned the route that would get him back there. A noise quickly turned him back to the ledge, though, where, to his surprise, two of the fleeing brutes were running back toward him with all speed!

And they were both looking more over their shoulder than ahead.

Luthien skittered back from the last kill and held tight to the wall, again using the magical camouflage of his magnificent cape. Peeking out from under the cowl, he saw the trailing cyclopian stumble, then, an instant later, go down on its face.

The remaining brute put its head down and howled in terror, running full out, skipping past the companion it had deserted, lying dead against the wall.

Out jumped Luthien; the one-eye broke stride for just an instant, then rambled ahead.

Both hands clenching tight to *Blind-Striker*, Luthien thrust out and dropped his back leg out from under him, falling low as the pierced cyclopian came right over him, turning a somersault and sliding back from the bloodied blade as it passed. It slammed down on its back onto the ledge, too dazed to rise in time, for Luthien came up and about, his blade diving into cyclopian flesh to finish the task.

It was no surprise to Luthien when his unseen ally came running along the ledge, bow in hand.

"I scored eight kills this day," Siobhan announced proudly.

"Then you have fallen behind," an exhausted Luthien informed her, holding aloft his dripping sword. "Fourteen, and that makes it sixteen to fourteen in my favor."

The half-elf eyed the young man sternly. "'Tis a long way to Carlisle," she said grimly.

The friends shared a smile.

"They are in full retreat," Shuglin informed the two kings, Bellick and Brind'Amour, when he found them among a group of Eriadorans and dwarfs near the middle of the long valley.

"In no formation," another dwarf added. "Running like the cowards they are!"

"A true rout, then," reasoned Bellick, and there was no disagreement. Losses to the joined human and dwarvish armies were amazingly light, but all reports indicated that the cyclopian dead would number near two thousand.

The dwarf king turned to Brind'Amour. "We must pursue with all speed," Bellick said. "Catch them while they are disorganized, and before they can find defensible ground."

The old wizard thought it over for a long while. There were many considerations here, not the least of which being the fact that the vast bulk of their supplies were still a couple of miles north of the valley. Bellick's reasoning made sense, though, for if they allowed the terror of the rout to dissipate, the Praetorian Guards would fast regroup, and would not likely be caught so unawares again.

"I follow your word in this," Bellick assured Brind'Amour, the dwarf recognizing the wizard's turmoil. "Yet I beg of you to allow my dwarfs to complete what they have begun!"

Every dwarf in the area cheered out at those words, and Brind'Amour realized that holding the eager warriors of DunDarrow back now would cause simmering feelings that his army could ill-afford at that time. "Go with your forces," he said to Bellick. "But not so far. Keep the one-eyes running. My soldiers will collect our wounded and our supplies, and set our camp there." Brind'Amour pointed to the southern end of the valley. "Return to us this night, that we might resume our joined march in the morning."

Bellick nodded, smiling widely beneath the bright hair of his orange beard. He reached up to clap Brind'Amour on the shoulder as he walked past, as he walked into a gathering mob of his eager subjects.

"All the way to Carlisle," began the chant, starting low and growing to a roar.

Chapter 20

VISIONS

Luthien commanded the main group of Eriadoran soldiers that day, setting the camp, tending the wounded, burying the dead. Though he doubted that the cyclopians would regroup and come back at them, he preferred to err on the side of caution. Scouts were sent up over the rim of the valley; archers were put in place on the valley walls, overlooking the encampment.

Brind'Amour spent the remainder of the day in his tent, alone, though soldiers venturing near to the tent often heard the wizard speaking in whispered tones. He emerged after sunset, to find Luthien and Siobhan organizing the nighttime perimeter. Many of Bellick's dwarfs, including Shuglin, had returned, all with tales of further punishment inflicted on their fleeing enemy.

"It all goes well," Brind'Amour remarked to Luthien and Siobhan when the three found a rare quiet moment.

Luthien eyed the wizard curiously, suspecting that Brind'Amour had spent the day in magical contact with the other arms of the invasion, a fact the wizard confirmed a moment later.

"Proctor Byllewyn and his force have swept down from the wall and encircled Princetown," the wizard said, "and the beleaguered folk, still without a garrison from the last war, and still without a wizard-duke to lead them, are close to surrender. This very night, the proxy mayor of Princetown meets with Proctor Byllewyn and Kayryn Kulthwain to discuss the terms."

Luthien and Siobhan exchanged satisfied nods; that was just what they had been hoping for. Princetown could have become a major obstacle to the eastern ground forces. If they had been held up for even a few days, they would have had no chance of getting to Carlisle on time.

"The eastern fleet has made the shores of Dulsen-Berra," Brind'Amour went on, "third of the Five Sentinels."

"Losses?" Siobhan asked.

"None to speak of," the wizard replied. "It seems that more of the independent islanders have joined our cause than have taken up arms against us."

"To the dismay of the Huegoths, no doubt," Siobhan quipped.

Luthien glared at her, not willing to hear such pessimism, but the half-elf remained steadfast. "Slaves must be replaced," she said matter-of-factly.

She was echoing Oliver, the young Bedwyr realized. Oliver deBurrows, my moral conscience, Luthien mused, and he shuddered at the thought.

"Not so," Brind'Amour answered to Siobhan's concerns. "The Huegoths remain far offshore, shadowing our vessels, and hopefully beyond the notice of Greensparrow. They have not joined in any of the limited action thus far, and have registered no complaints with Captain Leary."

The news was welcome, if surprising. Even Luthien, holding faith in the truce, had not expected the Huegoths to behave so well for this long.

"Your brother knows the truth, of course," Brind'Amour went on. "He understands our desires to keep the brutal Isenlanders away from innocents. But Ethan has assured King Asmund that the distant course determined for the longships is only to keep Greensparrow oblivious to Eriador's newest allies."

"Asmund believes him?" Luthien asked, somewhat skeptical.

"The Huegoths are behaving," Brind'Amour replied, and nothing more needed to be said.

"What of the western fleet?" Siobhan asked, and her concerns were clear in her voice, though she tried to hide them. That brought a sly smile from Luthien as he tried to imagine the half-elf and Oliver side by side. That vision was lost before it ever took form, though, for the mere mention of their fleet in the west sent Luthien's thoughts to Katerin. Luthien promptly reminded himself of his duty and squared his shoulders, but he could not dismiss his fears for his love. Never would Luthien demand that Katerin stay out of battle, not when the cause was this important, but he wished that she was by his side at least, that he might know every minute that she was all right. It struck Luthien then that perhaps Brind'Amour had arranged for Katerin to go far from him purposefully. And perhaps it was a good thing, the young Bedwyr had to admit. How well would he fight, how willing would he be to commit his forces to a daring battle, if he knew that Katerin was among those soldiers? She was as capable a warrior as anyone Luthien had ever known, and needed no looking after, yet with his heart so stung how could Luthien not hover over her?

"All the forces have come down from the northeastern reaches and from the three islands," Brind'Amour informed them. "They have gathered in full and will sail out from Port Charley in the morning, when the tide is high."

Better for both of them to be apart at this time, Luthien admitted, but that did little to calm his fears.

"All is in place, a most splendid start to the campaign!" Brind'Amour said cheerfully, his white teeth beaming from his hairy face.

With that proclamation, the meeting ended. As he and Siobhan walked away, Luthien noticed the expression on the half-elf's face and understood that she was harboring the same anxiety for her distant friend as he. No doubt, though, Siobhan was more tentative in her thoughts about Oliver. Luthien didn't mention their common worries; what would be the point?

"All the way to Carlisle," he said suddenly, imitating the dwarfish chant.

Siobhan looked at him, surprised, and then grateful for the reminder of the business at hand. "I will go out to the east," she announced, "and see that the watch line is secured."

"And I, to the west," Luthien said, and with a shared nod they split up.

Both were grateful for the privacy.

Brind'Amour's smile disappeared as soon as he entered his tent. Things had indeed begun full of hope and excitement, with early victories easily won. Their rout of the Praetorian Guards in the mountains exceeded even their highest expectations, as did the behavior of their Huegoth allies. But the wizard was experienced enough to temper his jubilation. Neither of the Eriadoran fleets had yet encountered Avon warships, and though Princetown was on the verge of surrender (if it hadn't already surrendered), the northern Avon city was never expected to be a factor. Eriador had already conquered Princetown, after all, before the last truce, and there was no garrison in place there, nor any of Greensparrow's wizard cohorts.

Early victories, easily won, but that had been an assumption before the invasion had ever started. It would be a foolish thing indeed for the Eriadorans and their allies to grow overly confident now that those expected victories had been realized.

Because, the wizard knew, the road ahead grew ever darker.

Brind'Amour's own central forces would soon be pressing down the Dunkery River, into the heartland of Avon, on their march to Warchester.

"Warchester," Brind'Amour said aloud. Aptly named, he knew, for he had been to the city often in times long past. The place was more a fortress than a city, with walls as high as those of Carlisle itself.

That run down the banks of the Dunkery would make this one battle with the Praetorian Guards seem as no more than a minor skirmish, for when they met organized resistance, Brind'Amour's army would likely be sorely outnumbered. Even if they struggled through, even if Warchester was taken, the weary Eriadorans would have another two hundred miles of hostile ground to cross before they ever reached the high walls of fortified Carlisle.

And the prospects for the western Eriadoran fleet seemed equally grim. Would the forty galleons and their fishing boat escorts survive their trek through the narrow Straits of Mann, right between the powers of Mannington and Eornfast? Baranduine had figured little into the preparations for war, but in truth, the wild green island to the west possessed a flotilla stronger than Eriador's, if all of Eriador's warships had been gathered together.

Even worse, by Brind'Amour's calculations, loomed the magical disadvantage. He was alone, and his type of magic, the powers gained through use of the natural elements—the fiery sun and the wind, the strength of a storm or a tree—had passed its zenith centuries before. Brind'Amour had battled Duke Paragor and Paragor's familiar demon, and had barely survived the encounter. How would he fare against Greensparrow's other allies, fresh with their hellish powers? And how would he fare against Greensparrow, who was as old as he, who had remained awake through the centuries, garnering his powers?

Indeed it seemed a desperate war to Brind'Amour, but he realized that, in truth, he had been given little choice. As he had openly proclaimed in Caer MacDonald, as long as Greensparrow sat in place on Avon's throne, there could be no peace. With Dukes Morkney and Paragor dead, Resmore broken in a dungeon in Caer MacDonald, and with Princetown still reeling and helpless from the last war, now was the time, perhaps the last true chance for Eriador to shake the lurking specter of King Greensparrow.

Brind'Amour sat on his cot and rubbed his tired eyes. He thought he was seeing things a moment later, when a great bird turned its wings perpendicular to the ground and slipped silently through the folds of his tent flap.

An owl?

The bird fluttered to a perch on the lantern holder, set halfway up the center tent pole. It eyed Brind'Amour directly, knowingly, and he understood that this was no chance meeting.

"Well, what are you about?" the wizard asked, wondering if his nemesis Greensparrow had personally come a'calling.

The owl turned its head slightly and Brind'Amour's next comment was lost by the image he saw in the owl's huge eyes. Not a reflection, but an image of a tower of stone, high and narrow and flat, set within the rugged mountains. A singular pillar of windblown rock.

Brind'Amour.

The call was distant, far removed, a whisper on the night breeze.

"What are you about?" the old wizard asked the bird again, this time breathlessly.

The owl swooped off the perch and out the flap, silent in flight.

Brind'Amour rubbed his eyes again and looked about his tent, wondering if it had been no more than a dream. He looked to his crystal ball, thinking that perhaps he might find some answers, but he shook his head. He had spent hours contacting his generals, east and west, and was too exhausted to consider sending his thoughts into the ball once again.

He lay back on his cot and soon fell into a deep slumber.

When he awoke the next morning, he was convinced that the incident with the bird had been no more than the dreaming delusions of a weary old man.

THE SEEDS OF REVOLT

How good it felt to Luthien: the wind in his face, the rush of ground beneath Riverdancer's pounding hooves! They were coming out of the mountains, back onto terrain where Luthien could ride his precious Morgan Highlander.

Riverdancer, after so many miles of plodding along painful, rocky ground, seemed to enjoy the jaunt even more than his rider. Luthien constantly had to hold the powerful white stallion back, else he would have easily outdistanced the other riders coming down from the foothills beside him, mostly Siobhan and the other Cutters.

As usual, they were the lead group, the spearhead for the Eriadoran army, and the single cavalry unit. Because of the difficult mountain terrain, only two hundred horses had been brought along, and more than a third of them could not now be ridden because of problems they had developed during the difficult trek, mostly with their hooves.

Riverdancer was fine, though, ready and eager to run on. Luthien tightened up on the reins, easing the horse into a steady, solid trot as they came to one last sloping expanse. Siobhan, astride a tall and slender chestnut, caught up to him then, and wasted no time in pointing out the smoke from a village not far distant to the south. Beside it wound a great silvery snake, the Dunkery River.

"It is called Pipery, according to Brind'Amour's map," Luthien informed her. "The northernmost of a series of mill towns set along the Dunkery."

"Our next target," Siobhan said grimly. She looked to both sides, to the hundred or so riders sweeping down beside her, then turned to Luthien. "Are we to split into smaller forces, or remain as one group?"

Luthien considered the options for just a moment. He had thought to break the unit into several scouting groups, but with Pipery in sight, the line for the army seemed obvious. "Together," he said at length. "We'll go south, then cut back northeast, to meet the Dunkery where it comes out of the foothills. Then south again along the river, scouting the path all the way to the town."

Siobhan peered into the rolling southland, confirming the course, and nodded her agreement. "The cyclopians will not wait for us to get to the town," she reasoned.

The thought did not seem to bother Luthien in the least.

The group moved south for a couple of miles, coming directly to the west of Pipery. In the shade of a pine grove, they gave their mounts a much-needed break, with Luthien dispatching several riders to scout out the area, particularly the trail back to the northeast, which they would soon be riding.

Those scouts moving directly east, toward the village, returned after only a few minutes, reporting that a group of two to three hundred cyclopians, including two-score cavalry riding fierce ponypigs, were fast approaching.

"We could outrun them back to the mountains," the scout reminded.

"We could outrun them all the way to Pipery," an eager Siobhan suggested.

Luthien's thoughts were moving somewhere in the middle of the two propositions. His group was outnumbered, but held a tremendous advantage of maneuverability. Ponypigs, resembling warthogs the size of large ponies, were brutal opponents, with strong kicking legs and nasty tusks, and cyclopians could ride them well, but they were not as swift as horses.

"We cannot afford to lose any riders," Luthien said to Siobhan, "but if this is part of Pipery's militia, then better to sting them out in the open than to let them get back behind the village's fortifications."

"No doubt they think us an advance scouting unit," Siobhan replied, "with little heart for battle."

"Let us teach them differently," Luthien said determinedly.

The young Bedwyr sent nearly half of his force to the north then, on a long roundabout, while he and Siobhan led the remaining riders straight on toward the approaching cyclopians. He spread them out in a line across a ridge when the enemy force was in sight, letting the one-eyes take a full measure, while he took the measure of them.

The scouts' information was right on the mark. The cavalry groups seemed roughly equal in strength, by Luthien's design. What the cyclopians didn't know was that they were facing a force of mostly Fairborn, with a well-earned reputation for riding and for archery.

Luthien scanned the green fields to the north, but his other forces were not yet in sight. He had to hope that they had not encountered resistance, else his entire plan might fall apart.

"With the cavalry in front," Siobhan remarked, referring to the fast-forming cyclopian ranks, riders on ponypigs forming a line in front of the foot soldiers. The half-elf smiled as she spoke, for this was exactly what Luthien had predicted.

Time to go, the young Bedwyr realized, and he drew out *Blind-Striker*, raising the sword high into the sky. Out came more than fifty blades in response, all lifted high.

A few quiet seconds slipped by, the very air tingling with anticipation.

Luthien jabbed *Blind-Striker* toward the sky before him and the charge from the ridge was on.

The cyclopians howled in response and the thunder of surging horses was more than matched by the thunder of charging ponypigs.

The elvish swords and *Blind-Striker* unexpectedly came down, the skilled Eriadoran riders deftly slipping them back into their sheaths. The close-melee weapons had been but a ruse, a teasing challenge to the savage cyclopians, for the Eriadorans never intended to battle in close combat. On Luthien's command, up came the bows.

A cyclopian's eye was a large and bulbous thing, and wider still seemed the eyes of the charging Praetorian Guards when they realized the ruse and understood that they would be under heavy assault before they ever got near their enemy.

Luthien Bedwyr felt like a rank amateur over the next few moments. He got his bow up and fired off a shot, barely missing, but though he was a fine horseman and a fine archer, by the time he got his second arrow in place, most of the Fairborn riding beside him had already let fly three, or even four.

And the majority of those had hit their mark.

Chaos hit the cyclopian ranks as ponypigs stumbled and fell, or reared in agony. Stinging arrows zipped through, felling rider and mount, dismantling the order of the cyclopian charge. Some one-eyes continued on; others turned about and fled.

And then a new rumble came over the field as the remaining Eriadoran riders swept down from the north, firing bows at the cyclopian foot soldiers as they charged.

Luthien drew out *Blind-Striker* again as he neared the leading cyclopian riders. He angled Riverdancer for a close pass on one, but an arrow beat him to the mark, taking down the one-eye cleanly. Luthien easily veered past the now-walking ponypig, crossing behind yet another cyclopian. The one-eye turned in its seat, trying to get its blocking sword out behind, but Luthien smacked the blade aside and stuck the brute in the kidney as he passed.

With a groan, the cyclopian slumped forward, leaning heavily on the ponypig's muscled neck.

Luthien spotted another target and charged on, his crimson cape flying out wildly behind him. The cyclopian, like most of its companions, had other ideas, though, and turned about and fled.

Luthien coaxed Riverdancer into a full gallop and ran the brute down, hacking his sword across the back of the one-eye's thick neck. He moved away quickly, not wanting to get tangled up in the ponypig as its rider slipped to the ground.

Many of the cyclopian foot soldiers turned to flee as well, but others formed up into a square, heavy shields blocking every side, long pikes ready to prod at any horsemen who ventured too near. That square marched double-time, right back the way they had come, toward Pipery.

The Eriadorans continued to nip at the one-eyes, particularly interested in running down any cyclopian rider who strayed too far from the main group, but when those Fairborn scouts watching the roads further to the east announced that a second force was coming from Pipery to reinforce the first, Luthien knew that the time had come to break off and await the approach of the larger Eriadoran army.

He eyed the field, satisfied, as he and his riders crossed back to the west. A couple of horses had been downed, with three riders injured, but only one seriously. The cyclopians had not gotten off so easily. More than a dozen ponypigs lay dead, or quickly dying, on the grass, and another twenty wandered riderless. Less than a quarter of the two-score cyclopian cavalry had escaped unscathed, with nearly half lying dead on the field, along with a handful of the foot soldiers.

More important than the actual numbers, Luthien's group had met the enemy again, on the enemy's home ground this time, and had sent them running in full flight. Luthien would continue with the scouting mission now, but he held few doubts that the larger Eriadoran army would roll through this part of their course. The road to Pipery, at least, would be an easy march.

Brother Solomon Keyes knelt in prayer, hands clasped, head bowed, in the small chapel of Pipery. A far cry from the tremendous cathedrals of the larger cities of Avonsea, the place had but two rooms: a common meeting room, and Solomon Keyes's private living area. It was a square, stone, unremarkable place; the pews were no more than single-board benches, the altar merely a table donated after the death of one of Pipery's more well-to-do widows. Still, to many in the humble village, that chapel was as much a source of pride as the great cathedrals were to the inhabitants of Princetown or Carlisle. Despite the fact that Greensparrow's cyclopian tax collectors, including one particularly nasty old one-eye named Allaberksis, utilized the chapel as a meeting house, Solomon Keyes had worked hard to preserve the sanctity of the place.

He hoped, he prayed, that his efforts would be rewarded now, that the invading army rumored to be fast approaching would spare the goodly folks of his small community. Keyes was only in his mid-twenties. He had lived practically all of his life under the court of King Greensparrow, and thus he, and most of the people of Pipery, had never before met an Eriadoran. They had heard the stories of the savage northlanders, though, of how Eriadorans had been known to eat the children of conquered villages right before parents' eyes. Keyes had also heard of the wicked dwarfs—the "head-bashers," they were called in Avon—for their reputed propensity for using their boots to cave in the heads of enemy dead and wounded. And he had heard of the elves, the Fairborn, the "devil's-spawn," disguising their horns as ears, running naked under the stars in unholy tribute to the evil gods.

And Keyes had heard whispered tales of the Crimson Shadow, and that one, most of all, had the people of his village trembling with terror. The Crimson Shadow, the murderer who came silently in the night, like Death itself.

Solomon Keyes was wise enough to understand that many of the rumors he had heard of his king's hated foes were likely untrue or, at least, exaggerations. Still, it was widely reported that somewhere around ten thousand of these enemies were nearing Pipery, whose militia, including the few Praetorian Guards who had come down from the mountains, numbered no more than three hundred. Whatever monster this force of combined enemies might truly be, Pipery was in dire trouble.

Keyes was rocked from his contemplations as the chapel door burst open and a handful of one-eyes stormed in. Praetorian Guards, the priest realized immediately, and not Pipery's regular militia.

"All is in place for the hospital," the priest said quietly, looking down to the floor.

"We have come for tithes," replied Allaberksis, coming in on the heels of the burly guards. The group never slowed, crossing the room and kicking aside benches.

Solomon Keyes looked up incredulously, staring at the withered old cyclopian, the oldest and most wrinkled one-eye anyone in these parts had ever known. Its eye was bloodshot and grayish in hue, its general luster long gone. There was a particular sparkle in the eye of Allaberksis now, though, one that Solomon Keyes recognized as pure greed.

"I have bandages," Keyes pleaded after a stunned pause. "Of what use is money?"

One of the Praetorian Guards stepped right up and shoved the priest to the floor.

"There is a box at the back of the altar," instructed Allaberksis.

"And you," he said to another of the brutes, "check the fool priest's private room."

"That is the common grain money!" Keyes roared in protest, leaping to his feet. He was met by another of the brutes and pounded down, then kicked several times as he squirmed on the floor.

Solomon Keyes realized the truth of the intruders. This group, like so many of the Praetorian Guards who had come down from the Iron Cross, was planning to flee to the south, probably on wretched Allaberksis's orders.

Keyes could not fight them, and so he lay very still, praying again for guidance. He breathed a profound sigh when the group swept back out of the chapel.

That relief was short-lived, though, for it didn't take the priest long to understand the implications of Allaberksis's actions.

Pipery was being deserted as a sacrifice. King Greensparrow's elite soldiers did not consider the small village worth saving.

The Eriadoran army camped within sight of Pipery, swinging lines far to the east and west, even launching cavalry patrols across the ground south of the village to make sure that very few one-eyes escaped. Brind'Amour had no intention of allowing Greensparrow's disorganized northern army to run all the way back to Carlisle, or to Warchester, perhaps, where they might regroup behind the protection of the city's high walls.

On one such expedition, Luthien's swift cavalry group had come upon a curious band of Praetorian Guards, led by the oldest one-eye the young Bedwyr had ever seen. The cyclopians were summarily routed, and in picking through their bodies, Luthien had found a purse clearly marked as contributions for the town's common good.

The young Bedwyr thought that significant, and was beginning to discern a possibility here, a hope for an easier march. He said nothing about it on his return to the camp, though, wanting to sort things out more fully before presenting his suspicions to Brind'Amour, who, for some reason that Luthien couldn't discern, seemed more than a bit distracted this evening.

"You fear the coming battle?" Luthien asked, prodding his old friend, as the pair walked across the central area of the large camp.

Brind'Amour scoffed at that notion. "If I feared Pipery, I never would have come south, knowing that Warchester and Carlisle lay ahead!" the wizard replied. He stopped by a water trough then and bent low to splash his face. He paused before his hand touched the water, and stood very still, for in that trough, Brind'Amour saw a curious scene, a now-familiar narrow and tall, flat-topped pillar of stone.

Brind'Amour.

The call floated in on the wind. Brind'Amour glanced all about, looking for the rocks that might have made such a reflection in the water, but no such tower loomed anywhere near.

"What is it?" Luthien asked, concerned. He, too, glanced all about, though he had no idea what he might be looking for.

Brind'Amour waved his hand in the empty air, all the answer Luthien would get from him at that time. The wizard considered the call, the subtle and personal call, considered the owl and now the trough, and suddenly thought that he had sorted out the answer.

And hoped that he did, for if his guess was correct, these curious events might well alter the course of the coming battle.

"Keep a good eye to the perimeter," the old wizard instructed as he briskly walked away from Luthien.

Luthien called after him, but it was useless; Brind'Amour would not even slow his swift pace.

Back in his tent, the wizard wasted no time in taking out his crystal ball. The image of the strange rock formation was clear in his mind, and after nearly an hour of exhausting divining, he managed to replicate it in the crystal ball. Then Brind'Amour let the conjured image become a true scene and he slowly altered the perspective within the ball, searching out landmarks near the tower that might guide him. Soon he was convinced that the formation was in the Iron Cross, not so far to the north and west, closer to the coast, surely.

The wizard released the image from the ball and relaxed. He considered his course carefully, realizing that this might well be a trap. Perhaps it was one of his peers from that long-past age, awake again and ready to join in with Eriador's just cause. Perhaps it was Greensparrow, luring him to his doom that Eriador continue without a king, and without a wizard to counter the magics of the dukes and duchess and king of Avon.

"Now is not the time for caution," Brind'Amour said aloud, bolstering his resolve. "Now is not the time for cowards!"

Brind'Amour considered again the desperation of this war, the complete gamble that had been accepted by all the brave folk of Eriador with the prize of true freedom dangling before them.

The old wizard knew what he must do.

Chapter 22

TRAPPING THE TRAPPERS

Brind'Amour slipped quietly from his tent later that night. The moon had already set and the stars were crisp, in those spots where they showed through the broken canopy of rushing black clouds. The wizard, energized by thoughts of the crucial task before him, walked spryly across the encampment, past the rows of sleeping soldiers, beyond the rolling thunder of several thousand snoring dwarfs, and beyond the perimeter line, enacting a minor spell so that even the acute senses of the Fairborn sentries could not detect him. Brind'Amour had neither the time nor the desire to answer questions now.

He walked another half mile, coming to an area of stony ground, a small clearing sheltered by thick rows of maple, elm, birch, and pine. He noted that many of the leaves of the deciduous trees were already beginning to turn a light brown; autumn was fast approaching.

With a deep, steadying breath, Brind'Amour brought the enchantment—no minor spell this time—into mind. Then he began to dance, slowly, each step perfectly placed, each twirl symbolic of what he was to become. Soon his arms remained out wide as he spun more quickly, dipping and rising through each turn, his arms waving now gracefully—too gracefully for a human, it seemed.

The darkness seemed to lift then, from Brind'Amour's perspective, as the wizard's eyes became suddenly sensitive; the landscape became distinct and surreal. He heard a mouse rustle through the grass, perhaps twenty feet away, heard the cricket songs as loudly as if they were resounding through the massive pipes of the Ministry's choir organ.

He felt a series of pinlike pricks along both his arms, and looked there to see his voluminous robes melting away into overlapping lines of soft feathers. The stings were gone in an instant, as the rest of the wizard's body began its change, as the feathers became a natural part of his new anatomy.

The ground went away in a rush as the great owl flew away, soft-feathered wings beating the air without a whisper of sound.

Brind'Amour knew freedom then, true freedom. How he loved this transformation! Particularly at night, when all the human world was asleep, when it seemed as no more than a wonderful dream.

Hardly registering the move, the wizard turned sidelong, wing tips perpendicular to the ground, as he sliced between a pair of close trees. He rose as he came out the other side, working his wings hard, then felt the warm air on his belly as he crossed near the first real mountains of the Iron Cross. Wings widespread, the wizard rose slowly into the night air, tingling from the mixture of currents and air temperatures. He soared through the night-blanketed range, weaving through valleys and riding the warm updrafts. Into the northwest he flew, to where the mountains were more rugged, impassable by foot, but merely a majestic wave for an owl to ride.

He flew for an hour, easily, wonderfully, then came into a region of sheer drops and broken, windblown pillars. He knew this region, had seen it clearly in his crystal ball.

Now the wizard slowed and took care to move closer to the sheltering cliffs. The landscape was exactly as he had viewed it in the crystal ball, and so he was not surprised when he turned around one bend, lifted up to clear a high jag, and came in sight of the singular, flat-topped rock pillar. It resembled the limbless trunk of an old, gnarled tree, except that its angles, twists, and turns through all of its five hundred feet were sharper and more distinct, seeming unnatural, as though some tremendous force had pulled it right up from the ground.

Brind'Amour flew past the pillar at about half its height, preferring to make his first run in view of the plateau from the other direction. Up he rose, in a gradual bank, coming about much higher, almost level with the pillar's flat top.

He saw a single figure atop the stone, sitting near the center of the roughly fifty-foot-diameter plateau. The person was huddled under robes, the hood pulled low, facing the glowing embers of a dying fire.

Brind'Amour passed barely thirty feet above the huddled figure, but the person made no move, took no note.

Asleep? the old wizard mused. And why not? Brind'Amour told himself. What would someone in a place so very inaccessible have to fear?

This time, the wizard's bank was sharper, nearly a spinning midair pivot. Brind'Amour came in even lower, not sure of whether he would make another scouting pass.

No time for such caution, he decided, and so he mustered his courage and swooped to the stone, landing across the fire from the figure, halfway between the huddled person and the plateau's edge.

"Well done, King Brind'Amour," said a familiar female voice even as the wizard began the transformation back into his human form. The figure looked up and pulled back the tremendous hood of her robes. "I knew that you would be resourceful enough to find me."

Brind'Amour's heart sank at the sight of Duchess Deanna Wellworth. He was not truly surprised, for he had been fairly certain that none of his wizard companions from that time long past had survived. Still, the fact that he had flown so willingly into such a ruse, and the reality that he was indeed alone, weighed heavily on his shoulders.

"My greetings," Deanna said casually, and her tone gave Brind'Amour pause. Also, he realized, she had referred to him as "King Brind'Amour." The old wizard didn't know what to make of it. He glanced all about, thinking that he should resume his owl form and rush away on the winds.

No, he decided. He would trust in his powers and let this meeting play out. It had to come to this, after all; perhaps it would be better to be done with it before too many lives were lost.

"And the greetings of Duke Ashannon McLenny of Eornfast in Baranduine," Deanna went on. "And those of Duke Mystigal of

Evenshorn, and Duke Theredon Rees of Warchester." As she spoke each name, the appropriate man stepped into view, as though walking from behind a curtain of night sky.

Brind'Amour felt a fool. Why hadn't he seen them through such a simple magical disguise? Of course, he could not have enacted such divining magics in owl form, but he should have flown to a nearby ledge and resumed his human shape, then scanned the plateau top more carefully before coming down. His eagerness, his desire to believe that one of his ancient brothers had returned to his side, had caused him to err.

The three dukes were evenly spaced about the plateau top. Brind'Amour scanned them now, seeking the weakest link where he might escape. Deanna Wellworth surprised him, though, and her three companions as well, when she lifted a round beaker of blue liquid before her, spoke a single word and threw it down. It smashed into the fire, which erupted into a burst of white, then went low, blowing a thick wave of fog from its sizzling embers. The wave rolled out in all directions, right past the four startled men. When it reached the edge of the plateau, it swirled upward, turning back over the stone.

Then the fog was no more, replaced by a blue-glowing canopy, a bubble of energy, that encompassed the plateau. All the plateau was bathed in the eerie light.

Brind'Amour was truly impressed; he realized that Deanna must have spent days, perhaps even weeks, in designing such a spell. He wasn't sure of the nature of the globe, but he guessed that it was some sort of a barrier, anti-magic or anti-flesh, designed to prevent him from leaving. Whether it would prove effective might be a different thing altogether, though, for the wizard was confident that he could counter anything one of Greensparrow's cohorts could enact.

But how much time did he have?

"You resort to treachery?" Brind'Amour scoffed, his tone showing his clear disdain. "How far the honor of wizards has fallen. Common thieves, is that what you have become?"

"Of course your ancient and holy brotherhood would never have done such a thing," Theredon Rees of Warchester replied sarcastically.

"Never," Brind'Amour answered in even tones. The old king stared long and hard at the upstart wizard. Theredon was a stocky, muscular man, nearing middle age. His hair was thick and black and curly, his dark eyes full of intensity. In truth, the man seemed more a warrior than a wizard, in appearance and likely in temperament, something Brind'Amour figured he might be able to turn against Theredon.

He shifted his gaze to Mystigal—Mystigal! What pretensions of power had caused this one to change his name? And of course he had changed his name, for no child in the age following the demise of the brotherhood would have been given the name of Mystigal! He was older than Theredon, slender and cultured, with hawkish and hollow features, worn away by the overuse of magic. A "reacher" Brind'Amour discerned, remembering an old term his brotherhood had used to describe those wizards who aspired to greater powers than their intelligence allowed. Any attacks from this one would likely be grandiose in nature, seeming mighty, but with little real power to support them.

The duke of Baranduine appeared as the most comfortable, and thus likely to be the most difficult of the three men. Ashannon McLenny was a handsome man, his eyes well-balanced with emotion, eager and calm. A clear thinker; perhaps this one would have been a candidate for the brotherhood in ages past. Brind'Amour let his measuring gaze linger on Ashannon for a while, then shifted it to regard Deanna. Brind'Amour knew her well enough to respect her. Deanna was a complete package: cultured, intelligent, beautiful, dangerous, and the wizard held no doubts that this one would have aspired to, and achieved, magical prowess in that time long past. She might prove to be the most formidable of all, and it was no coincidence that Brind'Amour's attack plans for Eriador had purposely avoided sending forces against Deanna's city of Mannington.

During those few moments he spent in scanning his adversaries, Brind'Amour whispered under his breath, enacting minor magical defenses. A coil of wire appeared in one hand and gradually unrolled beneath his sleeve, then under his robes until its tip poked forth beside his boot, securing itself against the stone. Next the wizard quietly gathered all the moisture from the air near to him, called it in but didn't concentrate it. Not yet. Brind'Amour set up a conditional spell to finish what he had started, and he had to hope that his magic would be quick enough to the conditional call.

"And where is Greensparrow?" Brind'Amour asked suddenly,

when he noted that the others, particularly Theredon and Mystigal, were exchanging nods, as if preparing their first assault.

Theredon snorted derisively. "Why would we need our king to pluck such a thorn as the pretender king of Eriador the wasteland?"

"So said Paragor," Brind'Amour calmly replied. That set cocky Theredon back on his heels a bit.

"We are four!" snarled Mystigal, bolstering Theredon, and himself, with the proclamation.

Now Brind'Amour called up a spell to shift his vision subtly that it might record magical energies. The strength of Deanna's globe surprised him once more when he realized the tightness of its magical weaving, but the other thing that surprised the wizard was that there apparently were no other magical curtains behind which other enemies might hide. No Greensparrow and, curiously, no demons.

He caught a sly look in Deanna Wellworth's eyes then that he did not quite understand. "There is no escape," she said, and then added, as if reading his mind, "No magic, not even a creature magically summoned, can pass through the blue barrier. You are without escape and without allies."

As if to accentuate Deanna's point, a horrid figure pressed its insectlike face against the top of the bubble then, leering down at the gathering on the plateau.

Brind'Amour recognized the thing as a demon, and he scratched his beard curiously, considering that the fiend was on the *outside*.

"Deanna!" cried Mystigal suddenly.

Brind'Amour looked from the fiend to the hawkish wizard. "Friend of yours?" he asked, a smile widening on his face.

Both Mystigal and Theredon squirmed a bit, an indication to Brind'Amour that the two suspected that their lead conspirator had erred, bringing up the shield before their allies, their true connections to power, had joined with them.

"Demon of Hell," Deanna answered Brind'Amour. "My fellows have come to greatly rely on such evil fiends."

We are not friends of King Greensparrow, nor can we any longer accept the truth of our ill-begotten powers, came a telepathic message in Brind'Amour's mind. He looked to Ashannon, the duke of Eornfast, recognizing the man as the sender, and then he understood that Deanna had not erred! Indeed the woman had used treachery, but her prey was not as Brind'Amour had first assumed.

A second fiend, two-headed and lizardlike, arrived beside the first, and both pressed and clawed wildly, but futilely, at the resilient bubble shield.

"Their mistake," Brind'Amour answered Deanna grimly.

Mystigal looked up to the dome, his expression showing deep concern. "What is this?" he demanded of Deanna, who now stood swaying, shoulders slumped and head down, as though her casting of the powerful globe had drained her.

The end of the question was snuffed out under the sizzling roar of Theredon's blue-streaking lightning bolt, the most common attack form offered by any wizard.

And one Brind'Amour had fully anticipated. The old wizard threw out his arm toward Theredon as the bolt began, felt the tingle in his fingers as his defensive magics countered the spell, catching Theredon's bolt on the edge of the conjured coil and running it down under Brind'Amour's robes to the stone beneath his feet. Brind'Amour felt all the hairs on his body dancing from the shock; his heart fluttered several times before its beat evened out. But in truth, the bolt wasn't very powerful, more show than substance.

"A tickle, nothing more," Brind'Amour said to Theredon. The old wizard looked up to the dome. "It would seem that the duchess of Mannington's spell is quite complete. You cannot access the powers of your fiend, or else your fiend is not so powerful!

"Yet I am of the old school, the true school," Brind'Amour went on, striding determinedly toward Theredon. He gave a few sidelong glances at Ashannon and Deanna, wondering what they might do next. "I need no diabolical allies!"

"Deanna!" Theredon growled, skipping quickly to the side, trying to keep as much ground between himself and dangerous Brind'Amour as possible.

The old wizard stopped and closed his eyes, chanting softly.

"Deanna!" screamed a terrified Theredon, knowing to his horror that Brind'Amour was about to hit him with something.

No energy came forth when Brind'Amour opened his eyes, but the old wizard's sly grin brought no comfort to Theredon. The muscular man backed to the far end of the globe. He saw his demon ally, both its grotesque heads pressed against the unyielding bubble. Theredon put his hands up to it, tried to touch it, to gather its power, but after only a few futile seconds, the frustrated wizard began pounding on the magical shield.

Brind'Amour took a step toward Theredon, shimmered and disappeared, then came back into view suddenly right behind the muscular wizard. The king of Eriador grabbed Theredon by the shoulder and roughly spun him about, then, before the younger and stronger man could even cry out, clasping a hand over Theredon's face. Crackling red sparks instantly erupted from Brind'Amour's fingers, lashing at his foe. Theredon cried out and reached up with trembling hands, clawing at Brind'Amour's arm.

Theredon's two-headed demon flew off, then returned at full speed, slamming the bubble with tremendous force, but merely bouncing away.

Behind him, above the screams of the demon and of Theredon, Brind'Amour could hear Mystigal chanting, and a moment later a ball of fire exploded in the air right between Brind'Amour and Theredon.

Fire, the single condition set upon Brind'Amour's waiting spell, was among the most predictable of wizardly attacks. At the instant the fireball blew, all the moisture Brind'Amour had gathered rushed out from him, blanketing him in a protective seal. When the flames of the not-so-powerful fireball disappeared, the old wizard was hardly singed, though wisps of smoke rose up from several places on poor Theredon's body, melting into the misty vapors that now engulfed the pair.

Brind'Amour looked back over his shoulder to see Deanna and Ashannon converging on poor Mystigal. The older, hawkish man scrambled away, crying out repeatedly to Deanna.

From the corner of his eye, Brind'Amour caught the movement as the buglike demon rushed at the bubble, then dove low, apparently boring right into the stone. A moment later, the ground under Deanna's feet heaved and the woman stumbled to the side, allowing Mystigal some running room. Theredon's frantic demon followed suit, and soon the floor of the plateau was rumbling and dancing, great rolling waves keeping all five within the globe struggling to hold their balance.

But Deanna's spell was well-constructed, the protective shield complete, even under their feet, and the demons could do little real mischief.

Theredon was on his knees by this point, grabbing weakly at Brind'Amour's arm, offering little resistance to the much more powerful, true wizard. Knowing that he had this one fully under control, Brind'Amour turned his sights on Mystigal, who was still calling out frantically to Deanna to come to her senses, and working hard to keep away from her and Ashannon.

Brind'Amour began another chant and lifted his free hand in Mystigal's direction.

Deanna and Ashannon worked in unison now, shifting so that they soon had the man cornered, then slowly closing in, Ashannon on the hawkish man's right, Deanna on his left.

The ground heaved under Ashannon's feet, knocking him toward Deanna, and Mystigal, with a shriek, ran out to the right, behind the stumbling duke. He only got a couple of steps, though, before Brind'Amour completed his spell and snapped his fingers. As though he was fastened to an overstretched cord, Mystigal rushed forward suddenly, his feet barely scraping the ground. He went right between Deanna and Ashannon, knocking them to the stone, and continued his impromptu flight all the way across the plateau, coming face-first into Brind'Amour's waiting grasp.

Red sparks came from that hand, too, and Brind'Amour wasted no time in bending the weakling man over backward, forcing him right to his knees.

Deanna and Ashannon collected themselves and eyed the spectacle of Brind'Amour's bared power from a safe distance. Ashannon motioned questioningly toward the trio, but Deanna shook her head and would not approach.

The old wizard tilted his head back and closed his eyes, concentrating fully on the release of power. Theredon's hands were tight about one arm, but the muscular man's grip seemed not so strong anymore. Mystigal offered no resistance whatsoever, just flailed his arms helplessly as the red sparks bit at his skull.

Brind'Amour attuned himself to his opponents' magic, that inner area of wizardly power. He felt the line of power there, the connection to the frenzied fiends. He felt the line bending, bending, and then, in Mystigal first, it snapped apart.

With a resounding whining buzz, the insect demon was hurled back to Hell and the ground under Deanna's bubble was quieter. As though he gained some resolve from that, Theredon growled and forced himself back to his feet.

Brind'Amour let go of Mystigal, who fell over backward to the stone, and put his full concentration on the stronger Theredon. The two held the pose for a long while, but then Theredon's core of power, like Mystigal's, snapped apart. Brind'Amour released him and he stood, precariously balanced, staring at the old wizard incredulously. Then, with all his strength, physical and magical, torn from his body, Theredon fell to the ground, facedown.

The stone beneath the old wizard's feet was quiet suddenly, as the two-headed demon joined its buglike companion in banishment, their ties to the world cleanly severed.

Brind'Amour spun about, facing the duke and duchess, not sure what any of this was about. He tried to look threatening, but in truth feared that either Ashannon or Deanna, or both, would come at him now, for he had little strength remaining with which to combat them.

The two looked to each other, then began a cautious approach, Deanna's hands held high and open, unthreatening.

On the ground, Mystigal groaned. Theredon lay very still.

"He will not awaken," Brind'Amour said firmly. "I have torn his magic from him, destroyed the minor wizard that he was!" Brind'Amour tried to sound threatening, but Deanna only nodded, as though she had expected that all along.

"We are not your enemy," she said, reading the old wizard's tone and body language. "Our common enemy is Greensparrow, and he, it would seem, has lost two more of his wizard-dukes."

With a sizzle and a puff, the blue-swirling globe vanished.

"Good spell," Brind'Amour congratulated.

"Years in perfecting," replied Deanna, "in preparation for the day that I knew would come."

Brind'Amour looked at her curiously. "Yet you performed the powerful magic without aid of your demon," he remarked suspiciously.

"I have no demon," she answered evenly.

"Nor do I," added Ashannon.

Brind'Amour eyed the duke of Eornfast skeptically, sensing that the man was not so certain of, or comfortable with, his position as was Deanna.

"I prefer the older ways," said Deanna. "The ways of the brotherhood."

Brind'Amour found that he believed her, though he could not have done much if he didn't. He was too tired to either attack the pair or flee the plateau. Deanna, too, seemed exhausted. She walked over slowly, bending low to inspect the pair of fallen dukes.

"Theredon is dead," she announced without emotion as she looked back to Ashannon, "but Mystigal lives."

Ashannon nodded, walked to the edge of the plateau, and leaped off into the night sky. Brind'Amour caught the flutter as the man transformed into some great nightbird, and then was gone.

Brind'Amour looked to Deanna. "Talkative fellow," he said.

"Duke McLenny knows that he has sacrificed much for this day," she replied. "Too much, perhaps, and so you must be content in the knowledge that he did not join with Theredon and Mystigal against you."

"But neither did he join with me," Brind'Amour pointed out.

Deanna didn't answer, just walked back to the center of the plateau and dropped some liquid on the dying fire. Immediately the flames roared back to life, bathing Deanna in their warm, orange glow.

"Bring Mystigal near to the warmth," she instructed Brind'Amour. "He does not deserve a cold death in such a remote, nameless place."

Those were the last words she spoke that night. She sat watching the fire for a long while, not even seeming to notice Brind'Amour, who, after laying Mystigal beside the flames, sat directly across from her.

The old wizard didn't press the point. He understood Deanna's dilemma here, understood that the young woman had just cast off the beliefs that had sustained her for most of her life.

TO KNOW YOUR ENEMIES

Luthien and Bellick went to Brind'Amour's tent together in the cool darkness before the dawn. The pair were full of enthusiasm, ready for battle once more. A lantern burned low on the pole just outside the entrance, but inside the tent was dark. The pair entered anyway, thinking to rouse Brind'Amour. The dawn attack was the customary course, after all, giving the armies all the day for fighting.

Little light followed them in, but enough for them to discern that the wizard was not inside.

"Must be out and about already, readying the plans," Bellick remarked, but Luthien wasn't so sure. Something was out of place, he realized instinctively.

Luthien moved to the wizard's bed and confirmed his suspicions that it hadn't been slept on the previous night. That was curious enough, but Luthien held a nagging suspicion that there was something more out of place. He glanced all about, but saw nothing apparent. All the furniture was in order, the table in the middle of the room, the stool beside it, the crystal ball atop it. Brind'Amour's small desk sat against the tent side opposite the bed, covered in parchments, maps mostly, and by several bags filled with all sorts of strange potions and spell components.

"Come along," Bellick called from the tent flap. "We've got to find the old one and get the line formed up."

Luthien nodded and moved slowly to follow, looking back over his shoulder, certain that something was wrong. He got outside the tent, under the meager light of the low-burning lantern, Bellick several strides ahead of him.

"The crystal ball," Luthien said suddenly, turning the dwarf about.

"What?"

"The crystal ball," the young Bedwyr repeated, confident that he had hit on something important. "Brind'Amour's crystal ball!"

"It was in there to be sure," said Bellick. "Right in plain sight on the table."

"He never leaves it so," said Luthien, moving swiftly back into the tent. He heard Bellick groan and grumble, but the dwarf did follow, coming in just as Luthien settled on the stool, peering intently into the ball.

"Should you be looking into that?" Bellick asked. Like most of his race, Bellick was always a bit cautious where magic was concerned.

"I do not understand why it isn't covered," Luthien answered. "Brind'Amour . . ."

Luthien's words fell away as an image, a familiar, cheery old face, thick with a tremendous white beard, suddenly appeared within the ball. "Ah, good," said the illusionary Brind'Amour, "it is morning then, and you are preparing to take Pipery. All speed, my friends. I doubt not the outcome. I do not know how long I will be gone, and I go only with the knowledge that Eriador's forces are secure. Righteous speed!"

The image faded away as abruptly as it had appeared. Luthien looked back to Bellick, just a stocky silhouette framed by the open tent flap.

"So the wizard's gone," the dwarf said. "On good business, I do not doubt."

"Brind'Amour would not leave if it wasn't urgent," Luthien agreed.

"The Huegoths, probably," reasoned Bellick, and the thought that there might be trouble involving Ethan put a sour turn in Luthien's stomach. Or perhaps the trouble was from the other way, from the west, where Oliver and Katerin sailed. Luthien looked again to the empty crystal ball. He reminded himself many times over that Brind'Amour's demeanor had been cheerful, not dour.

"No matter," the dwarf king went on. "We ever were an army led by two!"

Luthien understood that Bellick had just assumed control of all the forces, and he really couldn't argue with the dwarf, who surely outranked him. There was an issue, though, which Luthien had wanted to discuss with Brind'Amour before the assault began. At the end of the previous war with Avon, when he had wanted to press on to Carlisle, Luthien had held the conviction that victory would be possible because many of the folk of Avon might see the truth of the situation, might realize that the army of Eriador wasn't really their enemy. Luthien had come to agree that his expectations were likely overblown, but still, he couldn't accept the notion that all of Avon's folk, men and women much like the Eriadorans, would desire war against Eriador.

Bellick grunted and turned to go.

"Can you muster the lines yourself?" Luthien asked. The dwarf wheeled about, and though he couldn't see the details of Bellick's face, Luthien could sense his surprise.

"You're going to look for Brind'Amour?" Bellick asked incredulously.

"No, but I had hoped to secure King Brind'Amour's permission to go into Pipery, before the dawn, before the battle," Luthien replied.

Bellick glanced over his shoulder, then stepped into the tent, obviously concerned.

"To scout out their defenses," Luthien explained immediately. "With the crimson cape, I can get in and out, and not a cyclopian will be the wiser."

Bellick stood staring at the young Bedwyr for a long while. "That is not why you wish to go," the dwarf reasoned, for he had heard Luthien talking about the folk of Avon as potential allies many times in the last few weeks.

Luthien sighed. "We may have friends within Pipery's walls," he admitted.

Bellick offered no response.

"I came to ask permission of King Brind'Amour," Luthien said, standing straight. "But King Brind'Amour is not to be found."

"Thus you will go as is your pleasure," said Bellick.

"Thus I ask permission to go from King Bellick dan Burso, who rightfully leads the army," Luthien corrected, and the show of loyalty did much for Bellick as the dwarf stood straighter.

"You may be disappointed," Bellick warned.

Luthien shrugged. "At the least, I will scout out their defenses," he replied.

"And at the most?"

"Justice for the Avon populace," Luthien replied without hesitation.

"Go, and quickly," Bellick bade him. "We've less than two hours to the dawn, and I plan to eat my noontime meal in Pipery!"

Luthien didn't really know what he would do as he used the cover of darkness and his magical cape to slip silently over Pipery's wall, which was little more than a collection of ramshackle pilings.

He picked his way from darkened house to house, amazed at how few cyclopians were up and about. By all reports, and by his last encounter on the field, Luthien believed that the small village's garrison had swelled in number with the addition of those Praetorian Guards fleeing the rout in the mountains. But where were they?

The riddle was solved as Luthien crossed the town's main road, deep gouges cut into it from the passage of a huge caravan. Heading south, Luthien noted by the tracks, and not more than two days before. Across the road, the young Bedwyr came upon the town's stables, two buildings connected by long fences. The doors of the barn were thrown wide, but no nickers or whinnies came from within, and the corral was empty, save for a few horse carcasses that had been butchered for meat.

Luthien took a deep and steadying breath, not thrilled by the reality of war's dark threat. He wondered what other hardships the folk of Pipery, unwitting pawns in Greensparrow's grand game, might have suffered these last few days.

He composed himself immediately, reminding himself that he could not afford to waste even a second of time. He trotted from shadow to shadow along the side of the main road, then paused when he came to a fork, east and southwest. Directly across from him, Luthien spied the first light he had seen since entering the village, a candle burning in the window of a large structure, which appeared to be the town's chapel.

With a hopeful nod, Luthien darted across the road to the building's side. He considered the Ministry in Caer MacDonald, a place of spirituality, but also the chosen headquarters for Greensparrow's wretched Duke Morkney. Might that be the pattern even in the smaller villages? Within this chapel, might there be an eorl, or a baron, loyal to the king of Avon and holding Pipery under his iron-fisted rule?

A quick glance to the eastern sky reminded Luthien once again that he had little time to ponder. He slipped up to a side door, peeked in through a small window set in its middle, then, seeing no obvious enemies nearby, slowly turned the handle.

It wasn't even locked, and Luthien eased it open, fully aware that he might find the bulk of the cyclopian garrison within.

To his surprise, and relief, the place seemed empty. He quietly closed the door behind him. He had come in to a small side room, the personal quarters of the place's priest or caretaker, perhaps. The one other door lay open to the main prayer area. Luthien adjusted his shielding cape to ensure that he was fully covered, then moved up to the door jamb, peering around the corner.

A solitary figure was in the place, kneeling on a bench at the front of the chapel, facing away from Luthien. The man's white robe revealed him as a priest.

Luthien nodded and padded in softly, moving from bench to bench and stopping often, blending with the wall in case the man turned back. As he neared the front of the chapel, he quietly slipped *Blind-Striker* from its sheath, but held it low, under the cape.

He could hear the priest then, whispering prayers for the safety of Pipery. Most telling of all was when the man asked God to "keep little Pipery out of the struggles of kings."

Luthien pulled off his hood. "Pipery lays on the road to Carlisle," he said suddenly.

The priest nearly toppled, and scrambled furiously to stand facing the intruder, eyes wide, jaw slack. Luthien noted the bruises on the man's face, the split lip and the puffy eyes. Given the number of cyclopians who had come through the town recently, it wasn't hard for the young Bedwyr to guess where those had come from.

"Whether it is friend or enemy to Eriador is Pipery's own choice," Luthien finished.

"Who are you?"

"An emissary from King Brind'Amour of Eriador," Luthien replied. "Come to offer hope where there should be none."

The man eyed Luthien carefully. "The Crimson Shadow," he whispered.

Luthien nodded, then held up a calm and steady hand when the priest blanched white.

"I have not come to kill you or anyone else," Luthien explained. "Only to see the mood of Pipery."

"And to discover our weaknesses," the priest dared to say.

Luthien chuckled. "I have five thousand battle-hungry dwarfs on the field, and a like number of men," he explained. "I have seen your wall and what is left of your garrison."

"Most of the cyclopians fled," the priest confirmed, his gaze going to the floor.

"What is your name?"

The man looked up, squaring his shoulders defiantly. "Solomon Keyes," he replied.

"Father Keyes?"

"Not yet," the priest admitted. "Brother Keyes."

"A man of the church or of the crown?"

"How do you know they are not one and the same?" Keyes answered cryptically.

Luthien smiled warmly and pushed aside his cape, revealing his bared sword, which he promptly replaced in its scabbard. "They are not," he replied.

Solomon Keyes offered no argument.

Luthien was pleased thus far with the conversation; he had the distinct feeling that Keyes did not equate God with Greensparrow. "Cyclopians?" he asked, motioning toward the priest's bruised face.

Keyes lowered his gaze once more.

"Praetorian Guards, likely," Luthien went on. "Come from the mountains, where we routed them. They passed through in a rush, stealing and slaughtering your horses, taking everything of value that we Eriadorans would not find it, and ordering the folk of Pipery, and probably the village cyclopian militia as well, to defend to the last."

Keyes looked up, his soft features tightening, eyes sharp on the perceptive young Bedwyr.

"That is the way it happened," Luthien said finally.

"Do you expect a denial?" Keyes asked. "I am no stranger to the brutish ways of cyclopians, and was not surprised."

"They are your allies," Luthien said, his tone edging on accusation.

"They are my king's army," Keyes corrected.

"That speaks ill of your king," Luthien was quick to respond. Both men went silent, letting the moment of tension pass. It would do neither of them any good to get things worked up here, for both of them were fast coming to the conclusion that something positive might come from this unexpected meeting.

"It was not only the Praetorian Guards of the Iron Cross," Keyes admitted, "but even many of our own militia. Even old Allaberksis, who has been in Pipery since the earliest—"

"Old?" Luthien interrupted. Aged cyclopians were a rarity.

"The oldest one-eye ever I have seen," said Keyes, and the sharpness of his voice told Luthien that this Allaberksis was likely in on the beating he had received.

"Old and withered," Luthien added. "Running south with a small band of Praetorian Guards."

Keyes expression told him that he had hit the mark.

"Alas for Allaberksis," Luthien said evenly. "He could not outrun my horse."

"He is dead?"

Luthien nodded.

"And what of his purse?" Keyes asked indignantly. "Common grain money for the villagers, money rightly earned and needed—"

Luthien held up his hand. "It will be returned," he promised. "After."

"After Pipery is sacked!" Keyes cried.

"That needn't happen," Luthien said calmly, defeating the priest's outburst before it ever truly began.

Another long silence followed, as Keyes waited for the explanation of that most intriguing statement, and Luthien considered how he might broach the subject. He guessed that Keyes held quite a bit of influence over the village; the chapel was well-maintained and the villagers had trusted him, after all, with their precious grain money.

"We of Eriador and DunDarrow have not come to conquer," Luthien began.

"You have crossed the border in force!"

"In defense," Luthien explained. "Though a truce was signed between our kings, Avon's war with Eriador did not end. All along the Iron Cross, our villages were being destroyed."

"Cyclopian raiders," Keyes reasoned.

"Working for Greensparrow," Luthien replied.

"You do not know this."

"Did you not see Praetorian Guards coming out of the mountains?" Luthien countered. "Had they just gone into the Iron Cross, in defense against our march, or had they been there all along, prodding Eriador to war?"

Keyes didn't answer, and honestly didn't know the answer, though no Praetorian Guard caravans had been reported heading north in the few weeks before the onset of war.

"Greensparrow prodded us to march south," Luthien insisted. "He forced the war upon us if we truly desired our freedom."

Keyes squared his shoulders. His expression showed that he believed Luthien, or at least that he didn't consider the words a complete lie, but his stance became defiant anyway. "I am loyal to Avon," he informed the young Bedwyr.

"But Greensparrow is not," Luthien answered without hesitation. "Nor is he loyal to our common God. He allies with demons, I say, for I have battled with more than one of the hellish fiends myself, have felt their evil auras, have seen such a creature occupy the body of one of Greensparrow's henchmen dukes!"

Keyes winced; he had heard the rumors of diabolical allies, Luthien realized, and could not dispute the claims.

"How am I to know that you are not murderous invaders?" Keyes asked.

Luthien drew out his sword, looked from its gleaming blade to the blanching priest. "Why are you not already dead?" he asked.

The young Bedwyr was quick to replace the sword, not wanting to cause any more discomfort to the beleaguered man. "Pipery's fate is its own to decide," he said. He looked to the eastern windows then, and saw that the sky was beginning to brighten. "I do not demand your alliance or your fealty to my king, and on my word, your village will not be destroyed and your money will be returned. But if you oppose us, we will kill you, do not doubt. Eriador has come for war, and so we shall wage it with any who hold loyalty to evil King Greensparrow!"

With that, Luthien bowed and swept away.

"What am I to do?" Keyes called, and Luthien stopped and turned to face him from across the room.

"How am I to prevent my people from defending their own homes?" he asked.

"There is no defense," Luthien said grimly, and turned once more.

"Nor is there time!" Keyes pleaded. "Dawn is almost upon us!"

Luthien stopped at the doorway to the side room. "I can delay them," he promised, though he doubted his own words. "I can buy you the hours until noon. The chapel offers sanctuary, to all but one-eyes."

"Go then to your army," Keyes said in a tone that assured Luthien that the man would at least try.

More people, more cyclopians, were out and about as Luthien left the chapel, forcing him to alter his course several times. He made the wall before the dawn, though, and in the increasing light could see just how truly hopeless was Pipery's position. The wall was in bad disrepair—in many places it was no more than piled stones. Even at its strongest points, the wall loomed no higher than eight feet, and was not thick enough to slow the battering charge of Bellick's stone-crushing dwarfs.

"Do well, Solomon Keyes," Luthien prayed as he crossed out of the village, running fast across the open fields. For the sympathetic young Bedwyr, the image of the coming carnage was not acceptable.

A calm had settled over the fields between the Eriadoran encampment and Pipery, both sides waiting for the attack they knew would come this day.

And what a fine day it was! Too fine for battle, Luthien lamented. The sun dawned bright, the wind blew crisp and clean, and all the birds and animals were out in full, chirping and leaping.

Riverdancer, too, was in high spirits, snorting and pawing the ground when Luthien approached with his saddle. The white stallion leaped away as soon as Luthien had mounted.

Luthien could not ignore the nausea churning in his stomach. He always felt anxious before battle, but this time it was not the same. In every fight previous, Luthien had charged in with the knowledge that his was the just cause, and in the wider picture of Eriador's freedom, he considered the invasion of Avon a necessary and righteous thing. That did little to comfort him, though, when he thought of Pipery sacked, of men like Solomon Keyes lying soaked in their own blood.

Killing evil cyclopians was one thing, killing humans, Luthien now understood, was something altogether different.

He paced Riverdancer swiftly along the ranks, coming up to King Bellick and Shuglin as they reviewed the dwarven line.

"Good that you got back," Bellick remarked. "It would not do for you to be standing among them Avon and cyclopian dogs when we run them down!"

"We must hold our line," Luthien said bluntly.

The dwarf king turned about so abruptly that his wild orange beard slipped out of his broad belt.

"Until the hour of noon," Luthien explained.

"The day is not long enough!" Bellick roared. "They will see us now, and discover our strengths and weaknesses, and alter their defenses . . ."

"There is nothing that Pipery can do," Luthien assured the king. He saw Siobhan and several of the other Cutters approaching, along with a group of leaders of the Eriadoran army.

"They are helpless against our strength," Luthien finished, loud enough so that the newcomers could hear.

"That is fine news," replied Bellick. "Then let us go in and finish the task quickly, then march on to the next town."

Luthien shook his head determinedly, and Bellick responded with an open glare.

The young Bedwyr sat up straight in his saddle, looked all about as he spoke, for he was now addressing all who would listen. "Pipery will offer little defense," he said, "and less still if we delay through the morning."

A chorus of groans met that proposition.

"And consider our course carefully," Luthien went on, undaunted. "We will run through a dozen such villages before we ever see the walls of Warchester, with Carlisle still far beyond that. There are seeds of support for us; I have witnessed them with my own eyes."

"You have spoken with men inside Pipery's walls?" Bellick asked, not sounding pleased.

"With only one man," Luthien confirmed. "With the priest, who fears for his town's safety."

"And rightly so!" came a cry from the gathering, a call that was answered and bolstered many times over.

"How long?" Siobhan asked simply, quieting the crowd.

"Give them the morning," Luthien begged, speaking directly to Bellick once more. "They can make few adjustments to bolster their meager defenses, and we have the village surrounded that none may escape."

"I fear to delay," Bellick replied, but his tone was less belligerent. The dwarf king was no fool. He recognized the influence that Luthien Bedwyr held over the Eriadorans, the Cutters, and even a fair number of his own dwarfs, who remembered well that it was Luthien who had led the raid to free so many of their kin from the horrors of the Montfort Mines. While Bellick wasn't sure that he agreed with Luthien's reasoning, he understood the dangers of openly disagreeing with the young man.

"We will lose six hours at the outset," Luthien admitted. "But much of that time will be regained in the battle, unless I miss my guess. And even if the hours are not regained, I will ask that my folk march more swiftly beside me on the way to the next village." Luthien rose up in his saddle again and addressed all the crowd. "I ask this of you," he shouted. "Will you grant me this one thing?"

The response was unanimous, and Bellick realized that it would be folly to try and resist the young Bedwyr. He hated the thought of keeping his anxious dwarfs in check, and hated the thought of wasting so fine a morning. But Bellick hated more the notion of open disagreement between himself and Luthien, a potential split in an army that could afford no rifts.

He nodded to Luthien then, but in his look was the clear assumption that Luthien owed him one for this.

Luthien's responding nod, so full of gratitude, made it clear that he would repay the favor.

"Besides," Luthien offered with a wink to Bellick and to Siobhan as the ranks broke apart around them. "I now know where Pipery's wall is weakest."

As the hopeful word spread about Pipery, Solomon Keyes rushed to the wall and peered out across the open fields.

"They are standing down!" one gleeful man yelled right in the young priest's face.

Keyes managed a smile, and was indeed grateful, but it was tempered with the knowledge that he had but a few hours to do so very much. He looked up to the sky as though he might will the sun to hold in place for a while.

Bellick, Luthien, Siobhan, and all the other commanders of the army were not idle that long morning. With Luthien's information about the physical defenses and about the emotional turmoil within Pipery, a new battle plan was quickly drawn, analyzed, and polished, each segment run over and over until it became embedded in the thoughts of those who were charged with carrying it out.

They were back on the field before noon, ten thousand strong, speartips and swords gleaming in the light, polished shields catching the sun like flaming mirrors.

All of the cavalry was together this time, more than a hundred strong and sitting in formation directly north of the town. Luthien on shining Riverdancer centered the line, along with Siobhan. On command, all heads turned to face east of that position, where stood King Bellick dan Burso in his fabulous battle gear.

A lone rider galloped out to the town's north gates.

"Will you yield, or will you fight us?" he asked simply of the growling cyclopians gathered there.

Predictably, a spear came soaring out at him, and just as predictably, it came nowhere near to hitting the mark. King Bellick had his answer.

As soon as the rider returned to his place in the ranks, all eyes again went to the dwarvish commander. With one strong arm, Bellick lifted his short and thick sword high into the air, and after a moment's pause, brought it sweeping down.

The roar of the attack erupted all along the line; Luthien and his fellow cavalry kicked their mounts into a thunderous charge.

Not all the line followed, though. Only those dwarfs directly behind the cavalry began to run ahead, the charge filtering to the east, sweeping up the line like the slow break of a wave.

Luthien brought his forces to within a few running strides of Pipery's wall, then broke left, to the east, apparently belaying the line. Out of the dust cloud on the heels of the cavalry came the leading dwarfs, straight on for Pipery, and so it went as Luthien's group circled the city, every pounding stride opening the way for another grim-faced soldier. Luthien had named the maneuver "opening the sea gates," and so it seemed to be, the riders moving like a blocking wall and the foot soldiers pouring in like a flood behind them.

As soon as the pattern became apparent to the defenders, it was reversed, with those infantry to the west coming on in a synchronous charge. Luthien's cavalry by this time had swung far around to the southeastern section of the village, trading missile fire, elvish bow against cyclopian spear. None of the cavalry had been hit, though, a testament to the fact that cyclopians simply could not judge distance, and to Luthien's hopes that few, if any, humans were among Pipery's obviously thin line.

The young Bedwyr spotted the desired section of wall, a pile of boulders, wider than it was high. Luthien swung Riverdancer away from the village, then turned abruptly and came straight in for the target, Siobhan right beside him and the elven line slowing and widening behind the pair.

Luthien saw the cyclopian spearmen and pikemen come up to defend, waited until the last moment, then pulled hard on Riverdancer's reins, yanking the steed up short and skittering out to the left, while Siobhan skipped out to the right.

Opening the way for the elvish volley. Dozens of stinging arrows rushed in, most skipping off the stones, several hitting the mark. The defenders fell away, either dead, wounded, or simply in fear, and Luthien and Siobhan called out to their kinfolk and kicked their mounts into the charge once more.

Luthien tightened his legs and posted hard, heels low, the balls of his feet pressed in tight to the stirrups. He bent low and coaxed Riverdancer on, aiming the mount straight for the center of the boulder pile. Up sprang the mighty horse, easily clearing the four-foot obstacle, bringing Luthien into Pipery.

Siobhan came in right beside him, and they turned together, thundering down the road. Luthien spied two fleeing cyclopians and ran them down, Riverdancer crushing one of them, *Blind-Striker* cutting down the other. The young Bedwyr turned about to Siobhan, grinning as he started to call out his new total. He stopped short, though, for he found Siobhan similarly running down a pair of one-eyes.

Cyclopians huddled in terror at the base of that low wall as the riders streamed over it, twenty, fifty, ninety, coming into Pipery. None of them paused at the wall, and at last the brutes managed to stand up, thinking they had been spared, thinking to go out over the wall and run away.

Before they got atop the first stones, Pipery's barrier seemed to heighten by several feet as the human wall of Eriadoran foot soldiers greeted the cyclopians.

Chaos hit the streets of Pipery, riders rushing every which way, cyclopians trying to form into defensive groups, only to find, more often than not, that half of their number were dead before they ever joined in the formation. There were some pockets of stiff resistance, though, particularly in the north, where Luthien, Siobhan, and three-score other riders charged off in support.

Trapped between such forces, the cyclopian defenses quickly evaporated, each brute thinking to save itself. One by one, the one-eyes were slain.

It was Luthien himself who finally threw wide Pipery's north gate, and King Bellick dan Burso who stood right outside, ready to greet him. Luthien jumped back astride Riverdancer, then held out his hand to help the short dwarf climb up behind him. The fighting was fast diminishing, more a matter of chasing down single brutes than any real battles, and so Luthien and the dwarf trotted off to survey the battle scene.

"Not much of a defense," the dwarf king snorted, seeing how truly thin the line had been. Cyclopian bodies—almost exclusively cyclopian, Luthien noted hopefully—were strewn about in a long line, but in most places were no more than one or two deep.

"Where are they all?" the dwarf asked. "Did more of the folk get out than we figured?"

Luthien didn't think that to be the case, and he was pretty sure that he could guess where the rest of Pipery's defenders had gone. He called his cavalry into formation behind him and trotted south along the main road, to the fork facing the town's chapel.

When all the soldiers came into place around that structure and finally quieted, they could hear the soft singing of many voices emanating from within.

Bellick slid down then to put his dwarfs and the Eriadoran foot soldiers in place, and to manage the prisoner groups being escorted into the area. Luthien, meanwhile, took a slow circuit of the chapel, calming his battle-hungry companions on all sides. The dwarf king was waiting for him when he came back around to the fork in the road, and Bellick was not surprised by the plan Luthien had devised.

"You have guessed right thus far," the dwarf remarked, not of the mind to overrule the young Bedwyr.

Luthien slid down from Riverdancer, handing the reins to a nearby soldier. He dusted himself off and strode directly for the chapel's main door, motioning and calling orders as he went.

Without hesitation, without bothering to knock, Luthien entered to find several hundred sets of eyes staring back to regard him, expressions showing too great a mix of emotions for the young man to possibly sort through. He scanned the gathering, finally settling his gaze on Solomon Keyes, who stood at the pulpit at the front of the chapel.

"It is done," the young Bedwyr announced. "Pipery is free."

A woman jumped up from the edge of a pew and charged at Luthien, but several arms caught her before she had gone two steps, pulling her screaming back into the throng.

"Many had kin out there," Keyes explained evenly.

Luthien glanced back over his shoulder and nodded and a long line of human prisoners walked into the chapel, breaking away, running to their relieved families.

"There may be others," Luthien explained. "We have not sorted it all out as of yet."

"What penalty?" Keyes started to ask.

"No penalty," Luthien replied without the slightest hesitation. "They were defending their homes and their kin, so they believed." He paused, letting the surprised murmurs quiet. "We are not your enemy," he declared. "This much I have told you before."

As one, the crowd swung about to regard Keyes, who stood nodding.

"Pipery is free," Luthien went on. "And out of the war. Your gates are open, north and south, and you shall not hinder our passage, or the continuing line that shall come down from Eriador. Nor shall you deny any boats we put on the river from safe travel past your docks."

The murmurs began again, and were quickly silenced by Luthien's booming voice. "But we ask nothing of you," he explained. "What you give to us, you give of your own free will."

"Thieves!" one man yelled, leaping to his feet and pushing to the center of the open aisle. "Thieves and murderers!" he proclaimed, slowly stalking toward Luthien.

He stopped short when Bellick dan Burso entered, to stand at Luthien's side. "We are not your enemies," the dwarf king declared, and the blood spattered upon him could not diminish the splendor of his crafted armor, nor the dust covering him steal the flames of his fiery beard. But the sympathy that was in his heart could not diminish the intensity of his stern gaze.

Bellick let that gaze linger all about the room, then settled it on Luthien, who nodded for the dwarf to continue. "We are not your enemies unless you make of us your enemies," Bellick promised grimly. "Then know that Pipery will be sacked, burned to the ground!"

Not a person in the room doubted the imposing dwarf's promise.

Bellick pulled two large pouches from a cord on his back. "Your grain money," he explained, tossing them to the floor at the feet of the deflated rabble-rouser. "Taken from cyclopians fleeing Pipery. Taken from your King Greensparrow's cyclopians as they left Pipery to its doom. Decide then who are your enemies and who are your allies."

"Or decide nothing," Luthien added. "And remain neutral. We ask nothing of you, save that your swords are not again lifted against us."

He looked down at Bellick, and the dwarf up at him. "We will tend our wounded," Bellick announced, "and clear our dead from the field, that they do not lie beside the rotting cyclopians. And then we shall leave." The dwarf and Luthien turned to go, but were stopped by the call of Solomon Keyes.

"You may bring your wounded in here," the priest offered, "and I shall prepare your dead for burial, as I prepare the human dead of Pipery."

Luthien turned to him, somewhat surprised.

"My God and your God," Keyes asked, "are they not one and the same?"

Luthien nodded, managed a thin smile, and walked from the chapel.

FOR THE CAUSE OF JUSTICE

Bellick dan Burso was not ignorant of the many angry and suspicious gazes that settled over him as he walked with an entourage of bodyguards through Pipery's narrow streets. Luthien held illusions of friendship with all the common folk of Avon, and one day that might come to pass, but Bellick knew better than to hope for such allies so soon after battle. Aside from the cyclopians who had been slaughtered, more than a few of Pipery's human soldiers had been killed as well, and a fair number of families in the village now had a dead relative because of the invading Eriadorans.

Such a greeting rarely led to friendship.

Still, there were others in the town who managed a smile and a nod as the honorable dwarf king passed, and when Bellick arrived at the front steps to the chapel house, he found his own soldiers, set in place to guard over the Eriadoran and dwarvish wounded, relaxing on the stairs, enjoying food and drink with a handful of Pipery's citizens. The dwarven soldiers fumbled all over themselves, trying to get up, but the king waved his hand absently. No need for formalities now, not with the army preparing once more for a long and arduous march.

Bellick walked into the chapel, leaving his escorts on the front steps with the others. As the dwarf expected, he found Luthien inside, crouched near one of the pews, talking quietly with a wounded man.

"Brandon of Felling Downs," Luthien explained when Bellick joined them.

The dwarf nodded deferentially, taking note that the man had lost an arm. He seemed comfortable enough, though, on the pew, which had been converted into three end-to-end beds.

Bellick looked all around. "Which are ours and which of Pipery?" he asked.

"All mixed together," said Luthien.

The dwarf turned a sly look on the young Bedwyr. "Your doing?"

"I'll take a bit of the credit," Luthien replied. "But it was Solomon Keyes who assigned the cots."

Bellick snorted and started away. "Partners in crime," he said quietly.

Three rows down, Bellick came upon a pew of four beds, all holding dwarfs. One lay out straight, but the other three were sitting, throwing dice and chatting easily. Their smiles came wide indeed when Bellick addressed them; one even shoved the sleeping dwarf.

"Let him rest," Bellick bade them, then to the others, "We're putting out this day, south along the river. Any of you fit to join in?"

All four moved to rise, but Bellick could see that none were ready for the road. "Keep your seats," the dwarf king instructed. He told the healthiest of the bunch that he was in charge. "We'll be running supplies through here," he explained. "Keep them watched, and come along when the four of you are ready.

"When you are ready!" Bellick reiterated more forcefully, noting the hopeful expressions that came over his eager warriors. "And not a moment before!"

Bellick moved on then, inspecting each cot, stopping to say a short prayer over those most seriously wounded, offering encouraging words to the others. He had just completed his rounds, telling Luthien not to tarry too long, when he was met at the chapel door by Solomon Keyes.

The young priest wiped his dirty hands and held one out to the dwarf king.

Bellick took it, but turned it over instead of shaking it, taking note of the mud on the fingers. "You've been burying the dead," the dwarf stated.

"I have set others to the task," Keyes replied. "I have been offering final prayers, consecrating the sites."

"What of the one-eyes?" the dwarf asked, a hint of a challenge in his gruff voice. "Have you any prayers for them?"

"We built a communal pyre," Keyes replied indignantly, "and burned them. And I did pray for their souls."

Bellick's bushy eyebrows rose.

"I prayed that they would learn the error of their ways in the afterlife, and that they would find redemption."

"You're fond of them, are you?"

Now it was Keyes who gave a very dwarvish snort. "I hold no fondness for the ways of cyclopians," he replied. "But that does not mean that I hate the individual one-eyes."

"Perhaps some things are worth hating," offered Luthien, coming to join the pair.

"Perhaps I have no hate in my heart," Keyes replied easily.

"They beat you up good," Bellick reminded him. Keyes merely shrugged.

Luthien studied the man for a long moment and found that he was a bit jealous. He admired Keyes, not only for finding the courage to trust in the Eriadorans, but for holding such a generous heart.

"You are marching this day?" Keyes asked Bellick. "Surely your soldiers are weary from the fight, and the sun will set in a mere two hours."

"We've got no time to be tired," Bellick replied. "The road ahead is long, and every moment we waste gives Greensparrow more time to set his defenses."

"I will be ready to go in twenty minutes," said Keyes unexpectedly. Both Luthien and Bellick stared at him wide-eyed.

"You shall encounter many villages lining the road to Warchester," the priest explained. "Many in Pipery have kinfolk there. We do not want them killed."

"I thought you were to help with the wounded," said Luthien.

"I have enough people, trusted people, set in place to care for the wounded here," Keyes replied. "I, and a select handful of others, see our place in the march with King Bellick." He looked to the south. "I will save more lives out there than in here."

It took Bellick a few minutes to sort out the unexpected news, but the dwarf soon agreed. If Keyes could help weaken the defenses of the other villages half as much as he had done in Pipery, the road to Warchester would be swift and without great cost.

Luthien's elation was even greater, for he saw not only the tactical advantage of having such emissaries, but the moral one as well. With the Pipery spokesmen along, the number of deaths on both sides was sure to be reduced.

The young Bedwyr's optimism was guarded, though. He didn't really know how much influence Keyes might command away from Pipery. He also realized that no matter how swift and easy the march, it would stall at Warchester, a great and fortified city, its defenses complete with its own wizard-duke.

Where, Luthien wondered again, was Brind'Amour?

Though she was completely drained by using the powerful spell she had spent so long in perfecting, Deanna Wellworth did not sleep for the rest of that night on the plateau. She sat beside the fire, which Brind'Amour enhanced with some minor magics, though he, too, was obviously exhausted. Deanna cradled Mystigal's head on her lap, watching Brind'Amour as he gradually drifted off to sleep.

What had she begun? Deanna had set events into motion that were now above her control; had gone against her king and mentor in a conspiracy that could not be hidden and could not be reversed. Even if she killed Brind'Amour this night—and the thought crossed her mind more than once—she would not be able to hide the truth from Greensparrow. Because of her, three more of Greensparrow's dukes were gone: one dead, the other two, Mystigal and Resmore, broken.

Deanna tried not to focus too tightly on the events of this night. In truth, it was but a logical continuation of the course she had started upon when she had used Taknapotin against Resmore in the mountains. Greensparrow would make contact with the banished demon, if he hadn't already, and he would learn the truth of Deanna Wellworth, and of Ashannon McLenny. In those courageous earlier decisions, Deanna's course had been set, and this night was as much about her own survival as it was about helping Brind'Amour.

The old wizard awakened soon after the first slanting rays of dawn touched his face.

"He will live, I believe," Deanna said, indicating Mystigal, who was still unconscious.

"But his magic is no more," Brind'Amour replied, ending with a profound yawn. "The cord of magic within him has snapped."

"As with Duke Resmore?"

Brind'Amour chuckled, amazed at how perceptive this Deanna could be. His smile did not last very long, though, as he considered what he feared might be potential trouble. "What of the duke of Eornfast?" he asked bluntly.

"His business here was finished, and so he left," Deanna answered simply.

There was much more to it than that, Brind'Amour believed—and feared. Ashannon's demeanor had been aloof, almost icy. The duke of Eornfast had apparently gone along with Deanna's ploy, but was it because he agreed with her decision, or did he simply have no choice? Or even worse, Brind'Amour had to fear, did he have ulterior motives?

The old wizard's doubt showed clearly on his wrinkled face.

"Trust in Ashannon McLenny," Deanna begged. "He is a difficult one at times, but he holds no love for any who might claim rulership over his beloved Baranduine, be it Greensparrow or Brind'Amour."

"I never made such a claim," Brind'Amour was quick to respond.

"But shall you if your war goes well?"

Brind'Amour had to work hard to try and see things from Deanna's desperate point of view, in order to avoid insult at the remark. "Never have I claimed rulership over Avon!" he insisted. "Nor has any of Eriador at any time. When Bruce MacDonald ruled Eriador united, and had a disorganized Avon at his bidding, he never claimed anything but friendship to his kin from Baranduine."

"It is irrelevant anyway," Deanna said quietly. "All that matters is what Ashannon believes."

"And what does he believe?"

Deanna shrugged. "He agreed to banish his demon," she said with confidence, "and he has done so. And this was as much his plan as it was mine own. He has been a friend for many years."

"But would it not be in his interest to see Greensparrow weakened?" Brind'Amour reasoned. "The more difficult the war for Avon's king, the more easily Baranduine might slip from his grasp."

Again Deanna only shrugged. "We will have our answers soon enough," she said. "Now I must get back to Mannington to make my report to Greensparrow."

Brind'Amour looked skeptically at Mystigal, wondering what Deanna might be thinking to do with the broken wizard.

"I should like it if you would accompany me," Deanna said.

Brind'Amour's surprise was genuine.

"There is much we need to discuss," the duchess went on.

"Planning for the time after Greensparrow?"

Deanna chuckled. "We have much to do before we can ever hope for that," she replied. "For now, there are things you must know, and proof I must offer of my integrity in this matter."

Brind'Amour didn't disagree. For all he knew, this entire situation was some sort of an elaborate ruse designed to entice him into the confidence of conspirators who cared nothing for Eriador. He gave a long look to the towering mountains, wondering what progress Luthien and Bellick had made, wondering if Pipery had yet fallen.

Then he rose and stretched, and he and Deanna worked together, joining their strength to open a magical tunnel to the south.

Just a short while later, Mystigal was resting comfortably on a bed in Deanna's private quarters, while Deanna took Brind'Amour to meet the living proof that she had turned against Greensparrow.

Selna seemed more than a little surprised to see her lady and the bushy-bearded man who accompanied her, and her jaw dropped low when Deanna introduced the stranger as the king of Eriador.

"Greensparrow was the savior of Avon," Deanna explained to Brind'Amour. "So it has been said for more than twenty years."

"Do not do this, my Lady," Selna begged, but when she looked into Deanna's eyes, she saw no compassion there.

"Tell King Brind'Amour the truth, dear Selna," Deanna said, her voice dripping with threat. "Else I will have to make you admit things as I did before."

Brind'Amour did not miss the blanch that came over the older woman. He put a hand on Deanna's shoulder. "Pray tell me, dear Lady Wellworth, what was it that you did to this handmaid?"

"When I banished Taknapotin, my demon, I knew that one of

Greensparrow's informants had been removed from my court," Deanna explained. "But only one. Thus did I visit dear Selna here."

"It is not delicate to use magic in such a way," Brind'Amour remarked, recalling his own magical exertions over Duke Resmore.

"Not pleasant," Deanna agreed. She looked directly at Selna. "But I shall do it again, as often as necessary."

Selna was trembling visibly. "It was Greensparrow," she blurted suddenly. "He killed them; he killed them all! That night! Oh, my Lady, why do you keep forcing me to remember that horrible night?"

"Greensparrow murdered my entire family," Deanna said, her voice strangely devoid of emotion.

"All but one," Brind'Amour remarked.

"I was kept alive only because Greensparrow feared that he would not be accepted as king," Deanna explained. She looked to Selna, motioning for the woman to elaborate.

"Though she was but a child, Greensparrow meant to put Deanna on the throne if necessary," the handmaid admitted, lowering her gaze, for she could not look Deanna in the eye. "He would control her every action, of course, and then, when she came of age, he would marry her."

Brind'Amour was indeed surprised that the plan to conquer Avon had been so very devious, and had worked out so perfectly neatly. Again the wizard thought of that past time and the decision for the brotherhood to disband and go to their deserved rest.

"It never came to that, of course," Deanna added, "for the people of Avon exalted in Greensparrow. They begged him to hold their kingdom together."

"Then why was Deanna allowed to live?" Brind'Amour asked, directing his question to Selna. He saw something here between the woman and Deanna, something that Deanna, in her outrage upon learning the truth, might be overlooking.

"Ashannon McLenny of Eornfast," Deanna answered sternly. "He took personal interest in me, even willingly entered Greensparrow's court as a duke and accepted a demonic familiar, like all of Greensparrow's wizard-dukes—save Cresis the cyclopian of Carlisle, who is too stupid to deal with such fiendish creatures. Ashannon was a wizard in his own right, and a friend of my father's. While he abhorred the thought of dealing with Greensparrow, he had learned that Baranduine would be Greensparrow's next target, and he had not the forces to resist."

Everything was falling into place for Brind'Amour now. He understood the cool demeanor of Ashannon McLenny, the fire of Deanna, and something else, a player here whom Deanna did not fully appreciate.

"And how did Ashannon McLenny learn of the coming invasion?" the wizard asked.

Deanna shrugged—then gasped in surprise when Selna answered, "I told him."

Deanna's shocked expression made the older woman squirm. "I betrayed my dear Avon," she admitted openly. "But I had to, my Lady! Oh, I feared Greensparrow, and what he might do to you. I knew that I had to protect you until the events became a thing of the past, until you were no more a threat to Greensparrow."

Brind'Amour's snicker stopped the woman short, and turned both sets of eyes upon him. "No threat, indeed!" the wizard laughed.

Deanna managed a smile at that, but Selna, torn beyond reason, did not. Brind'Amour understood Selna fully now; she was the ultimate peacemaker, the wrinkle-smoother, and that could be a dangerous thing to her allies in times of political intrigue. Selna had betrayed Greensparrow to Ashannon, and would now betray Deanna to Greensparrow if given the opportunity, because in her heart she only wanted things nice and neat, peaceful and orderly. Selna would do whatever she thought best to end conflicts and intrigue, but while that was admirable, the success of such a course depended upon the mercy of kings, a trait Brind'Amour knew to be scarce indeed among the noble-born. In short, Selna was a fool, an unwitting lackey, though her heart was not black with ambition. In looking at Deanna, and measuring her stern demeanor toward the woman, it occurred to Brind'Amour that Selna had probably already spied upon Deanna for Greensparrow on other occasions, and that Deanna knew about it. Thus, Selna was no more a threat, Brind'Amour realized, not with Deanna so near and so watchful.

"My biggest fear in waging war was the balance of magical power," Brind'Amour said openly after he and Deanna left Selna's room, with Deanna pointedly locking the door from the outside and casting a minor enchantment to prevent any divining by other wizards into the room.

"Treat her with mercy," Brind'Amour advised.

"I will keep her safe and secure," Deanna replied, emphasizing the last. "When all of this is over, I will give back to her her life, though it will be one far removed from my court."

"Now only two of Greensparrow's wizards remain," Brind'Amour said, satisfied at that, "and one, at least, is on my side, while the other, I would hope, shall remain neutral."

"On your side?" Deanna asked. "That I never said."

"Then you are at least against Greensparrow," the old wizard reasoned.

"I am the rightful queen of Avon," the woman said bluntly. "Why would I not oppose the man who has stolen my throne?"

Brind'Amour nodded and scratched at his huge beard, trying to figure out exactly how much value Deanna Wellworth would prove to be.

"And do not think that the balance of magical strength has shifted so greatly," the duchess warned. "Mystigal, Resmore, and Theredon were minor spellcasters, conduits for their demon familiars rather than great powers in themselves, and neither I nor Ashannon hold much power anymore, now that our familiars have been banished."

Brind'Amour considered the barrier Deanna had enacted on the plateau and thought that she might be underestimating herself, but he held the thought private. "Still," he said, "I would rather battle Greensparrow alone than with his wizards allied beside him."

"Our powers were great because of our relationships with our familiars," Deanna explained. "If we achieved a higher symbiosis with them, even our lives could be extended."

"As Greensparrow's was obviously extended." Brind'Amour realized where Deanna's reasoning led. Brind'Amour was alive in this time because he had chosen the magical stasis, but Greensparrow had remained awake through the centuries. By now, the man should have died of old age, something even a wizard could not fully escape.

"So Greensparrow and his familiar are very close," Brind'Amour went on, prompting Deanna to finish her point. "A demon, perhaps a demon lord?"

"So we once thought," Deanna answered grimly. "But no,

Greensparrow's familiar is not a demon, but another of the magical beasts of the world."

Brind'Amour scratched his beard again and seemed not to understand.

"He went into the Saltwash those centuries ago to find his power," Deanna explained. "And so he did find it, with a beast of the highest order."

Brind'Amour nearly swooned. He knew what creature had long ago dominated the Saltwash, and had thought that his brotherhood had destroyed, or at least had imprisoned the beasts, as he had sealed the dragon Balthazar deep in a mountain cave.

"A dragon," he said, all color leaving his face.

Deanna nodded grimly. "And now Greensparrow and the dragon are one."

"Cyclopians," Luthien muttered grimly, seeing the slaughtered horses strewn about the fields. A single farmhouse, no more than a shell, stood on a hill in the distance, a plume of black smoke rising from it.

Luthien was walking Riverdancer, alongside Bellick, Shuglin, and Solomon Keyes. He reached up and stroked the horse's neck, as if offering sympathy to Riverdancer for the scene of carnage all about them.

"It might be that they're making our task all the easier," Shuglin remarked.

"The folk of Dunkery Valley have never held love for the one-eyes," Solomon Keyes explained. "We tolerated them because we were given little choice in the matter."

"You are not so different from everyone else in Avonsea, then," Luthien said.

Further ahead on the road, the line parted to let a pair of riders, Siobhan and another of the Cutters, gallop through. They pulled up in front of Bellick and Luthien.

"A village not so different from Pipery," Siobhan reported. "Four miles ahead."

"Alanshire," Solomon Keyes put in.

"How strong a wall?" Bellick asked Siobhan, but again it was Keyes who spoke up.

"No wall," he said. "The buildings in the central area of town are close together. It would not be a difficult task for the folk to pile crates and stones to connect them."

Siobhan nodded her agreement with the assessment.

"And how many soldiers?" Bellick asked.

"I can get in there and find out," Keyes answered. He looked back over his shoulder and motioned to the other men of Pipery who had come along.

Bellick regarded Luthien, and the dwarf's expression showed that he was suspicious of letting the priest go ahead of them.

"I can enter at dusk," the young Bedwyr said in answer.

"And I will be there to meet you," said Keyes. "With a full report of what we might expect from Alanshire."

"Some would call you a traitor," Bellick remarked.

Keyes looked at him directly, and did not back down in the least. "I only care that as few men are killed as possible," he stated flatly.

The Pipery contingent rode off, four men and a woman sharing three horses. Bellick and the others went about the task of spreading the Eriadoran line to encompass the village. The dwarf king's instincts told him to attack that same day, but after the situation in Pipery, he deferred to Luthien and to Keyes. If the night's wait would make the fighting easier, then the time would not be wasted.

Luthien rode out at dusk, taking Shuglin with him at Bellick's insistence. The dwarf king didn't fully trust Keyes, and said so openly, and he decided that if the priest had arranged a trap for Luthien, sturdy Shuglin would prove to be a valuable companion. Besides, the crimson cape was large enough that it could camouflage the dwarf as well as Luthien.

The pair reached the outskirts of Alanshire with ease, moving along the more open streets beyond the blockaded center; Luthien was certain that they could have made it this far even without the shielding cape. Now Shuglin came out from under it, and Luthien dared to pull back the hood. Soon after, the pair came upon Keyes and another man, an older, gray-haired gentleman with perfect posture and the sober dress of a old-school merchant.

"Alan O'Dunkery," Keyes introduced him, "mayor of Alanshire."

"It is a family name," the man said curtly, answering the obvious question before Luthien or Shuglin could ask it.

"The firstborn sons are all named Alan," Keyes added.

The gravity in the priest's tone seemed to escape Shuglin, but it was not lost on Luthien. This town was named after Alan's family; it was even possible that the whole river valley had been named for the family O'Dunkery, and not the other way around. This was an important man even beyond the borders of his small village, Luthien realized, and the fact that Keyes had convinced him to come out and meet Luthien gave the young Bedwyr hope.

"Brother Keyes has given me assurances that Alanshire will not be sacked, nor pillaged, and that none of our men will be killed or pressed into service," Alan O'Dunkery said sternly, hardly a tone of surrender.

"We'll not fight any who do not lift weapons against us," Luthien replied.

"Except cyclopians," Shuglin grunted. Luthien turned a sharp gaze on the dwarf, but Shuglin would not back down. "We're not leaving one-eyes on the road behind us," he said with a determined growl.

Luthien allowed the pragmatic dwarf the final word on that.

"You'll find few behind you," Alan said calmly. "Most have fled to the south."

"Taking much of Alanshire's livestock and supplies with them," Keyes pointedly added, reminding Shuglin that there were potential allies here, or at least noncombatants.

"How many cyclopians remain?" Luthien asked bluntly, the first information he had requested. This was a delicate moment, Luthien knew, for if Alan O'Dunkery told him outright, the man would be giving away information that would help the Eriadorans. "And if they are to make a stand at the wall, warn well any of your men or women who desire to stand beside them. Our fighters will not distinguish, human or one-eye, in the press of battle."

Alan was shaking his head before Luthien finished. "All the cyclopians that remain are in that building," he said, pointing to a tall, square structure that anchored the southeastern corner of the inner village. "In hiding, I would suppose, but in any case we will not allow them to come out."

Shuglin nearly choked on that revelation.

The Eriadoran army entered Alanshire the next day. There was no fanfare, no warm greetings from the populace, so many people who had lost so much in the cyclopian exodus. But neither was there any resistance. Bellick set up his line around the cyclopian stronghold and made only a single offer to the one-eyes: that he would accept their surrender.

The cyclopians responded with force, hurling spears and brutish threats from every window. With Alan O'Dunkery's permission, the Fairborn archers set the structure ablaze, and the one-eyes were summarily cut down as they came haphazardly charging out of the various exits.

Alan O'Dunkery and Solomon Keyes met with Luthien, Siobhan, and King Bellick that same day to discuss the next town in line, the influential woman who ran it, and the general mood of the place.

For the people of northern Avon, the purpose of this war was simply to escape with as little loss as possible. Greensparrow had erred badly, Luthien believed, by not sending his army north to meet the invaders. These people felt deserted and helpless, and it was not realistic for the king of Avon to believe that they would offer any resistance to so overwhelming an invading force.

The march to Warchester rolled along.

"Mystigal *and* Theredon?" Greensparrow asked angrily. "Both of them are dead?"

"Do not underestimate the power that Brind'Amour brought to the plateau," Deanna Wellworth replied. "Strong was the ancient brotherhood."

The skinny, foppish king leaned back on his throne, scratching at his hairless cheek and chin. "You are sure that he is destroyed?"

"I am *not* sure," Deanna replied. "It is possible that the wizard's spirit escaped, though his body was charred to ashes. I cannot understand the tricks of those ancient wizards, and have seen enough of Brind'Amour to respect him greatly. But I suspect that we will hear no more of him in the near future. I am confident, my King, that the army of Eriador is without a leader."

The news should have been welcomed in Carlisle, but Greensparrow scowled ominously. Brind'Amour ducked low behind a tapestry, fearful that the Avon king would somehow see through the fog of Deanna's divining mirror and through his own invisibility spell. The duchess of Mannington was equally nervous, the old wizard knew, judging by the amount of time she had spent in front of that mirror composing herself before mustering the courage to call to her king. When Deanna finally did cast the divination, it was in a trembling voice that only gradually steadied as she repeated the summons.

"It is possible that I will get to Resmore and free him," Deanna went on, trying to keep the king's thoughts full of information and empty of prying questions.

It didn't work. "Where is Ashannon McLenny?" Greensparrow snapped.

"Gone back to Baranduine to organize against the Eriadoran fleet," Deanna answered without hesitation.

Greensparrow's dark eyes flickered, telling Deanna that he would be quick to check on that.

"The dwarfs and men of Eriador have crossed through the northernmost villages," Deanna reported truthfully, information that Greensparrow undoubtedly already possessed. "Their path is for Warchester, I believe. I will go there personally, in Theredon's stead, and make our stand."

No response.

"What aid will Carlisle send to me?" Deanna asked. "Cresis and the Praetorian Guards?"

Greensparrow snorted. "You have not heard?" he asked. "A second army makes its way southwest from Princetown. Even now they approach the gap between Deverwood and the Iron Cross."

Behind the tapestry, Brind'Amour quietly sighed in relief.

"I will need Carlisle's garrison to deal with them," Greensparrow finished. "Warchester's forces, along with your own, should prove ample to destroy whatever has come south through the mountains.

"And I must keep my eyes to the river south of Carlisle," the king admitted. "The Eriadoran fleet in the west will be bottled in the straits and destroyed, without doubt, but another fleet has turned south of the Five Sentinels."

"And you have no ships left to stop them?" Deanna dared to ask, though she made sure that no trace of hope entered her voice.

Greensparrow scoffed. "I have thrice their number laying in wait," he said, "led by my finest sea captains. Still, if one or two of the rebels should slip through my galleons, I must be ready for them. Thus you are on your own, Duchess Wellworth," he said imperiously, signaling that the conversation was nearing its end. "Turn them back, or better, destroy them all. It will be far better if there are no organized defenders awaiting our triumphant return to Caer Mac—to Montfort!"

Greensparrow waved his hands and the image in the mirror clouded over and dissipated into nothingness. The glass quickly cleared and Deanna sat staring at her own reflection.

"So far, so good," Brind'Amour said hopefully, coming visible as he stepped out from behind the tapestry.

Deanna shook her head. "He will find a path to Taknapotin, who was my familiar demon," she explained. "Or he will make contact with the fiends of Mystigal or Theredon. We'll not hide the truth for long, I fear."

Brind'Amour nodded, unable to disagree, but he did walk over and put a comforting hand on Deanna's shoulder. "Long enough," he said. "You did well, Duchess, to deflect his curiosity, keeping him busy enough with the truth to have no time to unwind the lies. By the time Greensparrow understands that I live on, and that he has no remaining wizard allies in his cause, it will be too late."

"Even if he discerns such information this very night?" Deanna asked grimly.

Brind'Amour had no reply. The army was fast approaching Warchester, the fleet was sailing hard into the Straits of Mann. Mannington's many warships were already out at sea and Deanna could not possibly recall them without alerting Greensparrow to the truth. Even if Greensparrow learned the truth, even if all of Avon and a hundred dragons rose against the invaders, there was no turning back.

THE STRAITS OF MANN

The ugly little yellow pony skittered right, and then left, working hard to compensate for the rocking motion of the rough sea. Oliver seemed quite content up on Threadbare's back, though. His cheeks were rosy, his eyes bright, a far contrast from his last sea voyage, which he spent mostly at the rail.

"My horse, he likes the water," the halfling quipped to Katerin, whenever she happened by. She merely shook her head in disbelief.

The woman had little time to pause and consider the always-curious halfling, though, for the ship, *Dozier's Dream*, and the forty others sailing about it, would soon round a bend along the northwestern coast of Avon, moving into the narrowest part of the Straits of Mann. The stronghold of Eornfast lay less than twenty miles across the channel and Mannington just a few miles more on this side of the dark waters.

The lead ship, barely two hundred yards ahead of *Dozier's Dream*, hadn't even fully executed the turn when the enemy was revealed. Balls of flaming pitch streamed through the air, sputtering into the water all about the leading Eriadoran vessels. Crews tacked hard, turning out to the wider waters, dropping the sails to battle mast on those ships that could not escape.

"Katerin, to me!" cried old Phelpsi Dozier from the wheel.

Katerin rushed over to join with the weathered old mariner. This was his ship, the command given out of respect to Port Charley's oldest sailor, but Phelpsi was wise enough to understand and admit to his limitations. "Get 'em ready!" he said to Katerin. The old man paused when he glanced behind the woman, and like Katerin, shook his head. "And will ye get down from that stupid pony!" he yelled at Oliver.

"Horse!" Oliver corrected, and when Threadbare, as though the pony understood the old man's insults, stomped hard on the deck, the halfling promptly added, "And my Threadbare is not stupid!"

Most of the ships were turning to the west, putting out away from the coast, and as they sailed around the bend, Katerin saw the truth of their enemy. At least as many Avon sails were up to match the Eriadorans, forty to fifty war galleons, no doubt all manned by experienced crews, cyclopian and human. Katerin's fellows were skilled seaman, but only a handful in the entire Eriadoran fleet had ever waged battle upon ships of this size and caliber.

Where they were lacking in skill, though, the Eriadorans were determined to make up in sheer courage. So it was then for Katerin. She saw many ships turning out, and many Avon ships angling to intercept. The leading Eriadoran galleon on this side of the channel, though, would soon be surrounded, with nowhere to run. The ship took a flaming hit, then another, and the crew was soon too busy battling fires to consider the fast-closing Avonese warships.

Katerin called for full sail, straight on.

From his unusually high vantage point, Oliver saw what she meant to do, and recognized the risk that the woman of Hale was so willingly accepting. "Why do I always pick crazy-type peoples for my friends?" the halfling lamented.

"So says the halfling sitting on a pony on the deck of a ship," Katerin was quick to reply.

"Horse," Oliver corrected.

"If you sit up there that you might look important, then act important," Katerin scolded. "Put the archers in line, port side, and tell them to hold their shots until we're close enough to jump across. Same for the catapult crew!"

Oliver nodded, then paused, staring blankly at Katerin.

"The left side," the woman explained.

"I knew that," Oliver remarked, gingerly turning Threadbare about and clip-clopping off down the deck.

"Left," Katerin said again after him.

The lead Eriadoran exchanged heavy fire—catapult, ballista, and bow—with two Avon ships, one on either side. None of the three were sailing; none dared unfurl a sail in that barrage of bolt and flame. The rough tide battered the outer Avon ship the hardest, that one being to the starboard of the Eriadoran and thus the furthest out from the coast. Waves rolled against the Avonese relentlessly, driving both it and the Eriadoran toward shore and forcing all three of the ships even closer together.

Katerin tried to gauge her distance, and the speed of the drifting trio. She honestly didn't know if she could get between the Eriadoran and the Avon ship closest to shore.

"Ye've got the courage of a cuda fish," old Phelpsi Dozier remarked in her ear. "Or the brains!" he added with a snicker.

Katerin truly liked the old man, was even coming to love him. She had met Dozier on her first trip to Port Charley, when she was serving as an emissary for Luthien in the days when the revolution loomed no larger than the city walls of Caer MacDonald. Anyone looking at Phelpsi would think him frail, and perhaps simple, and yet he had managed to trap both Katerin and Oliver in the hold of his private boat, and now, with death staring them all in the face, he was as strong a shoulder as Katerin had ever known.

He continued to chuckle aloud, even when the Avon ship, realizing what *Dozier's Dream* meant to do, began firing at them, even when one crossbow quarrel cracked into the wood of the mainmast, barely a foot over Phelpsi's head. "Cyclopians never could shoot well!" the old man howled.

Katerin gained resolve from the snickering old Phelpsi, and used that strength to focus on her task. The tide pushed her ship relentlessly to port, and Katerin had to continually correct the course. Some rigging tore free and one of the sails began flapping wildly, but the damage could not slow the ship's momentum.

With only twenty yards separating them, it became apparent that *Dozier's Dream* simply would not fit between the vessels.

"Pull the reins!" Oliver cried to Katerin. "Or pull whatever a ship might have!"

"Get down from the pony," Katerin warned. She turned more to port, not wanting to clip the other Eriadoran, though the new angle put them even more in line with the Avon galleon.

"I am safer up here!" Oliver cried.

A barrage of arrows led the way for the charging Eriadoran ship; the catapult let fly, skipping a heavy stone across the Avon ship's decking, and *Dozier's Dream* crashed in, skimming the length of the Avon galleon. Rigging on both ships tangled and fell. Mast crosspieces smacked together and splintered.

Threadbare went into a short hop, landed firmly, and Oliver sailed over the pony's head, diving into a somersault, then a second, a third, even a fourth, along the deck, before he finally managed to stagger to his feet. He immediately turned toward Katerin, but overbalanced and fell headlong to the planks.

"Do not even speak it!" the halfling warned, but Katerin was paying him no heed, had no time to think of Oliver. Arrows buzzed the air all about the woman, and though *Dozier's Dream* was still moving forward, still crunching wood before the two ships settled in a tangled mess, the cyclopians were already coming over their rail.

Bolstered by the grateful cheering of the other Eriadoran crew, the crew of *Dozier's Dream* met the cyclopian charge, first with a volley of arrows, then with swords. Oliver regained his seat on Threadbare and plowed into a trio of one-eyes, knocking one into the churning water between the vessels.

One of the brutes recovered quickly, but hesitated before it rushed in at Oliver, obviously stunned to see someone riding on a ship! "Hey," the brute bellowed, "why is you up on that ugly yellow dog?"

In response, Oliver kicked Threadbare into a short hop, knocking the brute to the deck. Threadbare came on immediately, trampling the cyclopian, finally stopping with its back legs straddling the brute.

"Horse!" Oliver corrected. "But I am sure that you can see that now, from your better angle."

The cyclopian uncovered its face long enough to reach for its fallen sword. Before its hand ever got close, though, it had to cover once more, as Oliver placed his hat over Threadbare's rump, a signal he had long ago taught the pony, and the intelligent mount responded by kicking out, and then trampling the unfortunate cyclopian once again.

"A pretty horse, would you not agree?" Oliver asked.

"Ugly dog!" howled the cyclopian.

"They are so very stubborn," Oliver lamented, putting his hat back over Threadbare's rump, prompting the pony to action.

"Pretty horse!" the cyclopian yelled repeatedly, whenever it could seize a breath. It was too late for the brute to exact mercy from Oliver, though. The halfling kept his hat in place long enough for Threadbare to silence the cyclopian forever.

Those precious moments had put the halfling in a tenuous position, though. Glancing all about, Oliver soon realized that more cyclopians had come over to his ship than remained on the other. With his typical logic guiding the way, the halfling prodded the wonderful pony into a leap over the rails.

Threadbare hit the deck of the Avonese ship running, turning at Oliver's bidding toward the door of the cabin under the high rear deck, a door that had been smashed in by the catapult shot.

A huge and fat cyclopian came out of that hole, shaken and wounded, but still ready for battle, holding a gigantic mallet across its belt. Its bulbous eye widened even more, though the one-eye showed no fear when it took stock of Oliver and his pony thundering across the deck. The fat brute braced itself, legs wide apart, and smiled wickedly.

Oliver sincerely wondered if this had been a wise course. Considering the damage caused by the bouncing catapult ball, the halfling had figured the cabin to be empty—of living cyclopians, at least—offering him a fine place to relax, perhaps even to find a bit of wine and cheese.

Now he was committed. His first instinct was to continue the charge straight on, right into the brute, but he feared that this tremendous one-eye might outweigh both him and his pony combined! He pulled Threadbare to a light trot instead, bent low, and whispered into the pony's ear.

Oliver kicked hard on Threadbare over the last few paces, gaining a sudden burst of speed. The cyclopian howled and braced itself, but as quickly as he had started the charge, Oliver stopped it, falling off to the side, then dropping into a running crouch right under the belly of his pony.

On cue—Oliver's rapier tapping the pony's chest—Threadbare reared, kicking at the one-eye. The brute was too engaged to take note of the halfling as he ran out from under the pony and scampered right between the cyclopian's wide-spread legs.

Oliver fell into a roll and turned about as he regained his feet, rushing right back in, double-sticking with rapier and main gauche. Both blades bit hard, one on each side of the cyclopian's buttocks, and the brute reflexively skipped forward, right into the yellow pony's flailing forelegs. The cyclopian threw up its burly arms and frantically ran to the side, confused and battered. Threadbare chased it every step, biting at the back of its neck.

"I do hope that you can swim," Oliver remarked dryly as the cyclopian slammed against the rail, doubling over it, but catching itself quickly.

Threadbare never slowed, lifting his head high and ramming the brute right through the rail. The victorious pony reared again and neighed excitedly, then turned about to face his halfling rider.

"Join me for a spot of tea?" Oliver asked, motioning to the empty cabin.

The yellow pony snorted.

Oliver looked about and gave a great sigh. The fight was on in full, mostly on the decks of *Dozier's Dream*, and it remained fierce, though his side was obviously winning. "Very well, my equine conscience," the halfling said.

Threadbare hopped and Oliver ducked fast, as a crossbow quarrel split the air above his head. Then the halfling dodged to the side as a cyclopian fell over the rail of the poop deck, dropping dead to the main deck at Oliver's feet. The halfling looked back to regard Phelpsi Dozier, the ancient man obviously enjoying himself, patting an old crossbow, nodding and grinning wide, though few teeth remained in his mouth.

The ring of steel echoed across the decks of all four ships for more than half an hour, and when the fighting sorted itself out at last, the cyclopians were beaten, though many Eriadorans had been lost. Out in the deeper waters, the sailors from Eriador fared even worse, being outmaneuvered by the more skilled Avonese galleon crews.

Katerin organized what was left of the two crews, enough sailors to lightly man two ships. Unfortunately, the only ship of the four that could quickly put back out to sea was the Avonese vessel on the starboard side of the outer Eriadoran. Planking was put in place, and the crew went to work, changing the colors, untangling the rigging, and sorting out their positions. They left the three tangled ships, their own dead, and more than six hundred slain cyclopians behind, caught the wind in their sails, and moved out bravely to the west, into the crossfire of wild battle.

The fighting raged for several more hours, more men and brutes falling from sheer exhaustion than from arrows. Of the eighty-seven ships that had engaged, seventeen were either sunk or sitting helplessly, colors struck in surrender, drifting on the waves and wakes of passing ships.

And more than half of those seventeen were Eriadoran.

Katerin held out hope that they still might win out, but she realized that her fleet would be far weaker when it sailed out the southern mouth of the Straits of Mann, too diminished to be much of a factor even if they ever did reach the Stratton River and the seawall of Carlisle.

But they had to fight on, the determined woman realized, because every Avon ship that slipped under the waves was one fewer raider to strike at Port Charley, or at Diamondgate, or even her own home of Isle Bedwydrin.

"The one-eyes're good," old Dozier remarked, standing between Katerin, who was at the wheel, and Oliver, who remained atop his pony.

In truth, the pilots of the Avonese vessels were almost exclusively human, but Katerin could not disagree with Phelpsi, as much as she hated giving any credit at all to wretched cyclopians.

"There is an old Gascon saying," Oliver interrupted. "My Papa halfling, he once told to me, 'A fight is first of skill, then of heart.' And he also told to me," the halfling went on, striking a heroic pose for emphasis, " 'A one-eye, his chest is big, but his heart is oh so small!' We will win."

The simple confidence in the halfling's tone as he spoke the last three words, "We will win," struck Katerin profoundly. With a determined growl, she found the angle to intercept the closest Avonese vessel and daringly called for full sail.

Katerin took care this time not to entangle; there were simply too many free Avon ships for any Eriadoran to get caught up with one. Her crew was now much larger than before, more than four hundred strong, and as the ship slipped across the prow of the Avon vessel, the barrage of arrows raking the decks of the enemy ship took a mighty toll, including a score of bolts that cleaned out the two men and one cyclopian standing near the wheel.

Katerin's crew cheered her on; the catapult got off yet another shot as the daring woman cut the ship into a sharp one-eighty turn, bringing her around before the Avonese could replace their helmsmen and properly react. This time Katerin cut across the Avonese galleon's stern, and the volley started earlier, cleaning out the cyclopians, archers, and catapult crew from the poop deck. The Eriadoran archers got off a second shot, then a third, as the ship slipped past, and the catapult waited until the optimum moment to slam a ball of flaming pitch against the Avonese mainmast, which went up like a great candle.

Again the reply from the Avonese vessel was weak and without consequence, and Katerin knew better than to give this enemy a third try at her ship with her sails so very vulnerable. She took the galleon away, sails full of wind. Fighting against so many in such tight and dangerous waters was reckless, she knew; one ball of pitch could turn her entire deck into a conflagration, one flaming arrow could destroy a mast.

"Perhaps we should drop to battle sail," Oliver offered as the speeding ship closed in on a pair of Avonese vessels.

"You are the one who always claimed that cyclopians were terrible with bows," Katerin replied. "They could not hit the side of a mountain, so you said."

Oliver looked up and it seemed to him that those stretched sails were larger targets than any mountain. He regarded stubborn Katerin and shook his head helplessly.

Katerin didn't have to look at him to understand the stare, but she accepted the look and the risk. Now was the time for daring, even desperation that bordered on recklessness. She spotted a pair of Avonese vessels and angled accordingly.

Even determined Katerin had to back off, though, when she realized that the two galleons had spotted her and were calling back and forth, coordinating their response. With a frustrated snarl, Katerin cut hard to port, turning her ship low in the water. Her crew let fly, so did the Avonese, but the vessels were still too far apart and none of the three took hits of any consequence.

Katerin's frustrated expression melted into a grin a few moments later, though, when her crew began to cheer wildly. A trio of Eriadoran ships had come in at the Avonese from the other side when they had been intent on Katerin's speeding ship, and the Avonese had not been able to react appropriately. Both tried to turn their broadsides to the new threat, but they had gone in opposite directions and had actually tangled together. Now the crews of the two Avonese vessels were more engaged in fighting flames than in fighting Eriadorans, while the three Eriadoran vessels began to circle, archers and catapults pounding away. They pumped hundreds of arrows and dozens of balls of pitch and heavy stones into the Avonese galleons before more enemy warships sailed in, forcing the three Eriadorans to flee.

So I will be the taunting mouse for the Avonese cats, Katerin thought. She would be the distraction, the daring, darting little mouse, trying hard to stay out of the cat's claws, while her companion vessels found the openings left in her speeding wake.

Of the next eight ships that struck colors or filled with water, six were Avonese.

The spirits of all the Eriadoran crews began to rise, bringing new energy to continue the fight as the sun began its western descent. Katerin's spirits were perhaps highest of all, the fearless woman full of energy, full of the fight for Eriador. She would continue her wild run until one of her sails went down, she determined, and then she would find an Avonese ship to ram, that she might keep up the fight.

Something about the tone of Oliver's groan gave her pause, though, as profound a lament as the fiery young woman had ever heard. She looked to the halfling and then followed his gaze out to the north, the starboard side.

There she saw the end of the invasion, the doom of her fleet: a solid wall of sails, it seemed, lining the horizon. The vessels were not galleon size, but neither were they little fishing boats. "How many?" Katerin gasped. A hundred?

"Green flag!" cried a crewman straddling the mainmast, sighting the new fleet as he was trying to repair some of the rigging damage. "White-bordered!"

Katerin was not surprised. She had expected these newcomers, though not in such numbers. "Baranduine," she muttered hopelessly.

Phelpsi Dozier ambled over. "Not bad folks, the Baranduiners," he said. "Not like these damned cyclopians! I seen 'em often in the open waters. Might be they'd accept an honorable surrender."

The mere mention of the word sent Katerin's teeth to grinding. How could they surrender, thus laying open the entire western coast of Eriador? What would Brind'Amour and his forces do if

Greensparrow walked in the back door and flattened Caer MacDonald?

There came a burst of billowing orange smoke on the deck right before the wheel, an eruption out of nowhere, it seemed, and after the initial shock, Katerin thought she might get her answer. Had Brind'Amour come personally to her ship to speak with her?

When the smoke cleared, though, the woman saw not Brind'Amour, but another man, middle-aged, but undeniably handsome. His dress was practical for the weather and rigors of the sea, but fashionable and showed that the man was not wanting.

"My greetings," he said politely, giving a sweeping bow. His eyes locked on Oliver, the halfling all in his finery—purple cape, green hose and gauntlets, and wide, plumed hat—sitting astride Threadbare. "I am Duke Ashannon McLenny of Eornfast on Baranduine."

Katerin and old Dozier stared open-mouthed.

"And I am not amused by your show of silly wizard tricks," the halfling proclaimed, never at a loss for words. "Etiquette demands that you ask permission before you board a ship."

That brought a smile to Ashannon's face. "There was little opportunity," he explained. "And in truth, yours is the third Eriadoran ship I've boarded already. I must speak with a woman, Katerin O'Hale by name, and a man of Port Charley who is called Dozier, and a halfling . . ." His voice trailed off as he continued to stare at the most-curious Oliver.

"You would be Oliver deBurrows," Ashannon reasoned, for there simply couldn't be two such halflings in all of Avonsea!

"And I am Katerin O'Hale," Katerin interrupted, finding her tongue—and her anger. Her hand went immediately for the hilt of her belted sword. This was one of Greensparrow's wizard-dukes standing before her, and considering her past experiences with these men, she figured that Ashannon's demon ally wouldn't be far away.

"Fear not," Ashannon assured her. "I have not walked into your midst as an enemy. Some consider me a fool, perhaps, but I am not."

"Why are you here?" Oliver had to ask.

Ashannon swept his hand out to the north, forcing them all to look again to the incoming fleet. "A hundred warships," he began.

"You come asking for surrender," Katerin said grimly, and she wasn't certain that she could refuse such an opportunity. The Baranduine ships were fast closing on a group of several Avonese vessels, whose mostly cyclopian crews were standing at the rail, cheering wildly.

Ashannon smiled. "You will see," he said, turning to the north.

By the end of the first volleys, balls of smoking brown earth that exploded when they landed and scores and scores of arrows, most of the cyclopians on those three Avon ships were dead and fires raged on each of the galleons.

Katerin, Dozier, and Oliver snapped blank stares on the duke of Eornfast.

"I have met with Brind'Amour," Ashannon explained. "Baranduine is no friend to King Greensparrow. Pass the word to your fleet," he instructed. "I warn you, any of my ships that are attacked will respond." With a burst of smoke, the man disappeared, and a similar puff of smoke rising from the midst of the Baranduine fleet told the three startled companions which ship Ashannon marked as his flagship.

The fight was over hours later, in the dark, with thirty Avon galleons scuttled and ten others sent running, and a weary and battered, but now tripled, invasion fleet ready to move on. The Baranduiners sent skilled seamen to aid the Eriadorans, and gently passed over some peat bombs, the brown earthen balls that would violently burst apart upon impact.

Katerin and Oliver readily accepted Ashannon's invitation to board his flagship and sail beside him, the two of them intrigued and full of hope.

The fleet, more than a hundred strong, crossed out the southern end of the Straits of Mann, past the lights of Mannington, before the dawn.

Chapter 26

THE NIGHT OF THREE ROUTS

Though he had never been in this region before, Luthien Bedwyr needed no map to tell him which city was next in line. The Eriadoran army had thundered across a hundred miles and a dozen villages since coming out of the mountains. Resistance had been light, even nonexistent in some places, as the cyclopians—particularly the Praetorian Guards who had been routed out of the Iron Cross—continued to flee to the south, pillaging supplies as they went. That rowdy retreat had played well into Luthien's hands, turning the populace against Greensparrow. And with the help of Solomon Keyes and Alan O'Dunkery and other important Avonese, there had been minimum loss of human life to either side.

But now . . .

Luthien walked Riverdancer to the top of a small hillock. He peered south in the waning light of the day, following the silver snakelike Dunkery until it widened and dispersed into a shining blot on the horizon. There lay Speythenfergus Lake, and on its northern banks, along the strip of land between the Dunkery and Eorn Rivers, sat high-walled Warchester, its militia no doubt swelled by the thousands of cyclopians who had forsaken the villages to the north.

Below him on his right, Luthien's army plodded along, making steady progress. They would march long after sunset, setting their camp in sight of the mighty city.

How would the Eriadorans and mountain dwarfs fare against the fortifications of mighty Warchester? Luthien and his forces had never laid siege to a city, or tried to battle their way through towering walls of stone. They had won in Caer MacDonald by fighting house to house, but they had already been inside the city's walls when the battle had begun. They had won in Princetown by deception, luring the garrison outside of the city into a killing valley known as Glen Durritch. But how would they fare against a fortified city that expected them and had prepared for their arrival?

Luthien entertained the thought of convincing Bellick to go around Warchester, flanking Speythenfergus Lake on the east and marching straight out for Carlisle. The young Bedwyr understood the folly of such a plan, of course; they could not leave an entire cyclopian army behind them!

And so they had to go to Warchester, had to lay waste to the fortified city, and perhaps even turn west to the coast and attack Mannington as well. Not for the first time, and certainly not for the last, Luthien considered the apparent folly of their march and longed for the quiet rolling hills of Isle Bedwydrin.

"When Duke Theredon is not here, I am in command," the brutish cyclopian insisted in its sputtering lisp, poking its fat and grimy thumb into its barrel-sized chest.

Deanna Wellworth scrutinized the one-eye. She had always thought cyclopians disgusting and ugly, but this one, Undercommander Kreignik, was far worse than most. Its bulbous eye dripped with some yellow liquid, caking on the side of the brute's fat, oft-broken nose. All of Kreignik's teeth were too long and crooked, jutting out at weird angles over torn and twisted lips, and the cyclopian's left cheekbone had long ago been smashed away in a fight, leaving half of Kreignik's face sunken, and giving him a tilted, uneven appearance.

"I am a duchess, equal in rank to your missing duke," Deanna reminded, but Kreignik was shaking its ugly head before she ever finished.

"Not in Warchester," the brute insisted.

Deanna knew that she could not win this verbal battle. Since her arrival through a magical tunnel the previous night, she had been treated with outright disrespect. Like all of the other rightly paranoid wizards of Greensparrow's court, Theredon had put safeguards in place against the intrusions of any other wizards. The dead duke's orders to Kreignik, and probably to every ranking cyclopian below the one-eye, were unyielding; even Greensparrow himself would have trouble prodding the brute to comply. Kreignik likely wasn't the first cyclopian to rise to the rank of undercommander of Warchester. Men such as Theredon tested their subordinates by, for example, assuming the form of another duke, then challenging the loyalty of the cyclopian officers. Failure to follow Theredon's specific orders would mean a terrible, torturous death.

Kreignik had probably witnessed more than one such event. No threats and no logic that Deanna could use would sway the stubborn one-eye.

"I told you that Undercommander Kreignik would not fail at a critical time," came a call from behind the brute. Kreignik turned, and Deanna looked beyond the massive brute, to see Duke Theredon ambling down the hall.

Deanna winced at the sight. Brind'Amour, though he had altered himself to appear as Theredon, had the mannerisms all wrong, shuffling like an older man, and not walking with the confident and powerful gait of the strong duke.

"And you feared that my soldiers would not be ready!" the fake Theredon roared, clapping Kreignik on the back—an inappropriate action that made Deanna wince yet again. "Ready?" Brind'Amour roared. "Why, with all the cyclopians that have come down from the north, we are more than ready!"

Deanna noted the skeptical look on Kreignik's face and knew she had to do something to salvage the situation. "Why my dear Duke Theredon," she said with a laugh, "you have been drinking that Fairborn vintage I gave to you!"

"What?" Brind'Amour stammered, growing serious at the sight of Deanna, her lips drawn tight again as soon as the obviously mocking chuckle had ended. "Oh, yes," the old man improvised. "But not so much."

"I warned you of its potent kick," Deanna said, and Brind'Amour understood that she would have liked to really kick him then and there. "What good will you be in the coming battle?"

"What good?" the old wizard scoffed, and he assumed a more regal posture. "With the Praetorian Guards from the Iron Cross, I estimate that we outnumber the Eriadoran fools by nearly two to one. And we have the better side of the walls in our faces!" He snapped his fingers in the air before Deanna's unblinking eyes. "They could not take Warchester in a hundred years!"

Kreignik seemed to like that proclamation, so much so that the scowl melted from the ugly brute's face. Kreignik even dared to reach over and pat the imposter duke on the back, though Brind'Amour was quick to flash a scowl at the one-eye, backing it away.

"Perhaps they will not then attack," Deanna prompted. "But lay in wait in siege."

Brind'Amour laughed, and so did Kreignik, but Deanna was not amused. The plan, after all, had been to convince the cyclopian undercommander that retaining their forces in the city would be foolish and dangerous. Brind'Amour's words were true enough; even with Deanna and Brind'Amour working their magic, the Eriadorans had little chance of crashing through Warchester's fortified gate with the city so swollen by retreating cyclopians. Even if Luthien and Bellick somehow managed to enter and win out, their army certainly would be badly wounded, and with two hundred miles still to go to Carlisle.

Deanna's skin felt prickly as a wave of anxiety crept up about her. All of this seemed suddenly foolhardy; how could they hope to win out all the way to Carlisle? How could she, even with Brind'Amour and Ashannon, hope to defeat Greensparrow? The duchess firmly shook the thoughts away, reminding herself that Greensparrow's strength lay mostly in terror and in the hordes of cyclopians he had brought under his rule. Magic and demons and dragons were powerful weapons, but in the end measure, this war would be won by the resolve of the common soldiers and the cunning of their leaders.

Steadied once more, Deanna focused on the immediate task at hand, that of convincing Kreignik to go out from Warchester. She was about to try another course, when Brind'Amour abruptly stopped laughing.

"That is it!" the old wizard shouted in Kreignik's face.

The cyclopian backed a step, its expression twisted with confusion.

"Do you not see our opportunity?" Brind'Amour shouted, and danced about the corridor. "We can take the offensive, Kreignik," he explained. "We will go out onto the field and utterly destroy them. And we will catch this Crimson Shadow fool, and the fool Brind'Amour, too, if he is among their ranks. Oh, what gifts will King Greensparrow give to us when the Eriadorans are delivered to him!"

Kreignik didn't seem to buy it, though the brute had trouble hiding its intrigue at the possibility of such glory.

"We have no choice in the matter," Deanna quickly put in. "By all reports, there is a second Eriadoran army rounding the southern spur of the Iron Cross. If this army at our gates gets bogged on the fields outside Warchester, we can expect the second group to join up with them. Or worse, both armies will bypass Warchester altogether and march straight on to Carlisle."

"We will pursue them then," reasoned Kreignik. "We will catch them from behind and squeeze them against Carlisle's walls."

Brind'Amour draped an arm across the brute's wide shoulders. "Would you like to be the one who tells King Greensparrow that we willingly allowed the Eriadorans to get all the way to Carlisle?" he asked quietly.

The brute stood straight, as if slapped. "Catch them on the field!" he proclaimed. "Ten thousand Praetorians will go out this night!"

Brind'Amour tossed a wink Deanna's way, and the woman managed a slight nod and smile before Kreignik turned back to her. She noticed then that Brind'Amour went suddenly stiff, the grin flying from his face. He looked all about frantically, and Deanna had no idea what was so suddenly causing him such distress.

"The Fairborn wine," the old wizard stammered. "I must . . ." He gave a wail and ran off, leaving Deanna mystified.

Until a moment later, when King Greensparrow stalked around the corner at Deanna's back, flanked by an escort of five Praetorian Guards.

Deanna nearly fainted. "My King," she stuttered, dropping a respectful curtsy.

"What preparations have you made, Duchess Wellworth?" Greensparrow snapped. "And why have you not returned to Mannington, guiding the fleet against the Eriadorans?"

"I . . . I did not think so small an Eriadoran flotilla would prove a problem," Deanna explained. "My captains are more skilled . . . and Duke Ashannon will sail across the channel, no doubt." Deanna hardly knew what she was saying, was desperately trying to improvise. "The more immediate threat seemed this army. The speed and sureness of its approach has been remarkable—I could not leave Warchester unattended."

She noticed a frown grow on Kreignik's ugly face. The brute was not stupid. How could Deanna have been in on a "test" with Theredon, as the duke had claimed, yet now claim she thought Warchester had been unattended? Deanna's heart beat faster; it could all come tumbling down right here, right now. The under-commander said nothing, though, probably too afraid of Greensparrow's wrath should it speak out of turn.

Greensparrow mulled over the explanation for a moment, then nodded, though his dark eyes never blinked, and his gaze never left Deanna's eyes. "So you came into Warchester and assumed control," the king said.

"As we discussed," Deanna replied, resolutely not looking at Kreignik.

Greensparrow nodded and turned to Kreignik. "And what have you planned?"

"We will go out to destroy the enemy on the field," the under-commander replied.

Deanna held her breath, not knowing how Greensparrow would feel about such a daring move. The king, after all, understood that the Eriadorans could not possibly crush Warchester, especially since he believed that Brind'Amour was dead.

"This was Deanna's idea?" Greensparrow asked.

Deanna could tell by his suspicious tone that the king was prying for something. She wondered if Brind'Amour would reveal himself now, come out in open challenge to Greensparrow once and for all. Deanna felt faint with that possibility. Neither she nor the Eriadoran wizard had prepared for such an encounter; both were magically drained from their journey to the city, and Brind'Amour even more so from his impersonation. And to fight the Avon king in here, in the midst of an Avon stronghold, with more than fifteen thousand loyal cyclopians around him, was nothing short of foolish.

Kreignik straightened. "I only thought that . . ." it stammered. "The duchess was not . . . I mean . . ." Kreignik continued to stumble, even more so as Greensparrow's dark eyes flashed dangerously and the king began to wave his arms. Kreignik took a deep breath, visibly trying to sort out its thoughts, but before the brute got the next word out of its mouth, it was dead, lying in a smoldering heap on the floor. Deanna stared wide-eyed, and then turned her stunned gaze on Greensparrow, who stood shaking his head angrily.

Watching the action through a mirror in a side room far removed from the corridor, Brind'Amour, too, stared wide-eyed at the unexpected scene. The old wizard knew that he should break the connection—certainly he was taking a risk in divining so near to Greensparrow—but he feared that the Avon king had discovered them, that Deanna would need him. He got some relief when he glanced down to the yellow disenchanting powder he had set about the perimeter of the room the night before. Only the mirror was open to the palace, but even that was dangerous, Brind'Amour realized. He had detected Greensparrow quite by accident, by luck, and now he had to hope that the Avon king was not so fortunate. For Brind'Amour did not want a fight now, not here, not with Luthien oblivious to it all out on the field. At first he had considered throwing himself at the Avon king, in a desperate effort to finish this ugly business once and for all. That course would have gotten him killed, though, and Deanna, too, even if they managed to overcome Greensparrow. Brind'Amour lamented again the weakness of magic in these days. In times of old, if he and another wizard had fallen into a personal battle, then all the soldiers, human or cyclopian, in the area would have run for cover, would have been absolutely inconsequential in the magical fight. But now a sword could be a formidable weapon against a wizard, and those cyclopians standing defensively around Greensparrow certainly knew how to wield their swords!

So Brind'Amour could only watch and pray—pray that Deanna would make no mistakes, and that Greensparrow wouldn't happen to notice him.

"Cyclopians," the Avon king fumed. "This one's orders were explicit: only Duke Theredon Rees or myself could issue any commands concerning the Warchester garrison. Yet here he is, the fool, abiding by the requests of the duchess of Mannington."

"You disapprove of my plan?" Deanna asked, trying to keep the sincere relief out of her voice. "I thought that we had agreed—"

"Of course I do not disapprove," Greensparrow replied with a growling voice, obviously agitated. "I have Eriadorans coming at me from four sides. You destroy the middle here, while Ashannon crushes their flank in the straits, and the threat, if there ever was one, is ended.

"But do not think that your duties will be ended!" Greensparrow snapped suddenly, sharply, and Deanna jumped in surprise. "I expect the invaders to be crushed, slaughtered to the man, or dwarf, and then I charge you and Ashannon with our counterattack. Retrace Brind'Amour's own steps back to the north, while Ashannon sails to Port Charley. Your forces will meet in Montfort, which the upstarts call Caer MacDonald. Raise my pennant over the city once more, on your life!" He paused a moment, taking a full measure of the woman: recalling, Deanna knew, her failure in the Iron Cross. "Kill anyone who argues the point, and murder their children as well!" he finished, his eyes narrowing.

Deanna nodded with every word, glad that Greensparrow was still following his typically overconfident instincts, thoroughly relieved that he was too assured to suspect the treachery that she and Brind'Amour had attempted here in Warchester. Also, the king's orders left little doubt in Deanna's heart that she was following the correct course. When evil Greensparrow told her to murder children, he meant it.

He meant it as he had meant to murder Deanna's own brothers and sister that night in Carlisle.

It took all the woman's resolve and years of training for her to hold her thoughts private, and properly shield her emotions. She wanted to lash out at the evil king then and there, force Brind'Amour into the fight so that she could pay this wretched man back for the deaths of her family.

She grinned wickedly instead, nodding.

"You," Greensparrow snapped at one of his Praetorian Guard escorts. The brute immediately jumped forward, fearing a fate similar to that of Undercommander Kreignik.

"What is your name?"

"Akrass."

"Undercommander Akrass," Greensparrow corrected. "You are

to follow Duchess Wellworth's commands as you would have followed those of Duke Theredon Rees."

Akrass shook its head. "I cannot," the brute replied. "My orders are to stand by you, and you alone, to the death."

Greensparrow chuckled and nodded. "You have passed the test," he assured the brute. "But the test is no more, by my own words.

"Deanna Wellworth is the duchess of Warchester," he went on, then to Deanna, he added, "Temporarily."

This caught the five Praetorian Guards by surprise, and Akrass even dared to look back to the others.

Deanna nodded. "I will not fail in this," she said with clear resolve, and she meant every word, though her intended mission was not what King Greensparrow had in mind.

Not at all.

"You are leaving?" Deanna asked as Greensparrow suddenly swept away.

"I am off to the coast to see about Ashannon," he snarled.

Deanna was glad that he turned back to the corridor before realizing how pale her face suddenly went.

"You should fly to the east instead," she blurted, stopping Greensparrow short. He turned slowly to regard her.

"New information," she stammered, searching for something to tell this tyrant. "I fear that some Huegoths have joined in with our enemies. Their western fleet..."

Greensparrow's face screwed up with rage.

"I wanted to search it out more before speaking with you," Deanna tried to explain. "I cannot be certain. But now, I have other duties, more important." She straightened her shoulders, finding her courage. "You should fly out to the east and determine if the information is true. Ashannon will see to the Eriadoran fleet, and I will strike back to the north. We will await you in Montfort!"

Greensparrow let his gaze linger a bit longer on the woman, then turned and pushed through the Praetorian Guards.

Deanna nearly fainted with relief.

In a room not so far away, Brind'Amour sighed.

Luthien had heard the earlier reports that a great winged creature had landed on the fields south of Warchester. The descriptions had been vague—the army was still several miles from the city, and miles further from those southern fields—but the young Bedwyr could guess at what his scouts were talking about.

This time, he, too, spotted the beast, its great lizardlike form, widespread wings, and long, serpentine tail, as it flew far off to the south and east. Some on the hillock beside him called it a bird, but Luthien knew better.

It was a dragon.

Luthien's heart sank at the sight. He was one of the very few people alive in all the world who had faced a dragon before, and only dumb luck and the work of Brind'Amour had allowed him to escape. The young Bedwyr couldn't even imagine fighting such an enemy; he wondered if his entire army could even harm the great beast if it turned suddenly to the north and attacked.

Luthien shook that thought away; if such was true, then the dragon would have come north, breathing its fire and rending man and dwarf. The young Bedwyr looked back over his troops, and took heart. Let the wyrm come north, he decided, and they would put up such a barrage of arrows that the sheer weight of the volley would bring the beast down!

The dragon continued to the east, Luthien saw as he looked back, and was now no more than a speck on the distant horizon.

"Keep going," Luthien prayed quietly. He suspected that he would see this one again, though. It had landed south of Warchester, which meant that Greensparrow's allies included more than cyclopians and a handful of wizards.

"How could you tell him?" Brind'Amour asked, comfortable in his own form again when he and Deanna were alone in the locked and magically secured room.

Deanna held up her hands.

"Of the Huegoths," Brind'Amour explained impatiently, for she knew what he meant. "How could you tell Greensparrow of the Huegoths?"

Deanna shrugged. "It seemed the lesser evil," she replied casually. "If Greensparrow had gone to the west, as he had intended, then Ashannon and our fleets would be sorely pressed—likely destroyed even, when you consider the power such a wizard might exert over the cloth and wood of sailing ships. Even worse for us all, if Greensparrow flew west, he would likely discern the truth of it all. Flying east, he will spend many days confirming the information of the Huegoths, if they are as far offshore as you believe, days that we will need if we ever hope to get to Carlisle."

Brind'Amour was upset, but he understood Deanna's reasoning. There had to be a measure of truth within a web of lies, the wizard realized, and that truth had to be convincing. Deanna had thrown Greensparrow a bit of valuable information that she might keep his trust, something that she and Brind'Amour certainly needed. It was only that confidence Greensparrow held, in himself and in those he had subjugated, that had thus far kept him oblivious to the treachery. Still, it occurred to Brind'Amour that Deanna's goals and his own were not one and the same. Both wanted Greensparrow thrown down, but Brind'Amour didn't think that the duchess would shed many tears if the Eriadoran, dwarvish, and Huegoth forces were badly diminished in the effort.

He would have to keep a close eye on Deanna Wellworth. With that in mind, the wizard closed his eyes and began his transformation once more, assuming the form of Theredon Rees.

"Have you the strength for the illusion?" Deanna asked, drawing the wizard from his contemplations.

Brind'Amour stared at her blankly.

"Dusk is nearly upon us."

Brind'Amour nodded, catching on. Akrass was busy assembling the ten thousand who would go out from Warchester under cover of darkness.

"The mantle of Duke Theredon is ready to be donned," Brind'Amour assured her.

Deanna wasn't sure if that would even be necessary—or wise, since they would have to make up yet another story to satisfy the curiosity of Akrass. Greensparrow had publicly given her power over the entire Warchester garrison, after all, and Theredon was not needed.

Brind'Amour understood the same, but he wasn't about to let ten thousand cyclopians march out of Warchester under Deanna's control with his own forces so vulnerable if things were not handled just right. Not yet.

The pair left the room soon after to meet with Akrass, Deanna explaining quickly that since Theredon had returned—and wouldn't Greensparrow be pleased to learn that his duke was indeed still alive?—she was relinquishing command to him, but also that

Greensparrow's words concerning her own power still held, and she would serve as the duke's second.

Akrass believed it—what choice did the poor brute have?

They came out of the gates after sunset, the full moon rising in the east. "Theredon" and Deanna headed the procession, in step with the cyclopian Akrass, whose chest was swollen with pride. The one-eye wasted no time in beating any who ventured too near, or who showed even the least amount of disrespect.

Before they had gone very far, before the entire cyclopian line had even crossed under the huge gates, Brind'Amour put out a whistling call that was answered, a moment later, by a small owl, which flew down to the wizard's arm and cocked its head curiously.

Brind'Amour whispered into the bird's ear and sent it away, flying north with all speed.

"What do you do?" Akrass asked.

Brind'Amour scowled at him, reminding him that his newly granted power did not include questioning the duke of Warchester! The cyclopian lowered its gaze accordingly.

"Now we have eyes," Brind'Amour remarked to Deanna.

"Eyes and a plan," the duchess replied.

That plan was fairly simple: the cyclopians broke up into three groups, with three thousand going over the Dunkery River to flank the Eriadorans on the right, three thousand going over the Eorn River to flank the enemy on the left, and the remaining four thousand, including a fair amount of ponypig cavalry, going straight north, between the rivers, headlong into the Eriadoran encampment with the initial attack. The confusion caused within the Eriadoran army's ranks would turn to sheer panic, it was reasoned, as soon as the one-eyes came across the Dunkery and the Eorn, squeezing like a vise.

Of course, Brind'Amour and Deanna had other ideas.

Luthien, Bellick, and Siobhan were quick to respond when word reached them that a talking bird had entered the camp. The young Bedwyr prayed that this might be the work of Brind'Amour, even the wizard himself in a transformed body.

He was a bit disappointed when he found the owl perching on a low branch. It seemed oblivious, and though Brind'Amour often appeared that way, Luthien knew that this was not the wizard. Still there was no doubt that there was a bit of magic about the bird, for it was indeed speaking, uttering only one word: "Princetown."

"Brind'Amour has gone to Princetown?" Siobhan asked the bird.

"Princetown," the owl replied.

"At least we now know where the wizard has gone off to," Bellick remarked sourly, not thrilled to think that Brind'Amour would not rejoin them for their all-important attack against Warchester. As far as any of those in the camp knew, there was an enemy wizard ready to meet that charge.

Luthien wasn't convinced. He tried questioning the bird along different lines: "Are we to go to Princetown?" and "Has Princetown claimed allegiance with Eriador?" but all that the bird would reply was that one word.

Until Luthien and the other two turned to leave. Then the owl said suddenly, "Glen Durritch."

As one, the three turned back to the bird. "Princetown, Glen Durritch," grumbled Bellick, not catching on.

"Left, right, straight ahead," said the bird, and then, as though the enchantment put over the creature had expired, the owl silently flew off into the darkness.

Luthien's face brightened.

"What do you know?" Siobhan asked him.

"Only once have we gone against a fortified Avon city," Luthien replied. "And we won a smashing victory."

"Princetown," Bellick put in.

"But we did not actually battle against the city," Siobhan objected.

"We fought in Glen Durritch," said Luthien. Siobhan's face brightened next, but Bellick, who had come on the scene in Princetown near the end of the battle and really didn't know how things had fallen out so favorably, remained in the dark.

"Brind'Amour took the form of Princetown's Duke Paragor and sent the city's garrison out from behind the high walls," Luthien explained.

Bellick's gaze snapped to the south, toward Warchester. "You're not thinking . . ." the dwarf began.

"That is exactly what I am thinking," Luthien replied.

Siobhan called for the scouts to go out in force, and for the camp to be roused and readied for battle.

"This was a warning from Brind'Amour," Luthien insisted, joining Bellick as the dwarf continued to stare out to the south. "The garrison is coming out, and we must be ready for them."

For the three cyclopian groups, the one crossing the swift Dunkery had the most difficult time.

Even worse for the one-eyes, Bellick had realized that they would.

The cyclopian flank was split, a third already across the river, a third in the water, and the rest lining the eastern bank, preparing to cross, when the Eriadorans hit. The cavalry, led by Luthien and Siobhan, sliced down the eastern bank, while archers opened mercilessly on those brutes struggling in the water, their thrashing forms clearly illuminated by the full moon. At the same time, Bellick's dwarven charges overwhelmed those on the western bank, pushing them back into the river.

The waters ran red with cyclopian blood; even more brutes drowned in the swift current, their support lines chopped by dwarvish axes. Those one-eyes on the eastern bank were the most fortunate, for some of them, anyway, managed to run off into the night, screaming and without any semblance of order.

It was over quickly.

But though the rout was in full spate, the Eriadorans had just begun this night's work. Spearheaded by Luthien's cavalry, the force charged off to the south, determined to get to Warchester ahead of the remaining two cyclopian groups, to ambush them out on the field.

"It is empty!" Akrass roared, kicking at a bedroll—a bedroll stuffed with leaves and stones so as to appear full. Every fire in the vast encampment burned low, every blanket, every bedroll, covered nothing more than inanimate stuffing.

Before the cyclopian could even begin to express its outrage, the sounds of battle drifted in from the east, from the Dunkery.

"They have gone out to meet our flank!" yelled Brind'Amour, still in Theredon's guise but growing more weary by the moment.

Akrass called for formations, thinking to charge right off to the east and ambush the ambushers. With his duke's blessing, the undercommander did just that, so he thought.

The moon could be a curious thing when wizards were nearby. Simple spells of reflection could make the pale orb seem to shift its position. Similarly, spells of echo reflection could alter the apparent source of clear noise. And so the disoriented Akrass led his four thousand straight to the north instead of the east.

"Nice moon," Brind'Amour remarked to Deanna as they put their horses in line for the march, as the old wizard realized just how well Deanna had executed the enchantment.

"Simple trick," the woman replied humbly.

Brind'Amour was truly pleased. "Simple but effective."

The last of the Warchester formations trudged across the low and muddy Eorn without incident. They were too far away to hear the sounds of battle, or the rumble of the cyclopian thrust to the north, and so they, like Akrass's group, were caught completely by surprise when they happened upon the Eriadoran encampment, expecting to find the battle underway, but discovering nothing but empty bedrolls.

By that time, the fields to the east were quiet once more.

The cyclopian leader of this group, without Theredon or Deanna or even Akrass to guide it, ordered a full retreat, and so the force set out back down the Eorn, this time on the river's eastern bank. They looked over their shoulders every step, hoping that their comrades would come marching down behind them, but fearing that the charge from behind might come from the sneaky Eriadorans.

Their defensive posture was to the rear then, as in any good retreat.

Except that this time they got hit from the front, and then from both sides as the superior Eriadoran forces closed on them like the jaws of a hungry wolf. It took several minutes for all the one-eyes to realize that these were their enemies; many thought that they were being greeted, and then erroneously attacked, by the garrison that had remained at Warchester!

They figured out the truth eventually, those that were still alive, but by that time it was far too late. Confusion turned to panic; cyclopians ran off in every direction, though the dark silhouette of high-walled Warchester was clearly visible to the south. Some desperately called for the garrison to come out to their aid, but the one-eyes inside the high walls, with typical selfish cowardice, would not dare desert the defensible city to save their kin.

* * *

"Long enough," Brind'Amour and Deanna decided, though it was a moot point. The leading edge of the cyclopian force, Akrass riding among them, had come into a village—and recognized the place as Billingsby, a hamlet five miles north of Warchester.

Deanna trotted her horse ahead of the main group to meet with the undercommander as Akrass came thundering back from Billingsby.

"The Eriadoran wizard-king, Brind'Amour, has struck," she said in despair. "He has obviously deceived us and led us in the wrong direction!"

Akrass wanted to strike the woman; Deanna could see that.

"Greensparrow will blame me," Deanna said, intercepting the brute's intentions.

The furious cyclopian backed off immediately, figuring that if it attacked Deanna now, perhaps even killing her, Greensparrow's ire might fall squarely on its own shoulders.

"To Warchester!" the cyclopian undercommander howled, waiting for no commands from the wizards. Akrass galloped his pony-pig up and down the line, sweeping up the marching cyclopians in its wake, thundering back to the south.

By the time the battle was finished, the eastern sky had turned a lighter shade of blue, dawn fast approaching. Bellick's Cutter scouts came riding hard, informing the dwarf king that the third and largest force had swung about and was double-timing it back to the south, straight for Warchester.

King Bellick stroked his fiery orange beard and considered his options. His army was tired, obviously so, for they had fought two vicious encounters already. And with the daylight, and the warning cries that would no doubt come out from Warchester, it didn't seem likely that this third group would be caught so unawares.

Bellick split his forces, east and west, marching them out of sight of the city, with orders to let the one-eyes pass, then come in hard at the back of their line.

The men and dwarfs and Fairborn, bone-weary, covered in blood of kin and enemy, eagerly agreed.

The cyclopian line came in stretched thin, with the one-eyes too concerned with getting back to the safety of Warchester to consider their defensive posture. That march turned into an all-out rout when the Eriadorans appeared, striking hard at the rear flanks, chasing and killing the brutes all the way to Warchester's gates.

That was where Bellick and Luthien had determined to turn about for some much-needed rest, but unexpectedly, a moment later, the iron gates crackled with blue lightning—and then fell open wide.

For one horrible moment, Luthien feared that the entire Warchester garrison was about to come out at them. But then, as the lightning continued to crackle, consuming many Praetorian Guards standing near those gates, the young Bedwyr recognized the truth: that Brind'Amour had opened wide the city. All weariness washed from Luthien, and from the rest of the Eriadoran forces, with the presentation of such an opportunity. To Bellick's call, they charged ahead, howling and firing bows.

Chapter 27

THE WALLS OF WARCHESTER

The cavalry made the courtyard inside the gates and found it surprisingly deserted—even those one-eyes who had just reentered the city had fled for better ground. And that, Luthien saw with despair, would not be difficult to find. Warchester was surrounded not by one wall, but by several, all spiraling around the city proper and offering scores of defensible positions. Cyclopians were terrible with bows and even with throwing spears, but the defenders of the city were not all cyclopian, and Luthien could see just from this one area that those archers among the Avonese ranks would have many opportunities to fire their bows at the invaders. Luthien wished that he had the luxury of proper preparation, that he and Siobhan, Bellick, and some others could sit around a fire with a map of the city's interior and lay out organized plans. The young Bedwyr had been in enough large-scale battles to know the impossibility of that. He had pointed his forces in the right direction, but now, in the helter-skelter of pitched fighting, each warrior would have to make his own choices, each group would find new obstacles and would have to discern a way around them.

Luthien hated the prospects of this city fighting with so many miles yet to go, but the Eriadorans had gained the main gate, and this was an opportunity that simply could not be passed up.

Luthien prodded Riverdancer to his right, where the curving courtyard began to slope up. Most followed in his wake, some went to the left. Still others, mostly dwarfs, went straight ahead at the next wall, hoisting ladders or throwing ropes fixed with strong grappling hooks, then pulling themselves upward, fearless, seemingly oblivious to the many one-eyes who came to defend the high wall.

Luthien didn't have to go far to find a fight. Just around the bend, he came to a jag in the wall, behind which a score of cyclopians had dug in. Calling for Siobhan, he plunged ahead, cutting down the closest of the brutes with a mighty swing of his heavy sword. Riverdancer trampled yet another one, and then Luthien leaped the horse ahead, leaving the one-eyes behind to the throng coming hard in his wake.

Further around the bend, Luthien was able to gain a vantage point where he might look back to the inner wall directly across from the broken gates. He turned just as a dwarf went tumbling from its height, sliding off the edge of a cyclopian sword. But that brute, and others near it, were overwhelmed as a dozen other bearded warriors crashed in. The wall was taken.

An arrow zipped past Luthien's face, and he turned to follow its course in time to see it nail another one-eye right in the chest. The brute staggered, but was pushed aside as a wedge of cyclopians charged down the gap between the walls, heading Luthien's way.

The young Bedwyr and his cavalry unit met them and trampled them.

The central and highest area of Warchester, like all large Avonsea cities, was dominated by a tremendous cathedral, this one named the Ladydancer. Around the structure was an open plaza, which on quiet days served as a huge open marketplace. Now that plaza was swarming, the terrified populace desperate to get inside the cathedral.

But the doors were not yet open.

Deanna Wellworth, Brind'Amour, and Akrass the cyclopian stood on the balcony that opened above the cathedral's main doors. Over and over, Brind'Amour, posing still as Duke Theredon, called for quiet, and gradually the hysterical crowd did calm—enough so that the sounds of the battle raging along the outer walls of the city could be clearly heard.

That done, the old wizard stepped back, taking a place next to Akrass, and Deanna took center stage.

"You know me," the woman cried out to the crowd. "I am Deanna Wellworth, duchess of Mannington."

Several calls came back, some for the opening of the Ladydancer, others asking if Deanna's garrison would come to Warchester's support.

"What you do not know," Deanna went on, and her voice was superhumanly powerful, enhanced by magic, "is that I am the rightful heir to the throne of Avon."

The people didn't react strongly, seemed not to understand her point. Of course they knew of Deanna's lineage, at least the older folk among them did, but what did that have to do with the present situation, the impending disaster in Warchester?

"I am the rightful queen of Avon!" Deanna shouted. She looked to Brind'Amour and nodded, and before Akrass could even begin to digest that proclamation, the one-eye was dead, Brind'Amour's dagger deep into its back.

"I can no longer tolerate the injustices!" Deanna cried above the growing murmurs and open shouts. "I can no longer tolerate any alliance with filthy one-eyes, nor the truth of Greensparrow! You have heard the rumors of a dragon lighting on the fields south of the city. That was no Eriadoran ally, my people, but our own king, in his natural form!"

Like a giant wave caught between many great rocks, the crowd jostled back and forth, erupting in places, noisy everywhere.

"Hear me, my subjects of proud Warchester!" Deanna shouted. "This is no invading army, but a mercenary force hired by your rightful queen! This is my army, come from Eriador to restore the proper ruler of Avon to her throne!"

Brind'Amour heard a tumult behind him and casually turned about and threw his magical energy into the huge door of the balcony, warping the wood and sealing it tight. "You will start a riot," he stated, an obvious fact, given the level of commotion mounting below them.

"We need a riot," Deanna insisted.

Brind'Amour could not disagree. He had seen the defenses of the fortress called Warchester and knew that there remained several thousand cyclopians ready to fight in the place. Add to that the thirty thousand humans who called Warchester city their home and Bellick's forces were sorely outnumbered.

The old wizard stepped forward, dragging dead Akrass with him. Yet another enchantment—and Brind'Amour was fast exhausting the energy to cast such spells—made the cyclopian as light as a feather pillow, and Brind'Amour lifted the corpse high into the air above his head. "Take up arms against your true oppressors!" the fake Duke Theredon instructed. "Death to the one-eyes!"

That cry echoed back from a surprisingly large number of men and women, and the plaza erupted into chaos. There weren't many cyclopians about—most were down at the lower walls—but not all of the gathered people would heed Deanna's call. Thus the riot Brind'Amour had predicted began in full.

"Sort it out," he bade Deanna. "Find your allies and secure the Ladydancer. Get the wounded and the defenseless inside."

Deanna was already thinking along those same lines, and she nodded her agreement, though Brind'Amour, in a puff of orange smoke, was already gone to find Luthien.

Deanna continued to prod on her supporters, telling them to join together, to clearly identify themselves. Her speech was interrupted, though, as a heavy spear thudded down on the balcony just beside her. Turning, Deanna saw that several brutes had gained a perch on the tower high above her.

Her response—a crackling bolt of writhing black energy—only bolstered Deanna's support as it cleared that tower of one-eyes.

Turning back to the crowd, Deanna soon discerned a large group of organized supporters, working coherently and trying to get the innocents behind them, between them and the cathedral doors. The rightful queen of Avon turned and shattered Brind'Amour's stuck doors with yet another bolt, then fried the band of surprised cyclopians standing in the anteroom just inside. Soon the cathedral doors were thrown wide, and Deanna had her growing army of Warchester rebels.

The riot raged across the plaza.

Brind'Amour knew that his magic was nearing its end for this day. Despite the adrenaline rush and the wild fighting all about him, the old wizard wanted nothing more than to lie down and go to asleep. He used his wits instead, using his disguise to break up groups of cyclopians who were holding defensible regions of the wall by ordering them off on some silly business, weakening the line with improper commands.

It was more than an hour before the old wizard finally spotted some allies, a force of nearly a hundred dwarfs battling fiercely in ankle-deep water on the edge of a small moat surrounding one of the guardhouses. With no magical power to spare, Brind'Amour moved on. It took him another half hour to finally hear the thunder of hooves.

Coming to the edge of a high wall, Brind'Amour saw the forces squaring off on either side of a long and narrow channel: Luthien and a hundred riders, Fairborn mostly, at one end, and a like number of cyclopians on ponypigs at the other.

The charge shook the ground of all the huge city. Luthien's cavalry gained an advantage with a volley of bow shots, but unlike the encounters on the open fields, they could not strike and then turn away. This time, the forces came crashing together in a wild and wicked melee, many going down under the sheer weight of the impact, others held up in their saddles only because there was no room for them to fall.

Amidst it all, the weary old wizard spotted Luthien on that shining white stallion, his mighty sword chopping ceaselessly, his voice calling for spirit and for Eriador free.

But the cost, Brind'Amour pondered. The terrible cost.

Luthien and nearly half his force broke through, and a swarm of Eriadoran foot soldiers came into the channel behind them, finishing off the beaten cyclopians, tending the Eriadoran wounded, and running off eagerly after the Crimson Shadow.

The fighting soon got worse—by Brind'Amour's estimation, and by Luthien's—for it became, in many places, human against human.

It ended late that afternoon, except for a few pockets of fortified resistance, with another victory for Eriador, with Warchester taken. The price had been high, though, devastatingly high, the northern army taking casualties of four out of every ten. Nearly half of Bellick's fearless dwarfs were dead or wounded.

Support for Deanna Wellworth was strong among the populace, but not without question. The woman had taken credit for the attack, and every family in Warchester had suffered grievously. Still, those Avonese who came out of the Ladydancer that night spoke of the evil of Greensparrow and their common hatred of cyclopians, and, sometime later, of the mercy shown by the conquering Eriadorans, who were tending Warchester's wounded as determinedly as they tended their own.

Brind'Amour was glad to be back in his own form again, though he was so exhausted that he could hardly walk. He introduced Deanna to Luthien, Bellick, and the other Eriadoran leaders and told them all that had transpired.

"We have won the day," Siobhan declared, "but at great cost."

"We're ready to march on," a determined Shuglin was quick to respond. "Carlisle is not so far!"

"In good time," Brind'Amour said to the eager dwarf. "In good time. But first we must see what allies we have made here."

"And I must return to Mannington," Deanna added, "to find what forces I can muster for the march to Carlisle."

Brind'Amour nodded, but did not seem so encouraged. "Mannington is still a city of Avon," he reminded. "This battle might well be repeated in your own streets, but without the support of Eriador's army."

"Not so," said Deanna. "Most of my Praetorian Guards are out with the fleet, and no doubt at the bottom of the channel by now, and I have sown the seeds of revolt for some time among the most influential of my people." She managed a sly grin. "Among the bartenders and innkeepers, mostly, who have the ear of the common folk. Mannington will not be so bloody, and a large number, I believe, will follow me out to the south, to Carlisle, where we will join you on the final field."

It was encouraging news, to be sure, but for the Eriadorans, who had fought through fifty miles of mountains and a hundred miles of farmland, who had fought four battles over the course of one night and one day, the mere thought of continuing the march brought deep and profound sighs. They were tired, all of them, and they had so far yet to travel.

"Keep a transportation spell ready," Brind'Amour warned, "in case Greensparrow looks in on you and discovers the truth of it all."

"He will know soon enough," Deanna replied. "And he will not be pleased." With a comforting smile, and a pat of her hand on the old wizard's stooped shoulder, the proclaimed queen of Avon went off.

"Secure the city and our camp," Brind'Amour instructed Bellick. "We will stay five days, at the least."

"Time favors Greensparrow," the dwarf warned.

"Who could have anticipated the fall of Warchester in a single day?" Brind'Amour asked. "I had believed we would be bogged here for at least a week, perhaps even several, perhaps even leaving half our numbers behind to maintain a siege. We have the time, and need the rest."

Bellick grunted and nodded, and walked off with Shuglin and his other dwarven commanders to see to the task.

Luthien and Siobhan also went off, to determine what remained of their cavalry, and what new horses might be garnered within Warchester. They tallied their number of kills as they walked, after agreeing that they would not count, or even speak of, the men they had necessarily killed this day. Counting dead cyclopians was one thing, a relief from the pressures of the war, an incentive to keep up the good fight. Counting human kills would only remind them of the horrors of war, something that neither of them could afford.

"Sixty-three," Luthien decided for himself, and Siobhan's fair face screwed up as she admitted a total of only "Sixty-one."

Neither of them spoke it, but they both realized that the half-elf would find ample opportunity to catch up in the days, even weeks, ahead.

When the army left Warchester, six days later, they were well-rested and well-supplied, their ranks thick with soldiers indeed, for many of Warchester's folk decided to join in the fight against Greensparrow, to join in the cause for their rightful queen.

"It is as I told you it would be," a grinning Luthien said to Brind'Amour as they started out. "Avon will rise against Greensparrow in the knowledge that our cause is a just one. Perhaps we should have continued our last war from Princetown, after we together destroyed evil Duke Paragor."

"You did predict this," Siobhan admitted, riding along easily beside the pair. "Though I never would have believed that the folk of Avon would join in the cause of an invading force."

"They did not," Brind'Amour said in all seriousness. "Those who have joined have done so only because of one person. Had Deanna Wellworth not risen against Greensparrow, then our fight for Warchester would have been desperate and the army marching from Mannington would be marching against us."

It was sobering talk, a reminder of just how tentative this had all been, and would likely remain. Brind'Amour said nothing of the sea battle in the Straits of Mann, for he had not found the time or the magical energy to discern how his fleet had fared.

The old wizard could guess at the situation, though, had a good feeling about it all that he kept private until he could be sure.

The rout of Avon was on in full.

Greensparrow paced anxiously about his great throne, wringing his hands every step. He went back to the throne and sat down once more, but was standing and pacing again within a few short moments.

Duke Cresis had never seen the king so agitated, and the cyclopian, who had heard many of the reports, suspected that the situation was even more grave than it had reasoned.

"Treachery," Greensparrow muttered. "Miserable treacherous rats. I'll see them dead every one, that wretched Ashannon and ugly Deanna. Yes, Deanna, I'll take whatever pleasures I desire before finishing that traitorous dog!"

So it was true, Cresis understood. The duke of Baranduine and the duchess of Mannington had conspired with the enemy against Greensparrow. The brutish one-eye wisely held in check its comments concerning the irony, realizing that a single errant word could bring the full wrath of Greensparrow. When the king of Avon was in such a foul temper, most thinking beings made it a point to go far, far away. Cresis couldn't afford that luxury now, though, not with two Eriadoran land armies and one, possibly two fleets converging on Carlisle.

Greensparrow went back to the throne and plopped down unceremoniously, even fell to the side and threw one leg over the arm of the great chair. His kingdom was crumbling beneath him, he knew, and there seemed little he could do to slow his enemy's momentum. If he threw himself into the battle with his full magical powers, he would be putting himself at great risk, for he did not know the full power of Brind'Amour.

There is always an escape, the king mused, and that part of Greensparrow that was the dragon longed for the safe bogs of the Saltwash.

He shook that notion away; it was too soon for thinking of abdicating, too soon to surrender. Perhaps he would have to go to the Saltwash, but only after the Eriadorans had suffered greatly. He had to find a way . . .

"The Eriadoran and Baranduine fleet approaches the mouth of the Stratton," Cresis offered. "Our warships will hit them on the river, in the narrower waters where the great catapults lining the banks can support us."

Greensparrow was shaking his head before the brute was halfway finished. "They will sail right past the river," the king explained, confident of his words, for he had seen much in his days of dragonflight. "A battle is brewing on the open waters south of Newcastle."

"Then our eastern fleet will join in, and we will catch all the Eriadoran ships and those of treacherous Baranduine in between!" the cyclopian said with great enthusiasm. "Our warships are still the greater!"

"And what of the Huegoths?" Greensparrow snapped, and fell back helplessly into his throne. That much of what Deanna had told him was true, he had confirmed. A great Huegoth fleet was sailing with the Eriadorans in the east. In his dragon form, Greensparrow had swooped low, setting one longship aflame, but the wall of arrows, spears, even balls of pitch and great stones, that rose up to meet him had been too great, forcing him to turn for home.

He had gone to Evenshorn first, and there had confirmed that Mystigal was not to be found. Then, flying high and fast to the west, he had spotted the second Eriadoran army sweeping across the rolling fields between Deverwood and Carlisle, like an ocean tide that could not be thwarted. Still, it wasn't until Greensparrow had arrived back in Carlisle, his fortress home, that his spirits had been crushed. In the time the king of Avon had taken to go so far to the east and back, many had come running down from the region of Speythenfergus to report the disaster in Warchester, and word had passed along the coast and up the Stratton about Duke Ashannon's turnabout in the Straits of Mann.

Cresis appeared truly horrified. "Huegoths?" the cyclopian stammered, knowing well the cursed name.

"Evil allies for evil foes," Greensparrow sneered.

The cyclopian's eye blinked many times, Cresis licking its thick lips as it tried to sort out the stunning news. To the brutish general, there seemed only one course.

"One army at a time!" Cresis insisted. "I will march north with the garrison to meet our closest enemies. When they are finished, if time runs short, I will turn back for Carlisle to prepare the city defenses."

"No," Greensparrow said simply, for he knew that if the garrison went north, that second Eriadoran army would swing west and catch them from the side. Greensparrow was even thinking that he had better focus his vision on Mannington for a while, to see if treacherous Deanna had raised an army of her own to march south.

"Prepare the defenses now," Greensparrow instructed after a long silence. "You must defend the city to the last."

Cresis didn't miss the fact that Greensparrow had not said "We must defend the city to the last."

With a click of his booted heels and a curt bow, the cyclopian left the king.

Alone, Greensparrow sighed and considered again how fragile his kingdom had become. How could he have missed the treachery of Deanna Wellworth, or even worse, how could he not have foreseen the efforts of the duke of Baranduine against him? As soon as Deanna had reported the supposed fight with Brind'Amour, Greensparrow should have gone straight off to find Taknapotin or one of the familiar demons of the other dukes and confirmed her tale.

"But how could I have known?" the king said aloud. "Little Deanna, how surprising you have become!" He had underestimated her, and badly, he admitted privately. He had thought that her own guilt, his cryptic stories and those of Selna, and the carrot of ruling over Mannington, and perhaps soon in Warchester as well, would have held her ambition in check, would have kept Deanna bound to him for the remainder of her life. Greensparrow had long ago seen to it, using devilish potions administered by his lackey Selna, that Deanna would bear no children, thus ending the line of Wellworths, and he had sincerely believed that Deanna could prove no more than a minor thorn in his side for the short remainder of her life.

How painful that thorn seemed now!

His northern reaches had crumbled and four armies were on the move against him. Carlisle was a mighty, fortified city, to be sure, and Greensparrow himself was no minor foe.

But neither was Brind'Amour, or Deanna, or Ashannon McLenny, or this Crimson Shadow character, or the Heugoths, or . . .

How long the list seemed to the beleaguered king of Avon. Again that dragon side of him imparted images of the warm bogs of the Saltwash, and they seemed harder to ignore. Perhaps, Greensparrow considered, he had erred so badly because he had grown weary of Avon's throne, had grown weary of wearing the trappings of a mere human when his other side was so much stronger, so much freer.

The Avon king growled and leaped up from his throne. "No more of that, Dansallignatious!" he yelled, and kicked the throne.

I would have kicked it right through the wall, the dragon side of him reminded.

Greensparrow bit hard his lip and stalked away.

CAUGHT

They came in right between the twin tributaries that bore the name of Stratton, a scene not unlike the approach to Warchester, except that there was less ground leading to Carlisle. And the cities themselves, though both formidable bastions, could not have appeared more different. Warchester was a dark place, a brooding fortress, its walls all of gray and black stone banded with black iron, its towers square and squat, and with evenly spaced crenellations across its battlements. Carlisle was more akin to Princetown, a shining place of white polished walls and soaring spires. Her towers were round, not square, and her walls curved gracefully, following the winding flow of the Stratton. Huge arching bridges reached over that split river, east and west, joining the city proper with smaller castles, reflections of the main. She was a place of beauty, even from afar, but also a place of undeniable strength.

Luthien could feel that, even regarding the place from across two miles of rolling fields. He could imagine attacking Carlisle, the white walls turning brown from poured oil, red from spilled blood. A shudder coursed along the young Bedwyr's spine. The trek to Carlisle had been filled with terrible battles, in the mountains, across the fields, in Warchester, but none of them seemed to prepare Luthien for what he now believed would soon come, the grandfather of those battles.

"You should be afraid," remarked Siobhan, riding up beside the young man where he sat upon Riverdancer.

"It is a mighty place," Luthien said quietly.

"It will fall," the half-elf casually replied.

Luthien looked upon her, truly scrutinized the beautiful woman. How different Siobhan appeared now, all bathed and cleaned, than after the fights, when her wheat-colored tresses were matted flat to her shoulders by the blood of her enemies, when her eyes showed no sympathy, no mercy, only the fires of battle rage. Luthien admired this indomitable spirit, loved her for her ability to do what was necessary, to shut her more tender emotions off at those times when they would be a weakness.

The young Bedwyr dared to entertain an image then, of him and Katerin, Oliver, and Siobhan, riding across the fields in search of adventure.

"Do not tarry," came a call from behind, and the pair turned to see Brind'Amour's approach. "Bellick is already at work, and we must be as well, setting our defenses in place."

"Do you think Greensparrow will come out of his hole?" Siobhan asked skeptically.

"I would, if I were caught in his place," replied Brind'Amour. "He must know of the approaching fleets—he was told of the Huegoths—and his eyes have no doubt seen the charge of our sister army, sweeping down from the northeast.

"I would come out at this one force with all my strength," the wizard finished. "With all my strength."

Luthien looked back to the high walls of Carlisle, shining brightly in the afternoon sun. Brind'Amour's reasoning was sound, as usual, and the army would be better off taking all precautions.

So they dug trenches and set out lines of scouts, fortifying their perimeter and sleeping beside their weapons, particularly the tough dwarfs, who settled down for the night in full battle armor.

They didn't really expect anything until the next dawn; cyclopians didn't like to fight in the dark any more than did the men or dwarfs. The Fairborn, though, with their keen eyesight, thought little of the problems of night fighting, even preferred it.

And so did the dragon.

Greensparrow walked out of Carlisle as the midnight hour

passed, quietly and without fanfare. Safely out of the city, the king called to that other half, the great dragon Dansallignatious, the familiar beast he had joined with those centuries before in the Saltwash. The king began to change, began to grow. He became huge, black and green, spread wide his leathery wings and lifted off into the night sky.

Just a few minutes later, he made his first pass over the Eriadoran encampment, spewing forth his fiery breath.

But the invaders were not caught by surprise, not with the Fairborn elves watching the night sky. A hail of arrows nipped at the swooping dragon, and Brind'Amour, who had rested through all the ten days it had taken the army to march from Warchester, and for the week before that when they had remained in the captured city, loosed his fury in the form of a series of stinging bolts of power, first blue, then red, then searing yellow, and finally a brilliant white, cutting the night sky like lightning strokes.

Dansallignatious took the hits, one, two, three, four, and flew on to the north, scales smoking, eyes burning. The beast took some comfort in the havoc he had left in his wake, a line of fire, a chorus of agonized screams. Far from the camp, he banked to the west, then turned south, preparing another pass.

Again came the hail of arrows, again came the wizard's bolts, and the dragon flew through, killing and burning the earth below him.

There would be no third run; Greensparrow was spent and battered. He went back into the city satisfied, though, for his wounds would quickly heal, but those scores he had killed on the field were forever dead.

The next day dawned gray and gloomy, fitting for the mood in the Eriadoran camp. Many had died in the dragon strafing, including more than a hundred dwarfs, and the wounds of dozens of survivors were horrible indeed.

The Eriadorans prepared for an assault, suspecting that the dragon attack had been the precursor for the full-scale attack. They expected the gates of Carlisle to swing wide, pouring forth a garrison that numbered, by most reports, more than twenty thousand.

That indeed was Greensparrow's intention, but the plan was scratched, and the hearts of the Eriadorans were lifted high indeed, when the wide line of the Stratton south of Carlisle filled suddenly with sails! Scores of sails, hundreds of sails, stretched by a south wind and rushing to the north.

Siobhan spotted the banner of Eriador, Brind'Amour noted the green, white-bordered markings of Baranduine, and Luthien saw the froth of Huegoth oars.

"The dragon will come out against them, and leave them flaming on the river," Luthien said.

Brind'Amour wasn't so sure of that. "I do not believe that our enemy has truly revealed himself to those he commands," the old wizard reasoned. "Do you think that the folk of Carlisle know that they have a dragon for a king?"

"He could still come out," Luthien argued, "and later dismiss the event as the trick of a wizard."

"Then let us hope that we wounded him badly enough yestereve that he will not," Siobhan put in grimly.

The lead vessels never slowed, crossing under the high bridges east of Carlisle proper. Cyclopians crowded on those bridges, heaving spears, dropping stones, but the ships plowed on, returning fire, clearing large sections with seemingly solid walls of arrows. From Carlisle proper and from the smaller fortress across the river to the east, came catapult balls. One galleon was hit several times and sent to the bottom.

But the maneuverable Huegoth longships were on the spot in a moment, plucking survivors from the river, then swinging fast to the north, oars pounding to keep them in close to their companion vessels.

Despite the Stratton's sometimes formidable current, the ships passed the killing zone too quickly for the defenders of Carlisle to exact very much damage, and as if in answer to the prayers of those watching in the north, the dragon Greensparrow did not make an appearance. Nearly a third of the total fleet sailed on, their prows lifting high the water. An occasional catapult shot soared in, more often than not splashing harmlessly into the river, and even those attacks were soon enough put far behind the vessels.

Luthien took note of the wide grin that came over Siobhan's face, and he followed her shining stare to one of the lead sailing ships, a Baranduine vessel, which seemed to be in a race against a Huegoth longship. Both ships were still too far away for individuals to be discerned on the decks, even for Siobhan's keen eyes, with the exception of one remarkable silhouette.

"He is on his pony!" Luthien exclaimed.

"He always has to be the center," snickered Siobhan.

Luthien smiled widely as he considered the half-elf, once again trying to picture her with Oliver.

Lines of soldiers cheered the approach at a wide and sheltered region where the ships could drop anchor and the Huegoths and some of the smaller Baranduine vessels could even put in to shore. The ropes came flying in to them, were caught and secured, and the forces were joined.

"Luthien!" The call, the familiar voice, sent the young Bedwyr's heart fluttering. Throughout the weeks of fighting, Luthien had been forced to sublimate his pressing fears for his dear Katerin, had to trust in the woman's ability. Now that trust was rewarded as Katerin O'Hale, her skin darker from the days under the sun, but otherwise none the worse for her journey, came bounding down the gangplank of the lead Baranduine vessel, Duke Ashannon McLenny's flagship. The woman pushed her way through the crowd and threw herself into Luthien's waiting embrace, planting a deep kiss on the young man's lips.

Luthien blushed deeply at the coos and cheers that went up around him, but that only spurred Katerin on to give him an even more passionate kiss.

The cheering turned to laughter, drawing the couple from their embrace. They shifted to get a view of Oliver, still on Threadbare, coming onto the long gangplank.

"My horse, he so loves the water," the halfling explained. That may have been true, but his horse, like everyone else coming off the ships after weeks at sea, had to find its land legs. Threadbare came down two steps, went one to the side, then two back the other way, nearly tumbling from the narrow plank. Then back the other way, and back and forth, all the while making slow progress toward the shore.

Oliver tried to appear calm and collected through it all, coaxing his pony and praying that he wouldn't be thrown into the water—not in front of all these people! With some care, the halfling finally managed to get the pony onto the bank, to a chorus of cheers.

"Not a problem!" the halfling cried with a triumphant snap of his fingers, as he slid his leg over the saddle and dropped to the ground.

Unfortunately, Oliver's legs were no less used to the swaying of shipboard than were Threadbare's, and he immediately skittered to the left, then three steps back, then back to the right, then back again. He made a halfhearted grab at Threadbare's tail, but the pony was so named because of that skinny appendage, and Oliver slipped off, falling to his seat in the water.

The cheers became howls of glee and two men ran down to Oliver and scooped him up.

"I meant to do that," the halfling insisted.

That brought even louder howls, but they stopped abruptly, transforming into hushed whispers, when Siobhan moved near Oliver. Rumors about these two had been circulating and growing during the weeks and now everyone, Luthien and Katerin perhaps most of all (with the sole exception of wide-eyed Oliver!), wanted to see what Siobhan would do.

"Welcome back," she said, taking Oliver's hand, and she kissed him on the cheek and led him away.

The crowd seemed disappointed.

The time for greetings was necessarily short, with so many plans to be made and movements to be coordinated. Carlisle had not yet fallen, and the mere appearance of reinforcements did not change that situation!

The leaders met within the hour, Brind'Amour, Bellick, old Dozier, and Ashannon, along with Luthien, Siobhan, Katerin, and Oliver. Brind'Amour arranged for Ethan to keep King Asmund away for a short while, that he might first deal with his closest advisors, and with Duke Ashannon, who was still a bit of a mystery in all of this.

Ashannon and Katerin did most of the talking at first, with Oliver throwing in details of his own heroics.

"The Avonese fleet did not engage us south of Newcastle, as we expected," Katerin reported.

Brind'Amour seemed concerned, but Katerin was quick to put his obvious fears to rest.

"They were badly outnumbered and had little heart for the fight, especially when the Huegoth longships came into the lead of our eastern fleet," she explained. "They sailed south for Gascony, and there asked for refuge."

"Which the Gascons granted," Ashannon added. "But not without concessions."

Oliver conspicuously cleared his throat, and Ashannon yielded the floor.

"I met with my countrymen," the halfling explained. "The Avon-types were granted sanctuary, but only on condition that they declare neutrality. Greensparrow's fleet is out of the war."

"Most welcomed news," Brind'Amour congratulated. "Most welcomed!"

There were smiles all around, except for Katerin. "I have heard word of a force of five thousand coming down from the north," she said gravely.

"Duchess Deanna Wellworth and her garrison from Mannington," Luthien explained, and the tone of his voice told Katerin that these were not enemies.

"Deanna is a friend," Ashannon assured her. "And more importantly, she is a sworn enemy of King Greensparrow."

It proved to be a fine meeting, a meeting full of optimism, and now that the prongs of the invasion were closing in on Carlisle, Luthien and all the others dared to hope for victory.

Those hopes brightened with the dawn, as Deanna Wellworth's soldiers joined the line, and that same afternoon, the lead riders, Kayryn Kulthwain among them, came in from the northeast, heralding the approach of the second Eriadoran army, a force that was now larger than it had been when it left Malpuissant's Wall.

By mid-morning of the next day, Brind'Amour would have fifty thousand on the field encircling Carlisle, with supply lines stretching the breadth of Avon and the fruitful southern coast open to his warships.

Among the Eriadoran allies, there remained only one voice of dissent, a certain Huegoth leader who could not be put off any longer.

Luthien was with Brind'Amour when the king went to Asmund's longship. The younger Bedwyr hardly noticed the principals at the initial greeting, when he looked again upon his older brother. Ethan offered a hand to Luthien, but did not accompany it with a smile, nor a flicker of recognition in his cinnamon-colored eyes. Even after weeks moving in common cause, Ethan seemed as cold to Luthien as he had when the brothers had first found each other on the Isle of Colonsey.

Could it be that Ethan would never remember, or admit, who he truly was?

They had no time to discuss their personal situation, though, for Asmund descended on Brind'Amour like a great bear.

"We are warriors!" the Huegoth king roared. "And yet we have been sitting on the empty waves for weeks, our foodstuffs delivered by Eriadoran ships that have touched the shores of Avon!"

"We could not reveal—" Brind'Amour began, but Asmund cut him short.

"Warriors!" the barbarian roared again, looking for support from Torin Rogar, standing at his side. The huge Rogar nodded and grunted.

"I have not lifted my spear in many days," Torin complained. "Even the Avon warships turned from us and would not fight."

Brind'Amour tried to appear sympathetic, but in truth, after the beating his forces had taken all the way from Caer MacDonald, such eagerness for battle left a bitter taste in his mouth. The old wizard held little love for Huegoths, and for a moment seriously considered granting Asmund's desires, throwing the king and all his brutal warriors against Carlisle's high walls.

"I pain for battle," Asmund said hungrily.

"That you might replenish your slave stocks?" Luthien said bluntly. He noted Brind'Amour's scowl, and Ethan's, and he understood. Prudence told the young Bedwyr that they should keep the alliance solid at this critical juncture, but Luthien could no longer hold back his ire—at the Huegoths and at Ethan.

Asmund grabbed at the handle of the great axe that was strapped to his back; Luthien likewise put a hand to the hilt of *Blind-Striker*.

"You dare?" Asmund began. He thrust his fist into the air, a signal to his sturdy men that the meeting was at its end. Brind'Amour sucked in his breath, but Luthien did not blink.

"Perhaps Eriador would be wise to guard its coast," Asmund threatened.

"Is your pledge of honor so fragile that it might be broken by a few words spoken in anger?" Luthien asked, giving Asmund pause.

The king squared against Luthien, came very close to the young man, glaring down at him ominously. Luthien didn't back away an inch, and didn't blink.

"Friends do not fear to point out each other's faults," Luthien said in all seriousness, and he was taken aback a moment later, when Asmund suddenly bellowed with laughter.

"I do like you, young Luthien Bedwyr!" the king roared, and all his warriors stood more easily.

Luthien started to respond, again with grim confidence, but this time, Brind'Amour's scowl became an open threat and the young Bedwyr held his tongue.

The alliance was solid, for the time being, and after Asmund extracted a promise from Brind'Amour that the Huegoths could lead the charge against Greensparrow's fortress—a promise the Eriadoran king was more than happy to give—Brind'Amour and Luthien took their leave.

"When Greensparrow is properly dealt with, we will turn our eyes to the Huegoths," Luthien said as soon as he and Brind'Amour were back on land and away from Huegoth ears.

"What would you do?" Brind'Amour asked. "Wage war on all the world?"

"Promise me now that you will not let them leave the Stratton on ships rowed by slaves," Luthien begged.

Brind'Amour looked long and hard at the principled young man, wearing a stern and determined expression that the old wizard could not ignore. That dedication to principle was Luthien's strength. How could he possibly refuse to follow such an example?

"Asmund will be properly dealt with," Brind'Amour promised.

Chapter 29

THE SIEGE OF CARLISLE

They stood on the forward masts of the warships closest to Carlisle and on the hills outside of the city. Some brave ones rode their horses dangerously close to the white walls, waging a battle of words.

"We have fifty thousand on the field against you," they all said, as instructed by Brind'Amour and Deanna Wellworth. "Among our ranks is Deanna Wellworth, rightful queen of Avon. Surrender Greensparrow, the murderer of King Anathee Wellworth!"

Every hour of every day, those words were called out to the besieged people of Carlisle. Brind'Amour didn't really expect the Avonese within the city to rise up against their king, but he was looking for every possible advantage once the fighting did start. And that would take some time, the old wizard understood. An army could not simply charge the walls of a fortified bastion such as Carlisle.

They did wage a few minor battles, with the Eriadorans testing the strength of various points along Carlisle's perimeter. Asmund's Huegoths took the lead in most of these, but even the fierce Isenlanders knew when to turn about, and casualties remained light on both sides.

Meanwhile, other, more important preparations were underway, foremost among them the old wizard's work to keep Greensparrow busy. The Eriadorans could not afford to have the dragon coming out at them every night, or to have the wizard-king launching magical attacks into their ranks. Thus, Brind'Amour took it upon himself to engage Greensparrow, to test his strength, the powers of the ancient brotherhood, against this new-styled wizard. Alone in his tent the first night of the siege, Brind'Amour created a magical tunnel, reaching from his chamber to the tower Deanna had identified as Greensparrow's. This tunnel was not like the ones the wizard had used to transport Asmund or Katerin and Oliver, but one that would take him in spirit only to face the wizard-king.

Greensparrow was surprised, but not caught off guard, to see the ghostly form of the old wizard hovering before his throne.

"Come to scold?" the Avon king snarled. "To tell me the error of my ways?"

Brind'Amour's response was straightforward, a burst of crackling red sparks that burned, not into Greensparrow's physical body, but into his soul. A moment later, Greensparrow stepped from his corporeal form, spirit leaping forward to engage the old wizard. And thus they battled, as Brind'Amour and Paragor had battled, but in spirit form alone. It went on for exhausting hours, neither truly hurting the other, but draining each other, and when Brind'Amour broke the connection the following morn, he was weary indeed, sitting on the edge of his bed, head down and haggard-looking.

Deanna found him in that position. "You met with him," she reasoned almost immediately.

Brind'Amour nodded. "And he is powerful," he confirmed. "But not compared to what we wizards once were. Greensparrow came to power through treachery because he could not gain the throne through sheer might. So it is now. He rules, iron-fisted, but that iron fist is not one of magic, nor even one of his dragon alter-form, but of allies, cyclopian mostly."

"Do not underestimate his power," Deanna warned.

"Indeed I do not," Brind'Amour replied. "That is why I went to him, and why I will go to him again this night, and the next, and the next, if need be."

"Can you defeat him?"

"Not in this manner," Brind'Amour explained, "for I go to him in spirit only. But I can keep him occupied, and weary! This battle will be one of swords."

Deanna liked that prospect far greater than the thought of waging a magical battle against Greensparrow. Five armies had joined against Carlisle, and the besieged city had no apparent prospects for reinforcement.

In this situation, the biggest advantage for the Eriadorans was their dwarvish allies. Carlisle had been built to withstand the charge of an army, most likely a straightforward cyclopian force, but the designers had not foreseen the tunneling expertise of an enemy such as the bearded folk of DunDarrow. The dwarfs worked tirelessly, taking shifts so that the digging never stopped. They went down low, right under the river, so that the people within the city would not hear their work. Ashannon worked tirelessly as well, using his magic to shield the dwarvish work from Greensparrow's prying eyes.

On the sixth day of the siege, the first decisive encounter took place, in the smaller city across the eastern branch of the Stratton from Carlisle proper. Asmund led the Huegoth charge from the north, Siobhan's cavalry and the Riders of Eradoch in strong support. Several galleons braved the catapult fire from both banks to come in at the city along the river to the west, while Shuglin led two thousand dwarfs through their crafted tunnels, popping up at various strategic points within the fortress. Even more importantly, the dwarvish burrowing had weakened the substructure of the walls.

The north wall, its bottom carved out, crumbled under the weight of the charge, and in poured the vicious Huegoths and the cavalry. Luthien, Oliver, and Katerin, already within the city through dwarvish tunnels, spent more time sorting out innocents and ushering them out of harm's way than in fighting, for in truth there wasn't much fighting to be found. The garrison fled the minor city, along the bridges to Carlisle proper, almost as fast as the invaders entered it. And Greensparrow, who they assumed to be weary from his nightly encounters with Brind'Amour, made no appearance.

The place was conquered within an hour, and fully secured before the day was out.

The noose around Carlisle had tightened.

That same night, Luthien and Oliver, using the crimson cape and Oliver's magical grapnel, a puckered ball that could stick to any surface, made their stealthy way into Carlisle and walked the streets of Greensparrow's domain. They ventured into taverns, met with people in alleys, always whispering the name of Deanna Wellworth, planting the rumors that the invading army was, in fact, a force raised by the rightful queen of Avon.

The pair were out of the city again long before the dawn.

Also that night, Brind'Amour went again in spirit to meet the Avon king, but he failed, finding the way blocked by a disenchantment barrier akin to the one he had used on Resmore and again in the castle at Warchester. Up to that point, Greensparrow had been more than willing to battle the old wizard, but now, Brind'Amour realized, the wily Avon king had come to understand their strategy. His engagements with Brind'Amour were in part to blame for the fall of the section across the river; he could no longer afford the distraction of a nightly stand-off with his adversary.

The realization did not greatly worry Brind'Amour. He understood his foe better now, the man's strengths and limitations, and he was confident that his forces could strike hard and decisively, and that he, along with his fellow wizards, Deanna and Ashannon, would effectively neutralize the overburdened Avon king.

As he had proclaimed to Deanna on the second morning of the siege, this would be a battle of swords, not of magic.

"He cannot come at us across the river when our ships hold the waterway," Brind'Amour explained at a strategy meeting early the next morning. "And with us so close to his walls, he would not dare open the city's gates and try to break out to the north."

"We would be in Carlisle in a matter of minutes," Katerin reasoned, and though her estimate seemed overly optimistic, the point was well-taken.

"Time favors us," Siobhan thought it would be prudent to add.

"Does it?" asked Deanna Wellworth.

"The seeds of rebellion are being sown within Carlisle," Luthien answered before Siobhan could respond. "Oliver and I found many folk willing to hear of Avon's rightful queen, and of the treachery of Greensparrow."

"Of course, that might be only because I am so convincing," added the halfling.

That brought a chuckle—from all but surly Asmund, who was fast growing weary of this siege.

"I will not sit on the field and wait for the first snows of winter," the Huegoth said. Indeed, Asmund and his forces could not wait much longer. They had a long way to sail to get home, in waters that would grow more inhospitable with the changing season. Soon the winds would shift to the north, blowing in the face of Huegoth longships trying to make their return to Isenland and Colonsey, where a fair number of their women and children waited.

Brind'Amour sat back and let the chatter continue around him. Asmund wanted action; so did Kayryn Kulthwain and especially Bellick, who assured the others that at least twenty openings would be burrowed into Carlisle that very night, and that the substructure of several key points along the eastern and southern walls had already been compromised.

"They're thinking that we'll come from the north and east," the dwarf king remarked with a wink at Brind'Amour. "But they'll be only half-right. Mannington's and Luthien's riders will fake the attack from the north, while our ships put an army in the shallows of the river delta south of the city. We'll be in so fast, the one-eyes will still be standing at the north wall, wondering when your folk will attack," he said to Deanna. "And the rest of us will poke them from behind!"

It wouldn't be quite that easy, Brind'Amour knew, but it was a good point. Carlisle was ripe for plucking, and if they attacked and were not successful, they could always retreat to their current position and take up the siege once more, this time against a city weakened by battle. The coordination would be tricky, though, since so many various factions were together on the field, but the old wizard, the king of Eriador, decided then and there that the time for action had come at last.

"With the dawn," Brind'Amour said unexpectedly, silencing conversation and turning all eyes upon him. "Even before the dawn," he corrected, then paused to better sort out the plan, and the emotions of all of those staring at him.

And so it began, an hour before the eighth dawn of the siege, when Shuglin the dwarf came out of a tunnel into a quiet house just east of the plaza of Carlisle Abbey. All throughout the silent city, Bellick's forces slipped into position, while on the plain north of Carlisle, Deanna Wellworth's five thousand, along with the first army of Eriador, including Luthien, Siobhan, Katerin and Oliver and the Cutter cavalry, formed a long and deep line. South of Carlisle, Huegoths crowded into their longships, ready to storm the river fork, and in the east, Kayryn prepared her gallant riders for the mighty charge across the bridges.

The dawn was heralded by the blowing of a thousand horns—Eriadoran horns, Huegoth horns, Mannington horns—and by the thunder of cavalry in the north and on the stone of the eastern bridges, and by the roars of charging armies.

Luthien led the rush from the north, a feigned attack that kept the massive cyclopian force along Carlisle's northern wall distracted until the dwarfs within the city could organize. Then Carlisle's south wall crumbled in several places and on came the Huegoth charge, the army of Baranduine rolling in behind them. Kayryn herself led the thunder across the fortified bridges.

For more than an hour, little ground was gained, with Luthien and his forces stuck out on the northern fields, unable to find a breach in the intact and well-defended northern wall. In the south, Asmund's Huegoths met stiff resistance just inside the wall, and the Riders of Eradoch took brutal casualties on those narrow bridges. The waters of the Stratton ran red; the white walls of Carlisle were splattered with the blood of defender and invader alike.

Five of the leaders, Brind'Amour, Bellick, Deanna, and Ashannon, along with Proctor Byllewyn of Gybi, stood watching from the captured eastern region throughout that terrible hour, wondering if they had erred. "Did I underestimate Greensparrow?" Brind'Amour asked many, many times.

But then came the turning point, as Bellick's dwarfs, led by mighty Shuglin, gained the main courtyard and threw wide Carlisle's massive northern gates. Now Luthien's charge was on for real, the young Bedwyr and his forces pouring into the city, spreading wide in every direction like the finger flames of a wildfire.

Greensparrow, too, watched it all, from a high chamber in Carlisle Abbey. Duke Cresis came to him many times over the first hour, assuring him that the city was holding strong.

Then the cyclopian came in to report that the northern gate had fallen, and Greensparrow knew that the time had come for him to act. He dismissed Cresis (and the one-eye was glad to be away from the dangerous and unpredictable tyrant!) and went alone up the stairs of the Abbey's main tower.

From that rooftop, King Greensparrow saw the ruin of his life.

There was fighting in every section of the city. The north was lost, and the dwarfs were sweeping east to open the bridges, while the cavalry was thundering along the streets, winding its way to join in the fierce fighting at the south wall.

"Fools, all," the wizard-king sneered.

Greensparrow spotted a curious group of riders, noted particularly a man on a shining white stallion, a crimson cape billowing out behind him.

"At least, this," the king remarked, and his hands began weaving semicircles in the air, touching thumb to thumb, then little finger to little finger, the tempo gradually increasing as Greensparrow gathered his magical energies that he might strike dead the troublesome Crimson Shadow once and for all.

But before he could execute the spell, Greensparrow found his feet knocked right out from under him as the tower trembled under a tremendous magical assault.

Looking to the east, Greensparrow noted three forms: an old wizard in blue robes and holding an oaken staff, the duke of Baranduine, and the woman who would be queen. Brind'Amour struck repeatedly at the tower, lightning bolts reaching out from his staff to slam at the foundations beneath Greensparrow. Deanna and Ashannon were not so powerful, but still they threw every ounce of their strength at the king.

The tower swayed dangerously.

Looking back, looking all around, Greensparrow saw that he had become the focus. Even the Crimson Shadow and his cohorts had stopped their charge, were sitting astride their mounts and pointing.

"Fools, all!" the evil king cried, and then, in the daylight, before the eyes of so very many, the king of Avon revealed himself. He felt the pain, the torment, as his limbs crackled and expanded, as some bones fused while others broke apart. That horrible itch covered him head to toe, skin breaking and twisting, hardening into green and black scales. Then he was no longer Greensparrow; that part of the being that was Dansallignatious spread wide its leathery wings. And just in time, for the tower of the Abbey shuddered again and toppled.

All across the city, defender and attacker alike paused in their fighting to watch the fall, to see the king-turned-dragon hovering in the air above the cloud of rising dust.

A blue bolt of lightning reached out across the river and jolted Greensparrow, and with a howl of pain the dragon king swooped about. Cyclopian, Huegoth, Eriadoran, and dwarf—it did not matter—fell beneath the fiery breath as the great beast swept on. That part of the monster that was Greensparrow wanted to destroy the Crimson Shadow most of all, then turn east and across the river to engulf his wizard adversaries in killing fire. But that part of the monster that was Dansallignatious could not discriminate, was too taken up with the sheer frenzy of the killing.

And then, as the defense organized against the dragon, as walls of stinging arrows rose to meet his every pass, as warships sailed closer that they might launch their catapult volleys at the passing beast, and as the magical barrage from across the river only intensified, the dragon king saw the ruin and the loss and knew that it was time to flee.

Across the river Greensparrow soared, sending a last line of fire at the building where his principal adversaries stood ready. Deanna Wellworth was prepared, though, enacting a globe similar to the one she had used to trap Mystigal and Theredon on the high plateau. And though the area within grew uncomfortably hot, though Bellick's face beaded with sweat, and Byllewyn collapsed for lack of breath, when the dragon king had soared far off to the east, he left none of them truly hurt.

"Abdication!" screamed Bellick. "I know a running king when I see one!"

Tears in her blue eyes, Deanna wrapped the dwarf in a victorious hug.

Brind'Amour was not so full of glee. He started away in a great rush, bidding the others to follow. He led the way onto the nearest bridge and used his powers to their fullest to help clear the defense at the other end.

He would not explain his urgency, and the others didn't dare question him.

Somewhere far south of that point, Luthien Bedwyr was surprised when Riverdancer pulled up short so suddenly that Oliver, on Threadbare right behind him, almost wound up on his back. Siobhan and Katerin brought their mounts up a short distance ahead, looking back curiously at Luthien.

He had no answers for them, for he could not get Riverdancer to move. The shining horse held perfectly still for several moments, didn't even take notice when Threadbare bit him on the tail.

Then, despite Luthien's bidding, and fierce tugging on the bridle, Riverdancer swung about and pounded away. "Ride on to the south!" Luthien yelled, but his friends would not desert him, not when they didn't know whether his horse was taking him to allies or enemies.

Mighty Riverdancer soon outdistanced them, though, and Luthien breathed a sigh of profound relief when he turned into an alley to find Brind'Amour and the others waiting for him. The old wizard waved him down off the horse, then began whispering into Riverdancer's ear.

"What?" Luthien started to ask, but Deanna pulled him aside and shook her head.

Riverdancer neighed and bucked suddenly, and tried to pull away. Brind'Amour would not let go, though, and, his enchantment over the horse complete, he began instead to speak soothing words to the beast.

Luthien's eyes popped open wide—so did Oliver's, as the halfling led Katerin and Siobhan into the alley—when Riverdancer's sides bulged and expanded. The horse shrieked terribly, and Brind'Amour apologized and hugged the beast's head close.

But the pain passed as the bulges expanded, shaping into beautiful feathered wings.

"What have you done?" cried a horrified Luthien, for though the horse-turned-pegasus was indeed beautiful, this was his Riverdancer, his dear friend.

"Fear not," Brind'Amour said to him. "The enchantment will not last for long, and Riverdancer will bear no ill effects."

Luthien still found himself gasping at the appearance of the winged horse, but he accepted his trusted king's explanation.

"It must be finished here and now," Brind'Amour explained. "Greensparrow cannot get away!" He moved to the side of the magnificent beast, and obedient Riverdancer stooped low to help him climb into the saddle.

"The city will soon be yours," Brind'Amour said to Deanna. "Avon will soon be yours. I may miss your triumphant ascent to your rightful seat. Do not forget those who came to your aid, I beg."

"There are many wrongs to be righted," Deanna replied.

"If I do not return, then know that Greensparrow shall forever remain a problem to you. Keep your eyes to the Saltwash and your guard up high!"

Deanna nodded. "And for Eriador, whatever your fate, I promise independence," she replied. "Your army will not go north until a proper line of command has been established, be it King Bellick of DunDarrow, or Luthien Bedwyr, Proctor Byllewyn of Gybi, or Siobhan of the Fairborn."

Luthien was horrified that they were speaking so plainly of the possibility of Brind'Amour's death, but he quickly came to accept the necessity. Eriador could not be thrown into chaos again, whatever might now happen, and Luthien found that he believed Deanna's promise that Avon would no longer seek domination over his homeland. Still, given Deanna's last words, it seemed a real threat to Luthien that if Brind'Amour did not return, Eriador would split into tribal factions. Luthien could foresee trouble between Kayryn Kulthwain and Bellick, both so very proud and stubborn, perhaps trouble between both of them and Proctor Byllewyn!

Luthien's gaze went right to Brind'Amour, the brave wizard leaning low, stroking Riverdancer's muscled neck. On sudden impulse, Luthien ran to his horse, sliding Brind'Amour back almost onto Riverdancer's withers.

Brind'Amour put an arm out to stop him. "What are you about?" the wizard demanded.

"I am going with you," Luthien replied determinedly. "It is my horse, and it is my place!"

Brind'Amour looked long and hard into the young Bedwyr's cinnamon-colored eyes. He found that he could not disagree. Luthien had earned the right to join in this last and most desperate chase.

"If the horse will not carry us both, then select another as well," Luthien demanded. He looked back to Oliver, sitting, now nervously, on his yellow pony. "Threadbare," Luthien added.

"You want to grow wings on my precious horse that we might chase a dragon into a swamp?" Oliver asked incredulously.

"Yes," answered Luthien.

"No!" Brind'Amour emphatically corrected, and just as emphatic was the halfling's sigh of relief.

"Riverdancer will take us both," Brind'Amour explained, and Luthien was appeased.

"Luthien!" cried Katerin O'Hale.

The young Bedwyr slipped down from the horse and went to her at once, pulling her in a close embrace. "It is the proper finish," he said with all his heart. "It is the end of what I began when I killed Duke Morkney atop the Ministry's tower."

Katerin had meant to tell him not to go, to scold him for thinking so little of her that he would ride off on such a suicidal quest as to chase a dragon king into its swamp home. But like Brind'Amour, the young woman couldn't deny the sincerity in Luthien's eyes, the need he felt to see it through to the possibly bitter end.

"I only feared that you would go without bidding me goodbye," she lied.

"Not goodbye," Luthien corrected. "Just a kiss and a plea from me that you keep yourself safe until I can return to your side in this, the domain of Queen Deanna Wellworth."

His optimism touched Katerin, mostly because she realized that Luthien only half-believed that he had any chance of getting back to her. Still, she could not tell him to stay. She kissed him, and bit back the word "Goodbye," before it could escape her lips.

Then the gallant pair were off, Riverdancer as powerful in flight as he had been in the gallop, climbing high above the embattled city, noting the progress of their allies. Then Carlisle was far behind them, and the fields of Avon rolled along far beneath them.

The Saltwash was waiting.

THE DRAGON KING

A gray and hazy morning greeted the companions as the great pegasus set down on a patch of soft and mossy turf. They had flown throughout the afternoon and the night, straight to the east, but had not caught sight of the speeding dragon.

Luthien's fears were obvious: what if Greensparrow had not really gone to the Saltwash, but had merely flown out from Carlisle to rest before resuming the battle?

Brind'Amour would hear nothing of that disturbing talk. "Greensparrow knows that all is lost," he explained. "He revealed himself openly in his true and wretched form, and the Avon populace will never accept him as king. No, the beast went home, into the swamp."

As comforting as the wizard's confidence was, Luthien understood that filtering through Greensparrow's home in search of the runaway wizard would not be an easy thing. The Saltwash was a vast and legendary marsh, its name known well even in Eriador. It covered some fifteen thousand square miles in southeastern Avon. On its eastern end, it was often unclear where the marsh ended and the Dorsal Sea began, and on the west, where Luthien now stood, the place was deep and dark, filled with crawling dangers and bottomless bogs.

Luthien did not want to go in there, and the thought of entering the swamp in search of a dragon was almost too much for the young man to bear.

Brind'Amour was determined, though. "Take your rest now," he bade Luthien. "I have spells with which to locate the dragon king, and I will strengthen the enchantment on Riverdancer. We will find Greensparrow before the sun has set."

"And what then?" the young Bedwyr wanted to know.

Brind'Amour leaned back against the winged horse, trying to find a reasonable response. "I did not want you to come," he offered quietly at length. "I do not know that you will be of much help to me against the likes of Greensparrow, and do not know that I can defeat the dragon king."

"Then why are we here, just we two?" Luthien asked. "Why are we not in Carlisle, finishing the task, helping Deanna assume her rightful throne?"

Brind'Amour didn't appreciate the young man's sharp tone. "The task will not be finished until Greensparrow is finished," he replied.

"You just said—" Luthien started to protest.

"That I may not have the power to defeat the dragon king," Brind'Amour finished for him, the old wizard's eyes flashing dangerously. "A fair admission. But at the very least, I can hurt the beast, and badly. No, my young friend, it cannot be finished in Carlisle until the true source of Avon's fall is dealt with. We could have defeated the cyclopian garrison, and roused support for Deanna—no doubt that is happening even as we stand here talking—but what then? If we packed up our soldiers and marched back to Eriador, would Deanna truly be safe with Greensparrow lurking, waiting, only a few score miles to the east?"

Luthien had run out of arguments.

"I will go into the swamp later this day," Brind'Amour finished. "Perhaps it would be better if you waited here, or even if you took the road back to the west."

"I go with you," Luthien said without hesitation. He thought of everything he had to lose after he had spoken the words. He thought of Oliver and Siobhan, his dear friends, of Ethan and the possibilities that they might live as brothers once more, and most of all, he thought of Katerin. How he missed her now! How he longed for her warmth in this cold and dreary place! All the good thoughts of how his life might be when this was ended did nothing to change the young Bedwyr's mind, though. "We have been in this together since the beginning," he said, laying a hand on the old wizard's shoulder. "Since you rescued Oliver and me off the road, since you sent me into the lair of Balthazar to retrieve your staff and gave to me the crimson cape."

"Since you started the revolution in Montfort," Brind'Amour added.

"Caer MacDonald," Luthien corrected with a grin.

"And since you slew Duke Morkney," Brind'Amour went on.

"And now we will finish it," Luthien said firmly. "Together."

They rested in silence for only a couple of hours, their adrenaline, even Riverdancer's, simply too great for them to sit still. Then they walked cautiously into the swamp. Brind'Amour hummed a low resonating tone, sending it off into the moss-strewn shadows, then listening for its echoes, sounds that might be tainted by the presence of a powerful magical force.

The Saltwash quickly closed in behind them, swallowing them and stealing the light of day.

Luthien felt the mud seeping over the tops of his boots, heard the hissing protests of the swamp creatures all about him, felt the sting of gnats. To his left, the brown water rippled and some large creature slipped under the water before he could identify it.

The young Bedwyr focused straight ahead, on Brind'Amour's back, and tried not to think about it.

The fighting in Carlisle had continued through the night. There were no recognizable lines of defense in the city anymore, just pockets of stubborn defenders holding their ground to the last. Most of these were cyclopians, and they continued to fight mainly because they knew that the Avon populace would show them little mercy after twenty years of cyclopian brutality. The one-eyes had been Greensparrow's elite police, the executioners and tax collectors, and now, with the king revealed as a dragon, and long gone from the city, the cyclopians would serve as scapegoats for all the misery that Greensparrow had brought.

Not that all the citizens of Carlisle had taken up the cause of the returning queen. Far from it. Most had taken to their homes, wanting only to stay out of the way, and though many had surrendered and even offered to fight alongside the Eriadorans, more than a few continued their resistance, particularly in the southern sections of Carlisle against the fierce Huegoths.

To Oliver, Siobhan, and Katerin, and many others who had come from Caer MacDonald, it seemed a replay of the revolt in Montfort, only on a much grander scale. The trio had witnessed this same type of building-to-building fighting, and though they had been split apart from each other during the night, they understood the inevitable outcome and where it would lead. Thus Oliver was not surprised when he galloped Threadbare through the main doors of Carlisle Abbey to find Siobhan and Katerin, each leading their respective groups of soldiers, already inside, battling the one-eyes from pew to pew. The slanting rays of morning cut through the dimly lit cathedral, filtering through the many breaks in the wall of the semicircular apse, where the tower had crumbled.

"So glad that you decided to join in!" Katerin called to the halfling as he cantered past her, his pony thundering down the center aisle of the nave.

Oliver pulled Threadbare up short, the pony skidding many feet on the smooth stone floor. "We cannot let them have the cathedral," he said, echoing the reasoning that had brought Katerin in here, and Siobhan, and many others. It was true enough; in all of Carlisle, as in every major Avonsea city, there was no more defensible place than the cathedral. If the cyclopians were allowed to retreat within Carlisle Abbey in force, it might be weeks before the invaders could roust them, and even then, only at great cost.

The leaders of the army understood that fact, though, and so it did not seem likely that any cyclopians would find refuge in here. Siobhan's Cutters had gained the triforium, and from that high ledge were already raining arrows on the cyclopians in the nave, a force that was rapidly diminishing. Katerin's force had gained two-thirds of the pews in the main nave, and the northern transept, up ahead and to the left of Oliver's position, had been taken. In the southern transept, the defense was breaking down as terrified one-eyes ran out the doors, scattering to the city's streets.

"With me!" Oliver cried, bolting Threadbare ahead, barreling into a throng of cyclopians. Several went flying, but Oliver's progress was halted by the sheer number of brutes. The halfling's rapier flashed left, poking one in the eye, then swiped across to the right, cutting a line down another's cheek.

But Oliver soon realized that his call had caught his comrades by surprise, and that he had rushed out too far ahead for any immediate support.

"I could be wrong!" the halfling sputtered, parrying wildly, trying to protect himself and his pony. Cyclopian hands grasped at any hold they could find, trying to bring both rider and beast down under their weight. Other one-eyes came out of the pews behind Oliver, cutting off those, Katerin included, who were trying to come to the halfling's defense.

"Oh, woe!" Oliver wailed, and then he remembered that Siobhan was watching him, and that most important of all, he must not die a coward. "But I must sing in my moment of sacrifice!" he proclaimed, and he did just that, taking up an ancient Gascon tune of heroics and the spoils of war.

We take the town and throw it down,
Fighting for the ladies.
Whose so-sweet thorns bring out our horns,
Fighting for the ladies.

And so we kick, and punch and stick,
Fighting for the ladies.
And if we hurt, they bind with their shirts!
Fighting for the ladies.

Fighting for the ladies!
Take off your clothes to cover our holes,
Oh, won't you pretty ladies.
Then run away because we won the day!
Chasing naked, pretty ladies!

As he finished, the halfling shrieked and ducked as the air about him filled suddenly with buzzing noises. For a moment, Oliver thought that he was in the middle of a swarm of bees, and when he finally figured out that these were arrows swishing right by him, he was not comforted!

But then it ended, as quickly as it had begun, and the cyclopian press around Oliver and his yellow pony was not so great anymore. And then Katerin was up to him, scolding him for such a foolish charge.

Oliver hardly heard a word she said. He looked up to the triforium, to Siobhan and her Fairborn forces, already many of them moving along to seek out the next important target.

Oliver tipped his great hat to the beautiful half-elf, but Siobhan did not smile.

"My friends, they do not shoot so well!" she yelled down, imitating Oliver's Gascon accent.

Oliver stared at her, perplexed.

"She heard your song," Katerin remarked dryly. "I think she told them to shoot you dead."

"Ah," noted the halfling, tipping his hat once again and smiling all the wider.

"Gascon pig," Katerin said with a snicker, and turned away.

"But I am so wounded!" Oliver wailed suddenly, and Katerin spun about. "May I use your shirt to bandage my wounds?"

It was among the finest bits of riding that Katerin O'Hale had ever witnessed, for as she took a single threatening stride Oliver's way, the halfling swung Threadbare to the side and hopped the pony up onto a narrow wooden pew, running along in perfect balance.

Katerin looked helplessly to Siobhan, the both of them grinning widely at their irreverent little friend.

Then it was back to business, finishing off the one-eyes on this lowest floor of the cathedral, securing the nave, the transepts, and what remained of the apse. Soon the twin front towers were taken as well, but not before the cyclopians managed one breakout, led by a huge and terrible brute, dressed in regal fashion and wielding a beautifully crafted broadsword. Duke Cresis forged along at the head of the fighting wedge, crossing through the semicircular apse at the cathedral's eastern end, then turning into the southern transept. And when Cresis found that way blocked by a wall of Eriadoran defenders, the brute swung back to the east, down a narrow passageway and then through a cleverly concealed door on the left-hand wall. Cresis and twenty of his fellows had gained the catacombs.

"Throw burning faggots down the stairs," one Eriadoran offered. "Smoke them out, or to death—let the choice be on them!"

Others seconded the call, but Siobhan held reservations. The leader of that one-eye band had been identified as Duke Cresis, and the half-elf wasn't so sure that the brute should be given any opportunity to escape. "Perhaps there is another exit from the catacombs," she reasoned. "We cannot let so powerful a cyclopian slip back onto Carlisle's streets."

"Would any want to follow the brutes into the dark catacombs?" another soldier asked bluntly.

There came several calls for the dwarfs, but Siobhan silenced them. "We have no time to find Bellick's folk," she explained. "I am going."

A score of Fairborn were quick to line up behind her.

"I hate to leave my so-fine horse," Oliver lamented, but he, too, moved near to Siobhan, and Katerin was there at the same time.

"Four by three!" Siobhan ordered, and twelve archers took up positions before the closed door, four ranks of three each. "Do not wait to see," the half-elf explained, and she nodded to two men standing beside the door.

On a three-count, the men pulled the door open wide, diving out of the way as the first rank of Fairborn let fly. They dropped and rolled aside, and the second rank loosed their arrows as the first ran to the end, setting new bolts to their bowstrings. Then the third, then the fourth, let fly, and then the first again, and so it went, through two complete volleys, a score and four arrows bouncing down the stone walls and stairs.

Both Oliver and Katerin were handed lanterns, but Siobhan told them to keep the light down low. "Fairborn fight better in the dark than do one-eyes," she explained, and then she paused, studying closely her two friends, who were not of the elvish race.

"We're going down there beside you," Katerin said determinedly, ending the debate before Siobhan could even begin it. And so they did, three abreast, eight ranks in all, moving slowly and cautiously down the rough and uneven stairs.

They passed several dead cyclopians, the unfortunate first line of defense that had taken the brunt of the missile barrage, and then they came into the lower level.

Oliver's lantern seemed a tiny thing in here. The ceilings were low and close; Katerin and some of the taller elves had to stoop to avoid clunking their heads. The massive archways were even lower, their stones so thick that the whole of this area, built to support the tremendous cathedral above it, seemed one great winding maze.

The friends tried to stay together, but often they were forced to walk single file. Every archway presented four possible turns, and the floor was so uneven that being on the same line as a friend was no guarantee that the ally could even be seen. The torchlight did little to defeat the perpetual gloom, the cobwebs hung low and thick, and the archways were so numerous and imposing, and so low, that the area seemed more a winding, twisting nest of passageways than an open area dotted by columns.

"This was where the old abbey stood," Oliver reasoned, his voice low and muffled by the many cobwebs and blocking stones. "They built the cathedral right above it." As he spoke, the halfling turned a corner, coming upon a raised section of floor, three or four age-worn steps that led up to a stone box, an altar, or perhaps a crypt. Oliver could not be sure. He turned back to ask Siobhan's opinion, only to find that he had somehow split away from the others.

"I do so like the sky for my ceiling," the halfling whispered.

"One-eye!" came an echoing cry from somewhere in the distance, followed quickly by the ring of steel, and then a guttural grunt, followed soon by a Fairborn voice claiming, "They are in here still!"

"Siobhan!" Oliver called softly, trying hard to backtrack. He went through an archway, but every direction looked the same. "Left breast, right breast, down the middle, damn the rest," Oliver chanted, pointing in each direction. Then, as Gascon tradition demanded, the halfling went the way of the last "Damn the rest."

He heard more sounds of battle, individuals clashing but nothing large-scale. The cyclopians were indeed in here, hiding separately, looking to ambush.

Oliver went left at the next low arch, then, thinking he recognized the area as the entry foyer, came around a corner with a bright smile, expecting to see only the stairs leading back to the main floor of the cathedral.

His light was immediately swallowed by a pair of forms too large to be Fairborn, too wide to be Katerin.

The halfling squeaked and thrust forth his rapier, trying to get his lantern to the floor that he might draw out his main gauche. He thought that his slender blade would surely get the closest foe, but the form moved with the perfect balance and grace of a pure warrior, smoothly and deftly dodging.

Oliver thought he was about to die, but the shine of skin as the foe came around was ruddy and tan, not the grayish hue more common to one-eyes, and this opponent had two eyes—cinnamon-colored eyes.

"Luthien," Oliver began, but stopped short as he realized his error.

"Watch that blade, fool!" Ethan Bedwyr snarled, gingerly turning aside the still-poking rapier.

"What are you doing here?"

"I was told that Katerin had come in here," Ethan replied softly. "I promised my brother that I would watch over her."

A sly grin came over Oliver. "Your brother?" he asked.

Ethan had no time for such semantic games. He motioned to two other Huegoth companions who were still on the stairs, indicating that they should go to the right, then he and his immediate companion set off straight ahead.

Oliver bent down to retrieve his lantern and replace the main gauche on his belt, only to find himself alone once more. He looked to the stairs, tempted to go back up, but then he heard another cry from somewhere in the distance, a voice he recognized.

Siobhan and one Fairborn companion went down a dozen steps and turned a sharp corner, putting the sounds of the others far behind, then dared to crawl under a tiny door, no more than three-feet-square, barely large enough to admit a large cyclopian. The tunnel beyond was not much larger than the entrance, and the pair had to bend low, even crawling at points to continue along.

The darkness was complete, even to the sensitive eyes of the Fairborn, forcing Siobhan to light a hand lamp, a tiny lantern she had used often in her days as a housebreaker in Morkney-controlled Montfort.

She motioned for her companion, who was leading, to move on.

Finally, they came out into a higher area, the oldest catacombs in all the cathedral. Open crypts faced them from every wall, displaying the tattered skeletal remains of the first priests and abbots in Carlisle, perhaps in all of Avonsea. Most were lying on their back, but some, in more ornate crypts, were seated upon stone thrones.

Siobhan worked hard to steady her breathing as she noted one ancient corpse beside her, sitting tall and proud through the centuries, except that its skull was on the floor, probably the victim of hungry rats whose bones, too, were now likely resting in this place of death. The half-elf pulled her gaze away to see her companion bump his head hard on the curving ceiling of the next arch.

"Careful," Siobhan whispered, but then she cried out as her companion turned about and toppled.

Even in the dim light of her hand lamp, Siobhan could see the bright blood spewing from the elf's chest, which had been ripped from armpit to spinal cord.

Ahead of her stood the brutish cyclopian duke, that fabulous broadsword dripping elvish blood, Cresis's ugly face twisted with the promise of death.

There had only been a single, distant cry, and yells were becoming more frequent with each passing moment as more and more of the hunters happened upon hiding cyclopians. But Oliver had never been more focused in all his life. His mind, his soul, had locked on to that single utterance, and the maze seemed to sort itself out before him as he darted along, daring to turn up the flame in his lantern that he might better see the breaks in the uneven floor.

He paused in one wider area to jab his rapier into the butt of a battling cyclopian. Then, seeing that his prod had distracted the brute enough to give its Fairborn opponent an insurmountable advantage, Oliver ran on.

He passed through one archway without a look to either side, replaying that cry in his head, following his instincts and his heart.

Katerin spotted him and called out, and she, Ethan, and a Huegoth came in close pursuit.

But they could not keep up with Oliver in these tight quarters. They reached the top of a broken and uneven staircase, angling downward, just after the halfling had entered the little hole at its bottom.

Only the ring of steel told them that they had come the right way.

Siobhan was an archer, among the finest shots in all of Avonsea. But she was no novice with the blade, as Duke Cresis soon discovered.

The brute thought it had her by surprise, and so its first attack was straight ahead, a thrust for the half-elf's heart.

Out flashed a short sword, turning the brute's blade minutely as the half-elf turned her own body. A clean miss, and Siobhan countered lightning-fast, rolling her wrist to launch her blade in a diagonal line at Cresis's ugly face.

The brute fell back, stumbling over a block of stone into a wider area, the oldest altar in the ancient abbey.

Siobhan was fast to pursue, trying to press her advantage, but the same block of stone slowed her enough for the one-eye to steady its defenses.

"Duke Cresis?" Siobhan sneered.

Cresis snorted and did not bother to answer.

"I offer you the chance for surrender," Siobhan bluffed, and she prayed that the obviously powerful one-eye would accept. "The city is ours; you have no place to run."

"Then I will die with my sword in one hand and your head in the other!" the one-eye promised, and on Cresis came.

The broadsword flashed right, left, left again, and then straight down, the brute taking it up in both hands for the final attack. Siobhan parried and dodged, ducked low under the third swing and came up hard to meet the chop, her blade flat out over her head. She meant to catch the broadsword and turn it out wide, then step ahead, in close, and use the advantage of her much shorter sword in the tighter press.

Cresis's swing was far too powerful for that maneuver, and Siobhan found her legs nearly buckling under the weight of that vicious overhead chop. Her finely forged elvish blade held firm, though, stopping the attack short of her head, and she rolled out to the side, stabbing twice in rapid succession as she went, scoring one slight hit on the cyclopian's hip.

Cresis laughed at the minor wound and came in fast pursuit, thrusting his sword with every step. Siobhan danced desperately to keep out of the brute's reach. She came up hard against the block of stone that had once been an altar, and Cresis, thinking her caught, forged ahead.

Siobhan's balance was perfect as she went over the thigh-high block, falling prone on the other side as the cyclopian's blade swished the air above her.

Cresis leaped over, but the agile half-elf was already gone, scrambling out one end and putting her feet back under her. She reversed direction immediately, regaining the offensive, snapping her smaller blade at the brute's groin, then cutting it up so that Cresis's down-angled sword missed the parry.

The cyclopian fell back, a deep gash along its chin, its bulbous nose split nearly in half.

Siobhan could have asked again for surrender, and the brute might have agreed, but she was too far into the fight by then. She came on hard and fast, scoring again, this time putting the point of her sword deep into the brute's left shoulder, and coming in so close that she pinned Cresis's arms against the brute's torso.

But only for a moment, for Cresis howled in pain and heaved forward with all its considerable strength, launching Siobhan a dozen feet. She somehow managed to keep her balance and was ready when the brute came in at her again, with an all-too-familiar routine.

Right, left, left again, and then down, but this time, with only one hand on the sword.

Siobhan parried, dodged straight back, sucking in her belly, then ducked the third, coming up powerfully, seeing that Cresis had only one hand on the broadsword.

The blades met with a tremendous ring; Siobhan twisted with all her might, then stepped ahead, grinning in expected victory as the broadsword went out wide.

The light intensified as Oliver entered the chamber, to see his dear Siobhan in close with the huge and ugly brute. Cresis's sword was out to the side, not moving, but for some reason neither was Siobhan's readied blade diving for the one-eye.

Oliver understood when his love slipped away from the brute's chest, and more particularly, away from Cresis's left hand, which held a bloody dirk.

Siobhan managed a look at Oliver, then her sword hit the ground with a dead ring, and the half-elf quickly followed its descent.

Oliver was no match for Cresis and the mighty one-eye was hardly injured, but the halfling fostered no thoughts of retreat at that horrible moment. He roared for his love and leaped ahead, coming so furiously with his rapier, a ten-thrust routine, that Cresis could hardly distinguish each individual move, and the brute took several stinging hits along the forearm as it tried to maneuver the broadsword to block.

The cyclopian tried to square, but the enraged halfling would not relinquish the offense. Sheer anger driving him on, Oliver poked and poked, slashed at the broadsword with his main gauche, even catching the blade between the front-turned crosspiece of the crafted dagger at one point, though he had not the leverage to break the cyclopian's weapon or to tear it from Cresis's powerful grasp.

Still, it was Cresis, and not Oliver, who continued to back up, and Oliver found an opportunity before him as the cyclopian neared the altar block. Up the halfling leaped, and now Cresis had to work all the harder to parry, for Oliver's rapier was dangerously in line with the cyclopian's already-torn face.

"You are so ugly!" the halfling taunted, spitting his words. "A dog would not play with you unless you had a piece of meat tied about your fat waist!"

"I would eat the dog!" Cresis retorted, but the brute's words were cut short by yet another multiple-thrust attack.

Cresis was wise enough to understand that the halfling's rage was too great. If Cresis could keep Oliver moving, keep him sputtering and slashing wildly, the halfling would soon tire.

So the brute parried and started away from the altar, but then its one eye went wide with surprise as the main gauche came spinning, end over end. Up went the cyclopian's arm, blocking the dagger, but that wasn't the only incoming missile as Oliver ran to the edge of the altar block and threw himself at his enemy.

Cresis howled in pain again, his forearm burning from the stuck dagger. He tried to maneuver the broadsword to catch the flying halfling, but the brute's reaction was slow, its muscles torn and tightening.

Oliver crashed in hard, though the three-hundred-pound cyclopian barely took a tiny step backward. It didn't matter, for Oliver had leaped in with his rapier blade leading.

He was tight onto Cresis's burly chest then; he might have been a baby, clinging to its burly father. But that rapier had hit the mark perfectly, was stuck nearly to its basket hilt right through Cresis's bulky neck.

The cyclopian wheezed, sputtering blood from its mouth and its throat. It held on tight, tried to squeeze the life out of Oliver. But that grip inevitably loosened as the gasping brute's lungs filled with its own blood. Slowly, Cresis slumped to its knees, and Oliver was careful to get away, avoiding a halfhearted swing of the broadsword.

Cresis went down to all fours, gasping, trying to force air into its lungs.

Oliver paid the brute no more heed. He ran to his love, cradling her head in one arm and plunging his hand over the bleeding wound in the hollow of Siobhan's chest.

Ethan scrambled into the chamber then, followed closely by Katerin. "Ah my love!" they heard the halfling wail. "Do not die!"

"We cannot go on in this direction," Brind'Amour informed Luthien. The young Bedwyr pushed through some brush to join the wizard and saw the flat water, surrounding them on three sides.

They had spent nearly half an hour walking through the tangled and confusing underbrush to the end of a peninsula.

Luthien was about to suggest that they start back, but he held quiet as Brind'Amour moved behind him, the wizard staring intently at Riverdancer.

"The steed is rested," Brind'Amour announced. "We will fly."

Luthien didn't argue the point; he was thoroughly miserable, his feet wet and sore, his scalp itching from a hundred bites, and his nerves frayed, and though no monster had risen up against them, every one of the Saltwash's shadows appeared as though it hid some sinister beast.

So Luthien breathed a sigh of relief, filling his lungs with clean air as they broke through the soggy canopy. He squinted for some time, trying to adjust his eyes to the dazzling sunlight whenever it found a break in the thick cloud cover that rushed overhead. Logically, Luthien knew that they were probably more vulnerable up here than they had been in the cover of the swamp; Greensparrow would spot them easily if he bothered to look to the skies above his dark home. But Luthien was glad for the change anyway, and so was Riverdancer, the horse's neck straining forward eagerly. On Brind'Amour's suggestion, Luthien kept the horse moving low over the treetops.

"Do you see . . . anything?" Luthien asked after several minutes, looking back to the wizard.

Brind'Amour shook his head in frustration, then, after a moment's consideration, poked his thumb upward. "We'll not find the beast through this tangle," the wizard explained. "Let us see if the dragon finds us!"

The words resonated through Luthien's mind, inciting memories of his one previous encounter with a dragon, a sight that still sometimes woke him in the night. They had come out here for Greensparrow, he reminded himself, and they would not leave until the evil dragon king had been met and defeated.

Up went Riverdancer, a hundred feet above the dark trees. Two hundred, and the swamp took on different dimensions, became a patchwork of indistinct treetops and splotches of dark water. Still higher they went, the Saltwash widening below them, every shape blending together into one great gray-green quilt.

Flattening and blending, all the sharp twists of branches smoothed and blurred together in softer edges. All except for one, a single break in the collage, as though the Saltwash, like a great bow, had shot forward this singular, streaking arrow.

Luthien hesitated, mesmerized. What propelled the dragon at such speed? he wondered dumbly, for the mighty beast flapped its wings only occasionally, one beat and then tucked them in tight, speeding upward as though it was in a stoop!

Riverdancer snorted and tried to react, but it was too late. Luthien's heart sank as he realized his error, his hesitation. He looked into the maw of the approaching beast and saw his doom.

Then the world seemed to shift about him, to warp within the blue-white swirl of a magical tunnel. It ended as suddenly as it began, and Luthien found himself looking *up* at the dragon as it sped away from him.

Brind'Amour's staff touched his shoulder and the wizard called forth a bolt of crackling black energy that grabbed the dragon and jolted it.

Out wide went Greensparrow's wings, dragging in the air, stopping the momentum.

Luthien reacted quickly this time, bringing Riverdancer up high in a steeper climb, trying to come around behind the great beast.

But Dansallignatious, Greensparrow, ducked his head as he fell, turning his serpentine neck right about.

Riverdancer folded one wing and did a complete roll as the dragon breathed its line of fire. As he came upright, fighting to hold his seat and hold control, Luthien stared incredulously, watching a green, disembodied fist rush out from behind him. It shot through the air, punching hard into the dragon's midsection, and exploding there with enough force to hurl the beast many yards away.

"Hah!" Brind'Amour snorted, and snapped his fingers in the air beside Luthien's ear.

In less confident tones, the wizard whispered, "You've got to stay near to the beast, boy. Close enough so that if Greensparrow breathes, he'll burn away his own wing."

Luthien understood the logic of the reasoning, but saying something and doing something were often two completely different things—especially when one was talking about a dragon!

A second fist of magical energy went flying out, and then a third, and Luthien prodded Riverdancer in their wake, following their course toward the beast.

Greensparrow's winding neck swerved and the next fist shot by. The last one, though, scored a glancing blow, snapping the dragon's head out to the side. Still, Greensparrow seemed perfectly focused on the third missile, the living missile of the pegasus and its two riders, and Luthien nearly swooned, thinking suddenly that he had put himself and his companions right into the path of certain death.

"Hold the course!" Brind'Amour yelled, and Luthien, screaming all the way, obeyed.

The second flying fist, the one that had missed the mark altogether, had turned about like a boomerang, and came in hard, clapping the dragon off the back of the head just before Greensparrow could loose his fire. The beast pitched forward; Riverdancer flew in right over its bending neck. Luthien tried to draw out his sword, for he was close enough, almost, to hit the monstrous thing, and Brind'Amour's staff came forward once more as another bolt, this one red in hue, streaked down, sparkling from scale to scale.

Now the dragon roared and continued to duck its head, rolling right into a dive. Brind'Amour cried out in victory, so did Luthien as he started to bank Riverdancer into pursuit, but neither of them comprehended the vast repertoire of weapons possessed by a beast such as this. The dragon was rolling down, putting its head toward the safety of the swamp, but as the great bulk came around, Greensparrow kept the presence of mind to lash out with his long and powerful tail.

Riverdancer was turning, and that surely saved the steed's life and those of its riders, but still the pegasus took a glancing blow on the rear flank.

Suddenly the trio were spinning, holding on for their lives.

Brind'Amour came right off the horse's back and had to latch on with both hands to the cowl of Luthien's cape. He cried out, cursing as his staff plummeted out of sight, disappearing into the tangled background of the Saltwash.

Luthien righted the horse and wrapped one arm about the wizard as he continued to flail helplessly at Riverdancer's side.

The sun seemed to go away then, as the dragon soared past them, barely twenty feet to their right, great clawed feet reaching out. Luthien pulled hard to his left, turning the steed away, but a claw tore at Riverdancer's right wing, gashing flesh and snapping bone.

They spun over once more, this time in a roll that Luthien could not hope to control. Down they tumbled, and as they came around, Luthien saw that Greensparrow had folded his wings in a power dive and was in close pursuit, that awful fanged mouth opened wide.

But again came that blue swirl, as Brind'Amour opened a magical tunnel right below them. They were in it for only a split second, a split second that put them two hundred feet lower, barely at treetop level and several hundred yards to one side.

Falling again, too confused and surprised to even know what lay below, Luthien could only hold on and scream.

The pair and their wounded pegasus splashed hard into a muddy pool.

It seemed like minutes passed, but in truth it was but seconds before the two men and the wounded steed pulled themselves onto the soft turf at the pool's edge. Mud covered Brind'Amour's blue robes, turned Riverdancer's shining white coat a soiled brown, and coated Luthien as well—except for that magnificent crimson cape, which seemed to repel any stains, holding fast its shining crimson hue.

The companions hardly had time to take note of that, though. Riverdancer's right wing was badly broken and torn, the pained horse tucking it close to his side. Brind'Amour grabbed the bridle and led the steed into a thick copse, then cast some enchantment and motioned for Luthien to follow him.

"I cannot leave Riverdancer . . ." the young Bedwyr started to protest.

"The horse must revert to its natural form," Brind'Amour tried to explain, patting the air soothingly. "Riverdancer's wounds shall not be so great when the wings are gone, but even then, the horse will be in need of rest. And no use in trying to ride in this tangle anyway, against the likes of Greensparrow."

As if on cue, there came a deafening roar and a great shadow passed overhead.

"Come along," said Brind'Amour, and this time Luthien offered no argument.

To Oliver's surprise, and temporary relief, Siobhan opened her beautiful green eyes and managed a pained smile. "Did we get him?" she asked, her words broken by labored breathing.

Oliver nodded, too choked to respond. "Duke Cresis of Carlisle is a bad memory and nothing more," he finally managed to say.

"Half-credit for the kill," Siobhan whispered.

"All for you," Oliver readily replied.

Siobhan shook her head, which took great effort. "Only half," she whispered. "All I need."

Oliver looked back to Katerin, noting the streaks of tears on the woman's fair features.

"Half for me," Siobhan went on. "Fifteen and a half this day."

Oliver tried to respond, but couldn't understand the significance.

"Tell . . . Luthien that," Siobhan stuttered. "Fifteen and half for me this day. Final count . . . ninety-three and a half for me . . . only ninety-three for . . . Luthien . . . even if he kills . . . Greensparrow."

Oliver hugged her close.

"I win," she said, a bit of cheer somehow seeping into her voice. Then her timbre changed suddenly. "Oliver?" she asked. "Are you here?"

The light had not diminished, and Oliver knew that her eyes were not wounded. But she could not see, and the halfling realized what that foretold.

"I am here, my love," Oliver replied, hugging her, and keeping his voice steady. "I am here."

"Cold," Siobhan said. "So cold."

More than a minute passed before Katerin bent over and closed Siobhan's unseeing eyes.

"Come with us, Oliver," she bade the distraught halfling, her voice firm for she knew that she had to be strong for her friend. "There is nothing more you can do here."

"I stay," Oliver replied determinedly.

Katerin looked to Ethan, who only shrugged.

"I will finish the business in the catacombs," Ethan promised. "And return for you."

Katerin nodded and Ethan was gone, back the way they had come. The woman moved away from Oliver then, respectfully, and sat upon the altar block, her heart torn, as much in sympathy for poor Oliver as in grief for the loss of her dear half-elven friend.

"We must find my staff," Brind'Amour whispered.

"How?" Luthien balked, looking around at the endless tangles and shadows of the Saltwash. "We have no chance . . ."

"Sssh!" Brind'Amour hissed. "Keep your voice quiet. Dragons have the most excellent of hearing."

Again as if on cue, there came a great rush of wind and the canopy above the two exploded into a fiery maelstrom. Brind'Amour stood as if frozen in place, gaping at the conflagration, and only Luthien's quick reaction, the young Bedwyr tackling the wizard into a shallow pool and throwing himself, and his magical shielding cape, over Brind'Amour's prone form, saved the old man from the falling brands. Great strands of hanging moss dove down to the ground, coiling like snakes as they landed, their topmost ends burning like candle wicks. Not so far from the companions a tree, its sap superheated by the fires, exploded in a shower of miniature fireballs, hissing and sputtering as they landed on the pools or muddy turf.

"Up, and run away!" Brind'Amour cried as soon as the moment had passed, the blazing branches smoldering quickly in the dampness of the marsh.

Luthien tried to follow that command, stumbling repeatedly on the pool's slippery banks. In the distance, he heard Riverdancer's frantic neighing, and then, as he turned back in the direction of the area where he had left the horse, he saw the approach of doom.

He grabbed for Brind'Amour, thinking to pull the man back into the mud, but the wizard darted away. The cover was not so thick anymore—certainly not enough to shield them from the penetrating gaze of a dragon!—and Brind'Amour knew that to cower was to be caught.

No, the old wizard determined, they had come in here to battle Greensparrow, and so they would, meeting his charge.

Brind'Amour scrambled up to the trunk of an ancient willow, a graceful spreading mass that had accepted the first dragon pass as though it was no more than a minor inconvenience. "Lend me your strength," the wizard whispered to the trunk, and he embraced the tree in a gentle hug.

The dragon rushed overhead, looking about the area it had so brutally cleared. It let out a shrill shriek as it crossed over Brind'Amour, and immediately began its long and graceful turn.

Luthien called out a warning to the wizard, but Brind'Amour seemed not to hear. Nor did the wizard appear to take any note at all of the dragon. He stood hugging the tree, whispering softly, his eyes closed.

Luthien inched closer, not wanting to disturb the man, but keeping a watchful eye for the returning dragon. He started to call out to Brind'Amour again, but stopped, startled, when he noticed that the fingers of the wizard's hands were gone, as if they had simply sunken into the willow! Luthien looked to the man's face, was touched by the serenity there, then looked back to see that Brind'Amour's arms were in up to the wrists!

"Lend me your strength," Brind'Amour whispered again, but in a language that Luthien could not understand, a language of music, not words, of the eternal harmony that had brought the world into being, that gave the tree its strength and longevity, the language of the very powers that sustained all the world.

Luthien did not know what he should do, and when he looked back the way the dragon had flown, to see the creature speeding toward him once more, he could only cry out helplessly to his entranced friend and throw himself to the side, away from Brind'Amour and the willow, to the base of another large tree.

Greensparrow issued a deafening roar, culminating with the release of that tremendous fire. At the same moment, Brind'Amour cried out, as if in ecstasy, and a green glow engulfed the wizard, ran up his arms and to the tree, then up the tree, intensifying as it spread wide along the branches.

The hot dragon flames fell over them all; Luthien tried to dig a hole in the ground. His eyes burned and he felt as if his lungs would explode, and he could only imagine the grim fate that had befallen Brind'Amour, who was not protected by the marvelous crimson cape.

Indeed those fires did fall over the wizard, but Brind'Amour felt them not at all, no more than did the ancient willow. For Brind'Amour was a part of that tree then, and it a part of him, and while he had taken from it its ancient resilience, it had gained the wizard's sentience. Stooping, pliable limbs reached up from the swamp, swatting and entangling the dragon as it flew past.

Greensparrow was caught completely off his guard as one great limb whipped up to smack him right between the eyes and another caught fast on his left wing. Over and around the dragon spun. Wood bent and twisted and tore apart.

Now Brind'Amour did cry out in pain, and the sheer shock of the dragon hit destroyed his symbiosis with the tree, left him sitting on the wet ground, wondering why wisps of smoke were rising from his robes. He groaned as he considered the willow, many of its branches torn away, the trunk half-uprooted and tilting to the side, the whole of the ancient tree nearly pulled from the ground by the weight of its catch.

Brind'Amour wanted to go to the willow, to offer comfort and thanks, to try to lend his powers that it might better heal. He had other problems, though, for the dragon had been taken from the sky, to crash down heavily, clearing a swath a hundred yards long. But the beast was far from defeated. Greensparrow pulled himself free of the tangled and broken flora and righted himself, facing the wizard. One wing had been torn and would need time to heal; the dragon could not fly. Like a gigantic cat, Greensparrow crouched, tamping down his back legs, his yellow-green orbs locked on the puny man who had given him such pain.

A single leap brought him close enough to loose his fires once again, engulfing Brind'Amour.

But the old wizard was ready. With his magic, he reached down to the earth at his feet, drawing the moisture from it, meeting the dragon fire with a wall of water. Then he loosed his own response, a blazing line of energy that cut through the fires and slammed at Greensparrow.

Luthien huddled and trembled, blocked his ears from the thunderous roars of beast and flame. It went on and on, seconds seeming like hours. All that Luthien wanted was a single gasp of air, but that would not come. All that he wanted was to get up and run away, but his feet would not answer his call. Then the world started to slip into blackness, an endless pit, it seemed, and he was falling.

The sounds receded.

Then it ended, the fires and the energy bolt, and Greensparrow and Brind'Amour stood facing each other. Brind'Amour knew by the way the serpentine neck suddenly snapped back and by the beast's wide eyes that his resilience had surprised the beast.

"You have betrayed all that was sacred to the ancient brotherhood," the old wizard cried.

"The ancient fools!" the dragon replied in a snarling, resonating voice.

Brind'Amour was caught off guard, for the dragon's words did not come easily, every syllable stuttered and intermixed with feral snarls.

"Fools, you say," the wizard replied. "Yet that brotherhood is where you first found your power."

"My power is ancient!" the dragon answered with a roar. "Older than your brotherhood, older than you!"

Brind'Amour understood it then, recognized the struggle between the wills of this dual being. "You are Greensparrow!" he cried, trying to force the issue.

"I am Dansallignat . . . I am Greensparrow, king of Avonsea!" the beast roared.

Then the dragon flinched, an involuntary twist, perhaps, and Brind'Amour was quick to the offensive, hurling yet another bolt, this one white and streaking like lightning. The dragon roared; the wizard screamed in pain as all his energy, all his life force, was hurled into that one bolt. Magic was a power limited by good sense, but Brind'Amour had no options of restraint now, not when facing such a foe. He felt his heart fluttering, felt his legs go weak, but still he energized the bolt, launched himself into it fully, sapping every ounce of strength within him and hurling it, transformed, into the great beast.

He could hardly see the dragon, and wasn't really conscious of his surroundings anyway, but somewhere deep in his mind, Brind'Amour realized that he was indeed hurting the monster, and that it was transforming.

Finally the energy fizzled, and the wizard stood swaying, thoroughly spent. After a moment, he managed to consider his opponent, and his eyes went wide.

No longer did the dragon stand before him, nor was his foe the foppish king of Avon. Greensparrow and Dansallignatious had been caught somewhere in the middle of their dual forms, a bipedal creature half again as large as a man, but with scaly skin mottled green and black, great clawed hands, a swishing tail, and a serpentine neck as long as Brind'Amour was tall.

"Do you think you have defeated me?" the beast asked.

Luthien heard that call distantly, and the very voice of the beast, a whining, grating buzz, wounded him, stung his ears and his heart.

"You are a fool, Brind'Amour, as were all your fellow wizards," Greensparrow chided.

"And Greensparrow was among that lot," the wizard said with great effort.

"No!" roared the beast. "Greensparrow alone was wise enough to know that his day had not passed."

Brind'Amour had no response to that, for he, too, had come to believe that the brotherhood of wizards had surrendered their powers too quickly and recklessly.

"And now you will die," the beast said casually, moving a stride forward. "And all the world will be open to me."

Again, Brind'Amour could not refute the dragon king's words—at least not the first part, for he had not the strength to lift his arm against the approaching creature. He wasn't so convinced, though, that Greensparrow's claim about the world would prove true.

"They know who you are now," he said defiantly, his voice as strong and confident as he could possibly make it. "And what you are."

Greensparrow laughed wickedly, as if to question how that could possibly matter.

"Deanna Wellworth will take back her throne and her kingdom, and Greensparrow the foul will not be welcomed!" Brind'Amour proclaimed.

"If I can so easily defeat the likes of Brind'Amour, then how will the weakling queen, or any of her ill-advised allies, stand against me?" As he spoke, Greensparrow continued his advance, moving to within a few feet of Brind'Amour, who was simply too spent to retreat. "I will take back what was mine!" the beast promised, and the time for talking had passed.

Greensparrow's serpentine neck shot forward, maw opening wide. Brind'Amour let out a cry that sounded as a pitiful squeak, and threw up his arms before his face. Fangs tore his sleeves, ripped his skin, but the defensive move stopped Greensparrow from finding a secure hold, his snout butting the wizard instead and throwing Brind'Amour down to the ground.

At the same moment, the dragon king caught a movement to the side and behind, as a form uncoiled from its position at the base of a tree and rushed out at him.

Brind'Amour's companion! the dragon king realized. But how had he missed seeing that one?

Luthien took two powerful strides, bringing *Blind-Striker* in a two-handed over-the-shoulder arc that drove the blade hard against the beast's extended neck. He chopped again and again as Greensparrow tried to reorient and square himself to this newest foe. Green-black scales splintered and flew away. The beast's clawed hind feet dug trenches in the earth as it backpedaled.

Luthien, blinded by rage, screamed a dozen curses and pumped his arms frantically, refusing to give up the offensive, knowing that if he allowed the beast to gain its composure and its footing, he would surely be doomed. Again and again he launched his mighty sword, each swing culminating in a hit, sometimes solid, sometimes glancing. He kept Greensparrow backing, kept whacking at the twisting form with all his strength.

But then he slipped—a slight stumble, but one that allowed the dragon king to get out of reach, to gain its footing.

"The Crimson Shadow!" Greensparrow snarled. "How much a thorn you have been to me!"

Luthien put his feet back under him and started to charge once more, but skidded to a fast stop, realizing that to dive into that tangle of claws and fangs was certainly to die.

"For months I have been waiting for this moment," Greensparrow promised. "Waiting to pay you back for all the trouble. For Belsen'Krieg and Morkney, for Paragor of Princetown and for the ridiculous cries of 'Eriador free!' that have reached my ears."

Luthien stepped forward and swung, but found himself falling backward before the blade got halfway around, as the snakelike neck snapped out at him. He fell into the mud and scrambled backward. Greensparrow was laughing too hard to pursue.

"Watch him die, Brind'Amour," the dragon king chided. "Watch all your hopes torn apart."

Luthien glanced Brind'Amour's way, praying that the wizard was ready to join in then. But Brind'Amour could not help him, not this time. The wizard remained on the ground, barely holding himself in a sitting position. His magic was gone, expended in the enchantments, particularly that last bolt of power, his ultimate attack. It had taken much strength from the dragon, had even reduced it to this present form, but it had not destroyed Greensparrow.

Luthien studied his foe carefully. The dragon king was certainly wounded, had suffered a great beating from the tree and the energy bolts, and from Luthien's own wild attack. Large welts lined Greensparrow's neck, and his face was scored on one side. One of his wings was tucked neatly against his back, but the other hung out at a weird angle, obviously broken.

Slowly Luthien slid his foot back under him.

"Or perhaps I should not kill you," Greensparrow was saying, his gaze as much at the empty distance as at Luthien. "Perhaps I should bring you back to Carlisle, an admitted liar and enemy of the throne. Perhaps I could use you to discredit Deanna Wellworth," the beast mused, and looked back—to see that Luthien was up and charging!

Greensparrow snapped his head at the young Bedwyr, but too late. Luthien came under the descending maw, throwing up the tip of his blade, and Greensparrow's own momentum worked against him as *Blind-Striker* bit under the dragon king's bottom jaw, right through scales and skin, right through the flicking forked tongue and into the roof of his mouth.

Luthien continued forward and held on with all his strength, trying desperately to get inside the angle of the monster's flailing arms.

Greensparrow hissed and thrashed and Luthien could not hold the sword and stay in tight. His feet went out from under him as Greensparrow spun to the side, but *Blind-Striker* held fast and Luthien was pulled right from the ground.

A clawed hand swiped at his exposed ribs, tearing through his chain-link armor and the thick leather tunic below it as easily as if it was old and brittle paper. Bright lines of blood appeared, one gash so deep that Luthien's rib was visible.

Still he hung on, growling against the pain, but then the other blow came across, punching and not raking, a blow so fierce that Luthien flew away, taking his sword with him.

The dragon king's head jerked violently to the side as *Blind-Striker* tore free, and Greensparrow slumped to one knee, giving horrified Luthien enough time to scramble away into the cover of the swamp.

But the beast was fast in pursuit, sniffing and snarling, sputtering curses that rang in the ears of the young Bedwyr. Never before had he run from battle, not from Morkney, not from the demon Taknapotin. But this beast, even wounded as it was, was beyond both of them, was something too evil and too awful.

And so Luthien ran, stumbling, pressing his arm against his side in an effort to keep his lifeblood from spilling away. He heard the sniffing behind him, knew that Greensparrow was following the trail of dripping blood.

The beast was right behind him. Luthien gave a cry and ran on as fast as he could go, but caught his foot in an exposed root and went tumbling headlong.

All his sensibilities screamed at him that the trail had ended, that he was about to die!

A long moment passed; Luthien could hear the breathing of the monster, not more than a few feet behind him. Why didn't Greensparrow get it over with? he wondered.

His cape. It had to be the cape. Luthien dared to peek out from under the hood, could see the lamplight glow of those terrible dragon eyes scanning the ground. Luthien held his breath, forced himself to stay perfectly still.

He would have been found; he knew that Greensparrow would have sorted out the riddle soon enough, except that there came a crashing noise somewhere up ahead, and the white coat of Riverdancer flashed into view, running past.

Greensparrow howled, thinking that his young opponent had somehow gotten ahead of him, back to his horse. If the beast went airborne, it would be beyond his grasp!

That the dragon king could not allow, so he took up the chase, leaping forward, and stumbling over a form that he could not see.

Greensparrow hardly took note of the trip, and his heavy foot had taken the breath from Luthien. The young Bedwyr could have remained where he was, allowing the dragon king to run off in pursuit of Riverdancer, while he went back to Brind'Amour.

But Luthien saw his chance before him and would not pass it up, no matter the terror, no matter the pain. With a shout of "Eriador free!" the young Bedwyr launched himself forward, catching up to the beast even as it pulled itself from the ground. *Blind-Striker*'s tip bit hard, right between the wings, tearing through the scales and nicking the backbone.

Luthien kept going forward, leaped right onto Greensparrow's back, catching a firm and stubborn hold on the broken wing even as the beast tried to turn about.

Greensparrow threw himself into a roll, ducking his shoulder so that he would go right over the pitiful human. Luthien tried to leap free, got his blade out of the beast's back and pushed off the wing. He scrambled away as Greensparrow rolled, but the dragon king came up in a leap that brought him up to Luthien, and the man's breath was blasted from his lungs as Greensparrow came down heavily atop him.

He was pinned, nowhere to run, with the dragon king's terrible face barely inches away. They held the pose for several seconds, a strange expression, a look of confusion perhaps, on Greensparrow's dragon features.

Luthien knew that the torn maw could not bite at him, but his arms were pinned against his chest and he could not hope to block if Greensparrow gouged at his face with that array of horns. Desperately he struggled, to no avail. He couldn't even draw breath, and felt a pointed press against the hollow of his breast that he soon realized to be the tip of his own sword!

Luthien's eyes went wide. If that was the swordtip, then *Blind-Striker* was pointing straight out. But if the dragon king was on top of him . . .

"Foolish, wretched boy," Greensparrow said, his voice serene and his words accompanied by dripping blood. The creature managed a small, incredulous chuckle. "You have killed me."

Luthien was too stunned to reply.

"But I will kill you as well," Greensparrow promised, and Luthien had no words, and certainly no actions, to refute the claim as Greensparrow's neck lifted the horned head up high and put the sharp horns in line with Luthien's face. Even if the dragon king expired before he struck, the simple weight of the dropping horns would surely finish Luthien.

He tried to face death bravely, tried not to cry out. His concentration was shattered, though, by a thunderous roar to the side of his head, by the spray of muddy turf as Riverdancer charged up and spun about, then kicked out with his hind legs, connecting solidly on the dragon's head even as it began its descent.

Greensparrow's neck snapped out to the side violently; the head thumped hard against the ground.

The dragon king lay very still.

EPILOGUE

It took Luthien some time to extract himself from under the dead beast. Even after he had squirmed clear, he spent many minutes just lying in the muck, trying to catch his breath, praying that the searing pain would abate. Somehow he managed to get to his feet. And then he nearly collapsed, fell against his precious Riverdancer, merely a horse once again and with no sign of Brind'Amour's wings, and hugged the horse tight.

Luthien looked to the fallen dragon king, to see *Blind-Striker*'s crafted pommel poking into the air out the creature's back. Guiding Riverdancer, using the horse's strength, Luthien managed to get the dead dragon king angled so that he could retrieve the sword. Then Luthien led the horse back to Brind'Amour, and the young Bedwyr was relieved indeed to see that the wizard, though he was lying on his back, apparently unconscious, was breathing steadily.

It took a long while to get Brind'Amour across Riverdancer's back. That done, and with no desire to be in the swamp when night descended over it, Luthien led the horse away, following as direct a westerly course as he could.

Luck was with him, and sometime long after sunset, Luthien

emerged from the Saltwash onto the rolling fields of southeastern Avon. He meant to build a fire, but collapsed on the grass.

When he awoke to the slanting rays of dawn, he found a cheerful Brind'Amour standing over him. "This day you ride," the wizard said with a wink. "A long road ahead of us, my boy."

Brind'Amour helped him to his feet, and Luthien realized that his wounds were not so sore anymore. He looked to the one on his ribs and saw a thick muddy salve there, and he didn't have to ask to figure that Brind'Amour had added a bit of magic to the healing.

"A long road," the wizard said again, adding a wink. "But this time, the end of that road should be a better place by far!"

Indeed it was, for by the time the companions got back to Carlisle, Deanna Wellworth had assumed her rightful place as queen of Avon. Her speech to the doubting and frightened populace had been conciliatory and apologetic, but firm. She was back, by right of blood. They would have to accept that, but Deanna was wise enough to understand that the real test of her power, and the real reason for her return, was to improve the lives of those who looked to her for guidance.

Her reign, she promised, would be as her father's had been, gentle and just, for the good of all.

How much her hopes, and the hopes of those who supported her, were lifted on that morning when Luthien and Brind'Amour, both riding the healed Riverdancer, came back through Carlisle's shining gates, when news that the dragon king, evil Greensparrow, was truly dead!

That settled, Deanna acted quickly. She recognized Brind'Amour as rightful king of the free land of Eriador, and afforded the same autonomy to King Ashannon McLenny of Baranduine and to King Bellick dan Burso of DunDarrow. The four then struck a truce with Asmund of Isenland, though the subtle threat of war was needed to convince the fierce and proud Huegoth king to agree. For the three kings and one queen of Avonsea held a firm front in their demand that none of their subjects be held in slavery by Asmund's warriors.

The longships were emptied; men who thought they would never again see the light of day fell to their knees on the banks of the Stratton, giving thanks to God.

Asmund's warriors would row themselves home!

That business completed, Brind'Amour took to his own matters, arranging for the proper burial of those Eriadorans who had fallen, including the brave half-elf who had been his dear and valued friend, and who had been so instrumental in the change that had come over the land.

Luthien, too, could not hold back the tears as Siobhan was laid to rest, and only the sight of broken Oliver and the strength of Katerin gave Luthien the resolve that he, too, must remain strong for his halfling friend.

The first week after Deanna's ascent was filled with grief; the second began a celebration that the new queen of Avon declared would last for a fortnight. It began as a farewell to Asmund and the Huegoths, but seeing that the party was about to commence, the pragmatic barbarian changed his plans and allowed his rightly weary warriors to stay a bit longer.

On the first night of revelry, after a feast that left the hundred guests at Deanna's table stuffed, Brind'Amour pulled Luthien and Oliver, Kayryn Kulthwain and Proctor Byllewyn aside. "Greensparrow was right in dividing his kingdom among dukes," the king explained. "I will not be able to see the reaches of my kingdom from my busy seat in Caer MacDonald."

"We accept you as king," Proctor Byllewyn assured him.

Brind'Amour nodded. "And I name you again, and formally, as duke of Gybi," he explained. "And you, Kayryn Kulthwain, shall be my duchess of Eradoch. Guide your peoples well, with fairness and in the knowledge that Caer MacDonald will support you."

The two bowed low.

"And you, my dearest of friends," Brind'Amour went on, turning to Luthien and Oliver. "I am told that there is no duke of Bedwydrin, and no eorl, but only a steward, put in place until things could be set aright."

"True enough," Luthien admitted, trying to keep his tone in line with the honor that he expected would fall his way, though his heart was not in the assignment. Luthien had his fill of governments and duties, and wanted nothing more than a free run down a long road.

"Thus I grant you the title of duke of Bedwydrin," Brind'Amour announced. "And command of all the three islands, Bedwydrin, Marvis, and Caryth."

"Marvis and Caryth already have their eorls," Luthien tried to protest.

"Who will answer to you, and you to me," Brind'Amour replied casually.

Luthien felt trapped. How could he refuse the command of his king, especially when the command was one that almost anyone would have taken as the highest of compliments? He looked to Oliver, then his gaze drifted past the halfling, to Katerin, who was out on the floor, dancing gaily. There, in the partner of the red-haired woman of Hale, Luthien found his answer.

"This I cannot accept," he said bluntly, and his words were followed by a gasp from both Kayryn and Byllewyn.

Oliver poked him hard. "He does not mean to say what he tries to say," the halfling stammered and started to pull Luthien aside.

Luthien offered a smile to his diminutive friend; he knew that Oliver wanted nothing more than the comfortable existence that Brind'Amour's offer to Luthien would provide for them all.

"I am truly honored," Luthien said to the king. "But I cannot accept the title. Our ways are beyond the edicts of a king, are rooted in traditions that extend to times even before your brotherhood was formed."

Brind'Amour, more intrigued than insulted, cocked his head and scratched at his white beard.

"I am not the rightful heir to Bedwydrin's seat," Luthien explained, "for I am not the eldest son of Gahris Bedwyr."

That turned all eyes to the dance floor, to Katerin and to her partner, Ethan Bedwyr. Brind'Amour called the couple over, and called to Asmund as well.

Ethan's initial response to the offer was predictable and volatile. "I am Huegoth," came the expected claim.

Katerin laughed at him, and his cinnamon-colored eyes, that obvious trademark to his rightful heritage, flashed as he snapped his gaze about to regard her.

"You are Bedwyr," the woman said, not backing down an inch. "Son of Gahris, brother of Luthien, whatever your words might claim."

Ethan trembled on the verge of an explosion.

"You left Bedwydrin only because you could not tolerate what your home had become," Katerin went on.

"Now you can make of your home your own vision," added Brind'Amour. "Will you desert your people in this time of great change?"

"My people?" Ethan scoffed, looking to Asmund.

A large part of Oliver deBurrows, that comfort-loving halfling constitution, wanted Ethan to reject the offer so that Luthien had to take the seat, that Oliver could go beside him and live a life of true luxury. But even that temptation was not enough to tear the loyal halfling from the desires of his dearest friend. "Even Asmund would agree that such a friend as Ethan Bedwyr sitting in power among the three islands would be a good thing," Oliver put in, seeing his chance. "Mayhaps you have seen your destiny, Ethan, son of Gahris. You who have befriended the Huegoths might seal in truce and in heart an alliance and friendship that will outlive you and all your little Ethan-type children."

Ethan started to respond, but Asmund clapped him hard on the back and roared with laughter. "Like a son you've been to me," slurred the Huegoth king, who had obviously had a bit too much to drink. "But if you think you have a chance of claiming my throne . . . !" Again came the roaring laughter.

"Take it, boy!" Asmund said when he caught his breath. "Go where you belong, just don't you forget where you've been!"

Ethan sighed deeply, looked from Katerin to Asmund, to Luthien, and finally to Brind'Amour, offering a somewhat resigned, somewhat hopeful nod of acceptance.

It might have been simply the perception, the hope that embraced the kingdoms of Avonsea, but the ensuing winter did not seem so harsh. Even on those surprisingly infrequent occasions when snow did fall, it was light and fluffy, settling like a gentle blanket. And winter's grip was not long in the holding; the last snow fell before the second month of the year was ended, and by the middle of the third month, the fields were green once more and the breeze was warm.

So it was on the bright morning that Luthien, Katerin, and Oliver set out from Carlisle. Brind'Amour and the Eriadoran army had long ago returned to Caer MacDonald, Ethan Bedwyr to Bedwydrin, Ashannon McLenny and his fleet to Baranduine, and Bellick dan Burso to DunDarrow, all ready to take on the responsibilities of their new positions. But for Luthien and his two companions, those responsibilities had ended with the fall of Greensparrow and the official coronation of Queen Deanna Wellworth of Avon. Thus the trio had lingered in Carlisle, enjoying the splendors of Avon's largest city. They had spent the winter healing the scars of war, letting the grief of friends lost settle into comfortable memories of friends past.

But even Carlisle, so huge, so full of excitement, could not defeat the wanderlust that held the heart of all three, of Luthien Bedwyr most of all, and so, when the snows receded and the wind blew warm, Luthien, upon Riverdancer, had led the way to the north.

They rode easily for several days, keeping to themselves mostly, though they would have been welcomed in any village, in any farmhouse. Their companions were the animals, awakening after winter's slumber, and the stars, glittering bright each night above the quiet and dark fields.

The trio had no real destination in mind, but they were moving inevitably to the north, toward the Iron Cross, and Caer MacDonald beyond that. The mountains were well in sight, Speythenfergus Lake left far behind, before they formally spoke of their destination.

"I do not think Caer MacDonald will be so different from Carlisle," Luthien remarked one morning soon after they had broken camp. Again the day was unseasonably warm and hospitable, the sun beaming overhead, the breeze soft and from the south.

"Ah yes, but Brind'Amour, my so-dear friend, rules in Caer MacDonald," Oliver said cheerily, kicking Threadbare to move ahead of Katerin's chestnut and come up alongside Riverdancer.

Katerin did not smile as Oliver moved past her; her thoughts, too, were on Caer MacDonald, and the impending boredom promised by such a peaceful existence.

"True enough," said Luthien.

"So," Oliver began to reason, "if we creep into the house of a merchant-type and are caught—not that any could ever catch the infamous Oliver deBurrows and his Crimson Shadow henchman!" Oliver quickly added when his companions brought their mounts to an abrupt stop, both regarding him skeptically.

"Crimson Shadow henchman?" Katerin asked.

"We'll not go to Caer MacDonald as thieves, Oliver," Luthien said dryly, something the halfling obviously already knew. The halfling shrugged; Katerin and Luthien looked to each other and smiled knowingly, then urged their horses ahead once more.

"Why would we need to?" Oliver asked. "Of course, we shall

live in the palace, surrounded by all pleasures, food and pretty ladies! Of course I was only joking; why would I want to steal with so much given to me?"

Luthien's next question stopped his companions short again.

"Then what shall we do?" the young Bedwyr asked.

"What must we do?" Oliver asked, not understanding.

"Are we two to build a home and raise our children?" Luthien asked Katerin, and the woman's stunned expression showed that she hadn't given that possibility any more thought than had Luthien. "Are we all to serve Brind'Amour, then," Luthien went on, "carrying his endless parchments from room to room?"

Oliver shook his head, still not catching on.

Katerin had it clear, though, and in truth, Luthien had brought up something that the young woman hadn't really considered. "What are we to do?" she asked, more to Luthien than to Oliver.

The young Bedwyr regarded her, his face skeptical as he considered that the reality of their apparent future could not match the intensity of their recent past.

"What is there for us in Caer MacDonald?" the woman asked.

"Caer MacDonald is the seat of Eriador, where our friend is king," Luthien answered, but his statement of the obvious did little to answer the woman's question.

Katerin nodded her agreement, but motioned for Luthien to continue, to explain exactly what that might mean.

"There is important . . ." the young Bedwyr started. "We will be needed . . . Brind'Amour will need emissaries," he finally decided, "to go to Gybi, to Eradoch, to Dun Caryth, and Port Charley. He will need riders to take his edicts to Bedwydrin. He will need—"

"So?" Katerin's simple question caught Oliver off his guard, and defeated Luthien's mounting duty-bound speech before it could gain any momentum—not that the young Bedwyr was trying to instill any momentum into it!

"The war is over," Katerin said plainly.

Oliver groaned, finally catching on to the course the two were walking. He started to protest, to remind them of the luxuries awaiting them, the accolades, the pretty ladies, but in truth, Oliver found that he was out of arguments, for in his heart he agreed—though the halfling part of him that preferred comfort above all else screamed a thousand thousand protests at his sensibilities. The war was over, the threat of Greensparrow ended forever. And the threat of the cyclopians had been ended as well, at least for the foreseeable future. The three kingdoms of Avonsea's largest island were at peace, a solid alliance, and any problems that might now arise would surely seem petty things when measured against the great struggle that had just been waged and won.

That was why Luthien had refused the crown of Eriador when his name had been mentioned as possible king soon after the northern kingdom had gained its independence from Greensparrow's Avon. Oliver studied his young friend, nodding as it all came clear. That was why Luthien had deferred to Ethan for the high position that Brind'Amour had offered. That was, in truth, why Luthien and Katerin had been so agreeable to the idea that they should linger in Carlisle. They had spent months waging a just war, their veins coursing with adrenaline. They were young and full of excitement and adventure; what did Caer MacDonald really have to offer to them?

"I spent many hours with Duke McLenny . . . King McLenny, on board his flagship as we sailed along Avon's western and southern coasts," Katerin said sometime later, the trio moving again, but more slowly now. "He spoke to me at length about Baranduine, wild and untamed."

Luthien looked at her, a mischievous smile crossing his face.

Oliver groaned.

"Untamed," Katerin reiterated, "and in need of a few good heroes."

"I do like the way this woman thinks," Luthien remarked, promptly turning Riverdancer to the west.

Oliver groaned again. On many levels, he wanted to convince Luthien and Katerin to accept the life of luxury, wanted them to settle down with their baby-types, while he got fat and comfortable in Brind'Amour's palace. On one level, though, Oliver not only understood, but, despite himself, agreed with the turn in direction. Wild Baranduine, rugged and unlawful, a place where a highwayhalfling might find a bit of sport and a bit of treasure. Suddenly Oliver recalled the carefree days he and Luthien had spent when first they had met, riding the breadth of Eriador at the expense of merchants along the road. Now the halfling envisioned a life on the road once more, with Luthien and that marvelous cape, and with Katerin, as capable a companion as any highwayhalfling could ever want, beside him. His vision grew into a full-blown daydream as they moved along, becoming vivid and thoroughly enjoyable—until the halfling saw an error in the image.

"Ah, my dear Siobhan," Oliver lamented aloud, for in his fantasy, the group riding about Baranduine's thick green hillocks was four, and not three. "If only you were here."

Luthien and Katerin regarded the halfling, sharing his sorrow. How much more complete they, too, would feel if the beautiful half-elf was riding alongside!

"A couple of couples we would then be!" Oliver proclaimed, his tone brightening, his dimples bursting forth as that cheery grin widened on his cherubic face. "We could call ourselves the two-two's, and let the fat merchant-types beware!"

Luthien and Katerin just laughed helplessly, a mirth tainted by the scars of a war that would never fully heal.